BEL

"I hate you

"You grow tiresome, my love. Think of something else to say. Something sweet."

"Sweet? To you? I'd rather die."

"You may die of love before this night is over." He set down the cup. "But have no fear, I will resurrect you."

"On top of everything else, you are a blasphemer."

"Elen." He laughed, opening his arms and beckoning seductively. "Come here, my dearest wife."

Elen backed away. Perhaps she could reach the door and escape from him. Then she remembered the men stationed just outside. She was trapped.

Patric began to walk toward her. The blue cloak, slung so carelessly over his shoulder, billowed to one side as he moved, revealing his muscular flanks. Her eyes fixed upon his eager manhood. A surge of warmth shook her. . . .

FLORA SPEER

By Honor Bound

LEISURE BOOKS ❧ NEW YORK CITY

A LEISURE BOOK

Published by

Dorchester Publishing Co., Inc.
6 East 39th Street
New York, NY 10016

Printed in the United States of America

By Honor Bound

PART I.

A.D. 1039-1040.

DUNCAN'S WARS.

. . . That most disloyal traitor . . .

Macbeth, William Shakespeare

I could not love thee, dear, so much,
Loved I not honor more.

To Lucasta, Sir Richard Lovelace

1

The horsemen came toward evening. They rode northward from the pass through the mountains, and then across the purple-heathered splendour of the autumn hillsides. Dougal, who had been placed in charge of the household guard when Elen's father took most of the men south to fight with King Duncan, hurried down from his post atop the wooden watchtower and sought out Elen to give her the news.

"Can you tell me who they are?" she asked.

"No, lady, but there are not enough of them to be a danger. I promised my lord I would protect you with my life, and that I can easily do against these few men. Though my master be gone now, I will keep my word until I join him in heaven."

"Thank you, Dougal." Elen touched the grizzled old soldier's arm and tried to smile at him.

It was not easy to smile. It had been only a few days since they had news of the death of Colin, Thane of Laggan, who was to Elen not the famous warrior and trusted councillor of the king, but her beloved father.

They had had too little time together. Once she had grown old enough to leave her wet-nurse, Colin had placed his motherless child in a convent to be raised by the nuns. She had come home to Laggan less than a year ago, a shy, quiet girl of fifteen, and had assumed her duties as mistress of the fortified lakeside castle that was her father's stronghold.

Now that her father was gone, Elen knew what her fate must be. She was heiress to Colin's vast wealth. The lands he held in thanage from King Duncan and the title of Thane of Laggan would pass through her to her future husband, and on that husband's death, to her eldest son. She would not be permitted to remain unmarried for long.

Though her father, had he lived, would never have forced her to wed a man she disliked, Elen was aware that noble marriages were not arranged for reasons of affection. More practical concerns dominated such unions, and without her father's loving care for her welfare, she might be made to marry someone she found unlikeable.

She sighed deeply at the unwelcome thought, and went to give orders to the kitchen maids. If the riders proved to be friendly and there were to be guests at Laggan, she must have food and drink aplenty waiting for them.

She had entertained a faint hope that the horsemen might have been sent by her cousin, Macbeth of Moray, for it was he who had sent her the news of her father's death, along with a letter suggesting that Elen should leave Laggan and go to live with Macbeth and his wife until she married.

The riders were not Macbeth's men. They had been sent by King Duncan. Elen met them in the great hall, where Dougal and his well-armed guards watched over her with wary eyes.

The tall leader of the horsemen strode into her home with an air of supreme confidence, pulling off his heavy leather gauntlets as he approached her. He nodded curtly at Dougal.

"We are here in peace," he said. His voice was low-pitched and pleasing to the ear,

"Then you are most welcome," Elen replied, tilting her head upward toward his great height. She was tall for a woman, and there were men she could face at an equal level, but the man before her was a near giant, with broad, heavily muscled shoulders draped in a short, sky-blue mantle that was fastened with an ornate gold brooch. Beneath the hem of his mantle the edge of a dark brown tunic was visible, and below that, long narrow breeches stretched over muscular thighs and calves until they disappeared into soft leather boots bearing silver spurs.

Elen's strict schooling had left her no free time for romantic dreams. She knew little of men, having in her sheltered, secluded life met only male servants and a few of her father's friends who came to visit at Laggan and who were all enough older than Elen to seem ancient to her. She had never seen so fine a specimen of manhood as this one. Had she had romantic dreams, they would have taken a similar shape. Even in her innocence, Elen recognized virile, exhilarating masculinity when it stood before her.

"There is meat and ale, and a place to sleep for all of you," she said in a bemused voice.

"I thank you, lady."

Brilliant blue eyes looked down at her with unconcealed curiosity. He doffed his leather helmet, revealing his crisp, closely cropped auburn curls. Under a magnificent mustache, a wide smile displayed strong white teeth. His clean-shaven jaw was square, with a cleft in the center. He was not more than three or four years older than she was, Elen noted—no older than twenty at most—and yet he had the bearing of an experienced warrior.

Elen made herself pay attention to his words, and found they cooled the warmth that had flooded over her under his too-intent gaze.

"I bring you greetings from King Duncan," the young soldier said, his deep voice now husky with emotion, "and our king's message of consolation at the death of your father. Colin of Laggan was a brave fighter, one of our best. We will miss him. We need all of our strength to fight the Danes."

"You were not fighting the Danes when my father died," Elen replied crisply. "How went the siege at Durham?"

"Not well, lady." He looked somber. Then his smile flashed again. "I forget my manners. I am Patric mac Keith of Bute. I am commanded by King Duncan to conduct you safely to Dunfermline, where you will dwell under his protection. You are a king's ward now, until you marry."

Elen bowed her head to the inevitable.

"As was my father before me, I am the king's servant to command," she said.

She washed her face in clear water, then combed out her long, straight black hair, letting it flow freely over her shoulders to her waist, as was the custom for an unmarried maiden. She smoothed her dark blue woolen dress with nervous hands. Elen did not believe she was beautiful. She was too tall and thin, and much too pale for beauty. She had been told that often enough at the convent.

"And a good thing, too," Sister Devorgilla had said sternly. "Vanity is a sin, Elen. Rejoice that you have nothing to be vain about, and think instead of your immortal soul."

Still, she wished there were something about

her that he might find lovely. Giving in to sinful
vanity, she stared into the scratched bronze hand
mirror that had once been her mother's. She saw
only a blurred image in its imperfect surface.

"I wish I had a silver mirror," she murmured,
"and a red silk dress."

She squinted into the mirror again.

"It wouldn't help," she sighed.

Patric mac Keith warmed his hands at the fire
in the center of the great hall, watching the smoke
curl lazily up and out of the holes in the gable ends
of the roof.

The girl had shaken him. He had seen lovely
women before, the acknowledged beauties at
Duncan's court, all rosy-pink, with gold hair and
plump figures. They giggled and chattered cease-
lessly about clothes and men. And there were the
ordinary women, the youthful serving wenches
and farmers' daughters, many of them beautiful
and only too willing to accept the advances of a
handsome young warrior of noble family. He had
enjoyed as many of them as possible, for a fighting
man's life was usually short, and Patric was determined to make the most of whatever time he had.
Elen of Laggan was different from the talkative
females he had known before. There was a deep
quiet about her that offered comfort to his battle-
weary spirit.

She was beautiful in her own unique way. She
had eyes as mysterious as the night sky, eyes of so
deep a blue that they were almost black, fringed
with thick dark lashes. Her pale, translucent skin
stretched over delicate bones, punctuated by
those incredible eyes and her winged dark brows,
and the softest, most sweetly curved mouth he had
ever seen. He had handled a piece of coral once,
shown to him by a traveler from Rome. Elen's

mouth was the same rich color. Her figure was slender, her breasts a soft curve beneath her woolen robe, and her hands were long and slim, the delicate blue veins showing through the skin. She was fragile, lovely, a fairy creature who would shatter if handled too roughly.

That there was some as yet untried inner strength in her Patric dimly recognized, but his tired mind would not let him think on it. He was only grateful that her physical appearance had pushed the horrors of a foolish war out of his thoughts for a time. That brief respite was worth the long ride north.

"My lord?"

She stood before him, dark eyes questioning, coral lips parted in a gentle smile. Patric felt himself drowning in that smile.

She offered him a silver cup of honey-scented mead.

"You were far away, my lord," she said, her voice like music from the finest harp.

"Not so far. I was dreaming." He took the cup and emptied it, his eyes still fixed on her lovely face. Patric was wise enough to know he had finally met the one woman who could put all the others out of his mind forever.

Elen motioned to a servant to refill his cup.

"Will you sit? The meat is ready." She indicated a carved wooden guest's chair next to the high seat at the middle of the dining table. She took her place next to him on a low bench, leaving the high seat empty, for it was the rightful place of the Thane of Laggan. Members of her household mingled with Patric's men as they crowded about the table, devouring game birds and dark bread and cheeses, mead and ale, apples and nuts and clotted cream.

"Are there no other guests?" Patric glanced

around the dark, smoky room, seeing no one but servants, a few men-at-arms, and his own men.

"Our friends are fighting for King Duncan. Nearly every man in Lagganshire went with my father," Elen told him proudly. "But I have been well guarded. Dougal would protect me with his life, if need be."

Patric digested the hint of warning contained in her words, and reminded himself the mistress of Laggan Castle did not know him well enough to trust him completely. Given time, he could teach her to know, and to trust.

"Are you not lonely?" he asked, wondering if her heart were already fixed on someone else.

"My duties keep me busy."

"You evade my question."

She lowered her eyes, shyness overcoming her, and Patric was enchanted by this further evidence of her innocence.

"I—I have much work to do," Elen stammered. She wished she could think of something clever to say, something to make him laugh. He would think her a fool, stuttering and blushing, so unlike the polished and beautiful ladies he must meet at Ducan's court. She was not even a very good hostess, for although there was sufficient food and drink, there was nothing else to offer a guest.

"We lack entertainment," Elen said. "The harper went to war with my father, and we heard he was killed by my father's side." Her voice broke at mention of her father, but she recovered herself and asked, "Will you, or one of your men, sing or tell us a story?"

"Unlike King Duncan, I have no skill at music, lady, and my men are all rough soldiers," he replied.

"Then tell us a story," Elen urged. "Tell us of

the siege of Durham."

"Are you sure you want to hear such a tale?" He met her steady eyes in surprise. So, this innocent, fragile beauty did not flinch from hard truths. Good.

"Were you there?" Elen asked.

"Aye."

"Then tell me." She drew a deep breath. "Tell me how my father died."

The room quieted, as those about them awaited to hear what Patric would say. In the shadows, the servants edged silently closer to listen. Across the table from Elen, old Dougal drained his cup and called for more, then settled down to hear the tale.

"Eadulf, the Earl of Northumbria, had harried the Britons of Cumbria to the west, and had sent his men to raid the southern borders of Alba," Patric began. "King Duncan decided to put an end to Eadulf. He raised an army and invaded Northumbria."

"A great mistake, considering Eadulf's strength," Dougal observed, glaring into his ale. "The king is a rash young man."

"So said many of his councillors." Patric nodded at the elderly soldier. "You, and they, were proven right. The campaign was a disaster. I say this with no disloyalty to Duncan, for he now admits as much himself.

"We attacked Durham. We had a great army of both foot soldiers and horsemen, but we were badly beaten. Your father was slain early in the battle, lady," Patric said to Elen. "It was quick and relatively painless. Others were not so fortunate. Most of our horsemen got away, but the foot soldiers were killed, every man of them, and their heads were placed on stakes in the marketplace at Durham. I was told the English washed the face and combed the hair and beard of each man. I did not see it myself, for I was ordered to retreat with the king's party. We withdrew over the border into Alba."

"Him and his damned English!" Dougal exclaimed. "Duncan is more English than Scots. He even has an English queen. We need a Scottish king, someone who will pay attention to the needs of Alba, and not go looking for glory in another land."

"Be quiet, Dougal," Elen warned, but Patric chuckled.

"You are not the only man in Alba who says such things," he told the old warrior. "There was a near revolt among Duncan's lords after our defeat. Although all is peaceful now, I think the peace is only on the surface." Patric turned to Elen. "You are kin to the Mormaer of Moray, are you not, lady?"

"Macbeth is my cousin," Elen acknowledged. "So is his wife. Duncan is also my cousin. We all have the same great-grandfather."

"You are well situated, whatever happens."

"What do you mean by that?" She blushed a little under his close regard, but did not lower her eyes.

"Only that it is well to have kin on both sides of a quarrel. If there is a quarrel. Which there is not, at the moment. For the future, who knows?"

"That sounds like a riddle, my lord," Dougal said.

"Let us hope it remains a riddle unasked and unanswered," Patric told him. "And now, lady, with your permission, I will seek my bed. It was a long journey from the border and I am weary. We will speak tomorrow about plans for your trip to Dunfermline."

He was gone from the hall, leaving an

astonished Elen to stare after him. A manservant from among Patric's troop rose to follow him.

"That was not mannerly, to leave us so soon," Dougal remarked.

"He wishes to be alone for a time," the manservant said quietly as he passed Dougal's place at table. "My lord's brother fell at Durham, in that senseless battle. He saw the blow that slew his brother, yet could not help him."

"Then," said Dougal, "he must be one of those who quarreled with King Duncan afterward."

"Not so." The servant drew himself up proudly. "Patric mac Keith of Bute is among the most loyal of the king's nobles." With a stiff bow to Elen, the man followed his master out of the great hall.

Idiot, Elen told herself, you insisted he tell the story. How it must have hurt him to recall his brother's death—surely as much as it hurt me to hear how Father died. She paced barefoot across the chill floor of her bedchamber, turned and paced again.

"Please go to bed," Ava, her personal maid begged, worried by her mistress's unease. "You will make yourself ill."

"No." Then Elen noticed the little maid was shivering, and she took pity on her. "Very well. Now go to bed yourself."

After Ava had settled on her pallet in the corner of the room, Elen was unable to sleep. In the last few days her life had been turned upside down. Her father was gone forever, and in a day or two she must leave Laggan, not knowing when she would see her beloved home again. When she did return—if ever she did—it would not be as an innocent young girl. She would be some man's wife. The choice of that man was King Duncan's, and whomever he chose, she must obey.

Her thoughts turned to Patric mac Keith, with his blue eyes and that warm, bright smile of his. She had recognized him at once for what he was, a man with the polish and bearing of those southern Scots who favored King Duncan and who had frequent contact with the English. She knew this because her father had been like that, too, and so had those of his friends whom she had met. Her father had told her there were other men, most of them from northern Alba, who held tightly to the old tribal ways and believed that by the ancient Law of Tanistry not Duncan, but his cousin Macbeth, had the better right to be king. Yet Macbeth had pledged his loyalty to Duncan and, according to her father, had never failed the king. Nor had her father failed Duncan, even unto death. So, she believed, would Patric mac Keith be loyal. He was like her father in that, she was certain.

"Patric," she whispered into the still, dark night, trying the sound of his name, but carefully, so as not to waken Ava. "Patric."

Two days later Elen left Laggan. In the intervening time she had not spoken with Patric unless Dougal or Ava or both were present. She suspected her servants of protecting her from him. She was aware of Patric's watchful attention as she arranged for the maintenance of Laggan in her absence. She wondered why he stared at her so often. It made her self-conscious, made her feel strangely warm all over, and yet it was not entirely unpleasant to have him look at her.

When the day of departure came, Elen was determined not to weep, but it was difficult to leave her home, and harder still to leave Dougal.

"I will come with you," he had said. "I

promised your father I would keep you safe."

"I am under the king's orders to guard her well," Patric assured him. "Your duty is to remain here to watch over her inheritance until she returns."

Dougal grumbled and protested, and even swore an oath or two, but Patric had his way. When Patric and his men rode out of Laggan toward the mountains, only Elen and her maid Ava went with them.

Once the leave-taking was over, and her face was firmly set toward the southeast, Elen felt her spirits rising. The morning mist had lifted, showing them a bright, cool day, with an occasional breeze to whip stray wisps of blue-black hair about her face and sting a bit of rosy color into her pale cheeks.

They rode through the mountain pass in late morning, and then followed the path of a tumbling, foaming river, working their way along the deep glen through which the river ran. On all sides of them stretched the huge Caledonian Forest. Oak and alder and fir grew close together here. Beneath the branches an eerie silence lay, broken only by the sound of rushing water and the horses' hooves. Reindeer lived in the forest, along with wild boar, wolves, and wildcats, while golden eagles soared gracefully above the high mountain peaks, and schools of salmon swam in the rivers. It was a primitive world, beautiful and lonely. Only rarely did they see a dwelling of turf or stone, and seldom did they meet any other human beings.

They stopped well before nightfall. The men pitched tents and set a guard against marauding or curious beasts. They sat about the campfire eating dark bread and dried meat, and drinking ale.

"It's not dainty fare for a lady," Patric said,

"But it's only for a few nights."

"I don't mind," Elen told him. She, who had never traveled anywhere but to the convent where she had spent most of her life, and back to Laggan when her schooling was done, was enthralled by this adventure, which was made even more exciting by the presence of the broad-shouldered, handsome man now sitting beside her. "Do all travelers eat like this?"

The innocent question brought a laugh from the men who were seated nearby, and Patric grinned.

"Not all travelers," he said. "When the king travels, there are silken tents and linen sheets for his bed, fine tableware and his favorite cook, and more servants than you can count."

"Really?" Her deep blue eyes were wide.

"Really. And as for the bishop, when *he* travels—well, I had better not tell you about that. You would be jealous and think we are treating you very badly indeed."

"No, I wouldn't."

Patric grinned and said nothing.

"The bishop takes his own chickens along," Patric's manservant told her.

"Surely you're teasing me."

"I? Never." The man's face was a study in injured innocence. "The bishop likes his eggs fresh, that's all."

Elen gaped at the man, then caught him winking at Patric.

"Well, why don't you do the same for your master?" she demanded, then burst into laughter at the silly joke. "You were teasing me. Both of you were. Chickens!" She heard Patric's low, rumbling laugh blending with her own as his servant strolled away. She wiped her eyes, still giggling.

"That's the first time I've laughed since the messenger came from Durham," she said.

"You should laugh regularly. It becomes you." Patric reached out his hand. Before she could pull away, one finger had caught a drop of water from her cheek. He lifted it to his lips.

"A happy tear tastes sweeter than honey," he said softly, his eyes never leaving her face.

Elen sat immobilized, her breath caught in her throat. It seemed to her that the distance between Patric and herself was slowly diminishing. She did not know whether he was moving toward her, or whether she, pulled by some magical force, was being drawn closer to him. Her wits were addled, and she could think of nothing to say. She could hardly breathe. It was a lovely feeling.

Then one of Patric's men dropped a dagger and swore as it clattered onto a rock, and the moment was gone.

They were up at dawn the next morning, to continue their journey. Now grey mist closed about them and rain drizzled softly down, dripping off trees and slicking rocks dangerously. The great forest loomed around them, impenetrable and silent. They picked their way slowly along the lonely path.

There was no cheerful group about the campfire that night. The men huddled in their tents, trying to keep dry. Ava sneezed constantly and complained of the wet and cold until Elen told her sharply to go to bed.

Patric invited Elen to eat with him in his tent. They sat on folded blankets on the bare earth floor while his manservant handed them their food and then crept out, closing the tent flap against the rain and leaving them alone.

Elen was painfully aware of Patric, of the sheer physical strength of the man. He had the strangest effect on her. She had never known this awkward shyness with her father, or with his dearest friend the Thane of Lochaber, who was a frequent visitor at Laggan and was like an uncle to her, nor with her father's other friends who visited from time to time. Nor was she shy with old Dougal, or any of the male servants at Laggan. No, it was something about Patric himself that made her feel this odd mixture of fear and suspense and excitement. Whatever it was, she found she was beginning to like it.

After they had finished their bread and meat, Patric produced a shiny apple and cut it into neat slices with his dagger. She sat watching his hands as he worked. It was quiet in the tent. All she could hear was the softly dripping rain and the beating of her own heart. They were alone in a private world: a man, a woman, an apple. Like the Garden of Eden.

Patric offered her half the sliced apple.

"I could tempt you with this," she blurted, then ducked her head in embarrassment. How could she have said such a thing? What would he think of her?

Patric laughed softly. "Lady, you don't need an apple to tempt me. I need only look at you."

"Don't mock me, Patric."

She moved as if to leave the tent, trying to scramble to her feet, but he caught her arm and pulled her back. Unbalanced, she fell against his shoulder.

For a moment she stayed as she had landed, feeling the rock-hard muscles of his upper arm and shoulder. She shuddered at the sensation, consumed by a peculiar delight and a sense of certain danger. The warm, manly scent emanating from Patric's body was like a sweet, drugging potion. She wanted to remain where she was and let her senses slip into the delicious confusion now threatening to overcome her. She almost gave in to the feeling, before her convent training pricked at her conscience. Gathering her strength, she tried once more to move away from him, but his arms were around her, holding her close.

"Elen, look at me. Please."

Compelled by that whispered intensity, she raised her eyes. His face was so close. She had never been so close to a man before.

"I wasn't mocking you. You are beautiful." He bent his head.

Her first thought was that his luxuriant mustache was bristly, and it tickled. She forgot that when his mouth met hers. Her first kiss was not at all what she had imagined it would be. His lips were warm and hard and they ground against hers, and she felt herself being pulled across his chest, so that her breasts were crushed against him, and something was happening down inside her, something strange, and it was wonderful, wonderful. And then she could think no more.

It was a long time before he released her. One large hand, calloused and hard, a warrior's hand, held her face gently, tenderly, as he kissed her eyelids, her cheeks, her chin and nose, and then returned to her trembling mouth that burned to feel his touch again.

His hand slid lower, caressing her throat. She felt its warmth through her woolen gown as he laid it on her breast. She gasped, half in fear, half in pleasure, and he pulled away.

"We must stop," he muttered, trying to put space between them. In the narrow confines of his tent, it was impossible.

"I know. You should not—I should not let

you—we mustn't . . ." She stammered to a flustered halt.

She sat looking up at him as he knelt before her. He was so huge, so strong. He could overpower her if he wanted to, and she would be helpless to resist him. She dared not think about whether she would want to resist him or not.

His hand rested against her cheek, then dropped to her shoulder, where his fingers dug into her.

"I promised Duncan I would deliver you to him safely," he said. "The husband chosen for you will want a virgin bride. Come. I will conduct you to your tent now."

He pulled the tent flap open with a rough gesture and stepped outside. She rose and followed him. He did not touch her. He saw her into her tent and left without a word.

Ava was sleeping soundly. Elen lay down and pulled her woolen cloak about her. Her body tingled with strange new sensations, feelings unknown and unimagined until Patric kissed her. She touched her lips, finding them warm and slightly swollen. Her hand drifted down to cup the breast he had touched.

Perhaps he would want to kiss her again. She was unsure what her response would be if he did. She was honest enough to admit to herself that she had wanted him to continue kissing her, and to do whatever it was that he had begun with his hand, that had felt so marvellous. Sensuous pleasure reawakened as she pressed her own hand harder against her breast, recalling the feeling.

That must be what husbands and wives did together. She had learned the rudiments of human mating in bits and pieces from other girls in the convent and from comments made by Ava. It had sounded distinctly unpleasant. But if a man's touch could make her feel like this, then marriage, when it came, might not be so bad after all, if only the man were like Patric. Her dreaming ended abruptly as her training reasserted itself with a clear-eyed realization that until the marriage was made, her primary duty was to keep herself pure for her husband. In order to do that, she knew she would have to guard herself against Patric much more carefully in the future.

Patric's attitude toward her the next morning was polite, but distantly cool. Elen was certain he must think badly of her for letting him kiss and fondle her in that easy way. Soldiers, she had heard, often made free with maidens and then left them. She wrapped her cloak closely about her tense body and kept as far away from Patric as she could. She scarcely spoke to him that day.

It was impossible to ignore him as they sat about the campfire that evening, but Elen kept her maid close by. Ava's cheerful prattle helped to keep Patric at a distance, until she picked up a bucket and went to fetch water for her mistress to wash in. Elen was about to enter her tent when Patric's voice sounded directly behind her.

"Have I offended you, lady?"

It was too dark to see his face clearly. Only his eyes gleamed with reflected firelight. She was glad of the darkness. It would hide the scalding blood she knew was staining her face and throat. She could feel the heat of it.

"Lady?"

"You should not speak to me alone," she whispered.

His hand touched her elbow and she flinched. She heard his low laugh.

"Elen, we have done nothing wrong."

"You kissed me. You *touched* me."

"And if I am not mistaken, you enjoyed it. Elen, I need to speak with you. Walk with me a little. There, along the riverbank." He took her elbow again. The warmth of his hand through her sleeve ignited a tiny spark of response, and this time she did not pull away. They had walked a short distance from the camp and were surrounded by darkness before he spoke once more.

"You did like it when we kissed, did you not?"

"I don't know." Just in time she remembered her vow to be more cautious with him.

"Be honest, my sweet."

His hands were on her shoulders, turning her to face him. He was dangerously near, his face a pale blur in the darkness. Her knees began to shake.

"It is very important," he told her.

"Yes," she whispered defiantly. And then, unable to stop herself, she added, "I liked it when you touched me, too, though I know it was wrong. I never felt like that before. We can never do that again. I must wait until I am married to feel such things."

"Or betrothed. They taught you nothing in that convent, did they?"

"Please let me go now." If they stood like this much longer, with his hands on her shoulders and his warm breath on her brow, she would forget her careful resolutions.

"How young you are."

"You are not much older! Let me go, Patric."

His mouth came down on hers, hard and sweet, and it all began again, the delicious feeling she had been determined to forget. This time it was worse, because they were not kneeling in a cramped tent; they were standing face to face, and she could feel him, the whole muscular length of him, pressed tightly against her. When she wound her arms around his shoulders, her body seemed to grow taller, so they were mouth to mouth, and her breasts pressed achingly against his broad chest. His arms held her about her waist, which was now level with his own. She could feel his taut belly against her own softer abdomen. One of his hands slipped lower to press her even more closely against him, and it was tense thigh against tense thigh and thrusting hip against willing warmth.

She felt his tongue pushing against her lips and then entering her mouth in a wave of sweet sensation. Her eyes flew open and she began to struggle, but he gathered her even more tightly into his arms. There was a moment of half-hearted protest until, with a soft little moan, she yielded.

A glorious eternity passed before he lifted his head. She swayed when he loosened his hold on her. He had to steady her or she would have fallen. Her knees were like water.

"You feel it, too. I knew you did!" he exclaimed with boyish assurance. "I wasn't mistaken."

"This is wrong. You must let me go." Tears of shame and confusion were running down her cheeks. "If anyone saw us, I would be ruined."

"No, my sweet Elen, you don't understand. I can talk to the king and ask him—"

"Mistress?" Ava's questioning voice came out of the darkness. "Are you there? I was worried about you. I thought you were lost."

"I'm here." Elen disengaged herself from Patric's arms, thankful it was too dark for Ava to see much. "I'm coming now. Before I really am lost," she added under her breath.

"Elen, wait, please. Listen to me."

"Good night, Patric." And she hurried through the darkness after Ava.

2

They reached Dunfermline shortly after King Duncan himself arrived, leading the remnants of his army from the disaster at Durham. The palace and its grounds were a seething mass of confusion. Armed soldiers, wounded men walking or on litters or crutches, horses, and baggage carts crowded the courtyards, while richly dressed nobles jostled each other in the inner rooms and corridors. The clear, high music of church bells rang out over the din made by the discordant crowd.

Elen waited near the entrance, guarded by Patric's warriors, while he went in search of someone who could tell him where to deliver the king's new ward. Ava huddled close to her, wide-eyed in amazement at the noise and activity swirling around them.

Elen, her head high, stood wrapped in her dark cloak and the silent dignity she had assumed ever since Patric had kissed her so passionately by the riverbank. She had refused to speak to him at all during the remainder of their journey, ignoring the amused glances he sent her way. She was becoming increasingly irritated by his cocky self-assurance. He behaved as though he knew some wonderful secret.

Well, she wasn't interested in Patric's secrets. She was only concerned with saving herself from total ruin at his hands. The sooner she met King Duncan, and the faster he married her to one of his nobles, the happier she would be. That was her only hope of safety. When she had a husband to protect her, Patric would have to leave her alone.

"Elen? Lady?" He had returned and was speaking to her. She lifted her chin a little higher and he smiled in that annoyingly teasing way he had. "You are to stay with your cousin."

"I know that," she said coldly. "The king is my cousin. Take me to him."

"The king is too busy to see you today. You are to be lodged in your other cousin's quarters for now." Seeing her puzzled expression, he added, "You did tell me the sub-king of Moray is your cousin, did you not?"

"Macbeth, the Mormaer of Moray, is my cousin."

"His lady, Gruach, is here awaiting her husband's return with the army. I will take you to her."

"Thank you."

He grinned again, unabashed by her icy tone, and motioned for his party to follow him. Elen was quickly lost as they proceeded through corridors and interconnecting chambers, across courtyards, indoors and out, through the sprawling palace grounds until they came to a richly furnished apartment. Bright tapestries hung on the walls. Thick furs were draped over benches and carved wooden chairs. A fire burned in the hearth. A servant bade them wait and disappeared into an inner room. The men-at-arms remained outside, while Elen, Patric, and Ava waited in the splendid comfort of the room until Gruach joined them.

Gruach was only of medium height, but her proud carriage made her appear taller. At twenty-eight she was still beautiful. Her honey-blonde hair was braided and artfully arranged. Her grey eyes were warm. Her gold velvet gown swished against the rushes on the floor, and the jewels in her belt and at her wrists and neck winked in the firelight as she moved toward them.

"Lady," Patric said, bowing, "I bring you your cousin, Elen of Laggan."

"Duncan sent me a message. Thank you, Patric, for your good care of her." Gruach's voice was soft and sweet. She laid a gentle hand on Patric's sleeve. "I grieve with you for your brother, but I am told he died a brave warrior's death. I would expect no less of your father's son."

Patric bowed again.

"You may go now," Gruach said.

Dismissed so royally, Patric could do nothing but leave. Gruach smiled after him.

"He is a bit too sure of himself," she said, "but then, so was his father, until someone wiser and surer killed him."

Elen smothered a shocked gasp.

"Let me look at you." Gruach took Elen's hand and turned her toward the firelight. "You were a babe when last I saw you. How like your mother you are, with that beautiful hair. You are too thin and pale, but that can be remedied. With the right clothes and jewelry, you will be a lovely prize for some deserving thane. Duncan has commanded me to see that you are properly cared for, and I will do his bidding with pleasure. We will have to hurry, for my Macbeth is returning today with his men, and I must be free to attend him when he comes."

Gruach led Elen to another chamber as she spoke. "Is this your maidservant? Good. Bring your mistress's belongings in here. How fortunate that we have an extra bedchamber in this apartment. You will want a bath. Then we will see about your clothes. You will need something very grand for your presentation to Duncan.''

Gruach's voice went on and on, a melodic accompaniment to her firm direction of Elen's day. There was an undercurrent of barely subdued excitement about the woman. Watching her closely, Elen soon connected it to Macbeth. Gruach expected her husband to arrive at any moment and was desperate with impatience to see him.

None of Elen's gowns was suitable for court.

"This is dreadful," Gruach said. "Ava, find my maid. Tell her to bring my new red dress. Can you sew? Good, so can she. The two of you will alter it to fit Elen while I spend the afternoon teaching her how to behave before the king. Don't just stand there, girl. Hurry!"

"When will I meet the king and queen?" Elen asked.

"You will be presented to Duncan tonight at the welcoming feast. The queen sees no one but her ladies. She is ill and weak. She will not live long. I am the most important woman at Duncan's court."

The gown was being hastily refitted for Elen's slender figure, Gruach's instructions on court protocol had been repeated several times just to be sure Elen understood them, and the two cousins were sitting before the fire in the main room of the apartment, when Macbeth arrived at last.

The name Macbeth meant "son of life," and it had been well chosen for him. He appeared in the doorway with no announcement of his coming. He was simply *there*—big-boned and tall, ruddy-complexioned, with thick yellow hair and beard —and his presence filled the room with life and warmth.

"My love!" He opened his arms, flinging his bright blue cloak back over one shoulder.

Gruach rose from her stool and flung herself into his embrace. Their lips met in a hungry kiss that deepened into passion. They were oblivious to anyone else in the room.

For a moment Elen looked on in amazement. Then, afraid she was intruding, she looked away from her cousins and met straight-on the glowing dark eyes of the man who had followed Macbeth into the room. Something in his steady regard of her made Elen catch her breath, but she would not drop her own eyes. Then the man nodded and broke the oddly intimate contact.

"Who is this?" Macbeth had released his wife and was appraising Elen with a shrewd gaze. Gruach introduced them.

"You are welcome, cousin," Macbeth said. Elen found herself enveloped in his exuberant embrace. "What a beauty you are!"

"I don't think so," Elen demurred shyly, believing he was only trying to be kind.

"You must let a man decide that. What do you think, Talcoran? This is my aide, one of my most trusted companions." Macbeth clapped the dark man on his shoulder, pushing him toward Elen. "Well, what do you say, old friend?"

The dark man stared at Elen again, looking her over from head to toe with great seriousness.

"Very beautiful," he said at last.

"You see, cousin, I told you so." Macbeth laughed heartily. He slipped an arm about Gruach's waist. "My wife and I want to be alone now. We have been apart too long. You two stay here and talk. You should get to know each other."

He drew his wife toward a door at the far side of the room, and hurried her through it. The door closed firmly and a bolt could be heard sliding across it.

Talcoran cleared his throat and looked uncomfortable.

"Would you like some ale?" Elen asked nervously.

"Yes."

She poured a cup and brought it to him. He was not very tall. He was just a little shorter than Elen, and their eyes were level. His were dark grey, almost black. His hair was black and straight, his face swarthy, made even darker by a deep suntan and a black, neatly trimmed beard and mustache. He was thin. He looked wiry and tough, a strong veteran of war. In place of the bright garb of most noblemen, Talcoran wore plain dark clothes. They suited him. His simple, direct manner suggested that this man would care naught for gaudy fabrics or glittering jewels.

He drained the cup of ale, his eyes on her face all the while. There was something intense and very serious about him, which kept that close inspection from becoming insulting.

"Do you want more?" she asked.

"Yes." As she bent to pick up the pitcher from the hearth, he added in a softer tone, "I thank you, most sweet lady."

She rose abruptly at that, splashing some of the ale. He smiled at her. One front tooth was a little crooked. It gave him a rakish, almost a sinister look. His eyes were still fastened upon her face with that intent expression. Unnerved, she poured out the ale with a shaking hand while she searched for something ordinary to say to him that would break the awkwardness between them.

"You must be very thirsty after your long

ride."

"And hungry. It was a hasty retreat and a difficult journey home with inadequate supplies. And we left too many of our good fighting men dead in England." His voice was harsh, filled with the bitterness of defeat.

"If you wish to eat, I think there is some cheese, and some bread," she offered sympathetically. She almost told him about her father, to let him know she had at least a little understanding of how terrible war could be, but he spoke before she could say the words.

"It would be better," he told her, "If I found what I need somewhere else."

"But, I'm sure my cousins would want me to provide—"

"No. I must go." He rose quickly and a moment later the door to the corridor had slammed behind him.

What a strange man, Elen thought. He had no manners at all. She wanted to dismiss him from her thoughts, but the memory of his dark eyes haunted her for the rest of the day.

Gruach's maid and Ava helped Elen to bathe and dress. Ava combed her mistress's hair until it shimmered with blue-black light.

The gown Gruach had given Elen was of a deep wine-red wool, colored with the treasured dye made from cockles. It would never fade, not from exposure to the sun, nor from washing, however vigorous. The dress had a wide, curved neck and long, tight sleeves. The full skirt flared into rich, heavy folds that rippled when Elen walked. The girdle was of twisted cords of silk in the same dark red. It was a beautiful dress, expertly made and costly, and Elen was deeply touched by the gift, and the warm-hearted generosity that prompted it.

There was no decoration at all on the gown, which was unusual in an age of elaborate embroidered trim. It was only later that Elen realized Gruach must have intended the gown as a simple background for her spectacular collection of heavy gold jewelry. The simplicity pleased Elen. She added ony a delicate gold chain and a gold ring set with a pearl, both of which had been her mother's.

"Very suitable for a modest maiden," Gruach approved. She had changed to a gown of deep blue trimmed with fur, to which she had added wide gold braclets set with jewels, a heavy gold necklace, gold earrings, and a jeweled gold belt. Gold ornaments shone among her braids, holding in place a sheer silken veil that drifted softly about her shoulders. Several gold rings adorned her hands.

"This is my son, Lulach." Gruach indicated a fair-haired boy about twelve years old who had come into the room with her. He was dressed like an adult in a blue woolen tunic with a gold chain about his neck. "Lulach is attending the feast tonight because the young princes will be present. The king has commanded it."

"I don't like Malcolm," Lulach told Elen. "Donald is nice, but Malcolm always wants to fight."

"You must learn to fight, too, my darling," his mother admonished him. "That is what grown men do."

"When I have a big sword, I'll fight Malcolm and kill him." Lulach stuck out his lower lip.

"You must not say such things, my love. One day Malcolm will be your king, and then you must obey him."

"Not me!" Lulach turned his attention to

Elen. "When I am Mormaer of Moray, will you be my subject?"

Elen burst into laughter.

"I will be your most loyal subject, my lord," she said, making a low curtsy.

"Be careful," Gruach warned. "My son has a long memory."

"I did not know you and Macbeth had children," Elen said.

"We have none. I had two stillborn babes when first we married, and none since. Lulach is the son of my first husband, Gillecomgan, who was foully murdered." Gruach's lovely face twisted in pain. "That is why Lulach is so dear to me, why I cannot send him to be fostered by another family. I must keep him safe by my side."

"My father was burned alive," Lulach told Elen with childish relish. "He and all his men were locked inside his house and it was set on fire. King Duncan's grandfather ordered him killed. First he killed my mother's nephew, who was the next rightful king, and then he kiled my father so he couldn't become king, either. But no one can kill Macbeth. He's too strong for them all."

"Lulach, be silent!" his mother commanded. "You are speaking treason."

"But, mother—"

"Not another word." Gruach pulled herself together with a visible effort. "We must go now. We will be late."

"I thought we were waiting for Macbeth," Elen said.

"He is in attendance on the king. He will meet us there."

The great hall was brightly lit. Torches flamed along the walls, casting wavering shadows from the thick roofbeams against the high, peaked ceiling. Candles in tall holders burned on either

side of the king's raised chair. Nobles and their
ladies clustered in the hall, waiting for King
Duncan to appear. They were a colorful crowd,
arrayed in red or green or blue or saffron-gold, in
gowns of silk or wool, in tunics trimmed with fur
or with finely embroidered bands of gold and
silver thread. They wore jewelry of gold or silver
set with colored stones. They reeked of heavy,
musky perfumes.

The crowd parted, making room for Gruach,
wife of Macbeth mac Finlaec, and for her son and
her cousin. There were those who bowed low as
Gruach passed by.

They were just in time. They had barely
reached their places near the royal seat when the
king and his closest nobles appeared through a
side door.

Duncan did not look like a king to Elen. He
was no more than thirty, at least five years
younger than his cousin Macbeth. He was thin,
with light brown hair and a skimpy beard. Behind
the beard, his face was weak. Any one of his nobles
looked more kingly than he.

Macbeth was tall and magnificent in his deep
blue silk tunic. The chain of the Mormaer of
Moray lay in linked pairs of silver rings across his
chest, fastened with the broad penannular ring
which was his badge of office. He held himself
with great dignity, towering over the king. In his
own shire of Moray, Macbeth was king, and his
word was law. Even when he obeyed Duncan, who
was king of all Alba, Macbeth did not forget his
own rank.

Behind Macbeth a tall, handsome man with
brown hair and a solemn expression looked noble,
if not royal, and next to this man walked Patric
mac Keith.

Elen caught her breath as Patric's long-limbed, muscular form moved into view. She could not tear her eyes away from those auburn curls, that chiseled jaw. She was unaware of the other men who now filed into the hall behind Duncan.

Gruach nudged her, urging her forward, then Lulach, on her other side, pushed at her waist with his child's hand.

"Go and bow to the king," he whispered urgently.

Elen followed Gruach toward the king, aware of Lulach close beside her. She knew without looking that Patric was watching her.

Macbeth stepped forward, took her icy, trembling hand, and personally presented her to King Duncan.

Elen swept into a deep curtsy, her heavy red skirts flowing about her. She held it a moment too long and felt her cousin's strong hand lifting her. Under his golden brows, Macbeth's light blue eyes twinkled with amusement. The corners of his wide mouth twitched. Elen gave him a nervous smile, and then looked at King Duncan.

"Your father, the Thane of Laggan, was dear to us," Duncan was saying, in a voice too light and high pitched for command. "Although we deeply regret his death, we welcome you as our royal ward."

"Thank you, my lord." Elen met his eyes. They were pale grey, as colorless as the man himself.

"Our queen is ill, as you may have heard," Duncan told her, "and unable to care for you properly. Therefore, your cousin Macbeth has agreed to shelter you until we find you a suitable husband."

"I will do whatever you wish, my lord."

"Yes." The king turned away from Elen. "Is there no ale? No wine?" He snapped his fingers, and a golden, jewel-encrusted goblet was handed to him on a golden tray.

Macbeth and Elen moved away, and he dropped her hand.

"You did that very well," he said. "The shy, nervous young girl. Very effective." Before Elen could protest that she had not been pretending, Macbeth turned to speak to Gruach.

"You made a pretty bow," Lulach told her.

"Thank you, my lord." Elen smiled at the serious boy. "You helped me just in time."

"I like you," Lulach said. "When I grow up—"

He was interrupted by a sudden racket at the door by which Duncan had entered. Three young boys burst into the hall. The first was tall and dark, a wild-looking, unkempt child, whose knee-length silk tunic was stained and wrinkled. He was followed by a younger boy who led a toddler by the hand.

"That's Malcolm," Lulach said to Elen. "The one with the white hair is Donald, and the baby he's bringing with him is Maelmuire. Now I'll have to go sit with them. Malcolm is only eight years old and he never makes any sense when he talks. I would rather stay with you."

"The child has excellent taste," said a voice behind Elen, "but he is a bit young for you, don't you think?"

"Bancho!" Elen turned, exclaiming in delight.

The Thane of Lochaber wrapped Elen in his arms, his grey-streaked beard tickling her cheek as it always did.

"Run along, my young lord." The sturdy Bancho winked at Lulach, man to man. "The king requires you to entertain his sons, and a nobleman must do his duty, however unpleasant."

"I suppose I must." Squaring his thin shoulders, Lulach marched off toward the now squabbling royal children.

"I can't say I blame him. They aren't my favorite brats, either." Bancho looked at Elen with approval. "So you are the king's new ward? The way you look tonight, I don't think he will have any trouble finding a husband for you. I will miss your father, Elen. Colin was always a true friend."

"Thank you for those words, Bancho."

"And when you are married to some great lord, may I still visit you at Laggan and bounce you on my knee as I did when you were a wee lass?"

"Well, perhaps not on your knee," Elen laughed, "But you are always welcome at Laggan."

"Have you met Conal mac Duff? His wife is just a little older than you. She would make a good friend for you, Elen. You will need friends at court."

Bancho led Elen to the handsome, brown-haired man who had stood with Macbeth at Duncan's side.

"The Thane of Fife," Bancho said, "And his wife, Fionna. And this is Patric mac Keith."

"We have met before." Elen glared at Patric. He grinned back at her with his usual self-confidence.

"So you are the beautiful Elen of Laggan." Conal mac Duff's wife met Elen's eyes with an impish expression. "My brother has talked of you all day long."

"Your brother?"

"This great oaf is my brother." Fionna caught Patric's arm and laughed up at him. "I have tried to teach him manners. I hope he wasn't rude to you."

"He—he was very kind." Elen was much relieved when Bancho's hearty laugh cut across her stumbling words.

"Aye, I'll wager he was kind. He has an eye for a pretty lass. I must leave you, my friends. I should speak with several people I see here. Enjoy the banquet, Elen." With that, Bancho vanished into the throng of courtiers.

Elen looked from Fionna to Patric. Fionna was short and decidedly plump, and her curly hair was more golden-red than Patric's, but there was a distinct resemblance. They had the same square chin with a cleft, similar noses, and most of all, the same merry expression and easy confidence.

"Will you sit with us?" Conal mac Duff asked solemnly, indicating the banquet tables upon which platters of food were being piled.

"I think I must join my cousin Gruach," Elen began, but Patric interrupted her.

"Macbeth and Gruach are always at the high table with Duncan. Of course you will sit with us."

"But Lulach—"

"Lulach will eat with the young princes." Fionna took a place at a long table that had been set up close to Duncan's. "Sit here, next to me, Elen."

Unable to think of any further excuse to avoid Patric, Elen politely acquiesced. She found herself on the bench between Patric and Fionna, while Conal mac Duff sat on his wife's other side. Servants began to pass the platters of roasted game birds and boiled pork, bowls of turnips and cabbage and beans, plates of cheeses, breads and honey and apples and grapes. Cups were filled and refilled with wine or mead or heavy, frothing beer.

"You've never been to court before?" Fionna began in a friendly way.

"No, and my head is spinning. I can't remember the names of all these people."

"It will take you a while. Just ask me, my dear.

I know everyone here."

"Do you? Who is that man?" Elen indicated a black-haired, ugly man with a large, jutting nose, who sat the king's table.

"The one in the bearskin cape? That is Thorfinn the Mighty, ruler of Orkney, come south to negotiate with King Duncan. The king wants Thorfinn to make submission to him, but I don't think Thorfinn will. Like most Norsemen, he would rather be independent."

"He looks fearsome."

"He's really very nice. I'll introduce you to him if you like."

Elen watched the Norse giant hack at a joint of beef with a wicked-looking knife.

"No, I don't think so."

On her other side, Patric laughed at the look on her face. Elen had tried to ignore him, but now it was impossible. She and Patric were to share a wooden trencher. He neatly cut a piece of meat with his dagger and offered it to her, his graceful manners a notable contrast to the Viking at the royal table. As he turned toward her, she was aware of the provocative pressure of his firm-muscled thigh against her own. She was sure he was doing it deliberately.

"You cannot avoid me forever," he whispered, teasing her. "Do you like my sister?"

"Better than I like her brother."

He smiled. "I knew you would lose your shyness quickly once you were at court. I never imagined it would happen so soon."

"Do you treat all of the king's wards the way you have treated me?"

"I only kiss the beautiful ones. And I never kiss the boys. I do like it when girls kiss me back the way you did."

Elen stared straight ahead, her shoulders

rigid, knowing that waves of bright color were sweeping across her cheeks. She sensed Fionna watching her, knew Fionna's lips were opening to ask why she was blushing, and knew she would have to make some explanation.

She was saved by a disturbance. Across the hall, at another table, two men were quarreling. Elen saw Duncan say something to Bancho of Lochaber, who then hurried to speak to the disputing men. They subsided into their seats with obvious reluctance.

"What happened?" Elen asked. Conal mac Duff answered her.

"It was one of the northern nobles," he said. "They quarrel constantly with the men close to Duncan. They resent what they call Duncan's English manners and southern attitudes. They think he is neglecting the north of Alba, which is, after all, the heart of the kingdom. Duncan is planning to move his capital even farther south, across the Firth of Forth to Dunedin, and the northerners are freshly angered by that. I'll wager that was what the quarrel was about."

"The fools," Patric broke in. "Duncan is trying to bring peace to Alba, but he cannot do it if his nobles persist in making war among themselves."

"A stronger king could make them behave," Conal observed, "and our invasion of Northumbria had nothing to do with warring nobles, though our defeat there at Durham made many of them angry enough to war against Duncan himself. I think Macdowald will make trouble next."

"Stop it, both of you," Fionna said sharply. "I am tired of your constant arguing on this subject. You may want peace in Alba, but I want peace while I eat."

"Do you let her talk to you like this all the time, Conal?" Patric asked. "Why don't you beat her into silence? Most men would."

Fionna gave an outraged squawk.

"I could never beat her," Conal said. "She is too dear to me." He smiled down at his young wife with an expression of tender love.

"Then you are doomed to a lifetime of following her orders." Patric shook his head in mock sorrow. "Our father never could make her be quiet, either."

"Oh, Patric," Fionna began to giggle. "Can you not be serious for more than a sentence or two?"

"There have been times when I was serious," Patric said, his eyes on Elen, "but no one believed me."

"Fionna," Elen said nervously, "who is that tall thin man with the red hair?" Perhaps if she changed the subject Patric would forget about her and talk to whoever sat on his other side. For a while her idea worked, as Fionna pointed out various nobles and explained their positions at court. But sooner than she would have liked, Patric interrupted them with more teasing.

"Are you trying to guess who Duncan will choose for your husband? Have you considered that your cousin Macbeth might use his influence to claim you for his henchman, Talcoran? I must admit I respect that fellow. He's an honest man, and a remarkable warrior, if a bit rough. Or perhaps Macbeth will want you to wed his stepson Lulach. He will be a great nobleman one day, if Malcolm doesn't beat him to death before they both grow up. Of course, he's only a boy—you'd have to wait a year or two before you bed him." Patric leaned closer, his blue eyes gleaming dangerously, his voice dropping to a whisper. "Or would you rather marry me?"

Elen's heart gave a great lurch. She stared back at him for a long, breathless moment.

"I would rather throw myself into the sea," she said.

He shouted with laughter. Heads turned to look at them. Elen wished she could vanish in a puff of magical smoke.

"Lady, I think you lie," Patric sputtered between gusts of laughter. "You enjoyed my kisses. I have your own admission on that."

"Patric, whatever you are tormenting her about, stop it at once," his sister ordered. "You are making a spectacle of the poor girl. She will think everyone at court is as wicked as you. Leave Elen alone."

"I beg your pardon, sister. And yours, sweet Elen. Though I will tell you privately," he added in a low voice to the furious girl beside him, "that I have no intention of leaving you alone permanently."

After that, he obeyed his sister and did not disturb Elen with any further teasing. Instead, he spent the remainder of the meal paying extravagant compliments to the elderly woman who sat on his other side, leaving Elen to talk with Fionna and Conal. They, as if in apology for Patric's behavior, devoted themselves to conversation with her, pointing out important people, describing recent events at court, and doing everything in their power to make Elen feel comfortable.

When at last Duncan had retired and the guests had begun to leave, Patric took Elen's arm as she stood by the table. Before she could move away from him, his hand had moved down to weave his fingers between hers.

"Elen, I am truly sorry for what I said earlier. Sometimes my tongue runs wild when I begin to tease. Forgive me, please. I have no wish to hurt you, and my question was not a jest. I would have spoken to you during our journey, but you would not listen to me. Now we have little time. Before I speak with Duncan, I must know how you feel. I pray you do not despise me."

She raised her eyes to his. She saw there what appeared to be tenderness. As his strong fingers pressed her hand, she was once more overcome by the sweet confusion she now associated with Patric's nearness. Without full awareness of what she was doing, she responded with an answering squeeze of her own hand.

"Here is Gruach," said Fionna over Elen's shoulder, and Patric dropped her hand and stepped away from her.

"Fionna, I thank you for being so kind to my cousin this evening." Gruach was all smiles. "She is new at court and knows no one."

Now Macbeth and his aide Talcoran joined the group and began talking with Conal. Macbeth pointedly ignored Patric, though Talcoran exchanged a friendly word with him.

"I think we will be good friends." Fionna kissed Elen on the cheek. "Good night. We will meet again soon, I know." She left the great hall on her husband's arm.

Macbeth spared Patric a curt nod as he slipped a possessive arm about his wife's waist.

"Talcoran," Macbeth said, "You will escort my cousin Elen safely to my quarters. As for me, since I am not on campaign now, I will walk alone with my wife for a while before we go to bed." He and Gruach strolled off without another glance at Patric.

"I should attend the king," Patric said. He bowed stiffly to Elen, said good night to Talcoran, and then he, too, was gone.

Elen looked at Talcoran, feeling awkward.
Talcoran's expression plainly showed he wished
he were anywhere but in the royal banquet hall.
Elen almost felt sorry for him.

"We should go," she said. "They are dousing
the torches."

"Do you wish to take my arm?"

She felt a peculiar reluctance to touch him,
yet she did not want to offend him. He had been
placed in an uncomfortable situation. She
doubted he had any interest at all in escorting her
anywhere, yet he must obey Macbeth's order.

"That would be very nice," she said, as
politely as she could. "I don't want to trip and soil
my new gown." She forced herself to slide her
hand into the crook of his elbow. Through the
smooth wool of his tunic sleeve she felt warmth
and strong muscles. She made herself smile at
him. It was not necessary for her to look up to do
so, as she had to do with Patric. Talcoran's face,
level with her own, remained intent and serious.

"It is a beautiful dress," he said.

"I—thank you." she stammered. "It was
Gruach's."

He was silent as they paced through the
corridors and across the courtyard to Macbeth's
rooms. Elen began to understand that Talcoran
was shy, even more shy than she was, and she felt
a dawning sympathy for him. It must be dreadful
to escort an unknown woman and not know what
to say to her. She wondered what she would say to
Elen if she were Talcoran.

"You should have silk gowns," he said
suddenly. "You should wear silk. And a warm fur
cape in the winter."

"What a lovely idea. Then I'd never be cold."

"I wish I—" He stopped. They had reached
Macbeth's apartment. He opened the door and

waited for her to enter.

"Thank you for your good care of me, Talcoran."

"I was ordered to do it," he said gruffly, and walked away.

Elen found Lulach in her room, weeping in Ava's arms. His lower lip was bloody and swollen, and he had bruises on his wrists.

"He came looking for you," Ava told her. "I washed his face, but there's no repairing his new tunic."

"Lulach, what happened?"

"Malcolm beat me. He said I must let him, or when he grows up and becomes king, he'll cut off my head."

Elen was horrified. Having had no brothers, she knew she was ignorant of the scrapes boys got into, but this seemed unreasonably violent.

"Let's tuck you into your own bed before you catch a chill."

"Will you stay with me until I sleep?"

"If you like."

She did stay, sitting by his side and trying to distract him by telling him about Laggan.

"I hate Malcolm," Lulach murmured.

"Hush, go to sleep."

"He said I am a weakling. He calls me Lulach the Fool. I hate him."

3

The morning sun slanted through the narrow windows of the king's bedchamber. Patric's sharp glance took in the golden harp tossed carelessly into a corner, the overturned goblet that spilled the dregs of last night's wine onto a polished wooden table beside the bed, and the tumbled bed itself, its fur covering half on the floor.

Duncan had wrapped a gold silk cloak about himself; his skinny, nearly hairless legs and bare feet showed beneath the hem. His eyes were red-rimmed.

His latest mistress, a plump, golden-haired woman, eyed Patric with interest and drew her thin red silk robe over her nakedness rather too slowly for true modesty.

"Leave us," Duncan barked at her. "And tell Cormac to keep everyone else out of here. I want to talk to Patric alone."

"Will I see you tonight?" the woman murmured.

"I don't know. Go away."

The woman gathered up her belongings and slipped out the door. Duncan sank onto the edge of the bed and put his head in his hands.

"Christ, my head aches. Give me some water, will you, Patric? And the basin."

Patric brought the golden basin and poured some water into it. Duncan splashed the water on his face, then took the pitcher, drank from it, and spat into the basin. Patric watched him impassively.

"That's better." The king rose, pulling the cloak more tightly about his shoulders. "That damned Thorfinn. No matter what I promise him, he won't submit to me. What am I going to do about him?"

"He has his own ways, my lord. Perhaps you should be content to live peacefully with the ruler of Orkney as an equal ally."

"Never. Orkney must become part of Alba. I'll find a way. I'll think of something. I suspect Thorfinn has been plotting with my northern nobles. I know they are angry about the Northumbrian campaign. If I had won a great victory at Durham, they would proclaim me a mighty king, but as it is, they are close to revolt."

"Lochaber and Moray are loyal, my lord, and they are your most important generals. They will keep the others in line."

"Lochaber, yes. I trust Bancho. What about Fife? Is your brother-in-law my man, Patric? I never can tell about a quiet man who drinks as little as he does."

Patric repressed a smile at this assessment of Fionna's husband.

"Mac Duff is totally trustworthy, my lord."

"Good. He's rich and powerful. I need him. I wonder about Macbeth, though. Did you know he styles himself *Ri Alba* in Moray? King of Alba, indeed! I am King of Alba. He is King of Moray only, a sub-king, and that at my pleasure."

Patric knew that Macbeth's power in Moray was such that Duncan's pleasure, or his will, meant nothing there.

"He adheres to the old tribal customs, my lord," Patric said soothingly. "His title is more to please his subjects than to advance himself."

"I doubt that. Pah! I'm sick of them all." With a sweep of his hand, Duncan dismissed his fractious nobles. "That isn't why I wanted to talk to you. Patric, you have served me well. Almost alone among my nobles, you have never given me cause to doubt you. The loss of your brother at Durham was a blow to me, too. You deserve a reward for your loyalty and your suffering."

"I expect no reward for the loyalty I owe to you as my king."

"Don't talk like a damned courtier. I like you best when you are honest with me."

"I am being honest." Patric looked Duncan right in the eye.

"Perhaps you are, you idealistic young fool. How do you like Elen of Laggan?"

Patric was so taken aback by the unexpected question that he could find no ready answer.

"Why do you think I sent you riding like a madman to Laggan to fetch her to court? I wanted to give you a chance to meet her before all these other slavering hounds who call themselves men caught the scent of a great heiress. Do you want her or don't you?"

"Want her, my lord?"

"She's too thin for my liking," Duncan went on. "I want a woman in my bed with some fat on her bones, but what do you think? Her inheritance will make her look plumper."

Patric was irrationally annoyed at Duncan's words. Men commonly talked that way about women, but the subject here was Elen, and it was a subject on which Patric was sensitive.

"I like her well enough," he said cautiously, and watched Duncan explode into laughter.

"Well enough, indeed! One of the greatest heiresses in Alba, and you like her only well enough." Patric's king wiped his eyes, still laughing. "I'll give her to you for wife if you want, and afterward you may do as you wish for female companionship. Well, what do you say? Will you be the next Thane of Laggan? You do need a wife, you know. You must have an heir, since you are the only man of your family left alive. And I need a man I can trust to hold Laggan for me. It seems a suitable arrangement for both of us. Speak up, Patric. Will you accept or no?"

"If you wish it, my lord, I will be most pleased to wed her," Patric said formally, trying unsuccessfully to quiet the sudden excitement that flooded his mind as he finally comprehended that Duncan was serious. "Will you let me speak with her first to determine if she is willing?"

"Why wouldn't she be? Every woman at court would like to tumble into your bed. Except for my queen and Macbeth's Gruach, of course. Gruach. Now there's a hot-blooded wench, for all she's nearly thirty years old. I'd like to get my hands on her."

Patric stared dumbly at his king. He was well used to the crudities of soldiers in the field. Duncan's words did not shock him, nor did the sentiment behind them. He was himself aware of the thick air of sensuality that lay about Macbeth's lady. No, it was rather the speaker himself who failed Patric's youthful ideal of kingly behavior. A king should not speak aloud such thoughts about another man's wife. It was unworthy of his high rank. It was also foolish in a practical sense, for there were often unnoticed listeners about the court, who could carry tales to a jealous husband, and then . . . Patric, recalling the power of the Mormaer of Moray, did not want to think about what would happen then.

"Go on," Duncan was saying. "Go and ask her. But I have made up my mind, and whether she says yes or no, you will be betrothed at this night's feast."

Patric bowed himself out, more irritated and angry than he dared show. He was acutely conscious of having seriously damaged his cause with Elen by his stupid teasing at Duncan's feast two nights ago. Damn the man! Why couldn't Duncan wait a few days at least, let him approach Elen properly, as a serious suitor? As a king's ward, she had no real choice in the matter once the king had decided upon her husband, but Patric wanted a willing bride.

The poor girl was still mourning her father. She was like a shy, frightened bird. He must deal gently with her, he knew. He must resist the urge that shook him so violently each time he met her. He had barely been able to restrain himself that night in his tent. He had wanted to push her onto his pallet and throw himself atop her and make her his beyond all questioning. And then, the night by the stream, when she had responded so eagerly, he had been certain she felt as he did. Her avoidance of him since then was only proof of her innocence.

He had planned to discuss the matter with Duncan that very day, to request the thing Duncan had just so impulsively given him. He knew there would be objections from Macbeth, who felt no kindness or friendship toward southern nobles such as Patric mac Keith. He would overcome whatever objections Macbeth might make. He and Elen would be together, and they would be happy. She would come to love him if she did not already. He was certain of it.

At the memory of her fragile, trembling body

against his, he felt the heat flow into his loins. He cursed again as his healthy young body strained against his tunic. He found his way to the courtyard and sluiced his burning face with icy water from the wooden horse trough before he went in search of the Thane of Laggan's daughter.

He found her in the chapel. Elen knelt in prayer with her maid Ava by her side.

Patric got to his knees and sent up a fervent prayer of his own. Then he waited with growing impatience until Elen had completed her devotions. He intercepted her just outside the chapel door.

"What do you want of me?" she demanded, the red spots on her cheeks betraying her calm demeanor and the ice in her voice.

"I want to speak with you. I have the king's permission," he added hastily.

"King Duncan gave you permission to speak to me?" She looked as if she did not believe him.

"He commanded me to do so." Looking down at her lovely, bewildered face, Patric could not stop smiling.

"Then I must agree. I cannot disobey my king."

Ava had been listening to this conversation with undisguised interest.

"There is a garden next to the chapel," the little maid offered helpfully. "I could keep watch at the entrance to be sure you aren't disturbed."

"That will do very well," Patric said.

A high stone wall around the garden gave them complete privacy. Elen faced him with a touch of defiance in her manner.

"What is it you wish to say to me, Patric?"

He was only twenty, but Patric thought of himself as experienced and able to deal with nearly any situation. Now all of his self-confidence suddenly deserted him. Faced by the beautiful, delicate girl upon whom he had set his heart, his quick mind was a blank, his clever tongue silent.

"Elen," he managed at last, "marry me."

It was a far cry from the elegant speech he had hoped to make.

"What did you say?"

"King Duncan has said I may ask you to marry me."

Her comprehension was quick.

"You mean he has decided to give me to you. Along with Lagganshire and the title of Thane."

"Yes," he said. He could not tell if she was angry or not. "But only if you want it. I will not force you against your will. I may have given you reason to dislike me, and if you do, I will tell Duncan I refuse his offer of your hand. I don't care what he does to me. I won't marry you if you don't want it, too."

She looked at him as if she had never seen him before. Her midnight-blue eyes seemed to see into his soul. He had the uncomfortable sense that she was examining him with some ancient female knowledge he could never understand.

"Do you want to marry me, Patric?"

"I want it more than I have ever wanted anything in my life."

"I believe you. You and I both know we must obey the king, and yet you have contrived to give me a choice. You would let me say no if I wish it, and take the punishment for my disobedience on yourself."

He felt a sense of elation that she had understood his motives so quickly.

"I will marry you," she said softly.

It took a moment for her words to sink in. She had moved a step nearer to him.

"Will you kiss me to seal our bargain?" she asked shyly.

He touched her lips lightly, then drew back.

"Are you certain?" he asked.

"Yes," she breathed. "Oh, yes."

Their mouths met, warm and searching. Patric pulled his love against him. As her lips parted under the pressure of his tongue, he felt astonishment at the free offering of herself that she was making. She clung to him and gave back kiss for kiss in innocent passion.

Before all thought was swept away on waves of delight, Patric promised himself that he would treat her gently. Elen was so lovely, so precious, and she was his to protect. Certain of his happy future, he renewed his amorous attentions to his willing companion. . . .

Someone was coughing. Coughing again.

"Hsst! Mistress, master, please."

Unwillingly, Patric released Elen. Ava still stood at the garden entrance, her back to the lovers.

"What is it?" Patric asked.

"The priest is coming. He's here."

With great presence of mind Patric took Elen's arm, steadying her and leading her toward the gate. Her hair was badly mussed, but he hoped a priest would not notice that, and he silently thanked heaven that Ava was present. The three of them were at the gate when the priest reached it.

"Good day to you, father," Patric said politely.

"Good day, my children. Peace be with you." The priest entered the garden and began to stroll slowly down the path. As Patric steered Elen out of the garden she awakened from her kiss-induced trance.

"Do my cousins know of King Duncan's decision?" she asked.

"I do not think he told anyone before he spoke to me."

"He should have discussed it with them at once."

"Duncan is sometimes impetuous. He may have seen Macbeth after giving me permission to speak to you."

"I had better go to Gruach now and tell her."

"Shall I come with you?"

"No." Elen remembered her cousins' deliberate snub of Patric at Duncan's feast. She had a feeling they would be none too happy about her proposed marriage. "I'll do this myself."

Patric escorted the two women to Macbeth's apartments and kissed Elen before the door, in spite of Ava's giggles and the raised eyebrows of several passers-by.

"You should comb your hair," Ava advised once they were in Elen's room.

"I will. You may go. I want to be alone for a little while." She sat by the window, slowly drawing the comb through her hair and gazing dreamily out at the misty early autumn landscape.

She had never dreamed that such a wonderful thing could happen. Her previously mixed feelings about Patric had been immediately put right by his proposal. If he was to be her husband, it did not matter that he had kissed and fondled her on their journey from Laggan, and it was good that she had enjoyed what he did. It had taken only a day or two of observing Macbeth and Gruach to make Elen realize that such feelings were natural between husband and wife. She and Patric would feel toward each other as her married cousins did. She felt only a faint prickle of fear about what might happen once their bedroom door was closed. Whatever that mystery was, Patric would make it all right. Her body, gloriously alive after his most recent kisses and gentle explorations, assured her of that.

The only problem Elen could see was the response her cousins might make to the news, but even they could not deny King Duncan's command. She finished combing her hair and went in search of Gruach.

Gruach was not pleased.

"It is too soon after your father's death," she declared angrily. "It's disrespectful."

"It was the king's own decision," Elen said. "And I want to marry him, Gruach. I do."

"What do you know of such things?" Gruach was scornful. Then her eyes narrowed, and she took a step toward Elen. "What did you do on the journey from Laggan to Dunfermline?"

"Do? Nothing." Elen could not meet Gruach's eyes.

"You had better be speaking the truth, my girl."

"He kissed me," Elen confessed.

"And? Was there more?"

"No." How could she tell the angry Gruach how Patric had held her breast in his hand? As for what they had done this day, the way he had wrapped his arms around her so tightly she could hardly breathe . . . no, she could never tell anyone what she had felt then. "We are betrothed. It doesn't matter if he kissed me."

Gruach relented, her affection for Elen overcoming her anger.

"You are in my care, cousin, and you are very innocent. It is my duty to keep you safe for your future husband."

"I understand, and I thank you for your concern, but Patric and I have done nothing wrong."

"Well, since the king himself commands this betrothal, I suppose there is nothing to do now but see to it that you are properly dressed for the ceremony tonight. I'm glad we decided on cream-colored wool for your new dress. Will it be done in time?"

"I think so. Ava is sewing as fast as she can."

Macbeth was no more pleased than his wife had been. Duncan had personally informed him of his decision to marry Elen to Patric. The rage Macbeth dared not show before the king spilled out of him in his own chambers.

"I am your nearest living relative!" he stormed at Elen. "I should have been consulted before Duncan gave you away so quickly."

"I am very happy, cousin."

"Happy? Pah!" Macbeth spat into the rushes on the floor. "You know nothing about ruling a country. Duncan could have given you to someone who would be more useful to him than Patric of Bute. But Patric pleases Duncan because he is nearly as English as Duncan himself. English manners, English clothes, now even English laws. Duncan would discard all that is fine and good about Alba, all the old ways.

"Damn Duncan!" Macbeth's fist slammed into his hand. "The impetuous, spoiled young fool! He never thinks. First he invades Northumbria, where hundreds of good men are killed needlessly, including your own father, Elen. Next he insults Macdowald until Macdowald has quit the court and is near to open revolt. And now this ridiculous marriage!"

"Hush! Someone will hear you," Gruach cautioned, her voice low and urgent.

"Duncan wastes his authority," Macbeth said

in a quieter tone. "And someday soon, it will all be gone."

Macbeth, resplendent in his blue court tunic and his silver chain of office, led Elen into the great hall for her betrothal. There were murmurs of approval as she passed between the twin lines of watching courtiers. For the first time in her life, Elen believed that she looked beautiful.

Gruach's large silver mirror had shown her a slender young woman in a simple gown of the creamiest ivory wool, trimmed with bands of gold embroidery at neck and wrists and belted with a golden sash that Gruach had lent her. Her unbound hair streamed down her back. Her face was flushed with color. Her dark blue eyes sparkled. Her happiness was a tangible thing, apparent to anyone who looked at her.

It is Patric who has done this to me, she thought. She went joyfully to meet him where he stood before King Duncan's raised chair.

Afterward, she remembered nothing of the ceremony. She knew only that Patric's hand had held hers in a warm and steady grasp, and that he had given her a wide, heavy gold bracelet for a gift.

"The wedding will take place in one month," Duncan announced.

"My lord." Gruach moved forward, her flame-red gown a brilliant splash of color, her arms and neck weighted down with gold jewelry. "My lord, may I speak?"

"Certainly, cousin. What is it?"

"Elen is too shy to tell you herself, but she still mourns deeply for her father. She is also young, only sixteen, and newly come to court. She needs schooling before she will be ready to take her place as the wife of one of your great nobles."

Gruach paused to smile at Patric before continuing. "My lord, would you be kind enough to
delay the wedding for one year?"

No, Elen thought. No, I want to be with Patric!
She opened her lips to protest. Then Macbeth's
strong arm was across her shoulders, and his deep
voice boomed out over her feeble sounds.

"My lord, my wife is right. I, too, believe a
year's delay would be wise. In the meantime, I
would be happy to see to the administration of
Lagganshire, so that when Patric and Elen do
marry, she will bring him an even greater dowry
than she does now."

Elen fought back tears of disappointment. She
would not disgrace herself by crying before the
king. Beside her, Patric made an impatient
motion.

"Elen," he asked, "Is this what you want?"

Elen swallowed hard, forcing the lump in her
throat down so she could speak. No, it is not, she
started to say, but Gruach cut her off.

"Of course it is what she wants. I know my
cousin's heart. You see, she is so shy she cannot
tell you herself."

"Elen?" Patric persisted.

Elen was afraid she would dissolve into tears.
How could she defy her cousins before all of these
people, who would surely laugh at her—or worse,
think she was a rude, ungrateful girl when
Macbeth and Gruach had been so kind to her. She
found that she was so upset she could not shake or
nod her head, or even meet Patric's eyes. She did
not see the expression of deep hurt on his face
when he looked at her.

"Patric," Duncan said, "What is your opinion
of this? Are you willing to wait?"

Patric made the only correct answer.

"I am eager to wed, but I will do whatever you wish, my lord."

Still, Duncan wavered.

"It would be best, my lord," Macbeth insisted.

"Oh, very well. The marriage will take place one year from today," Duncan announced. "But you are still betrothed," he added to Patric, as though that were encouragement.

Through his pain and his humiliation, Patric reminded himself of his decision to go slowly with Elen. Perhaps he had not adequately controlled his boiling emotions in the garden that morning. Perhaps he had frightened her. He had not thought so from her eager response, but it might be that she had been trying to please him, and then later had unburdened herself of her fears to her nearest female relative. He would be more careful in the future, hold himself in check so as not to upset her.

Then he remembered that, unwed or not, she was still his betrothed. He could find time for them to be alone together, and gradually he would teach her not to be afraid of her feelings for him. He bent to kiss her cheek.

"No, no," Gruach said, laughing and drawing Elen away. "Don't embarrass the poor girl in public, Patric. You must wait until you are wed."

"That was unkindly done," Fionna whispered in his ear. "I don't think they want you to marry Elen at all."

"But I will," Patric replied. "Whether they want it or not."

Duncan had made his eldest son Malcolm ruler of Cumbria. Malcolm celebrated the event by pummeling Lulach until his nose was bloody.

"A wild, undisciplined, eight-year-old boy!"

Gruach exclaimed. "Has Duncan gone mad?"

"Why shouldn't he do this?" Macbeth replied. "Duncan's grandfather made him King of Strathclyde when he wasn't much older than Malcolm is now. That was to prepare the way for Duncan to become King of Alba, and now Duncan is ensuring Malcolm's succession in the same manner."

"Under the Law of Tanistry, you should have been king instead of Duncan. You should be the next king instead of Malcolm."

"Duncan's grandfather changed the law, and all the nobles swore to uphold the change. But you are not the only one in Alba who feels that way, Gruach. Several men have spoken to me today."

"And?" Gruach waited breathlessly for her husband's reply.

"Duncan is the king and has my loyalty. I have given him my oath."

Before Gruach could find an answer to that, Elen slipped out of the room. She had heard this same argument many times by now and it bored her. She was not on very good terms with her cousins these days. They had quarreled bitterly after Elen's betrothal.

"How could you have insisted on a year's delay?" Elen had asked. "You know how much I want to marry Patric."

"You are too young," Gruach said. "Wait a while."

"That's a stupid excuse. You were just my age when you married Gillecomgan."

"Elen, we want what is best for you." Macbeth was eminently reasonable. "There is more than your youthful affection for Patric at stake here. There are vast lands, all of Lagganshire, and an important title to consider. This is a matter of power. Love has nothing to do with the arrangement of such a marriage. You should know that without being told."

"The king said I could marry Patric. Why are you being so difficult?" The tears she had held back with such an effort in Duncan's hall now fell freely. Elen's face was wet with them.

"My dear girl, have patience." Macbeth enfolded her in his arms. "A year is not so long. In time, you will come to see we are only concerned for your welfare."

Elen understood it was useless to fight them. They honestly believed they were doing what was right for her. She would have to endure it. She drew on years of convent schooling to make herself obey them with the meekness that was her duty.

The hardest part was never seeing Patric alone. Whenever they met there always seemed to be someone else nearby. In the two weeks since their betrothal they had managed only one hasty kiss, when both Fionna and Conal were present.

Now, as Elen hurried toward the chapel, she met Patric with his brother-in-law. After greeting her, Conal asked, "Is Macbeth in his chambers?"

"Yes, they are talking about Malcolm."

"Everyone is talking about Malcolm," Conal said in his solemn way.

"How is Lulach?" Patric asked.

"He'll be all right once his nose regains its rightful size." Impulsively, Elen added, "I wish someone would stop Malcolm from beating him all the time."

"Lulach is too old to be so soft," Patric said in stern tones. "Gruach coddles him because he is her only child. If you want to help him, tell him to fight back. He's four years older than Malcolm, he ought to be able to win occasionally. He should be at weapons practice every day, too."

"He's not very warlike." Elen knew Patric's advice was good, but she could not help feeling just a bit angry with him. He could have been more sympathetic to poor Lulach. Then she noticed for the first time how serious both men looked.

"Tell Lulach he must become warlike very soon," Conal told her, his face grim. "And when you go to chapel, pray for us. We are going to war again before long."

4

Winter 1039 to Spring 1040.

Macdowald, the disaffected noble who had left Duncan's court in a rage, had turned to open revolt.

"He and his men have been seen near Forres, in my own Morayshire." Macbeth was coldly angry. "Duncan is sending Bancho and me north with an army to crush him. I'll have that devil's head on a pike for carrying his feud with the king into my lands."

When Macbeth and Bancho rode north, Patric mac Keith and Conal mac Duff rode with them. King Duncan remained at Dunfermline. He had been ill, and his physicians said he was not well enough yet to ride so far.

Elen and Patric managed one brief meeting before he left. Elen had gone to Conal's apartments to visit Fionna, and while she was there, Patric appeared.

"I ought to consult with my servants," Fionna said. "I want to be certain they are packing everything Conal will need. Will you excuse me for a little while?"

"Dear sister." Patric watched her disappear out the door with a knowing smile on his face. "I knew I could depend on you."

For the first time since the day of their betrothal, Elen and Patric were alone. They regarded each other warily from opposite sides of the hearth, each afraid to make the first move toward the other.

"You will take care, my lord," Elen said nervously. "I would like to see you come home safely." To her own ears the words sounded silly and too formal. Why could she never seem to say the right thing in exactly the right way, as Gruach always did?

"Elen." Patric's large hand moved toward her, reaching across the space that separated them. "Elen, my love."

Elen's right hand seemed to take on a life of its own. She felt it rising, stretching toward Patric's hand. She could not have controlled that movement no matter how hard she tried.

Their fingertips touched, parted, touched again. Their hands met, palm to palm. Elen's slender fingers vanished into his giant's grasp. He gave a gentle tug, stepping forward as he did, and she fell against his chest and rested there in perfect contentment.

"We should not be alone together," she murmured after a little while. "My cousins would be so angry if they knew."

"I care nothing for Macbeth, or Gruach either. I want you."

He was gentle at first, holding back so as not to frighten her. His kisses were light, falling softly on mouth and cheeks and brow. To his surprise, she moved firmly against him, put her arms around his neck, and kissed him back with growing ardor. He found it harder and harder to restrain himself.

"Patric," she whispered, "why don't you kiss

me the way you did before? Have I displeased you?''

"Never. But Gruach said you were afraid of me, and shy. I thought that was why you wanted the wedding delayed."

"I? It was Gruach and Macbeth. I wanted to marry you at once. I should have spoken out, but in front of the king and all those people, I couldn't. Oh, Patric, I was weak, and now you are going away to war, and who knows what will happen?"

"Do you mean that?" He was looking at her with a radiant expression that made her heart sing. "You do want to marry me, and at once?"

"Yes."

Suddenly she was swept off her feet. He spun around with her in his arms until she was dizzy. He laughed and laughed, and kissed her, and whirled her around again until they finally collapsed into Conal's big wooden chair that sat by the hearth. Elen cuddled on his lap, her legs over one arm of the chair, her head thrown back on his shoulder.

"My love," he said, still grinning broadly.

"My love," she replied, between happy giggles.

She was dizzy from all the spinning. His mouth found hers again while it was open in the middle of a giggle, and he was laughing, too. And then they were very, very serious. His laughing mouth was suddenly a fiery brand, igniting her being in a blaze of longing. Her fingers laced through his curly hair, pulling his head closer. She wanted to melt into him, to become one with him in the fire he had started.

He removed his lips from hers only to light a series of small flames across her cheek and down her throat. His hand cupped her breast, sending remembered heat curling deep into her innermost being. What she wanted most desperately at that moment was to be free of her clothes. She wanted to feel his hands on her flesh, though she knew his touch would sear her until she was only ashes.

She gritted her teeth against the feelings rising in her. She shouldn't, she mustn't. Macbeth and Gruach would be furious with her. But this was Patric, her betrothed. She was his, to do with as he wanted. There was nothing wrong in it, and she wanted to know again the delicious, heavy sweetness his touch created. She gave herself up to pleasure.

Patric shifted in the chair, holding her closer still, and now she was aware that he was pushing her skirt up over her knees. She felt his hand, hot on the skin of her inner thigh, his touch sending waves of heat upward toward the hidden center of herself that had begun to throb with a delicious ache.

He moved again, letting her feel his arousal. She looked at him with eyes wide and dark, and brilliant with newly awakened desire.

"Patric?" Her voice was full of wonder as she recognized how deep was his need of her, and how strong the control he had set upon himself.

"Ah, my love, now I know you don't fear me." His hand moved again, stroking along her thigh, sliding upward in a gesture of tender possession. "Were we in some private place, I'd make you mine right now."

"I am yours. I will always be yours."

"I know that at last. We were meant to be together, Elen, and nothing will keep us apart." His mouth lingered on hers once more as he stood up, still cradling her in his arms. Then he set her carefully on her feet. "I cannot see Duncan again before I leave for the north. He is still weak from his illness, and the physicians have limited his visitors. But I promise you, the day I return I will speak with him privately. I will tell him you have overcome the shyness of which your cousin Gruach complained, and we want to wed at once. We'll be married when I return, and then, my sweet, I will bed you with great joy.''

His youthful confidence carried her along, dissolving any reservations she might have had about Macbeth's ability to delay or prevent their marriage.

"I will come to you with joy," she said. ''Though I wish we need not wait. Patric, if you want, I'll go to your room with you now, before you must leave.''

His smile was rueful as he caressed her face.

''I know the dangers I face, love. I am deeply grateful for the gift you offer, but I'll not accept it just yet. I'll do nothing that might hurt you.'' His handsome face grew serious. ''I have a favor to ask of you, my sweet.''

''I'll do whatever you ask.''

''You will make an excellent wife,'' he teased, kissing the tip of her nose. ''It's not for me, it's Fionna. Will you be her friend, Elen? Did you know she's with child? I've heard the first babe is the most difficult. She is the only kin I have left, and I worry about her. She will be lonely once Conal and I are gone.''

''I'll be her friend gladly,'' Elen replied. ''And when you return, I will even more gladly be her sister.''

He thanked her with yet another tender kiss. When Fionna returned a short time later, she found Elen sitting demurely beside Patric, telling him about Laggan, so he could begin to learn of the domain that would soon be his.

"You were with him," Gruach said. "Alone with him."

"Have you set spies on me in his sister's household?" Elen was amazed at her own courage as she faced the older woman. For love of Patric she would anger even her dear cousin. "He is my betrothed and he is going to war. We only said good-bye."

"Well, you were alone only a short time," Gruach said in a softer tone. "I suppose there is no harm in it. Who knows what will happen in battle? I fear for Macbeth constantly."

"Then you must understand how I feel."

"Aye, I do." Gruach's arm went around Elen's slender waist. "I love you, and I only want what will be best for you, my dear."

"I know."

Elen wished that Gruach and Macbeth's conception of what was best for her was more in keeping with her own ideas on the matter. She said as much to Fionna the next morning while they watched the army ride out of Dunfermline. The co-generals, Macbeth and Bancho, led the way. Talcoran, Macbeth's most trusted aide, rode close behind his lord. Mounted on a great black stallion, garbed in leather helmet and a flowing deep red cape, Talcoran looked surprisingly noble, almost heroic. Elen noticed him with startled eyes before her attention was caught by the sight of the man for whom she had been looking.

Patric wore a blue tunic and cloak. Tall and proud on his snorting, prancing steed, which he easily kept under control, he was to Elen's eyes the handsomest man in the entire army. His glance met hers for a moment, and he raised one leather-gloved hand in salute before he passed by.

Patric and Conal mac Duff each rode at the

head of a detachment of their own men, as did many of the other nobles that Elen had met since she came to court. She sent up a silent prayer for the safety of all of them, and then turned to comfort Fionna, who was trying hard not to weep as she gazed after her husband's back.

"Don't worry about your cousins," Fionna said as they walked to her quarters after the army was gone. "No one wanted me to marry Conal mac Duff, but at last King Duncan commanded it. Now Patric loves Conal like a brother, though they argue all the time. Conal and I are very happy, or we will be once he returns safely from this campaign." Fionna patted her newly rounded abdomen. "You will be happy, too, one day soon. You'll see. My brother will make you a marvellous husband."

Dunfermline was quiet with most of the men gone. Gruach was often in attendance on the queen, who continued ill and kept to her rooms. To occupy her days, Elen divided her time between Fionna, who was rapidly becoming a valued friend, and Lulach. Following Patric's advice, she encouraged Lulach to attend weapons practice daily, and she tried to teach him to read, an activity the delicate boy much preferred. He would make a better priest than a warrior, but Elen knew there was no chance that Lulach would be permitted to follow his own inclinations. She sometimes thought that she and Lulach were little more than pawns being moved about a chessboard to suit the needs or ambitions of others.

Their nerves had been stretched to the breaking point before news came from the north. When they received word that a dusty rider had stumbled into King Duncan's presence with messages from his generals, the few nobles left at

Dunfermline, all of the ladies, and many of the servants began gathering in the great hall, to wait in anxious expectation. When Duncan appeared at last, a hush fell.

"There is good news," Duncan proclaimed, his words producing a raucous cheer. "Macbeth and Bancho have suppressed the revolt. According to the dispatches, there was little fighting for our men to do. At sight of the army drawn up for battle, most of Macdowald's men left his side and joined Macbeth. Macdowald's remaining supporters were easily defeated. There were few of our men killed, and fewer wounded. A great victory for Alba and the crown!"

Duncan himself led the cheers that followed this report. He was glowing with pleasure. Watching him accept the acclamations of his courtiers, Elen thought he looked more like a king than she had ever seen him look before.

"Perhaps he will become a better ruler as he grows older and wiser," she murmured to Fionna.

"So Patric believes," Fionna said. "Conal doesn't entirely agree with him, but Patric thinks time and experience will steady Duncan."

"It was not Duncan's victory, but Macbeth's," Gruach said, voicing a different opinion of the news.

"Bancho of Lochaber was there also," Elen reminded her.

"Aye. Bancho. That one." Gruach was thoughtful. Then she brightened. She had had her own messages from her triumphant husband. "But the battle was fought in Morayshire, on Macbeth's own lands, and he it was who put down the revolt and had Macdowald's head placed on a pike on the battlements of Forres Castle, as he had sworn to do. And now he is coming home to me." Her silver-grey eyes shone.

Elen could barely conceal her own excitement. Patric had promised he would speak to Duncan as soon as he returned. It was possible they would be married in just a few weeks.

"They will be home soon," she said to Fionna.

"I hope so." Fionna laughed as she regarded her rapidly expanding waistline. "If Conal is away much longer, he may not recognize me when he does see me again."

The joy over Macbeth's victory was short-lived, for soon came news from eastern Alba that the Danes had invaded from the sea. The weary army returned to Dunfermline only to learn it would have to march again in a few days.

"The Thane of Cawdor will hold the Danes off until we arrive," Bancho said. He had stopped in Macbeth's quarters to greet Gruach and Elen.

"I don't trust that man," Macbeth grumbled. "He is too ambitious." He was obviously tired, his usually ruddy face pale with lack of sleep, his blond hair and beard streaked with the dust of travel.

"So are we all ambitious, if it comes to that," said Bancho. He stretched, wriggling his shoulders and rubbing at a sore spot on one. "I wish we could dispense with this royal banquet tonight. I could well use a full night's sleep, but we can't cheat the king of his victory feast. Elen, have you seen Patric?"

"Not yet."

"What? If you were my betrothed, I'd have kissed you hello long before this."

"She will greet him at the banquet," Gruach said primly.

"Ah, I see. Well, you two will want to be alone." Bancho grinned at his co-general and cocked an eyebrow at Macbeth's lady. "I remember how it was when my wife was alive and

I returned from war. Elen, walk with me to the chapel. I've a few prayers to say, and I'm sure you have, too. Is this your cloak? You'll need it, the day is chill. Until this evening, my friend." Bancho and Macbeth clasped hands, and then Bancho hurried Elen out the door.

"They're keeping you from Patric, are they?" he said gruffly. "That's unfair. He won't tell you this himself, but I will. Young Patric fought bravely when we met Macdowald. Together, he and Talcoran saved Macbeth's life when he was surrounded by Macdowald's men."

"I had not heard that." Perhaps if Macbeth were grateful to Patric, he would not object when Duncan gave them permission to marry at once.

The chapel was empty except for a blue-cloaked shadow that stepped from behind a pillar. Elen's cry of happy astonishment was smothered against the shadow's broad chest.

"What a surprise!" Bancho chuckled. "Why, Patric, I had no idea you would be here. Now, I will leave you two alone while I give thanks for our victory. I feel certain the good Lord will understand a betrothed couple meeting in His house."

"Bancho." Elen reached out one hand to stop her father's old friend. "You planned this, didn't you, so Patric and I could meet privately?"

"I don't know what you mean." Bancho headed for the altar.

Because of the location and Bancho's presence at the other end of the chapel, their embrace was a good deal more chaste and restrained than either Patric or Elen really wanted it to be. Still, it was wonderful to feel Patric's arms about her again, warm and strong and whole.

"You are unhurt?" she asked. "I was so

frightened for you. I think I would die if anything happened to you."

"Nothing will happen to me." Patric laughed with all the carefree self-confidence of youth. "Let me look at you, my love. You've grown thinner. Once we are wed, I'll feed you well and plump you up a bit."

"Like Fionna?" she joked, and then blushed at the thought.

"Aye, like Fionna. She looks wondrous well, doesn't she? I'll fatten you in the same way, as soon as I can. Would you like that?" Again he caught her against his chest.

"Yes. Oh, yes. I want to bear your children. Have you spoken to the king?"

"Not about our marriage, no. There was no time for that when I saw him earlier. I can't do it tonight, either, with this great feast planned, and Macbeth and Bancho to be honored. I'll talk to him tomorrow. I'm sure he will agree to let us marry at once. It will be only a short wait now until we are together, Elen, my love."

But in the morning came the news that the Thane of Cawdor had rebelled against King Duncan and had gone over to the Danes. The new allies were ravaging the eastern coastline, and pushing even further inland.

"That damned traitor!" Macbeth's deep voice rang through the king's great hall. "My lord, I'll have his cursed head on a pike as I had Macdowald's. I'll make this land of Alba safe from invaders."

Elen, standing at one side of the hall with Lulach, could not share in the bloodthirsty cheers that now rose to the very roof-beams. Cawdor and the Danes had laid her hopes in ruins, at least temporarily. She felt Lulach's thin hand in hers.

"Patric will have to go away again, won't he?"

Lulach whispered. "He, and Macbeth, and Bancho. They all must go."

"I'm afraid so."

"I'm sorry, Elen. If I were king, I'd make everyone be happy and at peace. Why do they have to fight all the time?"

"Sometimes it's necessary, my dear." But in her heart, Elen was asking the same question.

Once more Elen and Fionna watched the army depart. There had been no time for Patric to speak to the king, not even time for Elen and Patric to meet again privately. There had been only a hasty good-bye kiss under Gruach's frowning gaze, before he was gone. She had a moment longer with Bancho.

"Thank you," she said, hugging him tightly. "Our meeting in the chapel was all we had. I am so closely guarded."

"It's to keep you safe, lass. You and Patric will have your days together, when the time is right. You are both young and it's hard to be patient, I know, but try." Then Bancho, too, mounted his horse and rode away.

The late autumn storms, which had most fortunately held off during the campaign against Macdowald, now descended upon them, followed by a sudden mid-winter chill. Duncan's army in eastern Alba lay bogged down in winter quarters, unable to move for ice and snow.

At Dunfermline the royal court endured a tense, lonely Christmas, cheered only a little by the entertainments Duncan provided. Among the diversions was a new song he had written, performed by Duncan himself. There were those who noted sourly that the king stayed warm and safe and had ample time for writing music while his army was near to freezing.

In early February, Fionna was delivered of a

healthy son. Gruach was present, but Elen, because she was an unwed maiden, was not permitted to see her friend until the next day. She looked in disbelief at the tiny creature who slept in a wooden cradle beside Fionna's bed.

"I want to name him Keith, for my father." Fionna was pale and drawn, with dark circles under her eyes.

"Was it very difficult for you?" Elen had a dozen questions about the ordeal Fionna had just undergone, but she was too shy to ask.

"Gruach and the midwife say it was a perfectly normal birth, but it took so long—a day and a night and part of another day. I'm so tired." Fionna sighed. "At least it's over now, and they say next time will be easier."

Fionna drifted into exhausted sleep, and Elen left. She had eagerly anticipated bearing Patric's children, but now, for the first time, she felt a thrill of fear. She knew that sometimes women died in childbirth. More often, the babies died, either at birth or shortly after. Could she bear to lose the child of the man she loved? She made herself think of something else, and went to find Lulach.

The Danes had been defeated and were retreating northward. Macbeth and Bancho returned to Dunfermline to a tumultuous welcome and great honors. Macbeth was given the lands and title of the traitorous and now dead Thane of Cawdor. He was everywhere acclaimed as a great general. His apartments were crowded day and night by friends and hangers-on.

Talcoran had been given new lands in Cawdor, bestowed by Macbeth from his own prize.

"I am happy for you," Elen told him.

"It means little," Talcoran replied in his

rough way. "I have no family, no heirs to leave my holdings to when I die. All of my kin were killed in a Norse raid years ago." He paused, his dark grey eyes probing at her.

"You will marry and have children one day," Elen said. He made her nervous. She wished he wouldn't look at her in that intense way, as if he were trying to see directly into her innermost thoughts.

"I will marry only if my lord Macbeth commands it. I am content to be alone."

I wish I were, Elen thought after he had left. Patric had not returned to Dunfermline. Macbeth had sent him north with the army, in pursuit of the retreating Danes. Elen suspected it had been done on purpose, to keep him apart from her. Watching the passionately happy reunion of Macbeth and Gruach, and the tender meeting of Fionna and Conal mac Duff, Elen felt more lonely than ever before in her life.

"Patric is well," Conal assured her.

"I want him here." She could not look at mac Duff's joyful face as he watched Fionna nursing their son. Would she and Patric never be together, never have their own children?

Several weeks after the army's return, Elen found Macbeth and Talcoran in deep conversation in Macbeth's chambers, while Gruach listened with undisguised excitement. For once, her cousins' apartments were free of visitors. Even Lulach was out, practicing with his sword in the courtyard.

"Come and sit with us, Elen. You may as well hear this," Macbeth invited her, reaching up a hand to draw Elen down onto a stool beside him.

"Something will have to be done," Talcoran was indignant. "But what? And when?"

"Aye, my friend. We must be careful, but you

are right. Alba cannot go on like this."

"What has happened?" Elen looked at the tense faces around her.

"Duncan has decided that since his brother-in-law Siward has been made the new Earl of Northumbria, there will be no need to keep an army on the southern border of Alba, or to fight in the south any more."

"But that is good news, Macbeth. That means there will be peace." Patric will be home to stay, she thought, but did not say it to Macbeth.

"There will be no peace," Macbeth told her angrily. "Duncan has just created his nephew, Moddan, Mormaer of Caithness. You know, I'm sure, that Duncan's grandfather gave Caithness and Sutherland to Thorfinn of Orkney years ago, Thorfinn being another of the old king's grandsons. Now Duncan is going to attack his cousin Thorfinn and try to take those lands back from him."

Elen remembered the Norse giant who had been at court on her first night there, and what Fionna had said about him.

"Is it because Thorfinn would not submit and acknowledge Duncan as overlord of Orkney?" she asked.

"That's right. Duncan has made his nephew Moddan general and sent him north to lead his army against Thorfinn."

"But you are the king's general!" Elen exclaimed. "You and Bancho."

"We are no more. Duncan has replaced us."

"Forgive me, cousin, I know little of warfare, but Moddan has never led an army before, has he? And shouldn't the army finish with fighting the Danes before it attacks Thorfinn? The troops must be tired after three campaigns in one year. Can they carry on two wars at once?"

"Lady, you are wiser than Duncan," said Talcoran. "If he had half your wits, he'd be a better king."

"It's intolerable," Gruach declared, rising from her bench to prowl about the room like some barely-restrained beast. "Macbeth, you cannot let this insult pass unanswered. Duncan had no right to remove you. You and Bancho saved him from total disaster at Durham after he led you all into that stupid siege. You had ample opportunity to unseat him then, when nearly half his nobles wanted to revolt. You alone prevented them. You, by your loyalty, kept him on the throne. Next you conducted two successful military campaigns for him, and see how he repays you."

"Peace, wife. Let me think."

Gruach whirled on him, her eyes ablaze.

"Peace is just what we will not have while that weak fool sits on the throne! He will destroy us all with this war against Thorfinn. No one can defeat Thorfinn. He is too strong. You said that yourself. And don't forget"—Gruach's voice rose as she warmed to her theme—"don't forget that Duncan's grandfather murdered both my nephew and my husband, my dear Gillecomgan. He burned my son's father. You swore to me before we married that those deaths would be avenged. How much more must we endure before you show that you are a true chieftain—and a true man?"

"He is the king."

"Not the rightful king. Not by our old laws. And even the rightful king can be removed when he fails in his duty."

"No. I have sworn to honor him as my lord. I cannot break my oath."

"He breaks his word to you every day. And to Bancho. To all of us."

Elen had never seen Gruach so distressed. She

rose and went to her cousin, putting an arm around her to comfort her, but Gruach brushed Elen aside and continued her tirade.

"There are many who would follow you, if you will but give the word. Talcoran, would you not follow my husband?"

"To the death." Talcoran had not hesitated. Macbeth clasped his shoulder.

"You always were a true friend. But I must think carefully about this."

"Don't think too long, husband. There are others who would willingly take your place if you delay."

"Is there no other way?" Elen was frightened by what had been said. She knew that if anyone had overheard them, and carried the word to Duncan, all of their lives would be forfeit.

"None. Duncan must be removed." Gruach was implaccable.

Elen caught Talcoran's eye.

"Can't you think of something?" she begged.

Talcoran cleared his throat. It was a habit Elen had noticed before. She thought it was because of his shyness when women were present.

"Is it not possible," Talcoran asked Macbeth, "that Thorfinn could be brought to an agreement?"

"Thorfinn the Mighty would never submit to Duncan." Gruach was scornful of this idea. Talcoran ignored her and spoke again to Macbeth.

"If Thorfinn wages war against Alba, the entire country will be laid waste. We have recently seen how the Norse fight, my lord, and what they do to women and children." Talcoran's eyes rested on Elen, then moved back to Macbeth. "When Thorfinn is done, he will be King of Alba, and there will be nothing left for Duncan—or you, or anyone else—to rule."

"I agree." Macbeth smiled grimly. "I know you, old friend. You have an idea. Tell it to me."

"Thorfinn has no reason to go to war against you. You have sent no army to take his lands away. It is Duncan alone who would take them back. Thorfinn knows this."

Talcoran stopped, thinking. Macbeth waited patiently until he spoke again.

"Make an alliance with Thorfinn. Treat him as an equal and do not challenge his control of Caithness and Sutherland. Thorfinn is not on good terms with the King of Norway, who is a constant threat to him. I think Thorfinn would like the idea of an ally on his southern border while he concentrates on Norway. When you are *Ri Alba*"—here Macbeth stood up and turned away with an expression of distaste, but Talcoran went doggedly on with his speech—"When you are king of all Alba, you will have a dependable friend at your back so you can deal with the English threat."

"Trust a Norseman?" Gruach cried. "Never!"

Again Talcoran ignored her and spoke directly to Macbeth.

"You know I met Thorfinn when he was at court last autumn. We talked together many times. I think he can be trusted."

"You always were a good judge of character." Macbeth was thoughtful as he considered Talcoran's suggestion.

"I read your character well when first we met, my lord," Talcoran said. "I have never been disappointed in you. Now I think you will not be disappointed in Thorfinn."

Once more Macbeth's quarters were crowded with visitors. Now they came not to congratulate him, but to discuss in low, angry voices Duncan's plan to reconquer the lands north of Alba. Bancho was often there, as was Conal mac Duff. Elen thought Duncan must have been aware of these meetings, yet she never saw him indicate by word or action that he knew.

It was a few days after Talcoran had first advanced his plan that Macbeth returned from the king's council looking grim.

"Where is my wife?"

"Attending the queen," Elen told him. She motioned for Ava to leave them, and when they were alone, she said, "You look unhappy, cousin."

"The court is moving north."

"All of us? Isn't the queen too ill to travel?"

"That matters not." Macbeth's bitterness overflowed. "Duncan will have us trail after him like the shimmering tail of some great, blazing comet. We must witness his defeat of the Danes, and behold his triumph as the mighty Thorfinn is vanquished forever and Duncan claims all the land right up to the northern sea for his own."

"He'll never do it!" Elen exclaimed.

"No, cousin, he will never do it, for if he did, his next target would be Moray, and I cannot allow that." Macbeth drew a deep breath and let it out in a great sigh that seemed to come from the depths of his troubled soul. Elen had to strain to hear his next words. "I have not wished for this, but there must be a change in Alba soon, and it seems I must lead it."

5

July 1040.

It was evening when Patric's manservant pushed back the tent flap and entered, followed by a boy whose clothes were covered with dirt and straw. By the light of the single oil lamp burning on his table, Patric recognized one of Duncan's attendants.

"This lad claims to be a messenger from the king," the servant said, giving the boy a shove toward the center of the tent. "He says he must put his letter into no hands but yours."

"It's true, my lord." The boy looked more closely at Patric. "Aye, it's you. I've seen you at court." He pulled a crumpled parchment from beneath his jerkin and handed it to Patric.

"When did you last eat?" Patric asked.

"Yesterday at noon. King Duncan told me to ride without stopping until I found you."

"Get him some food and a blanket," Patric said to his servant. "Let him rest. I'll call you if there is a return message."

"The king said there would be no need for an answer, and that I was to remain with you until you meet him."

"Until—? Very well. Go."

Patric pulled the lamp nearer and broke the royal seal.

Patric.

I write to you in my own hand because there is no one here I can trust, not even my own secretary.

Macbeth and Brancho have grown too rich and powerful. They forget that it is their king who heaped honors on them. They repay me with ingratitude and treachery. They speak of having submitted to royal authority, and then they do whatever they want.

I *will* be king of all Alba! I will bring these contentious nobles, and their lands, under royal control! I have relieved them of their commands and appointed Moddan my chief general. Now they are plotting against me—Macbeth, Bancho and Lochaber, all of the northern nobles. Even your brother-in-law sides with them. Only a few of the men of Lothian and Cumbria are with me. I know that you are one of the loyal ones.

I need a great victory. You must drive those damned Danes into the sea, while Moddan leads his half of the army into Caithness against Thorfinn. Once you have finished with the Danes, you must march after Moddan to reinforce him. I will sail northward with the navy, and we will trap Thorfinn between our two armies and the sea. After I have destroyed Thorfinn, no one will question my right to rule Alba as I wish.

I am so certain of victory that I have ordered the court to follow the army into Morayshire. I want them all to see Thorfinn kneel at my feet to make submission and plead for his life.

Pay no heed to plots or rumors contrary to my orders. We will prevail.

Until we meet in victory.

Duncan.

Patric sat staring at the document in his hands.

It is my death-warrant, he thought. They could beat the Danes; they were nearly finished already. But the overextended, exhausted army, with an inexperienced leader like Moddan, would never defeat Thorfinn, and Duncan and his little four-ship navy could not help.

I have a fool for a king. Only a fool would have dismissed military leaders of the quality of Macbeth and Bancho in the middle of a war. Patric could understand why the others had turned against Duncan, if that was truly what they had done, though Duncan's letter did not say that they were in open revolt.

But I can't desert him, whatever happens. Patric's grandfather and Duncan's were friends, his father and brother died fighting by Duncan's side, and Patric was pledged to serve him unto death. He could not break his oath and leave him, least of all when he was alone and in such distress. He needs Patric now, and Patric would not fail his king. He knew what his duty was.

Oh, Elen, my love, I will never see you again! He brushed the thought of Elen away before the sadness it evoked could unman him. He believed she would understand his loyalty to Duncan, for had not her father also died willingly in Duncan's cause?

He rose from the folding stool by his table and, crossing the small tent in two rapid steps, pulled the entrance flap aside and stepped into the night. A sentry snapped to attention.

"Wake my officers," Patric said. "I want to

meet with them at once.'' After the man had left, he threw the king's letter onto the campfire and watched it burn.

The fortified castle of Forres was cold and damp. It was August, and still summer in the south of Alba, but here in northern Moray there had been a great storm, and the winds off the firth whistled and moaned around the wide walls, then swirled out across the open moors that lay behind the fortress.

To this desolate outpost belonging to Macbeth the Mormaer of Moray, Duncan's court had come. His ailing queen, his nobles and their ladies, their priests and servants, filled the castle to over-flowing, whilst several detachments of the army camped with their leaders outside the walls. They were soon joined by Duncan himself and what remained of his inadequate navy, driven south-ward in defeat after a sea battle with Thorfinn of Orkney.

The king's red-gold banner floated bravely over the walls of Forres, although within there was naught but gloom. No sooner had Duncan reached dry land than he was stricken with a puzzling disease that kept him in his bed for days. He had scarcely recovered when word came that his nephew Moddan, in whom Duncan had placed all his hopes, had been ambushed and slain by Thorfinn's lieutenant, Thorkill Fostri. In the wake of Moddan's death, the remnants of his army made their way to Forres, where they added their numbers to the men already there.

It was not long before the castle and its environs reeked of its guests, of food cooking and peat fires, of animal and human ordure, of rotting food and unwashed bodies. Gulls circled above the walls, now and then diving down to scavenge some choice morsel from a rubbish heap. Their wild, forlorn cries added one more note to the sounds of horses, of shouted commands, of the ringing of the blacksmith's anvil, of the shrill voices of courtiers.

Elen picked her way carefully across a littered courtyard and into the castle, followed by Ava.

"Did you hear about the witches?" Ava was bursting with the latest gossip.

"I am sure you will tell me." Elen could not resist a smile, for all that her heart was heavy. The world seemed to be falling apart. Nothing was certain any more. The one hope she had had of the northward journey of Duncan's court—that she might see Patric at Forres—had proven false.

"I heard the story from Drust. You know Drust, Talcoran's aide? He was there, so it's not just gossip."

Elen wondered if the sparkle in her servant's eyes was for her tale or for Drust. She had seen the two together on several occasions recently.

They came at last to a niche where a narrow window pierced the stone wall. Elen paused, looking out toward the rugged mountains in the distance.

"Tell me here," she said. "At least it's quiet. I am not accustomed to living in a chamber with four other women. They giggle so."

"You should have your own quarters," Ava said.

"There is no room. You know that perfectly well. Let me hear your story, Ava."

"Well . . ." Ava moistened her lips in eager preparation for her speech. "The day before yesterday, King Duncan said he felt well enough to ride out with Macbeth and Bancho to observe the troop emplacements. Talcoran and Drust went with them, and some other men, too. When they stopped by a stream to water their horses, they were met by two ugly old women dressed in rags. At first King Duncan thought they were mad, and he wanted to leave the place, but when the women flew into a trance and began to prophesy, the king and his men knew they were witches." Ava paused to cross herself nervously. "Drust saw them with his own eyes, mistress."

Elen felt a chill along her spine. She knew as well as anyone that such creatures were real and powerful. She, too, crossed herself, as Ava went on with her tale.

"The witches told Duncan he would lose his throne, and his life, before the next full moon, and that his children must travel far from their native land before they dare return."

"No, it can't be."

"All the men there heard them. Duncan declared that these women must have caused his recent illness, and they should be punished for witchcraft. Do you want to know what happened next?"

"You will tell me whether I want to know or not." Elen wondered if the prophecy meant that Thorfinn would defeat and kill Duncan in the battle everyone knew would soon take place. Thorfinn was even now camped close by at Burghead, gathering his troops. Would that huge, black-bearded Viking be the next king of Alba? And if he were, what would happen to her kin and to herself? And Patric—would he die in battle for a hopeless cause?

Ava was talking again, continuing her story. In spite of her uneasiness about the tale, Elen made herself listen.

"Duncan had each of the witches put into a barrel and the barrels pierced all over with long spikes. They were rolled down a hill, and then they were dumped into the sea. Drust says it was a waste of good spikes. He says drowning is enough to get rid of witches. Drust says the king ordered everyone present to say nothing of what happened, because he says the king was afraid the troops would begin deserting if they heard of the prophecy. He says—"

"Drust says, Drust says!" Elen put her hands over her ears as she scolded her maid with unusual anger. "Be still! I've heard enough of this man of Talcoran's. Do not repeat this story to anyone else. The king has forbidden it. You will be silent on this, Ava."

"Yes, mistress."

As Elen listened to Ava's lurid tale, Patric rode through the gates of Forres, leaving his men camped some distance outside its walls. He had been summoned to a meeting of Duncan's council, and he was late. He met Talcoran outside the closed door. After a hurried greeting, Patric commanded the door wards to admit them, and together the two soldiers moved quietly into the council chamber.

Macbeth was speaking. He stood before the seated king with his legs spread wide and his huge fists planted firmly on his hips. His blue cloak was flung back over his shoulders, his golden head was held high and proud.

"We, your nobles, demand that you make peace with Thorfinn before Alba is destroyed."

Duncan had grown irritable since losing the sea battle with Thorfinn, and his recent illness had done nothing to improve his temper.

"You mean, before Thorfinn marches through your lands and ravages them," he sneered at Macbeth. "Before the harvests of Morayshire are trampled and bloodied in battle."

"I speak for all the men of Alba." Macbeth's steady gaze did not waver.

"You speak for yourself, Moray. Anyone with wits knows you crave this for your own head." Duncan touched the circlet of gold that sat upon his brow.

"No," Macbeth said softly. "You are mistaken, my lord. Those who know me well know I have never wanted your crown. Had we a good king, a strong and wise king who would make an agreement with Thornfinn and keep Alba safe against the English, then Moray would be enough for me."

"And have you not a good king now?" Duncan pounded on the arm of his chair like an angry child. "I will make you bow your head to me and mean it. When I have defeated Thorfinn you will all"—his eyes swept the room, taking in the faces of his nobles who were irritated or disgusted, according to each man's temperament, but not really surprised at yet another royal outburst—"*all* of you, I say, will bow the knee to me, and it will not be that false oath-taking you mouthed when first I became king, but true and total submission! And if you do not, I'll set your heads on pikes around the walls of Dunedin."

"Were you a true king of Alba, your new capital would be in the north, and not so near to England," Bancho growled, voicing a grievance felt by at least half the men in that room.

"Get out. Out of my sight, all of you. Go!" Duncan stood, his fury against these traitors now uncontrollable, his thin face blotched red with anger. "I hereby disband this council. I will rule alone. Leave me!"

For a moment it appeared that Duncan would personally push the men out of the room, but then, led by Macbeth, they all stalked out with great dignity. Talcoran was the next to last one to go. He turned and questioned Patric with raised brows.

"I'll join you shortly," Patric said, and Talcoran left him alone with Duncan.

"My lord," Patric began.

"They are traitors, every one."

"They are men who fear the loss of their lands and wealth. Calm yourself, my lord, for you must recall them."

"Do you dare say 'must' to your king?"

"Aye, for it is necessary. Those men are bound to you by their sacred oaths, and you need them. They must use their men-at-arms to fight Thorfinn for you. They are all the army you have. If you send them away, you have lost your crown."

Duncan's thin shoulders slumped.

"Why have I failed?" he asked querulously. "I wanted a strong, united kingdom. I wanted them firmly under my thumb so they would stop warring on each other and live in peace. I thought the English influence of my queen and her friends would civilize them, and instead they resent me for trying to change their customs. They are only tribal chieftains. Why won't they obey me? Damn them! I am the king!"

"You need them, my lord," Patric repeated.

"How like your father you are." Duncan was calmer now, the outburst over. "Keith of Bute always gave my grandfather good council, and me, too, while he was alive. I think you must have learned from him.

"I know you are right," Duncan added, sighing, "and I know most of the southern nobles will follow me, but the nothern men, Bancho and Macbeth and the others, are lost forever, I think."

"Macbeth and Bancho could not bear the final insult to their pride when you unmade them and made Moddan general in their place. The others, who look to Macbeth and Bancho as their leaders, felt the insult reflected upon themselves."

"I see that now." Duncan rubbed his face with his hands, a weary gesture. "It was a great mistake, and it is too late to remedy it. Patric, I have a commission for you."

Patric's heart sank. He had hoped for a meeting with Elen before what he believed would be Duncan's, and his own, final battle. Once more, he unhappily put the thought of Elen away and did his duty.

"I am yours to command, my lord," he said.

"There is no one more loyal than you, my friend. These are my orders, and I want you to swear to carry them out. If anything happens to me, if I am killed or captured, I want you to take my sons into England. Their uncle, Earl Siward of Northumbria, will give them sanctuary and will welcome you for their sakes. Remain with them and keep them safe until Malcolm can claim this kingdom for his own. My boy is only nine years old, and he must wait for manhood, but when he is grown, you must help him regain his inheritance."

Patric was deeply moved by Duncan's appeal. He did not question what Duncan had said, for he had no doubt that Thorfinn would soon defeat the men of Alba, and when that happened, the young princes would quickly be killed.

He knew full well what Duncan's commission meant. In order to carry it out, he would have to give up everything he held dear—his family lands in Bute, his homeland, the companionship of his dear sister and his brother-in-law—and most of all, he must give up Elen. He thought his heart would break as he faced that certainty.

But whatever his personal pain, however deep his love for Elen, he could not forget his honor. Patric did not care what others were doing, what excuses they used to themselves or to their associates to explain why they broke their oaths to their king. He only knew he could not break his own oath of loyalty to Duncan, for if he did, he would become something less than a true man. He would hate himself for the rest of his life, and, worse, he would be unworthy of Elen's love. He was bound by honor, and he believed that she would understand the painful choice he had to make. Taking a deep breath to help him shut away the bitter ache in his innermost heart, Patric went to his knees before his king and placed his hands between Duncan's own.

"I swear my sacred oath," Patric said, "that if the need arises, I will see all three of your sons safely to England, and I will never leave young Malcolm's side, except at his command or on his business, until he becomes King of Alba." He bent his head to kiss Duncan's hands. He did not see the tears in Duncan's eyes.

6

August 1040.

It was already too late for Duncan. Macbeth and Bancho and the other chieftains who followed their lead would tolerate no more insults from their king.

"It is time," said Macbeth, "for us to make our own agreement with Thorfinn. Give the order for our men to march."

Talcoran met Conal and Patric near the women's quarters.

"Will you come with us to Burghead, my lords?" he asked.

"I cannot," Patric replied. "I am sworn to stay with my king and to protect his children."

"I understand. I could not leave Macbeth, either." Talcoran clasped Patric's hand warmly. "We can respect each other as warriors, and dispense with personal animosity. I wish you well. And you, Conal? Do you go or stay?"

"I stay. I, too, remain loyal to the king, and Fionna does not want to leave the queen. Our duty lies here."

"I am fortunate," Talcoran said, "that my oath is to Macbeth and not directly to the king. It is one of the advantages of common birth. Farewell, my friends."

"He may have been born a commoner," Conal mused, looking after Talcoran's dark, wiry figure, "but his heart is noble, and there is no one braver in battle."

"Aye," Patric agreed. "I hope we never meet sword to sword. I would hate to have to kill him. Now, where is Fionna? I want to see her, and then I will arrange a meeting with Elen. Fionna can help me with that. She should know where Elen is."

Elen was in the room she shared with four other young women. While the others talked with great excitement and only a little fear about the battle that would soon be fought, Elen sat quietly on a stool and let Ava comb her hair and thought of Patric. She wondered what her cousin Macbeth would do next, and how it would affect her and Patric.

She had heard Patric was in Forres, that he was with the king. She must think of a way to see him. She would find a place, some small corner of the overcrowded castle, where they could be alone. Perhaps Fionna could help her. Elen decided she would seek out her friend as soon as Ava had finished with her hair. Fionna would surely know where her brother was.

Elen's heart lifted. After all the lonely months of waiting, she was certain she would soon be in Patric's arms again. And this time she would know all there was to know of love. She would overcome his scruples and they would possess each other completely while there was still time, for in this uncertain world, who knew what the morrow would bring? As she thought of Patric's hands touching her, the strength of his young body, she felt a warm flush and knew her cheeks were reddening. What did the fate of kingdoms matter, compared to what she felt for Patric?

A sudden loud knock at the door effectively quieted the chattering young women. There was a moment of ominous silence before one, braver than the others, opened the door to reveal Talcoran and Drust, his aide.

Talcoran's dark grey eyes searched the room, quickly lighting on Elen. His voice was rough.

"Lady, tell your maid to gather your belongings. You are to come with me. We are leaving Forres."

So it had happened. Macbeth had finally broken with Duncan.

"No." Elen rose from the stool, backing against the wall as if she were afraid Talcoran would sneak behind her. "No, I won't."

How could she go when she knew Patric was at Forres? Patric! He would protect her. He would speak to Duncan, ask the king to keep her at his court. Perhaps Duncan would even let them marry at once. She was still his ward. If he commanded it, she and Patric could be married that very day, and then they could never be separated.

"I must find Patric," she whispered to Ava.

"What is it, my lord?" the maid boldly asked Talcoran. "It will take some time to pack all of this." She indicated a pile of Elen's belongings, and an opened wooden chest from which spilled various articles of feminine apparel.

"You will pack at once." Talcoran brushed aside Ava's protest. "Drust will help you, and you will follow us immediately."

While Talcoran's attention was diverted from her to Ava, Elen took advantage of his momentary distraction. She made for the door and freedom.

Talcoran was too quick for her. He reached the door before she did, and in his hand was a long, sharp dagger. He pointed it directly at her heart.

One of the other women screamed. Elen met Talcoran with outrage.

"How dare you?" she challenged him. "Macbeth never told you to use force on me."

"He and his lady have gone to Burghead. He told me to take you there, where you are to stay with Gruach. He left the means to me."

"I am the king's ward. I am under his protection."

"He has none to offer you. You are coming with me."

Elen, glancing back into the room, saw Drust helping Ava to hastily dump her mistress's belongings into the wooden chest. Then she saw the four women with whom she had shared the room. They were huddled together, staring at Talcoran with expressions of terror. The only exception was a red-haired newcomer to court who looked fascinated by what was happening.

"Grania." Elen spoke to the girl. "Grant me a favor."

Grania nodded silently.

"Find Conal mac Duff or his lady, Fionna. Tell them what has happened to me. Ask them to tell my betrothed"—here Elen's voice rang out proudly—"to tell Patric mac Keith of Bute to rescue me if he can. If he cannot, if his duty to King Duncan prevents him, then tell him that my heart will always be his, and I will wait until this war is over and he comes to me."

"I know the Thane of Fife," Grania told her. "I will deliver your message."

"I will go with you now," Elen said, turning to Talcoran. "You do not need your knife."

"Nevertheless, I will keep it handy." Talcoran motioned with the blade, and Elen preceded him out the door. They walked through deserted rooms. Many of the men and women who had a short time before filled Forres Castle to over-flowing had now departed from it, some joining Macbeth, others returning to their homes to await the outcome of the war Duncan had begun. After a while, Talcoran said, "That was well-spoken, lady. Your betrothed has been my friend on more than one occasion. He is a brave man. You well deserve each other."

"Then let me go to him. My loyalty is with him and with the king, who is my kinsman. Release me, Talcoran."

"So is Macbeth your kinsman, and my loyalty is to him. I owe him everything. I will not betray his orders."

The dagger moved menacingly. Elen could do nothing but go with Talcoran to the stables, where horses awaited them, saddled and ready to ride. He helped her to mount and took her horse's reins in his own hands. Astride his great black stallion Talcoran led Elen away from Forres, away from Patric, and toward Burghead.

Macbeth's meeting with Thorfinn had been a successful one. Their agreement was celebrated with a great feast at which Gruach and Elen, along with the few other women present, were seated at the high table. Elen was placed next to Thorfinn himself. She marveled at the amount of mead he consumed.

"You do not eat," Thorfinn observed, looking at Elen over the rim of his golden cup. She was amazed to see a silver cross at his throat, hanging from a heavy silver chain.

"I did not know you were a Christian," Elen faltered.

"I am that." Thorfinn leaned toward her. His jutting nose was red from drink. He was the darkest man she had ever seen, even darker than Talcoran, and he was huge and powerfully built. Elen thought that if he wanted to, Thorfinn the Mighty could crush her with one finger. "Did you think all Norsemen are uncivilized, little girl?"

"I'm sure you are not," Elen said hastily.

Thorfinn smiled at her. His ugly face lit up in an expression of singular sweetness. Elen decided he was not so terrible after all.

"My mother," Thorfinn informed her, "was your father's cousin, so we are kin, as I am to Macbeth."

"Your mother was also sister to Duncan's mother," Elen reminded him sternly. "You are closer kin to Duncan. You were fostered at his grandfather's court, and it was old King Malcolm who gave you both Caithness and Sutherland."

Thorfinn roared with laughter.

"Are you still loyal to Duncan? A man who would take back a gift his grandfather bestowed? Duncan is a fool. He won't live long. Don't trouble yourself about such matters, little girl. You have a happy future before you. Leave war to men."

Elen wondered what Thorfinn meant about her future, but she had no chance to ask him, for Gruach, on Thorfinn's other side, now began to talk to him. When Thorfinn's skald, Arnor, took up his harp and began to sing a plaintive song of love and death, Elen was left with her lonely thoughts.

On the twelfth of August, Thorfinn, wearing his gilded battle helmet, and his new allies, the nobles of Alba, moved their combined armies out of Burghead to meet Duncan. Elen remained with Gruach, safe behind the thick, timber-laced stone walls of the ancient fortress that jutted out into the waters of Moray Firth.

The two women spent a good part of the following day in the chapel, praying. Elen wondered what the saints must think of them. She knew Gruach was asking heaven to grant victory to Macbeth and Thorfinn, while she, Elen, could only beg humbly that King Duncan and his queen, Conal and Fionna, and most of all, Patric, would be spared. Or if not spared, then at least granted a quick and painless death. Once Elen wondered wildly if her prayers and Gruach's would cancel each other out, like counters on some heavenly game board.

She was dry-eyed. She could not eat or drink or sleep. Gruach was in little better state. They forgot that they favored opposing sides in the bitter conflict. They knew only that women had no say in such important affairs, though they must bear the bitter aftermath of war. They were kin, close cousins, and now they clung together while they waited for news.

August fourteenth dawned grey and still. A heavy mist crept in from the sea and lay over the land for the entire day. Elen, leaving the chapel at midday, was oppressed by an unshakable dread.

"No one can fight in this," she whispered.

"Inland, the sun may be shining," Gruach said. "It may be the battle is already fought and won."

"Or lost."

They fell silent, and walked arm in arm from the chapel to Gruach's chamber, to spend the afternoon spinning and reading Gruach's prayer book.

The unbearable day seemed to go on forever. It was well after midnight when the messenger came. Elen went with Gruach to the great hall to hear the news.

The messenger was an old soldier, grey of hair and with a bloodstained bandage on one arm. Despite his obvious weariness he strode proudly into the hall. The guards stationed at Burghead crowded eagerly behind him.

Gruach entered and walked rapidly to the center of the room. She had donned her red silk gown, but had not taken time to arrange her hair. It hung down her back in a single, thick, honey-gold braid, as she always dressed it for bedtime.

Elen watched her with admiration. Gruach did not know if she would be given good news or dragged off to the dungeon to be held as a prisoner of war—or, indeed, if she would be murdered on the spot. That, or worse, was not unheard of when a battle was lost. But Gruach gave no sign of fear. She met the messenger with simple dignity.

"Speak," she said.

"Lady, I am charged by my lord Macbeth to tell you the battle is won, and to greet you as Queen of Alba. Duncan is dead, and Macbeth has been proclaimed king. My royal lady!" The man was on his knees before Gruach.

There was a motion as of a wave moving in from the sea, as every man and woman in the hall—officers, ordinary soldiers, ladies and serving wenches—knelt in the presence of their new queen.

Elen, too, fell to her knees, her mind blank. She had not had time to think of what Macbeth's message would mean for her. She was only grateful that Gruach would not be harmed. Then she felt Gruach's gentle hands on her shoulders, raising her to her feet.

"Cousin." Gruach's grey eyes were shining, her beautiful face was radiant. "I will need a lady-in-waiting. Will you serve me?"

"I am still betrothed to an enemy," Elen reminded her, "and I would gladly have seen Duncan win against Macbeth."

"That means nothing now." Gruach was

generous in victory. "We are kin, and you have done nothing to harm either me or the king." It was a moment before Elen's numb mind, dwelling now on Duncan and Patric, registered the fact that when Gruach said 'the king,' she meant Macbeth.

"There are nobles," Gruach went on, "brave men who fought against Macbeth with all their skill and strength, who will now make submission to him and be joyfully received as loyal subjects. Why should not you, our beloved cousin, also be welcomed?"

Elen wondered briefly if Patric, if he were still alive, would be among those men submitting to Macbeth. Somehow, she did not think so. If she were truly strong, she, too, would refuse, and bravely face death or exile. But Gruach's arms were open, and she was smiling her beautiful smile.

"My dear cousin," Gruach said.

Elen went into her loving embrace.

Macbeth returned to Burghead at midday. Gruach and Elen greeted him formally in the great hall. He strode in wearing upon his head Duncan's gold circlet, which was too small for him. It tilted rakishly over one eye as he embraced Gruach.

It was not until Macbeth, Gruach, Talcoran, and Elen were in Macbeth's private chambers that Alba's new king pulled off his crown and tossed it onto his bed with an irritated gesture.

"Talcoran, find me a metal worker. I will not wear that weakling Duncan's coronet. I want a new crown."

Talcoran hurried out, and Macbeth turned to Elen.

"I am thankful you are safe with us, cousin. I would not want you at Forres today."

"Even though I was brought here at knifepoint?"

"Talcoran is a bit rough at times." Macbeth grinned at her. "But he always obeys my orders."

"You know I did not wish to come. I wanted to stay with Patric."

Macbeth's face darkened at mention of Patric's name. He had listened to Elen's complaints about the manner of her leaving Forres when first she came to Burghead, and he did not want to hear them again. Then Gruach hastily diverted her husband's attention from the unpleasant subject.

"I have appointed Elen my first lady-in-waiting. With your permission, of course, my lord."

"You have it gladly. That was wise of you, Gruach. I have plans for our cousin."

Talcoran returned with a blacksmith. Macbeth explained that he required a new crown.

"I have little skill in such things, my lord," the blacksmith protested, "and no precious metals with which to work."

"I have enough gold for a dozen crowns," Gruach said. "If my husband the king will allow me, I will bring you my gold jewelry to melt down and use."

"Yes," Macbeth agreed, laughing at this idea. "Blacksmith, you will make two crowns, one for me and one for my queen, to wear when we ride into Forres Castle."

"My lord, as I said before, I have no ability in gold work."

Macbeth clapped the man on the shoulder.

"Just do your best for me, my friend, and it will be good enough. You have three days."

After the blacksmith had left them, Macbeth poured mead into four silver cups and gave one to each of them.

"Let us drink to peace and a plentiful harvest," he said.

"To peace in Alba," Talcoran echoed. "And to King Macbeth and his queen."

They drained their cups.

"Now," Macbeth said, "leave us alone. My lady and I have much to discuss in private, and much to celebrate."

Elen was halfway down the corridor toward her own chamber when Talcoran caught up with her.

"Lady, I would speak with you."

A stinging reply was on Elen's lips, but she did not say what she thought. She disliked this man for forcing her away from Patric, but there was something she desperately needed to know and it had just occurred to her that Talcoran could tell her. She put on what she hoped was a pleasant smile, and waited.

"I beg your forgiveness for unsheathing my knife against you."

"Surely for a soldier that is a small matter. You often use both dagger and sword."

"I have never killed a woman. I fight men. I would never have harmed you. Not you." His eyes were piercing into her in that intense way he had. "I had my orders, and it was necessary to make you go with me quickly."

"Before I could be rescued?"

He smiled, and his severe face softened. He cocked his head and smiled more broadly, and his one slightly crooked tooth gave him a jaunty, youthful look. Suddenly Elen found herself smiling back at him, her anger evaporating like the morning mist when the sun rises.

"Aye." Talcoran chuckled. "Who knows what those four fierce maidens in your room might have done to me if they had decided to release you? Not to mention your maidservant."

"Talcoran, you terrified them." Elen sighed. "I forgive you. I, too, always obey Macbeth's orders. Well, almost always," she amended, thinking of secret meetings with Patric.

She moved a step nearer to Talcoran, and laid one hand on his arm. She felt him tremble slightly at her touch, but his gaze, level with her own, was steady.

"I need your help," she said.

"I will do nothing that would harm Macbeth."

"I know that. I have heard the story. You saved his life. He rewarded you and raised you from a common foot soldier to high rank. I have heard that you saved his life a second time while putting down Macdowald's revolt. You and Patric mac Keith together saved Macbeth that day."

"What do you want of me?"

"Tell me if Patric is alive or dead."

"I do not know." Talcoran shook his head. "I never saw him in battle, but that does not mean he wasn't there. I have not heard that he was killed."

"I must know. Can you find out what has happened to him? Please?"

Her hand still rested on Talcoran's sleeve, and now his covered it. Not a large hand for a man, but strong and warm.

"Dead or alive, he is fortunate," Talcoran said. "I will see what I can discover."

Elen felt a faint surge of hope. Perhaps Patric had survived the battle. At least she would know. She knew she could depend on Talcoran.

7

Patric was alive and well. He had been ordered by Duncan to remain in Forres in readiness to take the young princes to safety, should that be necessary. He chafed at not being able to lead his own men into battle, but he obeyed. Now that the castle had been surrendered, he must find a way to leave it.

Bancho had been placed in charge of Forres, until Macbeth made his triumphal entry three days hence. Patric went to see Bancho.

"Submit to Macbeth," Bancho advised. "Your own brother-in-law has agreed to do that."

"Conal is a thane, with vast lands and wealth," Patric replied. "He wants to keep his property and his title to pass on to his son."

"You would have sons yourself," Bancho said, "were you to stay in Alba and marry Elen."

"It is partly because of Elen that I cannot stay. Macbeth dislikes me. He will never let me marry Elen. He did not approve of our betrothal, and now that he is king, I am certain he will end it. I cannot stay and watch Elen marry another man."

"I understand." Bancho's expression was sympathetic.

"There's something else preventing me, Bancho, and that is my oath to Duncan, which in

109

honor I cannot break. His death binds me even more closely to keep my word to him. I have told you about that, and you have said you understand. Give me leave to take his sons to England."

"Poor lads. Their father slain in battle, their mother dead of a broken heart. They are too young for such sorrow."

"They would be well cared for by their uncle Siward."

"Who would use them as weapons against Macbeth."

"If they remain in Alba, Macbeth will have them killed. He must, for there are those here also who will use them as weapons if he lets them live."

"Then they are better dead."

"Who will kill them? Will you?"

Bancho blanched.

"Will you kill your dead king's heirs?" Patric persisted. "Or do you think Macbeth will order Talcoran to do the deed? Talcoran, who owes everything to Macbeth and who will refuse him nothing? I think you suspect, as I do, what Macbeth's plans for Talcoran's future are. Would you see royal blood on his hands?"

"Elen," Bancho whispered.

"Aye." Patric's face was lined with pain. "We agree, then. Well, my friend Bancho, make your choice."

"Take them. I'll write the pass myself. Go at once. This evening. And if you are wise, you will find Elen and take her with you."

"She is too fragile for such a dangerous journey."

"I suspect that Elen of Laggan is stronger than you imagine," Bancho said dryly. "If you were to give her the choice, I feel certain she would want to go with you. She loves you."

"It is because I love her that I cannot take her.

Macbeth would declare her a traitor and confiscate all of Lagganshire as soon as Elen was across the border of Alba. How could I deprive her of her inheritance, take away all that once belonged to her father—lands, title, everything? It is one thing to choose for myself to give up all I possess. It is something very different to force such a choice upon the woman I love. I cannot do it. My heart is breaking, Bancho, but I must do what I believe is right."

"You are an idealistic fool." Bancho finished writing the safe-conduct pass and handed it to Patric. "I admire your steadfastness, lad. I only hope you don't regret what you are about to do."

"I'll see Fionna, then I'll be gone." Patric was at the door when he turned back. "Where is Duncan's body?"

"He was carried to Elgin after he was wounded in battle. He died there. We left his body, waiting for Macbeth's orders about it."

"Give it to me."

"What?"

"He was King of Alba. He should be buried at Iona."

"Are you mad? You would take three young boys and a corpse, and try to escape from Macbeth?"

"We have three days until Macbeth rides into Forres. He will be too busy until then to think about either Duncan or the princes. We will have a head start."

"If you believe that, you don't know Macbeth."

"Give me your leave, Bancho."

Bancho considered the man before him.

"What did Duncan ever do," he wondered, "to deserve a friend like you?"

"Why, that's easy." Patric smiled, looking like

his old cheerful self again. "He trusted me with an impossible task."

Fionna, with two other ladies-in-waiting, knelt in prayer beside the queen's bier. Patric entered the chapel and knelt behind his sister. His prayers for the dead queen were short, his active mind being occupied with more mundane matters than the repose of that good lady's soul. He reached out a hand and laid it on Fionna's shoulder. So deep was her concentration that she made no immediate response. Then she raised her head, saw whose hand it was, and smiled at him over her shoulder.

Patric was reminded of their childhood and the games of hiding-and-finding they had played through the rooms of their father's house, of Fionna's sweet smile and lighthearted laughter, and the tall older brother who always found both Patric and Fionna and made them pay a forfeit. All was gone—father, brother, house. Only he and Fionna remained, and now he must leave her.

Patric felt a sadness so deep he could hardly bear it. It was an ache different in kind, but equal in strength to the pain he felt knowing he would never see Elen again. Elen was a future he would not know, but Fionna embodied a past he could never forget.

She finished her prayers at last, and they moved into a dim corner of the chapel, where the candles placed around the queen's body cast long, flickering shadows.

"You are leaving now." Fionna knew of his promise to Duncan. She went into his arms, and he held her close as silent sobs shook her body. His own eyes were wet.

"Fionna," he said, "I want you to give a message to Elen."

"Elen? She left us. She went to Macbeth." In Fionna's voice was all the defeat and loss that Duncan's adherents now felt.

"She was forced to go. She had no choice. And she was so near. Had I but known when I spoke to Talcoran that day—" Patric controlled himself and lowered his voice. "I have no time to tell you what happened to Elen. Conal knows. Ask him what Grania told him. Will you give Elen my message? She will come to Forres with Macbeth, of that I am certain."

Fionna gulped back another wave of tears.

"What do you want me to say to her?"

"Tell her that I release her from our betrothal vows. I know Macbeth will not allow her to keep her pledge to me, and I understand. Tell her I wish her happiness. Tell her to forget me." Patric's voice broke on those last words.

"My dear." Fionna pulled her brother's head down onto her shoulder and stroked his burnished curls. "How torn your heart must be."

Patric allowed himself only a moment's self-indulgence before pulling away from Fionna and straightening his shoulders.

"My duty is with young Malcolm and his brothers," he said firmly. "I will write to you from England if I can." He embraced his sister one last time before turning resolutely away from the sight of her tear-streaked face.

Ava had gone to the servants' quarters and Elen was in bed, about to snuff her candle, when there was a knock at the door. She looked for her shawl but could not find it. The knock came again, more urgently this time. Elen pulled her loose linen nightdress more closely about her body and ran to the door in bare feet.

It was Talcoran.

"Lady, do I disturb you? I have news I thought you would want to hear at once."

"Patric." Elen's lips formed the word, but she made no sound.

Talcoran nodded.

"Come in." Elen stepped back, opening the door more widely, then shutting it behind the dark man.

Talcoran's eyes quickly searched the room, then came back to rest on her face.

He always does that, she thought. A well-trained soldier, making sure at once that there are no enemies lurking in the shadows to attack him.

She waited for him to speak, surprised as she was each time she stood near him, that he was a little shorter than she was. From a distance his tense, wiry strength gave him the appearance of greater height and fiercer aspect. One step away, as he was now, he was somehow less intimidating.

"There is not much to tell," Talcoran said. "I have learned that Patric mac Keith was ordered by King Duncan not to take part in the battle but to remain at Forres to guard his sons. One of my men saw him this midday. He was unharmed."

"Oh. . . ." As relief overcame her, Elen saw the room spinning and growing darker. There was a ringing in her ears, and her arms were like lead. Her knees buckled and would no longer support her weight.

She felt strong arms lifting her. Her head lolled upon a leather-coated shoulder. As her eyes fluttered open, she saw Talcoran's dark, worried face, and then the world was black.

When she regained her senses, she was lying on her bed. Talcoran hovered over her, holding a water jug in one hand while he splashed drops of water onto her face with the other.

"Elen, speak to me!" he commanded, as

though she were some disobedient soldier.

She could not answer at first. The tears she had resolutely held back for so many anxious days now poured out, cleansing her of her deep-seated fear that Patric was dead or horribly wounded. She could not stop crying.

Talcoran sat on the edge of the bed and took her hand.

"Don't. Don't," he begged. "I don't know what to do if you weep. How shall I help you?"

Elen sat up.

"Thank you," she gasped between sobs. "Oh, Talcoran, thank you. I'll never forget what you have done. No one else would tell me anything about Patric."

As a fresh burst of sobs shook her, Elen flung her arms around Talcoran and buried her face in his neck. Even in her emotionally overwrought state, she was aware of his hesitation, of a shuddering effort at restraint, before his arms enfolded her.

He held her carefully, sitting at rigid attention on the side of her bed until she had wept all the tears that were in her. Gradually, as her emotions quieted, she became aware of him again. The skin of his throat, where her face was pressed, was soft in contrast to the stiff black beard above it. His leather jacket was open at the neck, and she could see the beginning of the dark, silky hair that must cover his chest. He was clean, with a healthy male body scent that was distinctly pleasant.

Without thinking, she nestled a bit closer, seeking comfort, and his arms tightened about her. She felt a warmth, just the beginning of a sensation deep within her, a remnant of something she had once felt with Patric. Bewildered, she sat up and moved apart from Talcoran.

He looked at her with those disconcerting

dark grey eyes of his, as though he comprehended her confusion and recognized its cause more clearly than she did.

"I'm sorry. I never meant to make such a fool of myself," Elen whispered, wiping her eyes. "It was the relief."

He made no response. He just sat there on her bed, examining her very soul, the lines of his face and body tense.

"You are a good friend, Talcoran. I knew I could trust you."

Still he said nothing. Suddenly, he caught her hand in his and held it tightly. As his eyes bored into hers, he brought her hand to his lips, and pressed his burning mouth upon her trembling fingers. Her heart began to pound with heavy, painful beats.

"Talcoran?"

Abruptly, he stood, turning his back on her.

"You are distressed," he said over his shoulder as he moved toward the door, "and you are very young. You do not understand."

"Understand what? I know you have been a friend to me."

"You are so innocent that it would never occur to you that I might be stirred to do something I should not. Something that would harm you irreparably. Harming you would not pleasure me. Not at all."

"I am not so innocent," she said, trying to avoid recognition of the intimate meaning of his last words. "I have been betrothed for nearly a year."

A brief smile lit his face.

"Lady, I have no doubt that you remain a virgin. I have known enough experienced women to recognize an innocent one when I meet her. And now I think I should leave before we can be accused of something we have not done. Or worse, before we are accused of something we *have* done." He was deadly serious as he opened the door. "The next time you invite a man into your room at night, be certain your maid is here. It is much safer that way. And bolt this door after I leave. Guard your virginity well, lady. It is more valuable to your king than you realize."

Elen stared after him in amazement. What had he meant, her virginity was valuable to Macbeth? She shivered as it dawned upon her that his words could have only one meaning. Macbeth planned to marry her to someone, to seal a treaty or to bestow her father's lands and titles on one of his nobles.

"But I am betrothed to Patric," she whispered. Patric, who was safe and well, and with whom she would soon be reunited. "I love Patric. I will marry Patric or no one."

Even as the defiant words left her lips, she knew her betrothal would mean little to Macbeth. He disliked Patric and had opposed her marriage to him. Macbeth could easily dissolve Elen's oath to a man Elen felt certain would never kneel and call him king. To Macbeth, Patric was now a traitor, deserving only of death or exile.

Elen closed her eyes. She could see every detail of Patric's face. She could remember the way his hair curled under her fingers. She recalled the pressure of his mouth on hers, and his hands. Ah, those large, strong, gentle hands.

"Patric. Patric."

Macbeth rode into Forres in triumph, Gruach beside him as he formally took control of the castle that had been Duncan's last stronghold. Their new crowns, simple and roughly made but glinting bright gold in the sun, sat firmly on their heads while they accepted the cheers and salutes of the army and of those civilians who had come from all over the countryside to see the new king.

In the great hall at Forres Castle, those of Duncan's nobles who were left alive came to make submission to Macbeth. Most did so willingly, and if there were a few who hung back or pledged their fidelity grudgingly, they were scarcely noticed in the cheerful throng.

Elen stood close beside Gruach's chair, employed in her new role as lady to the queen. She watched as Conal mac Duff and Fionna knelt before the throne.

"You are most welcome to my court and my service," Macbeth told Conal. "As proof of my friendship toward you, I require you to keep the title of Thane of Fife, and to continue to administer the lands which accompany that title. When the time comes for you to die, both lands and title will pass to your eldest son without dispute."

"I thank you, my lord."

"Conal mac Duff," Gruach said, "I would like your wife to become one of my ladies. Will you grant her permission to do so?"

"Gladly, my lady," Conal replied.

So it was that later in the day Elen found herself in Gruach's chamber, alone with Fionna.

"How is young Keith?" Elen asked with stiff politeness.

"My son is well. Elen, I must—"

"Fionna, I—" They both laughed, and suddenly the tension between them was gone.

"Please," Elen said, "tell me where Patric is. I must see him. Is he imprisoned because he would not pledge himself to Macbeth?"

"He is gone." And Fionna delivered her brother's message.

"No. No." This pain in her bosom that made breathing impossible, this feeling of being shattered into a thousand ice-cold pieces, this must be her heart breaking, Elen thought.

"My poor dear, sit down." She felt Fionna's arms, guiding her to a stool.

"How could he leave me like that?" Elen whispered. "I love him. He said he loved me."

"He had his duty, his promise to Duncan."

"But why didn't he take me with him?" Elen's mind was a little clearer now, the first shock dissipating. "I would gladly have shared his exile. I was right here in Forres the day he came to see Duncan. He could have found me and protected me from Talcoran, and kept me here until the battle was over."

"I don't know." Fionna's voice trembled on the edge of tears. "That was such a confused day, with Duncan in such great distress and the queen so desperately ill. I don't know what happened."

Elen saw Fionna's anguished face and bit back the angry words she had been going to say, but they lay in her mind like cold, hard stones.

Patric lied. He had never loved her or he could not have broken his vow and deserted her like this. All he really wanted was Laggan. *And I a young and foolish girl, so ready to believe him!*

"What will happen next, Fionna?" she asked aloud.

"Conal says that tomorrow at the latest, Patric and the men who left with him, along with a few others who have gone into exile since Duncan's defeat, will be proclaimed traitors and outlaws, and their properties will be confiscated. All of the lands Patric inherited from our father and from our brother will belong to the crown after the proclamation. It is the way kings deal with such matters," Fionna added dryly. "It was to be expected."

"How can you bear it? I know how much you love Patric." I'm not sure I can bear it, Elen added silently to herself, the pain of Patric's defection still searing her heart. She heard Fionna's rueful laugh before her friend answered.

"We women don't have much choice in these matters, do we? I feel as though I am split in two. One part of me has gone with Patric, but the larger part of me remains here, with Conal and Keith, and I must endure the unhappiness of that division as best I can. Conal has done what he believes is right for our son and for Fife. Whatever happens in the future, I will not dispute his decision. I will stand by his side." Fionna drew herself up bravely. "I am pledged to Macbeth now. I will do as my husband wishes and serve the new king. And his queen. That task will not be hard. Gruach is kind, and she will not blame me for what Patric has done. Oh, Elen, I wish everything could be different, and Patric were here with us, and we were all happy, but we must accept what has happened and go on. We cannot look backward."

With that, Fionna came to kneel next to Elen and put her arms around her friend. A dry-eyed Elen laid her head down on Fionna's shoulder and the two held each other for a long, silent moment.

Its ancient name was Icolmkill, but later generations called it Iona. It was there that the kings of Alba were buried.

Low-lying and serene, its thick grass dotted with high stone crosses, the island had about it an air of sanctity. In the soft, moist atmosphere, delicate green ferns grew between the stones. Silence lay on Iona like a holy blanket.

On a morning of gentle sunshine in late

August of the Year of Our Lord 1040, Duncan mac Crinan was laid to rest. When the short service was over, Patric stood squinting against the misty light, gazing back toward Alba.

"We should hurry, my lord," one of his men reminded him. "Macbeth has surely sent men in pursuit of us, and we have tarried overlong in this place."

"We had no choice. It had to be done." Patric focused his attention on the ship that lay waiting offshore to take them to England. "Are the princes aboard?"

"Aye, my lord. The rowboat is returning for us now." The man chuckled. "I heard someone cry out that one of the princes was seasick."

"That will be Donald. Perhaps he will be better on the larger ship."

"We can hope so. I see the boat is waiting. Are you coming, my lord?"

"In a moment."

Patric spared one last glance for the purple hills of his homeland. They shimmered in the late summer haze.

Farewell, Alba. I will think of you constantly until I return.

Farewell, Elen. If I think of you, I will go mad. I will never think of you again. Never.

PART II.

A.D. 1040-1057.

MACBETH'S PEACE.

8

August 1040.

A great feast was held at Forres Castle to celebrate
the victory over Duncan. Thorfinn the Mighty was
there, and Bancho of Lochaber with his son
Fergus, a slender seventeen-year-old fresh from
his first battle. Conal mac Duff and Fionna were
present, sitting with Conal's friends, the Thanes of
Mar and of Angus, at a long table placed near to
the king. The three successful leaders—Macbeth,
Thorfinn, and Bancho—sat in the high seats at a
raised table.

At a table halfway down the hall, Elen was
squeezed onto a bench between Fergus and
Talcoran. She tried to make conversation with
Fergus, but he was infuriatingly uncommuni-
cative. Fergus answered a simple yes or no to each
of Elen's questions and picked at his food as
though he feared it would poison him. On his other
side, the vivacious Grania, now a lady to Queen
Gruach, met with no better success as she
fluttered her long eyelashes and smiled and tried
to flirt with Fergus.

Elen gave up. Her heart was not in the effort
to make clever conversation. Let Fergus find his
own way. She had tried to be kind to him for his

father's sake, but she would make no further
attempts. It mattered not at all. Since she had
learned that Patric had left Alba, nothing
mattered. There was a constant dull ache in her
bosom, as if her heart had been torn out of her
body, and lately she had begun to feel the
simmering anger of badly damaged pride.

"Are you ill, lady? You do not eat." Talcoran
examined her with the intensity she had come to
expect of him. She had not spoken to him since he
had stalked out of her bedchamber three nights
before. She blushed, remembering that he had
seen her in her nightdress.

"I am not hungry," she snapped at him.

"Do you grieve because Patric mac Keith has
been proclaimed a traitor?"

"Do not speak to me of that monster!"

"In Patric's eyes, we are the traitors," Talcoran said calmly. "Those whom we call loyal men
or traitors are dependent upon the fortunes of
their leaders. Had Duncan won the battle, I might
be the exile."

"Not you. You would have died on the battlefield, like a man. Patric mac Keith did not even
draw his sword." Elen spat out the last sentence
like a sour fruit.

"Bitterness does not become you, lady. Patric
was following his king's orders. Do not question
his honor." Talcoran bestowed a sardonic smile
upon her. "I remember that you, too, preferred
Duncan until I forced you into your cousin's camp
at knifepoint."

Elen glared at him.

"I hate you," she said between clenched teeth.
"I hate all men."

"That will pass. In time, your pride and your
heart will heal. You will forget Patric and love
again."

Elen regarded him with scorn. What could Talcoran possibly know of a woman's heart?

"Your cousin is about to speak," Talcoran said.

Macbeth had risen. In his red silk tunic, with a jeweled gold belt and a heavy gold chain across his broad chest, wide gold armbands on either wrist, he looked every inch a king. The rough gold crown he wore suited him better than a more elaborate, daintier circlet would have done. The crown gleamed softly atop Macbeth's thick yellow-gold hair. His beard was neatly trimmed, his blue eyes sparkled, his ruddy face glowed with happiness and triumph. He was all that a king should be. Everyone in that hall, friend and former enemy alike, felt the force of his personality. When he stood, the hall fell silent.

"I welcome you to my table," Macbeth said, raising a jewel-encrusted goblet. "I drink to your health and happiness, and to the well-being of the Kingdom of Alba."

"To Alba! To Macbeth!" Everyone in the hall rose, cups and tankards and goblets lifted high. "Macbeth! Macbeth! Macbeth!"

When the tumult had quieted a little, Macbeth continued.

"This day I have made a new agreement with my ally, Thorfinn of Orkney. Henceforth, Alba and Orkney will live in peace. There will be free and safe passage across our borders, and free trade between us. To Thorfinn the Mighty!"

Again the cups were raised, as another cheer reverberated around the hall. Thorfinn's men shouted and banged their cups loudly on the table-tops. A few tall Norsemen even leapt onto the tables, raising their arms toward the roof, stamping their booted feet, and shouting at the top of their lungs.

"Thorfinn! Thorfinn! Thorfinn!"

Macbeth threw back his head and roared with laughter, the sound carrying to Elen's ears over the noise of the exuberant crowd.

"Yet another cup must be drunk!" Macbeth cried. "To my loyal friend and the first general of my realm. To Bancho of Lochaber."

"Bancho!" Cups were emptied once more as the cheers continued.

"Bancho!" The cry went up from officers and common soldiers alike. "Ban-cho! Ban-cho!" Cups and fists drummed on tabletops. Young Fergus came suddenly to life, cheering and pounding with the rest. "Ban-cho! Ban-cho!"

Macbeth reached out a hand and pulled Bancho to his side. He flung a brawny arm about Bancho's shoulders, drawing him closer.

"Bancho! Macbeth! Bancho!"

Elen noticed Gruach, standing a little behind her husband. She was smiling an odd little smile as she watched Bancho.

Now Macbeth drew Thornfinn to his other side, and the three men stood arm-in-arm, accepting the acclaim, as the cheers grew louder.

"Bancho! Macbeth! Thorfinn!"

"I invite you all to Scone," Macbeth called over the din. "To Scone for my installation. And for another feast, even finer than this."

"The king! The king! The king! Macbeth!"

Elen felt Talcoran's hand on her shoulder. His other fist was in the air as he, too, raised his voice.

"Macbeth! Macbeth!"

Suddenly, forgetting her grief and pain, Elen was also caught up in the hysterical excitement, and she heard her own voice blending with Talcoran's rougher tones as the cheers rang out once more.

"Macbeth! Macbeth! Macbeth!"

The scene was entirely different the next morning, when Elen was in attendance on Gruach. Macbeth had learned it was Bancho who had aided Patric.

"You let him go, let a traitor escape? And with Duncan's body?"

"It seemed the best thing to do. Duncan should have decent burial." Bancho was quiet and calm, apparently unruffled by Macbeth's fury.

"And you think I would not have granted Duncan that? I myself would have taken his body to Iona. I would have arranged a royal funeral for him. But you and Patric mac Keith together have made it appear as though I begrudged Duncan even those last rites. You have shown me in a false light before my subjects. I will not forget this, Bancho."

"Dismiss me if you wish," Bancho said stiffly.

"What kind of fool do you think I am? If I dismiss you, your soldiers will go with you, and if you do not revolt against me, they will, for love of you. There will be war in Alba again, and which one of us will be king when it ends, eh? I'll tell you. We will both be dead, and Thorfinn will be king. Do you want that?"

"No, my lord."

"Then do not take my prerogatives to yourself. I was elected King of Alba, not you. I have your oath of fidelity. See that you keep it."

"I will, my lord."

"As for this matter of Duncan's body, we will say that when I made you commander of Forres Castle, I gave you leave to dispose of Duncan and his family in whatever way you saw fit. What you did, you did with my permission. We must appear to be united in this."

"I understand you, my lord."

"Would that you had understood me before you signed those safe-conduct passes for Patric!"

Bancho bowed his head in silence.

"Let nothing of this kind ever occur again, Bancho. I will tolerate no insubordination. I have too much work to do. You have my leave to go."

Bancho left, his back rigid with injured pride.

"You should have had him arrested," Gruach said.

"I would have liked to, but I could not. You heard the crowd cheering him last night. Nearly half the army belongs to him. I need him, and his soldiers."

"You are right, of course," Gruach conceded. "But be careful of him. He is too powerful, and too popular with his men. He could unseat you."

"Not now. I am firmly in control. But in the future? I will heed your warning, wife. We shall see." Stroking his golden beard, Macbeth turned to Elen. "You are pale and quiet, cousin, since your lover broke his vows and left you."

Elen raised her white face to his.

"I have forgotten him already," she said.

"Have you, indeed? I hope so, for I have better plans for you than ever Duncan had." Macbeth frowned. "Have you kept yourself virgin?"

Before a startled Elen could answer the blunt question, Gruach intervened.

"She is untouched, I can vouch for that. My servants or I watched her whenever she and Patric were alone together. There were kisses aplenty, and a fumble or two with his hands, but nothing more."

"Good. Well done, wife." Macbeth placed a resounding kiss on Gruach's ever-ready lips. "Our young cousin is a valuable asset. I know which of my men I will reward with the title Thane of Laggan, once I am officially installed as king."

Macbeth regarded Elen with satisfaction and a good deal of genuine affection. "What do you say, Gruach—shall she have a new silk dress for my installation at Scone? Green, I think, with gold embroideries, such as the princesses in the old legends wore."

"Bancho?"

Elen stopped the familiar figure. "I have not seen you since—"

"Since my quarrel with Macbeth?" Bancho moved back into the light of the window where she could see his face. "Don't be shy, Elen. Say it."

"He was unkind to you."

"He is the king. He must rule. From time to time some of us may not like his way of ruling, but we must accept it."

"I have no love for Patric mac Keith," Elen began.

"No?" Bancho looked at her with a sad smile.

"But I do think Patric was right to give Duncan burial, and to save his sons from death, and you were right to help him. Macbeth should not have insulted you for that."

"Aye." Bancho squared his broad shoulders. "That cut me deeply. I will not soon forget that insult."

"Be careful. There are those who are jealous of your power and of the love your men have for you."

"What do you know, lass? What have you heard?"

"Nothing but a murmur. Oh, how I wish life were simple again, the way it was before I came to court. Now nothing is what it seems to be, oaths are foresworn, and I am pulled in ten directions at once. I am constantly confused. I don't know where my true loyalties should lay. My heart is breaking.''

"You could not stay a child forever. No one can, though some of us might wish it.''

"Be careful, Bancho,'' Elen said again. "Guard yourself well. I fear for you.''

9

The kings of Alba enjoyed no priestly protection, no annointing or crowning by any priest's hand. Each king was inaugurated in a ritual that had its roots in a pre-Christian past so distant no storyteller or historian could recall its origin.

At dawn on a September morning in the Year of Our Lord 1040, Macbeth mac Finlaec was formally enthroned at Scone of the High Shields, on the bank of the River Tay, where a mound of earth marked the ancient spot.

The crowd had begun to gather before the sky was light. By the time the ceremony began, it numbered several hundred people.

Elen, in her new green silk gown, and Fionna, in blue silk, walked in procession with Gruach, who was clad in rich draperies of cloth-of-gold. A new, richly bejeweled crown sat upon Gruach's golden, braided coiffure. She was weighted down with heavy gold rings and bracelets, necklaces and earrings, and a wide gold girdle. Her gold brocaded cloak was lined with red-gold silk and fastened with two gold brooches and a gold chain.

Elen marveled that she could walk at all under the weight of her ornaments, but Gruach

moved with stately grace until she reached her
assigned position at one side of the mound. The
queen had no real part in the ceremony, but her
presence as a witness was important nonetheless.
Through her father, Gruach had her own claim to
the throne of Alba, and that claim strengthened
her husband's right to rule. It was also Gruach's
duty on this day to display both her beautiful
person and the magnificent wealth which Macbeth
possessed.

Once the queen and her attendants had taken
their places there was a pause, and Elen looked
around her. Although by ancient Gaelic tradition
anyone was free to attend this ceremony, the
ordinary people were in the background. The
nobles, each man carrying his sword and shield,
and a few wealthy landowners clustered nearer to
the sacred mound.

The Stone of Destiny on which Macbeth would
sit was directly in front of Elen. She could see it
over Gruach's golden shoulder. It was a large
stone, hollowed out, like a round chair, and
decorated with strange carvings: circles and
triangles and other markings Elen could not
identify. It was said that the Picts, who ruled Alba
before the Scots of Dalriada conquered them, had
made this ancient relic.

Perhaps Talcoran could tell her what the
carvings meant. He was half Pictish; he might
know.

Now the king's procession appeared. In
contrast to his gorgeously adorned wife, Macbeth
wore a simple white linen robe, bound at the
waist with a white silk cord. He was barefoot. He
wore no crown. The rising sun cast its rays upon
his hair and beard, making them shine like beaten
gold. An appreciative murmur rippled through the
crowd.

Macbeth was surrounded by his closest friends, all in their finest clothes and bearing ceremonial swords and shields. Conal mac Duff was in rich dark blue trimmed with silver, his brown hair and beard carefully combed, his handsome face solemn. Bancho of Lochaber wore bright orange-red. His greying beard and hair were a bit untidy, as though he needed a wife to brush and smooth him. Elen regarded him with deep affection.

Then she saw Lulach, pale and nervous and looking younger than his twelve years as he marched beside Bancho. He caught Elen's eye and gave her a quick smile.

There were others, all splendid and glittering, but now Elen's eyes lighted on Talcoran. He looked straight ahead as he walked, and in spite of his short stature, his dignity equaled that of the taller lords. He wore a grey wool tunic narrowly edged in silver and a darker grey wool cloak, caught with a magnificent silver brooch set with amber. His square Pictish shield was only lightly ornamented with silver.

How like him, Elen thought, admiration stirring in her. He will not robe himself as some of these courtiers do, in silks and gold and glitter. Talcoran is an honest soldier, and he will never try to be anything he is not. Perhaps that is why Macbeth loves and trusts him so much.

The nobles disposed themselves in a wide circle around the king. Macbeth stood alone before the stone, waiting for the ceremony to begin.

Elen knew that the day before he had been scrutinized in accordance with tradition. Elen and Grania had been excluded because they were both maidens, but Fionna and two other of the queen's married ladies had, with ceremonial formality,

examined the naked king and pronounced him
without blemish. Gruach had told her that this
custom had something to do with the fertility of
the land, but Elen had been unable to ascertain the
particulars   from   her   guarded   comments.
Privately, Elen thought the examination was a
heathen practice, and she wondered what Macbeth would have done had one of the women declared him physically defective and therefore
unfit to rule.

But then, she was certain Macbeth would have
told her that this entire ceremony had nothing to
do with Christianity. His enthronement was,
rather, intended to establish publicly that Macbeth's legitimate claim to the crown of Alba had
the support of all his nobles.

Macbeth now held a gold and silver staff of
office in his right hand. As a solemn hush fell over
the crowd, he seated himself upon the Stone of
Destiny. In total silence, Conal mac Duff and
Bancho of Lochaber draped about his shoulders a
gold-edged mantle of royal purple.

An aged seannachie, an historian-orator,
stepped forward. To authenticate his right to the
succession, Macbeth was addressed with all of his
titles, and with the names of all of his ancestors
back to Scota, daughter of Pharoah, and then back
to Noah. When this long recital was finished,
Macbeth stood. Lifting the hem of his robe so all
could clearly see, he solemnly placed his bare
right foot onto the soil of Alba.

"All hail Macbeth," the seannachie intoned,
"Married to Alba, High King of Alba. Hail, Macbeth."

At the orator's words, every warrior present
drew his sword and clashed it upon his shield
again and again, to proclaim Macbeth's power far

and wide. A shout went up, the same cheer Elen had first heard at Forres Castle.

"Macbeth! Macbeth!"

Behind Gruach's back, Fionna leaned toward Elen.

"The famous melodious shields make more of a clatter than music," she whispered, her joking words effectively breaking the spell that had held Elen entranced.

In the queen's chambers her ladies fluttered about, primping while they waited for the royal procession to the banquet hall to begin.

"Elen," Gruach said, "come with me. The king wishes to speak with you in private."

She took Elen's hand and led her through a door into Macbeth's private room. Elen caught her breath, dazzled at the sight of him.

Macbeth had changed his garments. He was now wearing a knee length cloth-of-gold tunic. A heavily wrought golden crown, set with amethysts and rubies, sat upon his head. A gold-trimmed mantle of royal purple swung from his wide shoulders in graceful folds.

Elen would have knelt, but Macbeth caught her by the shoulders and held her upright.

"No, cousin," he said, "let your obeisance wait until the banquet. I have asked you here to tell you privately what your fate will be. We must allow time for the banns to be published. That will delay the matter a little, but one month from today, you will marry my friend Talcoran."

"No!" The cry was wrung from the very depths of Elen's heart. She had known something like this would happen soon. She had tried to pretend it would never happen, had tried to put it from her mind. Now she wrenched her shoulders out of Macbeth's hands and went to her knees despite his efforts to stop her. "No, I beg you, cousin. If you have any love for me at all, don't do this."

"You grieve for Patric mac Keith." Gruach was practical as always. "You have some foolish idea that you care for him. That is because he is the first young man you ever saw who was not a near relative or a servant, and the first man to kiss you. You are an innocent in such matters. I tell you that you will soon forget him."

They did not understand, and Elen could not bring herself to explain. Patric had lied to her, broken her heart, destroyed her pride. She was now uncertain what she felt for him. He was, after all, a traitor. She felt utter confusion. Was Gruach right?

"Elen, don't be a fool," Gruach continued. "Talcoran will treat you kindly. Stand up. You will soil your new gown."

Elen stayed where she was. She lifted pleading eyes to Macbeth's handsome face.

"I don't want to marry anyone. Dear cousin, give me leave to retire to a convent. Laggan will revert to the crown, and you may then give it to Talcoran. As for me, I will turn over the few possessions that are my own to the church and end my days as a nun."

"Absolutely not. I forbid it. Stand up." Macbeth's blue eyes blazed at her. Elen forced herself to stand and face him with some semblance of dignity, but her mind was in turmoil. She no longer knew how she felt about Patric, or about anything else. She made herself dutifully pay attention to what Macbeth was saying.

"Patric mac Keith is a traitor. You are well rid of him. Listen to those who know more of the world than you do, and who have your best interests at heart.

"Talcoran has been faithful to me, a valiant warrior in my cause," Macbeth continued. "It is true he is not nobly born, but he is a good man. I will reward him and secure his permanent adherence to me by giving him Lagganshire and the title of thane. You must help me in this, Elen. You will be a good wife to him. Your coming marriage will be announced today."

"Please don't." Nearly swayed to consent by Macbeth's words and the force of his personality, Elen could barely whisper her plea.

"I command you."

Looking at her cousin's impassive face, Elen knew there was no hope left.

Macbeth had given her her own room in the palace. Ava was pleased and excited and chattered with giddy pleasure about her mistress's coming marriage. Elen heard nothing her maid said. She let Ava comb her hair and straighten her gown before the procession began, but she did not care to look into the silver mirror that Ava held up for her.

She took the gold bracelet Patric had given her as a betrothal gift and hid it at the bottom of her clothing chest. She could no longer wear it, but she could not part with it, either. Let the bracelet stay there, out of sight, like the feelings she also had to hide.

The magnificent procession wound its way slowly through the palace and into the banqueting hall. Elen scarcely knew where she was or what was happening. Like someone in a trance she marched behind Gruach, putting one foot after the other, her mind and soul a blur of conflicting emotions. Macbeth and Gruach reached the raised dais and stood before the royal chairs, their robes spread out around them.

"The golden couple," Fionna murmured. "May they always be so well-loved and happy."

Elen made herself look at them, at the King and Queen of Alba in all their gold-robed splendor. They were beautiful and powerful and she loved them both. They had taken her into their family circle, fed and clothed and been kind to her. They were her kin and she owed them her allegiance.

As she watched the royal couple, Elen came to a painful decision. She would try to forget Patric and survive as best she could in the new life Macbeth was forcing upon her. She would marry Talcoran and pretend to care for him if she could not care in truth, and no one would ever know how empty her heart was.

When Macbeth beckoned her forward, and called Talcoran to join her, Elen stood by that dark man's side and smiled, and put her hand in his, and agreed to give herself to him in marriage in one month's time.

Bancho sat next to Elen at the banquet, with Talcoran on her other side. For all her good intentions, Elen found it hard to hide her despair. She could eat nothing. She sat like a maiden carved of ice, not really aware of the people who offered congratulations to the newly betrothed couple and also to Bancho, who had that day been appointed to Macbeth's council. When Talcoran left his place to speak with Macbeth, Bancho took Elen's cold hand.

"Are you afraid of him?" Bancho asked.

"I feel nothing. I will do my duty," Elen replied through stiff lips.

"Ah, lassie, don't." Bancho scrutinized her pale face with anxious eyes. "You will make

yourself ill. I know Talcoran well. If you let him,
he will be a good husband to you. But do not give
him cause to imagine that your thoughts are set
upon another man. Like the rest of us, Talcoran
has his pride."

"He will have no reason to complain of me."

"It might improve matters between you if you
were to show some warmth, perhaps even a little
enthusiasm toward him. There are few men, in
Alba or anywhere else, who care to bed with a
statue."

"I will remember your advice."

"Remember also that I am your friend, Elen."

She had an almost overwhelming desire to
rest her head upon Bancho's shoulder and weep
and beg him to help her. Instead, she pulled her
hand away and gave him a quick little smile. She
had done with weeping. It never changed anything. She would weep no more.

When the banquet was over, Talcoran took
her to her room. Ava, seeing who was with her
mistress, quickly disappeared on some invented
errand.

Elen gave one nervous glance at the bed, then
stood unmoving in the center of the room,
watching the man who now controlled her life.

He drew nearer. Elen stared into his intense
grey-black eyes and thought she would faint. His
hands captured her face, holding her prisoner as
his lips sought and found hers. His mouth was
cool and dry. It was not horrible. She felt nothing.
Her arms hung lifelessly at her sides.

He wrapped his arms around her and pulled
her against him. His mouth was searching,
pressing harder on hers, as though he was trying
to evoke some response from her. Whatever he
wanted, she could not give it.

It was so odd not to reach up to kiss a man.

Patric was so tall that she had had to stretch. No! She would not think of Patric. Patric was a traitor. She must never think of him again. Never. Never.

"Never. Never." She was pushing at Talcoran, trying to break his hold on her. "No, never, never."

He let her go so suddenly she nearly fell. Abruptly returned to reality, she gaped at him, one hand pressed against her lips.

"Lady," he began, his voice ragged. Then he corrected himself. "Elen. My Elen. I know you do not want to marry me. I am not happy about our marriage myself. I would have preferred to continue a bachelor. Certainly I would rather not marry a woman who dreams of another man."

"I do not!" she flung at him, anger overcoming her fear and confusion. "I dream of no man. I wanted to become a nun."

A bitter smile twisted the corners of his mouth.

"I fear that cannot be arranged. We must both obey the king and make the best of it." His right hand stroked gently down the side of her face and cupped her chin. His smile was wistful now.

"Must you be so unwilling?" he asked.

"I will try to please you," she promised. "Macbeth only told me of his plans for me—for us—this noontide. I have had no time to grow accustomed to the idea."

"And do you think that you will grow accustomed, in time?"

"I do not know," she answered truthfully.

He dropped his hand. His face darkened.

"You have no choice," he said. He slammed the door behind him as he left.

10

October 1040.

The days passed quickly, too quickly for Elen.
When she was not in attendance on the queen, she
was besieged by seamstresses who measured and
fitted and draped and fussed over her until she felt
like screaming, for Gruach had decided that little
in Elen's wardrobe was suitable for the bride of a
wealthy thane. Elen must have new gowns of silk
and wool, delicate shifts of fine linen, warm
winter cloaks, shoes and stockings, and an almost
infinite variety of other items.

They nearly quarreled over the wedding
dress. Elen wanted to wear the green silk gown
she had worn for Macbeth's installation
ceremonies.

"You shall have a new gown," Gruach
insisted. "I have just the thing, some pale blue silk
that came from Byzantium. Fionna, see if it is in
the chest, there. Grania, help her. That lid is
heavy."

The bolt of fabric in question proved to be an
exquisite shade, so pale a blue it was almost silver,
stiff and heavy and enhanced by the silver threads
woven through it. Elen gave in, agreeing that it
would make a perfect gown, and Gruach happily

gave it to her as one of the many wedding gifts she was providing.

Elen saw little of Talcoran during this time. He was deeply involved in Macbeth's plans. Macbeth worked hard, weaving a deft skein of firm government about the once-divided land of Alba, binding it into one entity, and he kept his close associates busy with his new projects.

Hoping that memory of the great king who had originally united Scot and Pict would help in achieving unity, Macbeth announced that he would rule from Kenneth mac Alpin's old seat of government at Scone. He ordered changes and additions to the palace there, to make it more comfortable.

He organized troops of men to patrol the wilder parts of the countryside and enforce the king's rule, and Talcoran was placed in charge of these patrols. Elen was relieved that he was often absent from the palace, but she knew her reprieve would be a short one.

The final draft of the treaty with Thorfinn of Orkney had been completed and signed, and the mighty Viking had sailed north to his island homeland.

There was in Alba a sense that the government was in strong, capable hands. The hated English influence at court had been eradicated. The mormaers and thanes were firm in their support of King Macbeth. Most men looked forward to a new era of peace and prosperity.

Elen's wedding day was warm, with a soft, golden sun hanging in a misty sky, a reminder of summer in early October.

She felt as though she was standing outside herself, watching the quiet, slender girl who was being bathed and perfumed and combed and finally dressed in a gown of blue silk as stiff and pale as ice. For the last time, the black mass of her hair hung loose down her back. After that day it would be braided and bound up in the style of a married woman.

"You look lovely." Fionna gave Elen a quick hug.

"I wish..." Elen stopped. She would not voice that wish. She told herself once more that Patric was a traitor. She had to stop the unexpected thoughts of him that crept into her head unbidden whenever she let down her guard. She must put him out of her mind. From this day on she must think only of Talcoran, that strange, dark man, who, once she was his wife, would have power of life and death over her.

"I know." Fionna hugged her again. "I, too, wish it were different, but we cannot change what has happened. Try to be happy, my dear. Don't look back. Forget the past. We will be friends no matter what the future brings."

The wedding ceremony took place in the porch of the church, as was the custom. Macbeth and Gruach were the witnesses. Elen made her responses in a firm voice, stating clearly that she came to Talcoran of her own free will and that she agreed with all the provisions of the contract. At the end she offered her lips for Talcoran's kiss with apparent willingness.

The solemn mass inside the church afterward passed through her mind in a blur of candlelight and priestly vestments and incense. The magnificent feast Macbeth had provided for her and her new husband lasted all that day and into the evening. When Elen thought she could bear no more of noise and music and coarse jests, Gruach herself, accompanied by Fionna and Grania, led her away from the banquet hall.

They did not take her to her former chamber. Talcoran had been given an apartment in the palace, and it was to his bedroom that they conducted her. Elen's possessions had been moved there during the feast, and now all was in readiness for the bride.

Her friends removed the blue silk gown, her undershift, stockings and shoes, and slid over her head a shift of linen so sheer and fine that it settled on her shoulders and swirled about her body like a mist. Her hair was combed again.

Gruach kissed her.

"Get into bed," she said.

Elen had just slipped beneath the covers when the door burst open and Talcoran was pushed into the room. He was followed by Macbeth, Bancho and his son Fergus, Conal mac Duff, and a few other nobles who were his friends. They were all full of wine and mead, and laughter and ribald jokes. Even the usually solemn mac Duff was smiling broadly.

Talcoran's clothes had been removed, and he was wrapped in his dark woolen cloak. Macbeth stepped forward and stripped the garment off his shoulders, leaving Talcoran naked. When Elen looked away, blushing, there was a roar of laughter.

"Put him into bed," Macbeth ordered.

Mac Duff and Fergus pushed Talcoran under the covers. He sat bolt upright beside Elen.

"I call you all to witness," Macbeth declared, "that Talcoran and Elen of Laggan have been bedded together."

"Shall we stay and witness the rest?" inquired one overly jubilant noble. "We should make certain the marriage is legal."

"No," Gruach said, arching a brow at her husband. "It is time to leave."

"Aye." Macbeth laughed. "We've done our work for the night. Now it is Talcoran's turn. You know what to do, my friend."

"Do you need any help?" asked the drunken nobleman.

"He does not!" Macbeth chuckled, pushing the fellow toward the door. "Let us leave them."

There was another burst of laughter from the men. Grania pretended embarrassment, and young Fergus put his arm about her. As the revelers filed out, Bancho winked at Elen.

The door was scarcely closed before Talcoran leapt out of bed to bolt it securely. When he headed back to the bed he faced a wide-eyed Elen.

She had never seen a naked man before this night. Although Talcoran was not as tall as most of the other men she knew, he was well proportioned. Strong muscles rippled as he walked toward her. His legs were straight, his hips narrow, his belly flat. There was a mat of smooth, silky black hair on his well muscled chest. She knew from experience the wiry strength of his arms. She was surprised to see that he was tattooed halfway up each forearm with a ring of tiny blue circles. There was another small design on his left shoulder: a circle, a triangle, and some other mark that looked like a tiny fish. He had narrow hands and feet.

He stood by the bed, his proud look challenging her, his masculinity clearly evident. She could feel her cheeks growing hot. Feeling compelled to say or do something, she fastened her attention upon the tattoo on one of his arms.

"What is that for?" she asked, indicating the marks.

"It is a Pictish custom. You have not married a Scottish nobleman, Elen."

"I married the man chosen for me by my

king." She regretted the words as soon as they were out of her mouth. She had not intended to remind him that she was an unwilling bride. But he did not seem to notice either the words or her embarrassment.

He leaned toward her. He caught at a strand of her hair that had fallen forward over one cheek, and wound it about his fingers.

"Black as a raven's wing," he murmured. "You are beautiful, wife." He drew the last word out, savoring it.

"I do not think so," she said. "I am too tall and thin."

"Will you contradict your husband?" There was a teasing note in his quiet voice, a tone he had never used with her before. "I think you are beautiful."

"I had thought you would prefer a shorter woman." Afraid he would misunderstand her and be angry, she added quickly, "Someone blonde and pink."

"It does not matter that we are the same height." He sat beside her now, still playing with her long, soft hair. "A man cannot grow taller than God meant him to be, but he can increase his stature among men by his deeds."

"If that is true, then you are a giant, my husband." Elen stumbled over the unfamiliar word, but she was rewarded by a smile from Talcoran. "I have never heard anyone say aught of you but that you are honest and brave and loyal to your king."

"He has rewarded me well." Talcoran's hand had strayed to her shoulder. He pushed at the wide neckline of her linen shift. His lips found the hollow of her throat and lingered there.

She began to tremble. She wanted to shove him away, but she dared not. She was his possession now. She must be a good wife to him. She must try to please him.

He seemed to sense her fear. He withdrew from her throat, then spoke as if he had read her mind.

"I know I am not the husband of your choice, Elen. But if we deal fairly with each other, it is possible that we will not be unhappy together. I will never be cruel to you so long as you are honest with me."

She suddenly recalled a night more than a year ago, when he had escorted her to her room after a royal feast, and she had realized how shy he was. She had felt sympathy for him then, and now she felt the same emotion. How dreadful it must be to be made to marry a woman who did not want him. How sad to try to be kind to her and receive nothing in response.

She made herself touch him. She smoothed back the straight black hair and traced the harsh planes of his dark, tanned face. His skin was cool and smooth. She stroked his bristly beard and outlined his firm mouth with her fingertips.

He sat still, waiting patiently as she ran her fingers along the corded muscles of his neck and felt the strength of his shoulders. When she laid her hands flat upon his chest, a shudder went through him. He stood up with a sudden movement.

"I have a gift for you," he said.

He went to a carved wooden chest that stood against the wall. He lifted the lid and took out an object. Returning to the bed, he put it into her hands. It was a smooth white pebble, painted all over with small blue circles, like the designs tattooed on his arms.

"It is a charmstone," he told her, his dark face serious. "It is used to treat sick people, and it will keep you safe."

"Another Pictish custom?" she teased lightly, meeting his eyes with a smile.

"I want you to have it, for luck."

"I will treasure it. Talcoran"—her voice began to shake as she continued, knowing what they must do in a few minutes, fearing it, yet unable to deny a tiny flame of excitement that had begun to burn inside her—"the room is cold. Would you not be warmer in bed, beneath the covers?"

"I have no doubt I would." He got into the bed beside her and gathered her into his arms. She shivered as she felt the length of his naked body through her shift, and the weight of his arm across her waist, but it was not a totally unpleasant sensation.

His mouth covered hers and she willed herself to respond to him. She was surprised that it was so easy. He was gentle, teasing her with soft, light kisses on her face and throat and shoulders. His kisses went on and on, never stopping, but never advancing to anything else. He did not speak, but somehow she understood that he would do no more than this until she indicated that she wanted him to go further. Eventually, she did. Her arms went around his neck and she pulled his head down to hers for a longer, harder kiss.

Still he was gentle, treating her with maddening care, and she could have wept with the sudden need that welled up in her. She wanted something more. She wasn't sure what.

"Please, Talcoran—I don't understand," she gasped. She found to her astonishment that she was writhing against him, aching for his touch, wondering if he would ever put his hands on her. "I want, I want."

At her words, he changed. The cautious gentleness was gone and in its place was a boiling, seething passion, as Talcoran appeared to lose all control over himself. His mouth bruised hers when he forced her lips open and thrust his tongue into her, seeking her response with fierce determination.

She was caught in a whirlwind. Where before Talcoran had lured her with his measured, slow kisses, now everything was happening too fast. She could not stop him; she could not even make him go more slowly. He kissed her again and again, following his own inner rhythm, heedless of her feeble attempts to hold him off so that her heart could slow its furious pounding while she gathered her wits and cleared her mind. He was coaxing, urging, no, *forcing* into life feelings she had never known she had, sensations she had never dreamed existed. She realized that her own self-control was slipping.

He tore at her shift, pulling it off her shoulders and finally tearing it down the front in his eagerness to reach her body beneath it. Through the blinding, dizzying sensations of yet another violently sensuous kiss, she felt his hands on her bare breasts. He was doing something to her nipples, something that created an exquisite wave of pulsating heat deep inside her.

He dragged his mouth away from hers. She tried to pull him back. She experienced a desperate, painful need to drink from his lips again, but he denied her longing, and his mouth fell on her breast instead, with a moist, sucking motion that drove her near to madness.

She twisted and moaned and thrust her hips at him, no longer knowing or caring what she was doing. His hands caressed the smooth skin of her flanks with long, languorous motions that should have calmed the fever building in her, but instead only made it worse.

She cried out as he buried his face in her belly, and his hands stroked lower, over her hips and buttocks, caressing, sliding across the surface of her thighs, his palms flat on her inner thighs as he separated them. His fingers touched her in the most secret spot of all, probing gently. She was suddenly aware of his stiff manhood throbbing against her thigh.

"Elen." His voice was a hungry gasp. "I will try not to hurt you."

She nodded, not really certain what he would do next, conscious only of the dull, gathering ache in the center of her body that must end soon or she would die of it.

She felt something pushing against the place that ached, something soft, yet hard, that thrust, and thrust again, and then, meeting an obstruction, began to hurt her. She moved her hips to get away from the discomfort, but in her confusion she pushed against him, and with a long, tearing slide, he was inside her.

Her scream of pain was smothered by his mouth, and then his full weight was on top of her. He would not release her mouth, he was sucking the very life out of her, and now he was moving inside her, hurting her again. She tried to make him leave her alone, but he was too strong for her to push him away, and all of her efforts seemed only to fuel his passion to an incredible level of intensity.

Gradually, amid her struggles, she became aware that something peculiar was happening. The pain had stopped, and in its place faint ripples of pleasure flowed out of the center of her being, lovely warm sensations.

She ceased to fight him, recognizing that it was Talcoran who was creating this unexpected delight. Her body was moving by itself, matching

Talcoran thrust for thrust. She sensed there was something more that would happen, something just beyond her reach. She clutched at him, pulling him harder against her, wanting whatever it was, that sweet, elusive thing.

"Elen, Elen," Talcoran gasped. He stiffened and buried his face in her neck before he cried out again. "Elen!"

It was over, and the soft, lovely feeling was gone.

"No," she moaned. "Not yet. Talcoran, don't stop."

There was total silence. Then she heard a muffled laugh from somewhere near her left ear.

"Lady, was that an invitation?" Talcoran's mouth found hers in a kiss so deep and tender it nearly made her weep. "I regret I cannot accomodate you at the moment. But soon, my sweet. Soon."

He settled on one elbow and pulled the shreds of her shift across her breasts.

"I seem to have inflicted more damage than I intended." He bent his head and kissed the tip of a breast that peeked out from a tear in the fabric. It was sensitive from his previous assault on it. She uttered a soft cry. "I'm sorry it was necessary to hurt you, Elen."

"It was only for a moment." She stared at him, amazed at the feeling of tenderness that flooded over her. She touched his face with a hand that shook a little. He turned his head to kiss her fingers.

"It will be better the next time," he promised.

"It was very nice this time," she whispered shyly, ignoring the hungry ache that was only slowly releasing its grip on her.

"I hope that's true." He laid his head on her breasts. His steady breathing soon told her he was asleep.

She pulled the fur cover up over his shoulders and smoothed down his hair. He had forgotten to put out the candle.

Let it burn, she thought. She wriggled down into the bed, fitting herself against him. If he wakes, he may want to do that again, and if he does, I want to see his face.

11

Talcoran had already left when Elen awakened the next morning. She was conscious of a sharp sense of loss. She had wanted to wake beside him. She wanted him to kiss her and put his hands on her and do the thing he had done last night, so that she could feel again that lovely warm sensation and perhaps achieve whatever it was that lay beyond, that she had just sensed but had not quite touched.

Ava told her he had gone out, saying he had some business of the king's to attend to. He had not said when he would return.

Wondering if, in her innocence, she had displeased him in some way, Elen got out of bed and prepared to attend the queen. Ava produced several bronze hairpins and began to comb Elen's hair. Today, for the first time, the rich, thick mass of her hair was braided and twisted and pinned up in the ornate arrangement of a married woman.

"My lord Talcoran told me to give you this," Ava said, handing Elen a little carved wooden box.

Inside it lay six small gold balls, ornaments for her braids. Ava twisted them securely into her hair as she arranged it, then stood back to observe the effect.

"You look well, my lady," Ava said. "Is he a good husband?"

"You should not ask such a thing." There was no reproach in Elen's voice, only a note of wonder. She touched the hair ornaments with gentle fingers. Then she put the charmstone Talcoran had given her into the little wooden box.

"I will keep this near me," she said.

Fionna was with Lulach in the queen's quarters when Elen arrived.

"Gruach is sitting with the king, listening to petitions," Fionna said. "Grania and the others are with her. She thought you would prefer to spend your day privately and asks that you bear Lulach company."

Her former pupil produced his prayer book and a slate. Elen began once more instructing him in his lessons.

"My mother says, now that you are married, I must have a priest to teach me," Lulach said.

"That sounds like a very good idea. Talcoran and I will have to leave court soon and travel to Laggan, so that he can inspect his new lands."

"But not until spring. You must stay at court for Christmas. It is so nice now that Malcolm has gone. Besides"—Lulach gave her a sly look—"if you wait until spring you may be big with child, and then you can't travel, and you can stay here longer."

"Lulach!" Elen shook her head at him, trying to appear stern, but secretly amused as he assumed a wise, adult expression. "Whoever put such a thought into your head? You are growing up too fast."

"I'll be thirteen next month, and I've become an expert with the broadsword. My weapons instructor says so. And Macbeth discusses affairs of state with me now," the boy added proudly.

"Does he?" Elen thought her cousin probably did talk to his stepson of such matters, although surely in a much simplified way. Knowledge of the art of ruling men would be an excellent thing for the child who might one day be King of Alba.

Lulach's physical growth and ability to learn had been slow compared to other boys of his age until the past summer. Now he was so newly-sprouted tall, with his bony wrists and knees and his awkward attempts at playing adult, that Elen felt a surge of tender affection for him. She wanted to put her arms around him and hug him as she used to do, but she feared his youthful masculinity would be insulted by any suggestion of coddling.

"You have become a man, my prince," she said, feeling suddenly old.

"I know," he replied gravely, and she repressed a smile.

"Do you miss Patric?" he asked suddenly.

Elen realized that she had not thought of Patric since she had been robed for her wedding. After last night with Talcoran she could never think of any other man. Talcoran. At the memory of him, her body stirred with that strange, aching need. Perhaps Lulach was right and she would soon be with child. Perhaps it had already happened. Talcoran's child.

"I hardly remember Patric," she said, and thought she spoke the truth.

Lulach appeared relieved at her answer.

"I'm glad. He's a traitor to Macbeth. But at least he took Malcolm away. If I met Patric again, I'd thank him for that before I killed him."

"Let us hope," Elen said fervently, "that neither of us will ever meet Patric mac Keith again."

It was early evening before Macbeth and Gruach returned to their chambers. Talcoran arrived soon after, to report to Macbeth on some matter.

Elen observed her new husband closely as he spoke with the king. Why had she never realized before that in his own harshly rugged way Talcoran was handsome? How smooth and sleek was the dark hair that hung to just below his ears. How beautifully straight his nose was, how fine the high cheekbones above his thick beard. And his hands—those slender, sensitive fingers that had lit unexpected fires in her body—how strong and beautiful they were.

She saw him looking at her with a glowing expression in his eyes. Drawn by an irresistible force, she crossed the room to him, moving lightly, as though her feet skimmed above the rushes on the floor and never touched it at all. She wanted to throw herself into his arms. She knew he had read her thoughts. She expected to feel herself blushing, but oddly, there was no disconcerting rush of blood to her face, only a warmth at her heart as she smiled at him.

Perhaps, she thought, I cannot blush now that I am a wife.

Then Talcoran, who in public had always been so cold and self-contained, bent toward her and kissed her lightly on the mouth.

"I'll join you soon," he whispered, before he followed Macbeth out of the room.

"So," Gruach said behind her, "it goes well after all. Your hair looks lovely pinned up like that. Very becoming. Did Talcoran give you the ornaments?"

"Yes." Elen looked after the men, the fingers of one hand lightly pressed to her softly parted lips, as if she would bring back Talcoran's kiss.

Gruach's arm was about her waist.

"I was right about him. I knew it. Are you content now, cousin?"

"I think so. It is not—" Elen hesitated, unwilling to say too much, lest the spell that Talcoran had woven about them should be broken. "It is not at all what I expected," she finished.

"It never is." Gruach's grey eyes were misty. "I remember when first I wed my Gillecomgan, all of the world was suddenly strange to me. And strangely beautiful."

"And Macbeth?" Elen could not resist the question.

"I was not an innocent girl when I married Macbeth, nor was he a boy. We were both full grown, man and woman together, and he is magnificent, splendid, a great golden lion. A king." Gruach's breast heaved with emotion. "There is no one like Macbeth, or ever will be again."

How different this night was from the previous one. Then she had been numb and fearful. Now she waited with urgent expectation for Talcoran to appear in their bedchamber.

Wrapped only in a loose, flowing robe of deep green wool that opened down the front, Elen leaned back in Talcoran's wooden chair while Ava unbound and combed her hair. The golden ornaments, Talcoran's gift, lay on a table beside her. She fingered them, feeling their delicately chased surfaces, admiring the way they shone in the candlelight.

She looked up as the door opened and Talcoran came in. He stood watching her, his eyes following Ava's hands as she drew the horn comb through the heavy smoothness of her mistress's hair.

No one spoke. Talcoran was a quiet man, and

Elen could find no words to express what she felt
at the sight of him. He unbuckled his heavy leather
belt and laid it, and the broadsword that hung
from it, carefully on top of the wooden chest in the
corner. He pulled off his tunic and folded it neatly,
placing it next to his belt. His boots followed. Clad
now only in his narrow woolen breeches, he sat on
the end of the bed, watching the women until Ava
had finished with Elen's hair.

"Leave us," Elen said at last, and Ava scurried
out.

Once she was gone, Talcoran rose and
removed his breeches, then came to stand behind
the chair. He began to stroke Elen's hair with
gentle, caressing motions. He picked up the heavy,
fragrant weight of it and buried his face in it.

Elen felt excitement mounting in her. When
his arms went around her, she laid her head back
against his waist. His supple hands brushed along
the length of her slender throat, then moved lower
to push her robe apart. She felt his lips against her
hair and then his cheek on hers as he sought the
sensitive spot at the base of her neck. His hands
never stopped, up and down on her throat, up and
down, moving lower with each stroke until his
fingers slid around her breasts and rested there.
One thumb flicked across a nipple. She caught her
breath. He chuckled softly and pulled away from
her. He moved around the chair and bent over her,
one hand on each wooden arm. Intimidated by his
naked strength and the rapidly growing evidence
of his enormous desire for her, she would have
retreated, but there was no place to go.

His mouth tasted her sweetness, withdrew,
returned again. Her lips parted, and when next
they met his, received his tongue. He began a
tantalizing exploration of her inner mouth that

left her weak. She made futile moaning sounds deep in her throat.

When he had begun kissing her she had grasped his wrists. Now she raised her hands to push him away so she could breathe. She shoved at his shoulders once or twice before she found her fingers had become entangled in his hair. With a groan, she gave up her effort to separate herself from him. When he would have pulled back, she held him there, and now she tasted his mouth, sucking at his tongue, pulling him more deeply into her, giving back all that he had given her.

They broke apart at last, both gasping for air. Talcoran straightened and looked down at her with a frown. Afraid she might have done something wrong, she watched him fearfully.

"Elen," he said between deep breaths, "do you truly want me?"

She wondered at his question after her passionate response to his kisses. She sensed that he did not want to hear a complicated discussion of the vague longings she had experienced all day. She would be hard put to explain to herself exactly what were her conflicting and tumultuous emotions toward this near stranger who was her husband. How could she hope to make him understand what she did not understand herself? She knew what he wanted of her that night. Perhaps it was enough that at that moment she wanted the same thing of him.

He watched her closely, standing before her in naked masculine splendour, virile and unashamed, waiting for her answer.

"My lord," she began, and stopped. No, there would be no formality here, not in this private place. He had told her on their wedding night to be honest with him. She looked him straight in the eye.

"Talcoran," she said, "I want to do what we did last night, but I don't want it to end. There is something more, something I almost touched. I want to find it."

His smile seemed to light up the room. He bent toward her again. She thought he would kiss her, but he did not. Instead, he caught her at the waist, pulling her up. With awesome ease, he lifted her into the air and slung her over his shoulder. Her robe slid onto the floor in a soft heap, forgotten.

He was so strong that her weight was nothing to him. She was bent double over his shoulder, looking down the length of his back to his heels. Her long hair was dragging on the floor, and he was laughing. She had never heard Talcoran laugh before. She marveled at the husky, joyful, male sound of it.

She tried to turn herself right side up as he carried her the few steps to their bed. She pushed herself up and clutched at his shoulder, unbalancing them both.

They went down, landing on the bed, sprawling in a tangle of limbs and hair. They were both laughing now. He rolled over on top of her and held her down while he kissed her breasts and shoulders and her willing mouth.

"Elen," he breathed, "my sweet, dear wife."

It was there again, the thing she had felt the night before, and it was growing. It filled her heart and spilled over to create gloriously warm and sweet sensations wherever Talcoran's mouth and hands touched her.

He explored every curve and crevice of her body. He began with her mouth. He had prepared her well before they reached the bed and she was eager for more. Her lips opened like a dewy, coral-pink rose, and he assaulted them with loving brutality, not letting her turn away until he had driven her to the edge of a sweet, moaning anguish that begged him to stop and pleaded for more at the same time.

He moved on, to her throat, finding again the pulse in the hollow there and teasing at it with tongue and lips, while the blood surged ever more strongly through her veins in a pounding, throbbing rhythm of growing desire.

He found her breasts and played there a while, nibbling and sucking, smiling with pleasure when she arched her back and thrust the sweet mounds at him and begged him not to stop.

He moved lower, his own feverish intensity growing ever more apparent. She began to realize how great had been his self-control the night before, even when she thought he had lost it. He had kept himself under tight rein as long as possible, trying not to hurt her, and perhaps sacrificing some of his own pleasure in that effort. Tonight there would be no holding back.

She ceased to think. She became a writhing, moaning creature of desire, driven by the fires that now he lit in her. She felt his hair beneath her fingers, but she did not know she pulled at it. She clutched his shoulders, not realizing she raked great bloody scratches on them. He lifted his head with a startled cry and her nails tore at his face in her frenzy.

He caught her hands, holding them securely at her sides while she thrashed and cried and begged him with broken, nearly incoherent words, to help her, help her.

She whimpered in her desperate need when she felt him pushing at that place where he had entered her body before. She tensed, expecting the pain she had felt then, not caring if it hurt again.

But there was only the faintest twinge of discomfort as he plunged deep into her burning,
heaving flesh.

He released her hands and she wrapped her
arms and legs around him, unaware of her actions,
intent only on what was happening inside her.
There was a core of fire, deep within her being,
and with each movement that Talcoran made,
each stroke into the interior of her deepest self, he
touched that core and sent great molten waves of
undulating fire rippling out from the center,
through every pore and fiber, every nerve and
muscle, until she was fire itself, blazing, burning,
searing light and heat, and Talcoran was
consumed within her, and they were completely,
totally one, an unquenchable flame of white-hot
passion that burned and burned and would not,
could not, end.

They lay spent, wrapped in each other's arms.
Talcoran was still inside her, a softer, gentler
thing that stirred echoes of fiery passion when he
moved against her. Her inner body still intensely
sensitive, she reacted at once, thrusting against
him, and heard him chuckle. His mouth was as
sweet as honey when he kissed her. He withdrew
from her and lay down beside her, pillowing his
head on the dark waterfall of her hair.

"I must remember to thank Macbeth for
forcing us to marry," he said, tenderly tracing the
outline of one soft breast with a slender finger.
"Our king little knew what a treasure he was
giving me."

She did not know why it was that his slightest
touch was so pleasing to her. She moved until the
palm of his hand rested firmly on the curve of her
breast, then gave a happy sigh.

"Am I a treasure?"

"Oh, yes." He smiled, and drew his hand slowly from her breast across her abdomen, down to rest between her thighs in a possessive gesture that stirred her deeply. The fire leapt up for a moment, then subsided into a comfortable warmth when he removed his hand. "And you, wife, are you content?"

"You said that I must always be honest with you."

"Yes." He waited, the air between them vibrating with sudden tension.

"Then," she whispered, "I must tell you that I was sorely disappointed not to find you in our bed this morning, for I wanted you then. I yearned for your presence all the day long. A short time ago I thought I would die of wanting you. You may not think it possible after what we have just done, but, heaven help me, I want you again. You look at me or touch me, and I am in turmoil. How can I be content when I feel like this?"

"You do not regret our marriage?"

"Only your absence when I would be with you constantly."

"Elen." He pulled her into his arms with rough tenderness, holding her against his chest. His voice was strained, as if he choked back some overwhelming emotion. "I left this morning because I knew I had hurt you and I feared you would be angry with me. I, who go into battle without hesitation, flinch at the thought of your rage."

She tried to look at him, but he held her head firmly against himself. Perhaps he feared what she would see in his face.

"Then you must care about me," she said. "I thought you disliked me. You said you did not want to marry me."

"I have wanted you since first I saw you," he

whispered harshly, holding her so tightly she could hardly breathe. "But I am only a rough soldier. I never dreamed you might be given to me as wife. I have never bedded a noblewoman before. I have never even bedded a virgin. I thought you would hate me for what I did to you."

He had loosened his grip on her a little, and now Elen sat up and looked at him. His eyes were suspiciously bright. She wondered if there were tears in them, then dismissed the thought. This, after all, was Talcoran.

"Did you find hatred in your bed tonight?" she asked, and smiled at his expression.

"You did say you wanted me again?" he asked.

She saw that he wanted her. She tried to look calm and unconcerned, though now the flame was burning high in her, too.

"I have promised always to be honest with you, my husband," she told him in mock seriousness. "I cannot deny that I want you."

"Show me," he commanded.

The land of Alba lay at peace during that golden autumn and throughout the silver winter that followed. Fionna was with child again, along with two other of the queen's ladies—the result, Gruach noted dryly, of soldiers returning home from war unscathed.

Elen had had hope for herself, then was disappointed to find it was not so. Since Talcoran's passionate interest in her continued unabated, she had little doubt that it would not be long before she, too, grew rounded and content like the others.

She was surprised to find her husband and the solemn Conal mac Duff becoming fast friends. Mac Duff plainly admired Talcoran's honesty and unaffected manners. When their courtly duties permitted it, the two couples often spent evenings together, the men bent over a chessboard, the women busy with spinning or needlework, amid quiet laughter, gossip, or plans for the future.

The Christmas celebrations that year were marred only by the arrival of news from Northumbria. Patric mac Keith and the three young princes in his charge had safely reached the English court. Malcolm and Maelmuire were to live with their Uncle Siward, Earl of Northumbria. Donald had been sent to Ireland for schooling.

"Well enough for the present," Macbeth said. "Siward is new to his title and is too weak to attack Alba."

"He may not always be too weak," Talcoran cautioned.

"True, but we'll worry about that when the time comes, if it ever does. I have other things on my mind, a kingdom to set to rights."

Elen noticed that Fionna slipped away during this discussion. Later she found her weeping in a far corner of the king's reception room and hurried to her friend's side.

"At least I know now that Patric is alive," Fionna sobbed. "I should be happy about that, but I miss him so much."

"I wish I could help you. I don't like to see you unhappy."

"Don't you ever miss him, Elen? Don't you ever think about him?"

"How could I? I have a husband now. I scarcely remember what Patric looks like." She would not admit, even to herself, that she could still feel crisp auburn curls beneath her fingers, still remember the touch of a wide, warm mouth on hers. She turned away from Fionna with a vaguely guilty feeling. "I must speak to Talcoran."

12

January to September 1041.

Shortly after the twelve days of Christmas feasting were over, Elen began to believe her hopes would be realized. By early February she was certain. She waited to tell Talcoran until they were snuggled together, warm and peaceful after an evening of lovemaking.

"I am with child," she said.

"You have made me very happy," he told her between kisses. "It could not have come at a better time, now that we have put away our swords. With a strong and just king we will have peace. Our sons will grow up in a land that is prosperous and peaceful."

"Strange words for so fierce a warrior," Elen teased him.

"I want no more battles. I want you and our child, nothing else."

Within a week Talcoran had decided it was time for them to make their long-overdue journey to Laggan.

"I should see my new lands," he told her, "and I want our son to be born at the place that will be his home."

Fionna and Conal were returning to Fife for the birth of their own child in early June.

"As soon as I am well enough to travel, we will come to you at Laggan and stay until your babe is born," Fionna promised. "You should not be alone with only servants to attend you for your first child."

"If this continues, I will soon have none of my ladies left to attend me." Gruach was only half joking. "I must give both of you my blessing, since your husbands wish you to go, but promise to return to my service as quickly as possible. I love you both, and I will miss you terribly."

Elen had never felt so well. Unlike some of her friends among the queen's ladies, she suffered only a few days of morning nausea before her body adjusted to pregnancy. Now, in the spring of her eighteenth year, she was blooming. Her skin had taken on a soft, rosy sheen. Her figure had lost its youthful angularity. Her breasts, formerly small, delicately rounded globes, had enlarged to rich, womanly mounds and become exquisitely sensitive, a fact that delighted Talcoran when he discovered it.

He had been reluctant to touch her after she told him she carried his child, fearing he might harm her or the baby if he continued his frequent, vigorous lovemaking. Elen soon changed his mind. Always receptive to his advances, she endured her enforced celibacy for just two nights before becoming the agressor.

"You must not neglect me again, Talcoran. I cannot bear it," she said. "I need you."

He stretched beside her, sated and at peace.

"I am glad to hear it," he said. "I thought I would go mad. I need you, too, Elen."

In late March, they set out for Laggan. They traveled slowly, Talcoran insisting that Elen must not overtire herself. She rode the tamest of palfreys, Ava riding beside her in case she should want something. With Talcoran close by, Elen thought only once or twice of her last trip along this path through the forest wilderness, when Patric had taken her to court. That earlier journey seemed to her now to have taken place in another lifetime, when she had been a shy, innocent girl, fearful of the future.

The trip was uneventful, and on a soft, early spring evening they came at last to Laggan. The sky was a delicate blue, fading to pink in the west. A crescent moon was reflected in the gently ruffled waters of Loch Laggan. The silhouette of Laggan Castle loomed beside the lake, solid and comforting. Behind the log palisade they could see the outline of the peaked roof of the great hall, and the two-storied living quarters attached to the hall. The kitchen and storage rooms, stables and outbuildings spread out on the opposite side of the great hall, ending in the cluster of turf and stone cottages where servants and a few of the farmers lived.

"There is our home," Elen said, and felt Talcoran's hand covering hers in the gathering dusk. His face was in shadow, but she sensed his pleasure.

Old Dougal was a little greyer and a bit more wrinkled, but his eyes still sparkled and his step was firm.

"I welcome you, my lord," he said to Talcoran with great formality. "Welcome to the new Thane of Laggan. And welcome to you, too, lady."

When she removed her cloak, Dougal noted Elen's expanded waistline.

"So we will soon have young ones running about," he said with a broad smile. "It will bring some life into this lonely place. Your father would be pleased, lady."

That night the Thane of Laggan slept in the

master's bedchamber, and made love to his wife until it was nearly dawn.

The days ran into one another in a sunny, peaceful blur. Talcoran took control of his new lands as though he had always been a nobleman, making changes with a sure sense of what was right, bringing his intensity and his own sense of purpose to Laggan. Elen observed him with growing admiration as, with a diplomatic skill worthy of Macbeth himself, Talcoran overcame the resistance of the people of Laggan to new ideas.

Even Dougal, at first reserved and wary, was won over by his new master. Talcoran rode out occasionally to oversee the troops of Macbeth's men who patrolled this part of Alba, keeping the king's order. When he did so, he left Dougal in command of the castle, stating that he had full confidence in Dougal's reliability and loyalty.

While Talcoran made the lands of Laggan his own, Elen bustled about the castle, ordering rooms cleaned, inspecting the larder, preparing for the guests they expected later in the summer and for the baby she wanted so much. She chose the room where her child would be born, and she and Ava prepared linen cloths for the birth, and swaddling clothes for the new baby.

A messenger arrived from Fife with the news that Fionna had been safely delivered of a second son, on the first of June.

"A good omen," Talcoran promised that evening as the household drank a toast to the Thane of Fife and his family. "Now I am certain that ours will be a healthy son, too."

As the summer progressed and Elen grew steadily larger, she no longer moved with her old light step. She sat more often, and complained of an aching back. One night, after an awkward coupling, Talcoran pulled her against him and nuzzled at her neck.

"This must be the last time until the child is born, Elen. I would not harm either of you."

"No," she protested, "I don't want to sleep alone." Her days had been full, and with Talcoran beside her each night, possessing her body until she fell into satisfied slumber, she had not had time for the terrors that consumed other pregnant women.

"I am your husband, and I order this. After tonight you will sleep in the room you have prepared for the birth. I cannot lie in the same bed with you and not touch you."

He was her lord, and she must do as he commanded, but now Elen found her confidence deserting her. She lay alone in her new, small room with Ava snoring softly on a pallet nearby and worried, while all of the night demons she had previously rejected gnawed at her mind. Even the charmstone Talcoran had given her, which she kept in its carved box by her bed, seemed to have lost its magic.

Worse even than her fears for herself and her child was her concern for her marriage. She had never doubted Talcoran's fidelity, but how could a man as vigorous, as virile as he endure months of abstinence? She began to eye the women of the household, wondering if he took one of them to his bed in her absence. They were an unlikely lot. Most of them were too old or too young or too dirty, and she knew Talcoran was fastidious. But if he was desperate, anything was possible.

She found herself watching Ava, who was young and plump and pretty, although she knew full well that Ava was preoccupied with Talcoran's aide, Drust. In her year and a half at court, Elen had learned to accept many things that would have shocked the naive girl she had once been. One of those things was that it was not at all unusual for a man to lie with his wife's personal servant if the wife were not available. Talcoran was seldom seen in the same room with Ava, but that meant nothing.

Elen became even rounder and more awkward, and her hands and feet began to swell. Her head ached every day. She was ugly and lonely and certain that Talcoran must be unfaithful. She clung to the charmstone he had given her, as if that would keep him close to her. She slept with it under her pillow.

That summer was unusually hot and airless. The fields were heavy with ripening grain. Early apples dropped from the trees and lay on the ground, their pungent odor as they rotted speaking to Elen of autumn and decay and death.

Then in mid-August Fionna and her family came to Laggan like a crisp breeze, dispelling morbid thoughts and unhealthy fears. At a year and a half, Fionna's red-haired son Keith toddled about on unsteady feet, getting in everyone's way and generating frequent laughter with his damp, toothy smile and his tendency to sit down in the most unlikely places. The new baby, named Ewen, was plump and sweet-smelling and slept most of the time.

The day after their arrival, Talcoran and Conal rode off to meet with some of Macbeth's men who patrolled Lagganshire, leaving the women alone. It took Fionna less than half of that day to drag out of Elen all the dark imaginings that had tormented her for weeks. Characteristically, Fionna addressed first the problem most important to Elen.

"Talcoran is not unfaithful," she said flatly,

shaking Elen a little. "He adores you. He has said nothing to me, but I suspect from the way he watches you that he is worried about you, just as Conal worries about me when I am with child. He doesn't talk about his feelings because he doesn't want to frighten you."

"I am so ugly." Elen covered her face with her hands. "I can't bear to look in the mirror."

"I always feel that way, too. It will be much better once the baby comes." Fionna was briskly sensible. "I admit you are very large, but you look perfectly healthy to me. Come for a short walk. You need to get out of this hot room. It is cooler by the loch. We can talk more there. Ava, bring some cushions for your mistress to sit on if she tires." As Ava ran to do her bidding, Fionna giggled. "Surely you can't imagine Talcoran would want that silly girl? My dear, I think the heat has addled your wits."

One week later, Elen was awakened toward dawn by a sharp pain in her lower back. Thinking that, like so many recent aches and pains, it would go away if she walked a bit, she got out of bed.

Ava, who had been sleeping on the floor at the foot of her mistress's bed, scrambled to her feet at Elen's surprised cry. A gush of water poured onto the chamber floor, soaking Elen's nightdress.

"What is it?" Elen stared down at the lower half of her body in blank astonishment. "What has happened to me?"

"It is your time, mistress. We should call the lady Fionna."

"No, not yet. She will still be asleep. I think you are mistaken, Ava. I feel nothing."

"You will," Ava promised. "You will."

Elen walked, dragging the damp shift about her ankles, back and forth across the room, until she was sure there would be a deep groove worn in the stone floor.

As soon as the castle began to stir with the day's activities, Fionna was summoned. She arrived with a shawl wrapped over her nightdress, her red-gold curls tumbling down her back. She shot one knowing look at her damp, bedraggled friend and took immediate command of all arrangements.

"Ava, get that soiled shift off her at once. You should have had sense enough to do that without me telling you. Elen, keep walking. I'll be back as soon as I dress." Fionna paused at the door. "I'll send my maidservant to help with the preparations. She was with me when Ewen was born. She will know what to do."

Ava helped Elen into a clean shift of heavy, coarse linen. The maid Fionna sent arrived with a bundle of fresh rushes, and together she and Ava strewed them on the floor. The clean straw mattress on which Elen would give birth was laid on top of the rushes.

Meanwhile, encouraged by the two women, Elen walked, back and forth, back and forth.

"Good, that's fine." Fionna had returned. "We will need warm water to wash the babe when it is born. I want the bed aired and freshly made up, so it will be ready for your mistress when this is over."

The maids hurried to carry out her orders.

"Elen, I think you are foolish," Fionna went on. "You should have a midwife here."

"No. No," Elen gasped, bending over and clutching at her swollen abdomen. She waited until the contraction had ended, then straightened and faced Fionna. They had been through this argument before. "The only midwife near by is a dreadful old hag. She's a witch—I'm certain of it. I don't want her near me. I want you to be here."

"Very well, then." Fionna put her arms around Elen and steadied her as another contraction came. "You know I'll stay with you. Now stop worrying and concentrate on the work before you."

Elen's discomfort was mild at first, but by mid-morning the pains were regular and strong enough to make her catch at Ava's shoulders so she could stand during them.

Talcoran arrived, looking worried. He took Elen's hands just as a contraction seized her. She gripped his wrists and held on tightly until it was over. Talcoran, the brave warrior, turned white.

"Go out of this room," Fionna ordered. "This is woman's work. Go away."

"Elen." She felt his lips on her moist forehead and realized he was trembling.

"Go," she said, trying to smile at him. "Fionna will call you when the child is born."

"Keep walking," Fionna urged after Talcoran had left. "It will make the babe come faster. Ava, take her other arm on your shoulder as I am doing. Now, walk."

Supported between the two women, Elen tried to keep her legs moving. With scarcely focused eyes she saw Fionna's maidservant carry a wooden cradle into the room and laid out the child's garments beside it.

"This will encourage you," the woman said kindly. "Think of the child to come."

By noon, Elen could walk no longer. The pain and the downward pressure of a great weight were too much for her. She knelt on the straw mattress, supported by Fionna and Ava, and pushed and pushed until she thought her heart would stop from the effort.

"Push harder," Fionna ordered.

"I can't. I'm so tired." Elen's head fell back.

"Lay her down, lady," Ava suggested, "And let her rest a little. It will make what is to come easier for her."

Elen lay down on the straw, and for a moment the pain left her. She nearly dozed, but it began again, and suddenly all she wanted was to be rid of her burden.

Ava lifted her and sat behind her so Elen could lean against the servant. Ava's plump arms were around her waist, pushing down hard on her swollen belly.

"What are you doing? Let me go." Ava held her fast while a grinding pain of incredible intensity convulsed her exhausted body. With the strength of rising panic, Elen began struggling against Ava, crying out loudly when she could not get free. Fionna's voice came out of the red mist in front of her.

"Push, Elen. Harder, harder. Push!"

She was being torn in two. Some monstrous thing was killing her. She screamed and tried to fight back, but Ava still held her. Someone was separating her legs and touching her. Was it Talcoran? Why was he doing this to her? He had never hurt her after that first time.

"Talcoran!" She heard her own voice, ragged and hoarse, but it was Fionna, not Talcoran, who answered her.

"Push again. Once more. That's good. Just once more, Elen."

She no longer knew where she was or even who she was. She only knew she had to be free of this thing that was killing her in its struggle to be free of her body. From somewhere deep inside the heaving, panting, sweating, bleeding creature that was herself, Elen found the strength for one final effort.

She took a deep breath and pushed as hard as she could, pushed until her ears rang and the world began to go black. Something slid out of her, something wet and slippery, and there was a gush of hot liquid against her thighs, and then she was light as air, floating upward into the blue August sky, and somewhere a baby was crying.

Her head was pillowed on Ava's lap and the little maid was weeping while she dabbed at Elen's face with a damp cloth.

"Ava, stop that nonsense and help me."

That was Fionna, Elen knew, although she could not open her eyes to see what was happening. She had never been so tired. Her head was down on the straw mattress now, and she heard water being poured out, and people were doing things to her body. The pains began again.

"No," she muttered weakly, "no more."

"Only a little longer," Fionna assured her. "You have a fine son. Let us finish this, then you can see him."

She was not sure what happened to her next. There was more pain, mercifully brief, and she felt totally empty. Fionna bathed her and gave her wine to drink—Talcoran's best Rhinish wine—and then Fionna and Ava and the other maidservant dragged her to her feet and got her into the bed.

The baby began to cry again, and her breasts ached.

"I want my son."

"Here he is." Fionna put a tiny swaddled bundle into her arms. He had the wrinkled red face of an aged stranger.

"He looks just like his father," Ava cooed.

Elen began to laugh. She was so weak and tired that she began to cry at the same time, but she could not stop laughing.

"I have never seen anyone who looked less

like Talcoran," she said between happy sobs.

"That is odd, for I have no doubt that I am his father." Talcoran sat on the side of the bed and poked a long finger at his son, who promptly began to scream. Now Talcoran laughed, too. "He is perfectly healthy, I see. Or rather, I hear." He leaned forward and kissed Elen.

"Hello, wife," he said softly. He held her free hand. "I thank you for our son."

"It was you who gave him to me."

"I will give you others as soon as we can have them."

Fionna made a sound as near to a snort as she could possibly manage.

"That is just what Elen does not need to hear today," she said. "What Elen needs is rest. Ava, take the baby away to its cradle. Say good-day to your wife, Talcoran, and leave."

Talcoran did not move.

"Lady, do you speak to your husband in that way?" he asked lazily.

"Frequently. He values my good sense."

Elen expected Talcoran to make some sharp answer, but he did not.

"Fionna, let me have a few moments alone with Elen. Please."

Surprisingly, Fionna capitulated without an argument.

"I'll go tell Conal the good news. Come along, Ava."

Before the door had closed behind them, Talcoran was kissing Elen's hands.

"She thinks I am a thoughtless fool," he muttered.

"No, she thinks you are a man who has just met his first son. Talcoran, I want to ask a favor of you."

"You may have anything it is in my power to

give you."

"Could we call him Colin, for my father?"

"Colin mac Talcoran," he said softly. "So that one day there will be another Colin, Thane of Laggan. I agree."

She felt the tears rising again. She wished she were not so weak and tired. She wanted to tell him how much it meant to her that he had immediately understood her request, but that would have to wait until later. Her eyelids drooped.

"I must let you sleep now, or Fionna will scold me again," he told her.

He kissed her lips. As she saw his dark, rugged face hovering above her with tender concern, she found the strength to say at last the words that had lain in her heart for so many months, that she had never dared speak before, even in their most intimate moments.

"Talcoran," she whispered as she slipped toward the deepest sleep she had ever known, "I love you. I love you."

Bancho of Lochaber rode into Laggan Castle.

"Talcoran and Conal are hunting," Elen told him. "You will see them at the evening meal. You will stay a few days, I hope."

"Only a day or two. Are they always so ugly?" he asked, frowning at the baby in Elen's arms. "I don't remember Fergus at that age. I was away from home fighting for most of his first year. I do remember you, Elen. You were a pretty little thing."

"Girls are always prettier than boys," Fionna said tartly, "As you would know if you ever paid any attention."

Bancho laughed. "We have missed your tongue at court, lady." He settled into a big wooden chair near the firepit, which had been his special place for as long as Elen could remember. "That is why I am here. I have a message from Macbeth. Which I will deliver," he added before Fionna could speak, "only when Colin and Talcoran are here, too."

They ate heartily that night, of grouse from the day's hunt, venison, and fish from the loch, cheese and apples and mead and ale.

"This is like the days of my youth," Bancho remarked, loosening his belt. "There was always good food at Laggan."

"I haven't seen so many at our table since my father died," Elen said, looking down the long board at Bancho's men, and Conal mac Duff's troop of retainers, and Talcoran's men-at-arms, all sitting with Dougal and the men of Laggan. Servants moved along the tables, offering platters of meat or bread, and pitchers of foamy beer. "Laggan Castle has come alive again."

"I am sorry to spoil your happiness, Elen, but you must leave Laggan in a few days. I am here with a summons from Macbeth. You are all to return to court at once."

"But why?"

"The king commands it."

"My son is only two weeks old," Talcoran said. "Neither Elen nor the baby can possibly travel yet. Elen will remain at Laggan until she is stronger."

"Macbeth wants you all at court," Bancho insisted.

"I am Thane," Talcoran said softly. "In Lagganshire, I am absolute ruler, as you are in Lochaber. I will go to court, but my wife will remain at home for another month."

"Well," Fionna murmured as the women left the table to prepare for bed, "I never thought I would see Talcoran defy Macbeth."

"It's not defiance, it is only care for me," Elen replied. "Macbeth should understand that. I know Gruach will."

As she and Fionna mounted the stairs to their bedchambers, Elen looked back into the great hall. The men still sat at table, their cups before them, talking companionably. It was a pleasant scene, yet her heart was heavy as she watched them. She believed that Bancho had not told them everything.

Even more than her foreboding about a return to court she dreaded separation from Talcoran. She had not moved back to their bed-chamber yet, for the baby wakened several times each night to be nursed and would disturb him, and Fionna had warned her to wait until her body was completely healed before chancing another pregnancy. As she recovered, she found her desire for Talcoran reviving. She knew he was eager for her to return to their bed, for he had told her so. Now they were to be apart for a month. The spectre of the blonde beauties at court rose to haunt her before she firmly dismissed the thought. Talcoran wanted her. He would wait.

13

Her clothes and other personal belongings had been put away in their usual places. The apartment in Macbeth's palace at Scone appeared unchanged. It was hard to believe that she had been away for more than half a year, but the baby sleeping in Elen's arms was proof of that.

"Welcome, mistress." Her husband's sturdy aide stood by the door.

"Drust, where is your master?"

"He is with the king. He ordered me to bring this woman to you, and to tell you he will dine privately with you this evening." Drust pushed forward a blonde woman of about thirty, while his eyes strayed toward Ava, who appeared to be deeply involved in folding linens.

"Thank you, Drust." Elen regarded the man with barely concealed amusement. "I think after our long journey from Laggan, all of my servants will need a rest. Tell the men who rode here with me that they are free until tomorrow morning." As Drust turned to go, Elen added, "And you, Ava. Once you have prepared me to meet my husband, you will have the evening free, too." She heard Drust chuckle as he went out.

Elen now turned her attention to the woman Drust had brought her.

"Who are you?" she asked.

"I am called Briga." The woman spoke Gaelic with a strong accent. "I am a Dane. My family had settled peacefully in the east of Alba, but we were all captured when King Duncan's army fought those Danes who had invaded Alba."

"That was two years ago." Elen spoke sharply. She preferred to forget the time of which Briga spoke. "What have you been doing since then?"

"I was given in service to a noble lady." The woman seemed uneasy. She lifted pale blue eyes to Elen's. "Mistress, your husband told me to speak honestly to you, that you would not condemn me."

"Then do as he ordered."

"My former mistress's husband lay with me. I did not want it, but he forced me. He hurt me." She wrung her hands, looking frightened. "He kept doing it. He beat me when I tried to resist him. Finally, he got me with child. When she found out, my mistress dismissed me."

Elen looked at the woman's scrawny form. Did Talcoran expect her to take in this odd, foreign creature? Her hair was matted and uncombed, her face and hands were dirty, and her dress was stained across its tight bodice. Elen knew her husband well enough by now to know that he usually had a good reason for whatever he did. She wondered what his reason could be for this.

"Go on with your story," Elen commanded.

"My baby was born two weeks ago. I have more than enough milk, but she could not drink it. There was something wrong with her. She died yesterday." The woman began to weep, tears streaking through the dirt on her face.

"Where did my husband find you?" Understanding was dawning on Elen.

"I was living in the stables. I had a little corner. My baby was born there. But some of the men who work there tried to do to me what my master had done. The Thane of Laggan stopped them. When he heard my story, he told Drust to bring me to you because you need a wet nurse."

Elen smiled. She had ample milk to keep young Colin happy. Talcoran wanted her back in his bed, that was it, and very likely he also wanted another son. But if they lay together and she conceived again, there would be no more milk for the child they already had. Colin needed mother's milk until he was at least a year old, perhaps older. There was no other suitable food for a baby. Winter was coming, the time when many babies died, especially those who were weak from lack of food. However much he desired his wife, Talcoran would allow nothing to occur that would harm his son. Thus, the wet-nurse.

Another thought occurred to Elen. She would soon resume her position of lady to the queen. Attendance on Gruach would require long hours away from Colin, when she would not be able to nurse him. She was sure Talcoran had thought of that, too.

She inspected Briga carefully. In spite of her thinness, the woman had big breasts. Her bodice strained over them. Her claim of an adequate supply of milk seemed truthful. In fact, now that Elen looked more closely, those spots on Briga's bodice were certainly milk stains.

"You are dirty," Elen said. "You smell of the stable."

"Mistress, nothing would please me more than a hot bath. I was not always so." Briga looked down at herself with distaste.

"If I accept you into my service, you must have nothing to do with men. If you get with child and your milk stops, I will dismiss you."

"I understand." Briga met Elen's eyes squarely. "After what has happened to me, I do not care if I never touch another man. But I want to hold a baby in my arms again."

Elen wondered how she would feel if Colin were taken from her. She hugged her son more closely to her bosom and felt him stir against her. She did not think she could bear losing him. Her heart went out to the bereft woman before her.

"Very well. Ava, see that this woman has a bath, and find her some clean clothes. When she is ready, bring her back here. You will begin your work tonight, Briga. For the time being, we will both nurse Colin, so I can stop slowly. I have heard of women who became ill and died because they stopped nursing too suddenly."

"So have I, lady. If we are careful, I think we can manage without too much discomfort to you."

So it was that Talcoran, returning to his chambers after nightfall, found a clean and smiling Briga, who offered his freshly fed and sweet-smelling son for inspection, then whisked the baby off to another room. A young manservant appeared, stripped Talcoran of his courtly garb and helped him into the wooden tub of water that steamed before the hearth. Talcoran contemplated the closed door that led to his bedchamber, then subsided into the tub with an expectant grin.

A short time later, his eager nakedness barely covered by a dark red robe, he dismissed the manservant and, bearing a silk-wrapped package, entered the bedroom.

Elen came to meet him. Her heavy, milk-laden breasts were clearly discernable under her pleated linen shift. Her hair hung loose over her shoulders in the way he liked best.

Talcoran's breath came quickly at the sight of her. He felt his manhood rise in imperative need and wondered if he could control himself until she desired him, too. He wanted to do nothing to hurt her, but it had been so long, so very long.

Elen watched her husband as he came through the door. Would he still find her desirable, with her newly rounded breasts and her thickened waistline? Had there been other women since he returned to court without her? She found that she did not want to know. She vowed that she would never ask him.

She was astonished at the depth of her need for him. She did not want to satisfy the urge at once. She wanted to draw it out, and waiting, lure him and tease him and make him her own, as he had been before she had grown heavy with his child.

"Ava prepared food for us," she said, indicating a table laden with fowl and roast beef, dark bread and clotted cream, and a great silver bowl of apples she had brought from Laggan.

"These are from your own orchard," she said, touching the bowl. She indicated the chair drawn up to the table. "Will you sit and eat?"

"Must I eat by myself?" he asked, taking his place. "Will you not join me?"

"I will serve you."

He realized that they were completely alone, all the servants gone. The room was still, with a heavy expectancy in the air. He cut a piece of beef and began to eat. She poured mead into a golden goblet for him. The honey-rich fumes infiltrated his senses with subtle pleasure as he drank.

He could not concentrate on food. He could only think of the woman who stood before him in the fullness of her rich, moist femininity. He pushed

his wooden plate aside. When he stood, she backed
away a few steps, toward the bed. He picked up
the silk-covered package he had laid on the table,
and followed her.

"This is for you," he said, and tossed the
package into the center of their bed.

She turned her head to look at it, a smile
curving her lips.

"What is it?" she asked.

"Open it and find out."

She knelt on the bed and reached across it to
pick up the parcel. Every lushly rounded line of
her body showed through her shift. He thought he
would die if he could not take her at once. With a
great effort he controlled himself. She had been
through a difficult childbirth. He ought to be
gentle with her, as if it were the first time all over
again.

She unfastened the silk wrapping and brought
forth a heavy gold necklace set with garnets.

"Talcoran, how beautiful." The midnight-blue
eyes she raised to him were full of love. "Oh, my
darling, thank you."

"You deserve more than gold for what you
have given me."

Her arms were around his neck, her sweet
mouth close to his.

"Elen," he groaned, wanting her kiss, yet
fearing that if he took her offered lips he would no
longer have the strength to withstand the desire
that now drove him. He desired her with a
burning, unquenchable need that had made it
impossible for him to think of any other woman.
This woman, and this one alone, had insinuated
herself into his heart and his mind, but nothing in
Talcoran's life as a warrior had prepared him for
the feelings Elen had awakened in him. Now that
she was mother as well as wife and lover, he

hardly knew how to treat her. He backed away from the bed.

Elen read something of his confusion in Talcoran's face.

"Will you put it on for me?" she asked, holding out the necklace. When he hesitated, she added, "The clasp is difficult. I don't know how to work it."

She had moved into the center of the bed, so that he had to kneel on the covers to reach her. She lifted the mass of her straight black hair away from her neck, revealing the fragile nape.

She felt him fumble as he draped the heavy gold links about her neck, then fumble again with the clasp. How odd for Talcoran, who was always so sure of himself. When the necklace was on, she sat unmoving, still holding her hair away from her neck, feeling his breath on her skin, waiting, her head bowed.

At last, at long last, she felt his lips on her neck, moving gently down her spine, while his hands caressed her shoulders. She moved languidly, leaning back and rubbing against him with lazy, cat-like motions.

His mouth slid to that spot at the base of her throat where the pulse beat, and the heavy, throbbing sensation began in her veins, as all of her senses came alive in one warm, intoxicating wave of pleasure.

She tugged at her shift, pulling it up. She felt his hands helping her, lifting it over her head. He tossed the flimsy linen aside, leaving her with nothing on but the gold and garnet necklace. She heard his robe slide to the floor, but she did not see it, for he was kissing her back and she felt molten fire licking up and down her spine.

She caught his hands and pulled his arms around her. When she sat back she was aware of his erect manhood prodding at her buttocks. She wriggled against him and heard his delighted exclamation.

There was no need to coax him further. She had finally succeeded in convincing him that she was not a fragile flower he might crush. She gave herself up to the delirious onslaught of his passion.

He pulled her around to face him and his mouth touched hers. How long it had been since they kissed, more than a month, and then it had been nothing like this. His lips ground upon her again and again, moaning and gasping, his tongue plunging into her, urging her to meet him with equal need.

He bore her back onto the bed, his hands and his mouth searching hungrily, seeking out all the remembered special places, the warm, dark crevices, the soft mounds and curves, exploring her richly altered body as though it were a freshly discovered land he was determined to claim for himself.

Her newly rounded belly, her hips now curving in a more womanly line, her legs unchanged in their slender length, all received his most fervent attention as he covered her delicately sensitive skin with kisses, stirring in her a storm of vibrant, utterly shameless passion that matched his own.

She caught at his head, held him to her so she could kiss and tease, her hands stroking and luring him until he begged her to stop lest it end too soon. She clutched at him to pull him closer to her, wept and moaned in frustration when he moved away, nibbled at his lips, kneaded his shoulders, locked her fingers in his hair and held his mouth against hers for long, searing, flaming, impossibly deep kisses.

She bent over him while he caressed her heavy, swinging breasts, stroking and pulling gently, his fingers circling the dark, sensitive nipples. She saw the milk begin to seep, coming slowly in pearly, translucent drops. He saw it, too, and fastened his hungry mouth on her and began to suck. An explosion shook her body as he tugged and suckled and swallowed, and she screamed in unbearable delight.

"Ah, Talcoran, Talcoran!" she cried, pulling him on top of her as she sank back onto the bed. "Love me, please love me now."

He plunged into her as a man dying of heat and thirst plunges into a cool lake. He was rough, almost violent, but it mattered not at all because she was with him, riding high on the crest of a pounding, growing wave, and at the same moment that she cried out in joy, he shouted with relief as their bodies exploded with the ecstatic release of months of frustrated denial. It went on and on, it would never stop, she knew they would both die of joy before this incredible, endless, surging sweetness was over.

"Elen." Above her Talcoran ground out the word, barely able to speak. "Elen, I . . . love . . . you. Elen!"

The great, pounding wave had receded, leaving her limp, inert, on the beach that was their bed. She lay for a long time without moving. A deeply tanned hand caught her chin, forcing her face around until she met her husband's eyes.

"I do, you know," he whispered. "I love you, though I have never said it before. I will always love you. Always."

It was a small party, a private feast in the king's own chambers for fifteen or twenty friends. Elen wore her new gown of wine-colored silk and the gold and garnet necklace Talcoran had given her.

She smiled across the room at her husband. In the weeks since she had rejoined him at Macbeth's court, Elen and Talcoran had drawn closer to each other than they had ever been before. All of the doubts that had plagued her during the past summer were gone. At last she was certain of his love for her, and of her own for him. Their nightly lovemaking was deeper, richer, more passionate than anything she had dreamed was possible. She thought childbearing had something to do with it. There was no question that she was more receptive to his advances since their son had been born.

"Elen, you are daydreaming again." Gruach laughed at her. "You are like a young girl, yearning over her first love."

"Not young any more, but fortunate, certainly," Elen answered. "And happy."

"So is Talcoran, if I am any judge of men. Would that my own husband were so happy." Gruach's lovely face darkened. "There will be trouble with England before long."

"Well, my good thane." Macbeth had been strolling about the room, chatting with his friends. He paused before Conal mac Duff and took a long gulp of mead from a golden cup. "What news have you had from that accursed traitor, your brother-in-law?"

Conal stiffened. Out of the corner of her eye, Elen saw Fionna edging nearer to her husband.

"I have no contact with Patric mac Keith," Conal declared.

"What, not even a letter inquiring after his sister's health? After two years' time? How thoughtless." Macbeth glared at Conal and tossed down another swig of mead. The room had grown quiet. Everyone's attention was centered on the king and Conal.

"I am not so fortunate as you," Macbeth went on. "I have had news of him. Would you like to know what your brother-in-law is doing?"

Conal said nothing.

"He is attempting to stir up England against me!" Macbeth exploded. "He and that damned Siward, who calls himself Earl of Northumbria, are trying to convince King Edward to send an army into Alba. And young Malcolm now styles himself King of Cumbria, though he is but eleven years old."

"It was King Duncan who gave Malcolm that title," Fionna said boldly. "You cannot blame that on Patric."

"Do you favor your brother and that puking infant over me, lady?"

"No, my lord, I do not," Fionna answered promptly. "My husband and I are loyal to you, as well you know."

"Do you let a woman speak for you?" Macbeth sneered at Conal.

"My wife knows my heart well," Conal said, putting a protective arm around Fionna's waist.

"See that you both show your loyalty," Macbeth muttered, and moved on to speak with the Thane of Atholl.

When the party had ended, Elen and Talcoran strolled to Conal's chambers with their friends.

"I have some wine newly arrived from the Rhineland. Come in and try a cup," Conal said.

Fionna was plainly still upset, but she seconded the invitation, and the four friends entered the mac Duff's chambers. But Elen saw Fionna wipe away a tear when she thought no one was watching.

"What is wrong with the king?" Conal asked. "Why did he speak to us that way in public? He knows full well I am loyal to him. I cannot help what Patric does."

"He was greatly angered at the news," Talcoran said. "He will think better of it, and tomorrow he'll say he's sorry."

"Aye, but in private, and those who heard him attack me publicly will never hear the apology."

"It is a difficult situation for both you and him," Talcoran said soothingly.

"It is impossible!" Fionna cried, no longer trying to hide her tears. "Do you know how hard it is to have my beloved husband on one side of this quarrel and my dear brother on the opposite side? Sometimes I feel as though I'm torn in two, and I fear for them both."

Elen went to her friend, but Fionna shook off her comforting arms.

"What are we to do, Talcoran?" Fionna asked. "What will happen if the English attack Alba with the intention of putting Malcolm on the throne?"

"That is not likely to happen soon, my love." Conal patted his wife's hand. "Edward of England has enough problems at home just now. I doubt he'll start a war in the near future, no matter how persuasive Patric and Siward are."

There was a silence, broken finally by the sound of Talcoran clearing his throat. Elen looked at him in surprise. She had not heard him do that for a long time. He looked nervous, as he sometimes used to do before they were married.

"This is more than just a quarrel," Talcoran said. He leaned forward in his seat, intense and serious, his dark face shadowed. "I, too, am torn by it. I will tell you something that perhaps I should not say. Macbeth has ordered me to report to him any sign that your loyalty to him has lessened.

"I owe Macbeth everything. He raised me from common soldier to the rank of thane. He has given me riches, land, and my dear wife. I would never betray him. But Conal, you have been my friend since the very first day I spent as Macbeth's aide. In the name of our friendship, I beg you, do nothing that will force me to report ill of you to him."

Conal clapped a hand on Talcoran's shoulder.

"I promise you, on my oath sworn to him at his investiture, that I am loyal to my king. The only thing that could possibly change that would be a betrayal of his kingly oaths by Macbeth himself—if he betrays this Alba, this land to which he was wed at Scone. Or, if he unjustly harms me or my wife and children, then vengeance must be taken. I know Macbeth, and I do not think either of these things will ever happen. Macbeth may be angry right now, but he is a fair man, a good king and, more important, he is not a fool. You have nothing to worry about, my friend."

"And you," Talcoran said to Elen later, when they were alone in their bedchamber. "Must I worry about your loyalty, too?"

"How can you even ask such a thing?"

"You loved Patric mac Keith once. You were betrothed to him."

"Are you jealous? Of a traitor?" Elen stared at her husband in amazement.

"I want to know what you feel for him."

"Has Macbeth asked you to spy on me, too? I don't know what has happened to that man. He has changed in the last year."

"The duties of kingship weigh heavily on

him."

Elen threw off her robe and got into bed.

"I don't know about that," she said, "but I do know that he and the queen are not so close as they once were. Gruach is often lonely."

"You are changing the subject," Talcoran said, climbing into bed beside her. "Tell me what you feel for Patric mac Keith."

"I have forgotten him." Elen put her arms around her husband. "It is you I love. I had not thought of Patric for months until Macbeth mentioned his name tonight. But I will very quickly learn to hate him if he comes between us. I want nothing between us, Talcoran. Nothing at all."

"There is nothing between us, not even your shift." He chuckled, diverted by the knowing exploration of her nimble fingers. He groaned with pleasure. "You are a witch. I never should have taught you to do that."

Later, when he finally slept, Elen lay with her arms around the lover who was her husband and thought about Patric. She had spoken the truth when she told Talcoran she seldom remembered Patric. So much had happened to her since last she and Patric met. She could not even clearly recall his once beloved face. She wondered briefly if he were well and what he was doing at that moment, before consigning him once more to the dead past and forgetting him.

14

June 1042 to May 1043.

In the early summer of 1042, Elen and Talcoran returned to Laggan. There had been some trouble with an outlaw band in the northern shires, and Talcoran was commissioned to lead the king's patrols to destroy the outlaws.

Young Fergus of Lochaber went with them at Bancho's request.

"The boy will get himself into trouble yet," Bancho told them. "He has been moping about and drinking too much ever since that lady of Gruach's was married."

"You mean Grania," Elen said.

"That's the one. Fergus imagines he is in love with her. Love!" Bancho snorted. "Did you ever hear anything so silly?"

Behind Bancho's broad back, Elen and Talcoran exchanged smiles.

"I think it was cruel of Macbeth to marry her to that old man," Elen replied. "He is seventy if he's a day, and she loathes him. And now her husband has taken her from court to live in his fortress on a mountaintop somewhere."

"You sound just like Fergus. I want him away from court before he does something that cannot be fixed. If he should meet the king some night when he is drunk, God knows what he might do or say for the sake of his precious Grania. Take him to Laggan, I beg you. With any luck you'll keep him there until Grania is a widow, and then if he is still interested in her, I'll see what I can do for them."

Elen was with child again. She expected the baby to be born in mid-November.

"How wonderful," Fionna said when Elen told her. "My baby is due in December. We are staying at court this time, so we can help each other. You will return from Laggan in time?"

"Talcoran promises we will be back at court by late August."

But the outlaw band would not be caught, and the departure from Laggan was repeatedly postponed. The autumn storms began early that year, bringing days of rain and sleet so heavy that the men-at-arms could not leave the castle.

Elen was distraught. She was heavier and more awkward than she had been with her first pregnancy, and this time she had been sick nearly every day. To make matters worse, her household seemed to be in constant uproar.

There were too many men cooped up by the bad weather. Fergus tried to help Talcoran, but he was desperately unhappy without his Grania, and frequently got drunk and quarreled with the soldiers.

Briga was trying to wean Colin in anticipation of the new baby she would have to nurse. She was ill and irritable from her aching breasts, and Colin, not happy at being made to drink from a cup, cried almost constantly.

It was with a feeling of utter defeat that Elen ordered the room in which Colin had been born cleaned and aired so she could move into it.

"I'm frightened," she said to Talcoran one

evening. She pushed a heavy lock of hair off her forehead with weary hands, swollen like her feet to unrecognizable plumpness. "How I wish Fionna were here."

"I am going to send Dougal for the midwife tomorrow," he told her. "She will stay with us until your time comes."

"No, I won't let that witch near me."

"If I order it, you have no choice."

"Talcoran, I beg you. I have Ava, and Briga will help. Don't bring that dreadful old woman into my home."

Talcoran exclaimed with impatience as Elen went to her knees before him. He lifted her roughly to her feet.

"What nonsense is this? I'm trying to help you, woman." He peered at her intently, seeing the terror in her eyes. "What is it, what's the real reason for this fear?"

"She is the woman who attended my mother when I was born. My mother bled to death. My father always thought it was the midwife's fault."

Talcoran folded her in his arms, soothing her.

"I never knew. I wondered why you refused her the last time. I didn't insist on her presence then because Fionna was here. Very well, I won't call her."

Elen pressed a hand against her back.

"I am so uncomfortable," she complained, and then laughed at Talcoran's expression. "Don't worry, you still have another month and a half to wait for your next son."

As it happened, he did not have to wait very long at all. The pains began that night, shortly after she went to bed. Her first labor had taken only half a day, and Fionna had promised the second would be faster and easier, but Elen walked alone all night, and then through the day that followed, with Ava and Briga supporting her. By nightfall she could no longer stand or even kneel. She lay on the straw matress on the floor whimpering with each pain.

Talcoran's worried face swam before her.

"I must call the midwife," he said.

"No, no, you promised," she panted. "I would rather have the man who births the horses."

"You are mad with pain. I am going to send Dougal."

"My lord." Elen heard Briga's heavily accented voice. She could only catch a few words of conversation through the unremitting pain that gripped her. "No time . . . she will die . . . if you will let me."

Talcoran was pulling her up, forcing mead down her throat with grim determination. She choked.

"Swallow it," he ordered. "And keep it down. There will be more pain and this will ease it."

"My lord, you must leave," Briga said. "This is not a man's place."

"I can hold her for you."

"The kitchen maid will hold her. Ava and I will do what we can."

They were giving her more mead. Her head was swimming and the pain was becoming worse.

Talcoran let her go. Unfamiliar hands took her and held her down on the straw mattress. She had no idea what they did to her. She only knew she had never borne such dreadful, flaming pain. Mercifully, she had to endure it for only a few moments before she fell into a deep, black pit.

When she opened her eyes the sun was setting in gold and pink spendor. She was unable to move. It was not until Briga appeared that she was even aware she was still alive.

"You have slept a day and a half. Now you

must eat," Briga said, and began to spoon hot broth into her. Elen swallowed obediently, too weak to say anything.

"You have another son," Briga told her, and Elen fell asleep again.

Sometime during the night she opened her eyes to find Talcoran hunched on a stool by her bed. He held her hand tightly in his as though he would transfer some of his strength to her. Still she could not speak. She felt the tears pouring out of her eyes, and she exprienced a deep sadness as though some great tragedy had occurred.

"My love," Talcoran whispered, "I thought I had lost you. We must never do this again. I could not bear to live without you."

She did not understand what he was talking about, but he had called her his love. She dropped into peaceful slumber once more.

Elen recovered slowly. She lay for days unable to move or to rouse herself to any but the simplest answer to queries about her health.

"I have never seen so much blood," Ava told her one day. "It was all over the floor. It took half the night to clean it up."

Elen said nothing. Ava finished washing Elen's face, then began to braid her hair.

"We all thought you would die. Thank heaven Briga was here. She knew what to do. Did you know the baby was turned the wrong way?"

"No."

"And now she is nursing him. He is so tiny. Briga says babies born before their time seldom live, but her milk is plentiful and he is growing. Have you seen him?"

"No. Please stop."

"Stop braiding your hair?" Ava looked startled. "Am I pulling it too tightly?"

"Stop talking. I'm tired."

When she was stronger, Briga brought the baby to her. He was impossibly small, with a fringe of dark hair and large blue eyes. Elen, sitting up for the first time since his birth a week before, took him in her arms. He stared up at her, unblinking.

"How wise he looks."

"He is a good baby, mistress."

"We need to find a name for him."

"I thought you knew. Oh, mistress, I'm sorry. I should have told you."

Talcoran had come into the room while Briga was speaking.

"It's all right, Briga," he said. "Elen, we feared he would not live through the first night, and so we had him baptised at once. His name is Aiden."

"Aiden." Elen touched the baby's petal-soft cheek with one finger. "Yes. I like that name." Her son gave a soft, mewling cry, then a stronger one.

"I'll take him away and feed him." Briga picked up the tiny bundle and left the room.

"She saved your life," Talcoran said.

"I know, Ava told me. We must never let Briga want for anything, even when we no longer need a wet nurse."

"Agreed." Talcoran examined her face. "You are getting better. You have a little color now."

"It's all the red meat and wine you've been making me swallow, even when I didn't want to."

"I have been so worried about you." Talcoran held both her hands tightly. "Elen, we must not have any more children."

Her wits were so foggy these days that it took a while for his meaning to sink into her mind.

"No," she said at last. "Don't leave me alone."

"We have two strong sons. That is enough. I

don't want to risk losing you. When you are well enough, choose any room you want for your chamber. You may have the finest silks to hang in it, I'll bring carvers to Laggan to make you a new bed if you like. But we will not lie together again."

"No!" She lifted her weak, heavy arms and put them about his neck. She rested her head on his strong shoulder and wept. "Talcoran, I love you. Don't do this to me."

He sat like a man made of stone, completely unresponsive to her—or so she thought until a large, hot drop of moisture fell upon her bare neck, then another. She lifted her head and gaped in utter astonishment.

His face was impassive, his eyes blank, but fierce Talcoran was weeping. She tenderly touched his cheek, wiping away a tear. Slowly he focused on her face.

"My love," she whispered.

He came to life then, crushing her in his arms, raining kisses on her face and throat, and his scalding tears mingled with hers.

"How I love you!" he cried. "I want no other woman. I pray God I have the strength to stay away from your bed. If you bear another child it will surely kill you. Elen, Elen, what are we going to do?"

They remained at Laggan that winter. Elen was not well enough to travel, and the outlaw band Talcoran had been ordered to bring to justice had disappeared into the hills at the first snow.

Elen's strength gradually returned. Anxious to leave the room in which she had given birth, with its unpleasant associations, she moved into the bedchamber she had occupied as a young girl. Its narrow window faced south, and the pale winter sun shone in, bringing both light and a faint hint of warmth.

As soon as she was able to sit up for a length of time, Talcoran carried her down the wide stone staircase to the great hall. There she sat each evening, ensconced in her father's big chair by the firepit, wrapped in furs and shawls, with her feet propped on a low stool to keep them above the chill drafts that scudded along the stone floor.

"You need to be with people," Talcoran said. "It will cheer you up, and you can direct the household from here."

Bancho came for Christmas.

"It's lonely at Lochaber," he said. "I miss my friends, and my son."

"I thought you were at court," Elen responded. "I hoped you would have news of Fionna."

"I knew you would ask," Bancho said with a laugh, "so, last week when one of my men rode from Scone to Lochaber, I got most of the court gossip from him. Fionna had a daughter the day before my man left. She will be named Elen, in your honor."

"How lovely!" Elen exclaimed. "Are you returning to Scone when you leave here, Bancho? May I give you a letter for Fionna?"

"I'll not go back to court for a while, lass. Why don't you have one of Talcoran's couriers carry your message?"

"What's wrong?" Talcoran asked, hearing, as Elen had, the odd note in Bancho's voice.

"Our king is none too fond of me these days." Bancho stretched his legs toward the fire and leaned back in his favorite chair. Talcoran handed him a cup of ale and Bancho tasted it appreciatively before continuing. "Macbeth has never forgiven me for letting Patric mac Keith take

Malcolm and his brothers out of Alba. Not to mention my giving Patric a pass for Duncan's body."

"But he made you his chief general," Elen said.

"Aye, lass, and that's part of my problem. I lead the army and I am a mite too popular with my men for Macbeth's ease of mind."

"Macbeth should know you are his man," Talcoran said quietly.

"Aye, he should." Bancho sipped at his ale and stared into the fire. "Sometimes I wonder what demons our kings wrestles with in the dark of night. Since there are no wars to fight, it seemed wise for me to quit Scone for a while. I'll go back in the summer and be as charming as an old man can be."

He was growing old, Elen realized. He was the same age as her father had been, which would make him nearly fifty. There was new silver in his dark hair and beard, and he moved more slowly now. Well, she was no longer young herself. She would be twenty on her next birthday, and Talcoran had just turned thirty.

How quickly time passes, she thought. How short our lives are.

Just as Elen began to feel well again, the bitter cold came. Beneath the full winter moon, wolves howled into the January nights. Servants took to their beds with the illnesses that came every winter.

Young Colin developed a severe cold that left him with a heavy cough and a perpetually runny nose. Aiden continued to thrive, but Elen worried about him. He was so small. If Briga should fall ill and lose her milk, what would happen to her fragile younger son?

Then she herself caught Colin's cold.

"Stay in bed," Talcoran advised. "Keep warm. I don't want you to be ill again."

His advice was useless. Within three days, Elen was coughing constantly, with a high fever. She lapsed into delirium, plagued by fantastic dreams. It was a week before she was well enough to ask about her children. When she did, Ava burst into tears, horrifying Elen.

"Aiden has died," Ava told her bluntly. "Briga went to give him his morning feeding one day, and he lay dead in his cradle. Briga blamed herself and wouldn't eat, until she fell ill just like you, and her breasts were clogged with milk and we thought she would die, too."

Elen struggled to make some sense of this confused story. All she had really heard was that her son was dead.

"Where is Talcoran?" she asked. "Where is Colin?"

"Colin is well, thank God, and my lord Talcoran sits below in the hall. He is very unhappy, mistress."

"Tell him I want to see him."

Talcoran came at once. He stood erect, as stiff and cool and self-contained as he had been when first she knew him. She could tell he had been drinking heavily. She held out her arms to him, wanting to comfort and be comforted. Talcoran did not appear to notice.

"Ava tells me you are better," he said, his speech abnormally clear and careful.

"Oh, my dear love," Elen whispered, tears filling her eyes. "Let me hold you."

Still he made no move toward her.

"The weather has cleared," he told her. "My men and I leave tomorrow to search for those outlaws. I do not know how many days we will be gone. Dougal will remain in charge of Laggan Castle. I can leave Fergus, too, if you wish it, my lady."

Elen looked at him in despair.

"Do whatever you want," she said.

Talcoran was gone for nearly a week. By the time he returned Elen was out of bed and had begun to resume her duties. He paid little attention to her. He threw himself into work, planning new stables to be built the following summer and a building to house his men-at-arms more comfortably. He sat up late at night, dictating to his secretary long reports to be sent to Macbeth at Scone. He ate too little. He drank constantly and deeply, although he never showed the effects of it.

Elen was in little better condition. She had grown thin again. All the soft roundness of motherhood she had developed after Colin was born now wasted away in grief over Aiden.

Only Colin brought any joy into Laggan Castle that late winter. He had begun to walk, and he stumbled cheerfully about the great hall, gurgling with baby laughter, his deep blue eyes bright with mischief. Briga, who was recovering slowly from her own illness, cared for him tenderly.

Elen grew closer to both Briga and Ava. After the ordeals of the past months she felt they were more her friends than her servants. In her increasing isolation from Talcoran, she needed them.

She spent long hours on her knees in the tiny chapel that opened off one end of the great hall, praying for both Aiden and Talcoran until the priest himself warned her about the effect the chilly room would have on her fragile health.

Spring came but slowly. There was a soft

breeze one evening, then a faint touch of green on the hillsides. There were a few early flowers scattered here and there, and the ice that had clogged rivers and streams was gone. Briga took Colin to play in the new grass by the loch.

Inside Elen's heart, something that had lain cold and frozen throughout the winter began to thaw as the days grew longer and warmer. She sat alone in her chamber one afternoon, enjoying a rare respite from her duties. She tossed the household keys carelessly onto a table. She really should check on the supply of ale, and one of the kitchen maids had warned her that some of the dried meat had started to rot. They probably hadn't dried it properly, and she had neglected to see for herself how they had stored it. She hadn't had time before Aiden was born.

She watched a fluffy cloud sail slowly across the blue sky. A sweet-scented breeze blew through the open window and touched her cheek, reminding her that she ought to see if Talcoran's room had been aired. He had ridden out earlier in the day. She would do it while he was gone. She hurried along the corridor to the master's chamber and pushed open the door.

She was halfway across the room before she saw him sprawled naked across the bed with an empty cup in his outstretched hand. She tiptoed to the bed and looked down at him as he slept.

There were dark shadows under his eyes. When had he grown so thin? She stretched out a trembling hand to touch the ribs that clearly showed beneath the waxy skin. She snatched her fingers back before they made contact with his flesh, and picked up the cup instead. It smelled of mead.

He had forbidden her this room. She should not be here. She turned to go. She took two steps away from the bed and stopped, then turned back to look at him again. He was her husband and she wanted him. She knew that he needed her. She stripped off her clothes and lay down beside him.

He did not move. After a moment she kissed his unresponsive lips. She thought she saw his eyelids flutter, but he gave no sign that he was aware of her.

She tucked her head under his chin and snuggled against him. She was deeply touched by his familiar warmth. She thought fleetingly that if they had had each other to cling to, perhaps the dreadful winter just past would not have been so bad. She would not dwell on that. Her heart would forever ache for the loss of Aiden, but what was done was done, and this was today. She would disregard Talcoran's qualms about lying with her. They could begin again.

Her fingers traced the tattooed design on his left shoulder. Then she ran her hand along his chest, feeling the muscles now grown stringy from lack of nourishment. She would repair that damage, make him eat more meat and good brown bread and cheese. She felt his belly, hollow and empty, and gently caressed his flanks. They were sinewy, with not a trace of fat on them.

Oh, my love, she thought, I have been so preoccupied with my own grief and ill health that I have neglected you.

She came to his manhood, lying small and shriveled on its bed of black hair. All of Talcoran's hair was smooth and silky, even in this most private place. She took him in her hand.

He had lain unconscious while she fondled him, but now he stirred, turning his head and flinging one arm over his eyes. His other arm closed about her, holding her against his side. He muttered something she could not understand, then lapsed into mead-induced sleep once more.

With fingers light as a butterfly's touch, she continued her caresses. She felt her own body growing warmer, felt the languid moistness beginning. Surely, even if he was drunk, he must soon begin to be aware of her. . . .

At last he began to respond, as she knew he would. He sighed deeply and the arm about her waist tightened. She strained upward, reaching for his lips.

He came alive with frightening suddenness.

"Damn you!" He thrust her aside, and in the same furious movement rolled off the bed and stood glaring down at her. "What in the name of all the fiends of Hell do you think you are doing?"

Elen stretched on the bed and smiled at him. Surprised at her presence he might be, but his desire for her was now obvious.

He saw her looking. He snatched a fur off the bed and wrapped it around his waist.

"You looked so lonely sleeping here," she said. "Will you join me, my love?" She patted the still-warm spot beside her invitingly.

"How dare you come into my room? I have forbidden you. My God, woman, don't you know—" He broke off, looking at her with a hungry expression.

"It is spring, Talcoran," she said. "Let us love the afternoon away in celebration."

A few months ago he would have leapt upon her and left her breathless with his kisses and his intense, demanding passion for her. Indeed, he would not have needed half the coaxing she had been forced to today. But it was a new Talcoran, a dark, bitter man who stood watching her with cold scorn.

"Get up and dress yourself," he said. "I have done with you. Do not come to my bed again."

"I know you want me. We need to love each other." Reluctantly, she left his bed. She tossed her hair back over her shoulders and saw the flickering emotion in his eyes as he watched the movement. She came to face him, put her hands on his shoulders and tried to kiss him. "Please, Talcoran," she begged.

He stepped back, clenching his jaw.

"Get out," he said. "I will not be the instrument of your death."

"You do want me." She watched him carefully, seeing no change in his hard expression. "Briga helps me in the stillroom, did you know that? She knows a great deal about herbs and their properties."

"What of it?"

"She says there are herbs we could use to make an infusion to drink that would keep me from conceiving."

"I have heard of such potions. It is a sin to use them, and they can kill. I will not allow you to take the risk, either for your body or your soul."

"No, my love, they are only simples and the old remedies for illnesses that women have made for generations. They have that special effect in addition to their other properties. There is no harm in them."

"No."

"Talcoran, I beg you—"

She had never seen him so angry. He drew himself up, and to Elen he suddenly seemed much taller than she was, overwhelming, powerful.

"Woman, will you continue to defy me? I don't want anything to happen to you. You dare not have any more children. I will not allow you to use wicked potions, and most definitely I will not lie with you. Now get out, and stay out of my room!"

Under his cold, angry eyes, she dressed. She

was at the door, pulling it open, when he spoke again.

"Elen." He sounded exhausted and infinitely sad. "It is for your good that I do this."

She did not answer him. She could not look at him. She wandered with dragging feet back to her own room and sat dumbly in her chair, her hands idle in her lap, staring out the window.

"I'm angry, too," she murmured at last. "How could you treat me so? I love you."

She ached with unsatisfied desire. Almost equally unpleasant was the humiliation of Talcoran's rejection. There was nothing private in the way they lived at Laggan. Someone surely had heard Talcoran shouting at her. By now every man and woman in the castle would know that the Thane of Laggan wanted nothing to do with his wife.

"How can it be for my good," she whispered to the empty, lonely room, "when it hurts so much?"

15

Autumn 1043.

Elen tried to pretend nothing had happened, that all was as it once had been between her and Talcoran. Before others he treated her with the same grave courtesy he had always shown. In private, he ignored her.

There were nights when, half-mad with longing for him, she could not sleep at all, nights when she carried a pitcher of mead to her lonely room and drank herself into a stuporous slumber.

When Briga learned of this, she cornered Elen in the stillroom one afternoon and scolded her mistress severely, forgetting in her concern that she was only a servant.

"If you have no thought for yourself," Briga said, "think of Colin. He is still a baby. He needs you."

"You don't understand," Elen began.

"I understand more than you think," Briga interrupted. "My master is a stubborn man, and he loves you too much for his own peace. We can but hope that one day he will come to his senses. Here, drink this."

Briga handed her a thick clay cup filled with a steaming brew. Elen inhaled the scent.

"This smells good. What is it?"

"Lavender and mint, and one or two other herbs. It will soothe you. I'll bring you more at bedtime, to help you sleep."

Elen hesitated, looking doubtfully into the liquid, then sniffing at it. Briga understood her qualms.

"Do you think I'd do anything to harm you, mistress? I'll make another cup if you wish, so you may see everything that goes into it."

"I trust you, Briga." Elen drained the cup, and drank the one Briga brought to her chamber at bedtime. Her sleep that night was long and dreamless.

After that she resorted occasionally to Briga's concoctions when she could not sleep. They never left her with a headache as the mead did. There was sage, dried and ground into a powder and dissolved in hot water, to calm the nerves, or cowslip wine, which helped Elen to sleep when she had a headache, or chamomile. Her favorite remained the lavender and mint infusion Briga had first given to her.

After a while Elen became accustomed to the lonely way of life Talcoran had imposed on her, but she was not happy with it, and she felt a deep resentment toward her husband for his arbitrary decision. He would listen to nothing she had to say on the subject, dismissing all her arguments with his insistence that bearing another child would kill Elen and he would not chance it.

She was grateful when they finally returned to court. Macbeth had begun a progress through his kingdom and was at Forres when they returned. Soon after, he moved to Aberdeen, then to Scone, then to Dunfermline and back to his capital at Scone again. The continual travels of this itinerant court suited Elen's mood. While

Macbeth and his administrators and councillors attended to local affairs and received royal tribute from landholders and nobles in each place they stayed, and the men and women of his court ate and drank all of the provisions available until it was time to move on, Elen applied herself to her duties as lady to the queen and tried not to think of her desolate marriage.

In November, a rumor circulated through Macbeth's court that Duncan's second son, Donald, now ten years old, had been taken to live on an island in the Hebrides.

"That is much too close," Bancho grumbled. "I hope no idiot has a plan to invade Alba and put that lad on the throne."

"Thorfinn of Orkney controls the western islands," Talcoran reminded him, "and his friendship with Macbeth remains unshaken. I think we can trust him to stop any schemes of that sort."

"I hope you are right," Conal mac Duff put in. "Life is too sweet these days. I have no more taste for war." He smiled at Fionna as she poured frothing ale into his cup and then moved on to refill Bancho's.

"You have the nicest apartments in the palace," Bancho told her. "I feel at home every time I come here."

"You are always a welcome guest." Fionna patted Bancho's silver-streaked head. "I saw Fergus yesterday. He certainly looks happier now that Grania is back at court."

"Have you talked with Macbeth?" Elen asked Bancho. "Will he let Grania and Fergus marry soon? She has been a widow for almost six months now."

"Unfortunately, she is a *rich* widow. I think Macbeth does not want to hand over so much land and other property to a son of mine. Well, it can't be helped. Not everyone can be as happy as the four of you are." Bancho cocked an eyebrow at Elen, unaware of the irony of his words. "How do you feel, lass? You do look better than you did last winter."

"I am in excellent health, thank you." Elen rose and kissed Bancho on the cheek.

"There's something to be said for old age," he joked, winking at Talcoran and Conal. "All the lassies feel free to kiss and fondle me. I find I like it."

"You are not so harmless as you appear," Elen teased him. "I've heard some stories about you, old friend. I must leave you now. I am to attend the queen this evening."

She left the room without a glance at Talcoran. She was certain Fionna had noticed and would comment later, but Elen told herself she no longer cared what people thought.

Gruach and Macbeth were talking in one of the queen's private rooms. Elen heard them as she went through the anteroom. At first she thought they were discussing the rumor about Donald, but she was wrong.

"Bancho may be in contact with Siward of Northumbria," Macbeth was saying as Elen crossed the room. "The question is, would he betray me? He has too much power, too many armed men at his disposal." He broke off, seeing Elen in the doorway.

"If you wish, I will leave," Elen offered.

"No, not at all. Come in, cousin." Macbeth put his arm across Elen's shoulders.

In a bright blue tunic trimmed with fringe and gold embroidery, he was as dazzling and as charming as ever. He sat her down on a cushioned chair and poured wine for her with his own hands, while Gruach inquired with genuine concern about her health and that of her son.

"Colin is well," Elen said. "And what of Lulach? I have heard little of him since we returned to court."

"He remains at the monastary at Loch Leven for schooling," Gruach informed her. "I think he would like to be a monk, but we have other plans for him."

When Macbeth had left them, Gruach became very serious.

"What did you hear before you came into this room?" she demanded.

"Only something about Earl Siward. I wasn't thinking of that. I was thinking of Bancho."

"What about Bancho?" Gruach snapped.

Elen knew she had made a mistake. Gruach thought she had been eavesdropping. She would have to lie her way out of it. She hated lying, because she was so bad at it. Perhaps a half-lie would do.

"We were talking a little while ago," she said, "about Grania and Fergus. You know of course that they want to marry? Bancho said he would speak to Macbeth about it. I was thinking of that when I came in here, so I didn't really hear what you said." She hoped that would satisfy Gruach.

"Grania and Fergus." Gruach was thoughtful. "Perhaps that is not such a bad idea. I should have thought of it myself. Their marriage would please Bancho, would it not?"

"I'm sure it would. Bancho loves his son dearly. Anything that makes Fergus happy—"

"—would bind Bancho more closely to us in gratitude," Gruach finished for her. "And Grania's inheritance from her late husband would pass to Fergus and their sons, not to Bancho."

"Will you speak to Macbeth for them?"

"Yes, I will. In the meantime, do not mention this to anyone. And do not speak a word of anything you may have heard between Macbeth and me. Have I your promise on that?" Gruach's voice was suddenly sharp.

"I would never do anything that would cause any trouble for you or for Macbeth."

It was late when Elen left the royal apartments that night after helping Gruach prepare for bed.

"The king will join me soon," Gruach said. "Go to your husband."

"Good night, my lady."

"I'll talk to Macbeth about Grania," Gruach promised. She smiled at Elen. "Later tonight, when he is in a good mood."

"Thank you." At least Gruach was happy. The strains that had appeared in her marriage after Macbeth became king now seemed to be resolved, and they were as close as they had been when Elen had first known them.

Elen slipped out of the royal apartments into a back passage that provided a shorter way to her own rooms than the usual path. She did not like wandering about the palace late at night. She knew there were rats near the kitchen, and she feared the dark shadows that lurked at corners and alcoves. She picked up her skirts and hurried.

Two strangers appeared at the far end of the dimly lit corridor, two rough-looking men who tried to hide their faces from her as she scurried past them. Something about them frightened her. She knew they had turned to look after her.

"Who?" asked one man.

"Meeting a lover," she heard the other say. Then she heard a guffaw, and the sounds of their boots as they went on their way.

"She reached the end of the passage and turned a corner into a more brightly lit hall. She stopped to catch her breath and let her heartbeat return to normal. She wondered who they were, and what business men like that could have in a corridor leading only to the king's chambers. Perhaps there was another exit she knew nothing about. That must be it. They were only taking a quicker way, just as she had done. Her heart had stopped its frightened pounding. She took a deep breath and went on to her rooms.

"Where are Bancho and that son of his? I expected them at my table tonight." Macbeth was clearly annoyed.

"I have not seen them since mid-afternoon, my lord," Talcoran replied. "They went riding together and said they would be back by nightfall."

"They should be here. I planned this feast especially for them. I have something important to tell them, good news for Fergus."

Gruach caught Elen's eye and smiled before speaking to the king.

"Surely they will return soon, my husband. Perhaps one of the horses has cast a shoe and they must walk it back."

"Perhaps. Well, let us eat. We will not wait any longer. You there, bring me wine."

It was a strange meal, with the guests of honor missing, and it ended early. Elen attended the queen when she returned to her bedchamber. A serving girl, asleep before the fire, scrambled to her feet as Gruach entered and hastened to help Elen undress the queen.

"Where are Fionna and Grania?" Gruach demanded. "They should both be here. Elen was with me last night. Tonight she should be free from her duties. Where are those silly wenches?"

"I do not know, mistress," the serving girl said. "Neither of them has been here."

"Send for them at once."

"My lady," Elen spoke up, "it may be that one of Fionna's children is ill and she could not come."

"Then she should have sent a message to me saying so. Was there such a message, girl?"

"No, mistress." The serving girl looked frightened.

"Grania has no such excuse," Gruach fumed. "She was with us when we went to the great hall, but where is she now? That ungrateful wretch! I coaxed and pleaded with my lord last night until he agreed to allow Grania to marry Fergus. That is why we planned this evening's feast, to tell them so, to honor Bancho and his son, and none of them had the decency to appear."

"It is very odd," Elen agreed. She wondered if Grania had slipped out to meet Fergus, if the two of them were off in some quiet corner of the palace making love. Could Fergus possibly be so irresponsible as to insult the king by not going to a banquet in his own honor in order to be alone with Grania? And if so, where was Bancho?

"Cousin," Elen said as she helped Gruach into her nightgown, "did they know that Macbeth had agreed to the marriage?"

"I hinted about it to Grania this afternoon. She was overjoyed. I am certain Macbeth said something to Bancho, and most likely to Fergus, too."

"Then I do not understand where they can be." Elen wrinkled her brow in puzzlement. "Since no one else is here, I will attend you tonight. May I use this girl to send a message to Talcoran?" He would not know if she was absent from their apartments, but Elen would observe the proprieties in front of the queen.

"Of course. Thank you, Elen. At least you are faithful. You and Talcoran."

Once Gruach was settled in bed, Elen withdrew to the anteroom and sat down by the fire. It was her duty as the queen's lady to remain there throughout the night in case the queen should want something. She had spent many such nights, but usually one or two of the queen's other women had been with her, and they had whiled away the time gossiping or telling stories.

She wondered where Fionna was. It was unlike her friend to stay away with no explanation.

And what of sweet, foolish Grania, who had been singularly unchanged by her brief marriage to an aged thane? Elen did not want to be present when Grania met the queen after this.

Grania may have lost the thing she wanted most by this evening's nonsense, Elen thought. Macbeth may change his mind and not let her marry Fergus after all.

She was growing drowsy. She pulled her shawl about her and shifted into a more comfortable position in the big wooden chair.

She was nearly asleep when Macbeth came into the room. He moved silently on bare feet, but she half opened her eyes, feeling his presence. He had thrown a saffron-gold woolen robe over his nakedness. Under it, his bare legs were long and straight, covered with golden hair. When he saw her, he gave a muffled exclamation and drew the robe about himself. He walked to her chair and stood watching her.

"My lord?" Elen forced herself awake and started to rise.

"No, don't stand." He put a large hand on her

shoulder to keep her in the chair. "I thought you were sleeping. Are the other women with the queen?"

"The others did not come tonight. The queen is alone except for me."

He tilted her chin up to look into her face. The firelight shone on his yellow-gold hair and beard and flickered across the gold wool robe and the golden-haired arm and the hand that held her chin. There were a few more lines on his face than there had been four years ago when she had first seen him, but they did not detract from his appearance. To her eyes they only made him look wiser, more kingly than ever.

"You are a lion," she murmured, still not fully awake, "a great, golden lion, fierce and powerful and noble."

"I only wish I were." He sighed, his face darkening. "There are things a king must do that are not noble at all. God, how I wish they were not necessary! Sometimes I feel there's quicksand wherever I put my feet. Are you happy, Elen?"

She could not answer the unexpected question. She felt that he would easily detect a lie if she told one, and she did not want to explain the truth. She tried evasion.

"Are you, my lord?"

"Happiness is not for kings. It would comfort me to know that you are happy." He dropped onto a stool across the fire from her. She was surprised by his action, and even more surprised by the impassioned words that followed. "You know I did not want to be ruler of Alba. I fought against deposing Duncan for as long as I could. Having been Mormaer of Moray, I thought I knew how dangerous great power can be, how it can destroy all a man would build and finally corrupt the soul if he does not use it wisely. That was one of Duncan's faults, that he did not use his power wisely. Still, when the time came for me to take the crown, I believed I was strong enough to resist the dark temptations that must sooner or later come to all rulers. But hard though it is to resist temptation, how harder still it is to give in to it, and then have to live with the terrible results. There are so few I dare trust now. So many plots against me.''

He stared at her, but she was certain his eyes did not really see her. He looked at something beyond her, some distant, tormented place in his own heart, and his face was suddenly altered, becoming older and drawn, as if his spirit was in deep pain. In that silent moment Elen saw a stranger sitting before her, a man more changed by the lonely burdens of kingship than she had previously realized. Then he shook his golden head and she felt he had rejoined her once more.

''What I have done,'' he said, rising, ''I cannot undo. Goodnight, Elen.'' He kissed her on the forehead and went into his wife's bedroom, leaving her to ponder what it was that gnawed at him and troubled him so deeply.

The king habitually rose early. On this morning he sat in the queen's bedchamber eating bread and cheese and drinking ale as he watched his wife dress. Elen thought he looked more at ease than he had the night before, with the dark thoughts and suspicions gone. That must be Gruach's doing. She always had a comforting effect upon her husband.

''I like to see you together, my love,'' Macbeth remarked, ''You so fair and golden, Elen all black and white. You make a pretty pair.''

"Thank you, my lord." Elen made a mock curtsy and the two women laughed.

"Has Grania come yet?" Macbeth asked.

"No." The queen's good humor vanished and her eyes flashed cold grey fire.

"That is odd. Very odd," Macbeth mused. "Perhaps I should have a search made. Is she not in her room?"

"No." Another flat reply from Gruach. "I sent a servant to look."

Elen watched Macbeth turn his head and come to full, wary alertness at the sound of footsteps in the anteroom. His hand went to his waist in a sudden gesture, as if to draw a dagger, but he had none with him, for he still wore only his saffron-dyed robe.

"Who's there?" he called. He relaxed visibly at the voice that answered him.

"My lord? May I speak with you?"

Macbeth nodded, and Gruach called out, "The king is in my room, Talcoran. You may come in."

Talcoran appeared, booted, spurred, and with his black cloak wrapped about his shoulders. Above the great silver brooch that fastened it, his dark face was somber.

"I apologize for intruding into your private room, my queen, but I have news that will not wait."

"You do not intrude, my friend." Gruach rose from the stool where she had been sitting while Elen arranged her hair. "Would you like Elen and me to leave while you speak with the king?"

"No, lady. You may as well hear from me what the whole palace will soon know."

Now Macbeth, too, was on his feet, towering over his friend.

"Well?" he asked, and Elen had the strangest

sensation that Macbeth knew what was coming next.

"It's Bancho. We found him lying in a ditch. He had been stabbed. Twenty times. He is dead." Talcoran's terse phrases and low voice somehow conveyed more grief and loss than loud emotional cries could have done.

"Fergus?" Macbeth snapped out the question.

"Missing. No sign of him. He is not in the palace nor anywhere within a mile of here."

"Ohhh—!" Gruach reeled, her face bloodless. Elen, pale and in a state of shock herself, caught the queen and guided her to the bed, where she sat staring at Macbeth with terrified eyes.

"Oh, my love, what have you done?" Gruach whispered.

"Lie down, my lady. Put your head back," Elen urged.

"Talcoran, I will dress and come with you." Ignoring his now crying wife, Macbeth left the room.

As she bent over Grauch's weeping form, Elen sensed Talcoran just behind her.

"Are you all right?" he asked.

"Yes. No. I'll manage."

"I know you will. You are stronger than most women." Talcoran regarded the weeping queen on the bed. "Be careful, Elen. This is a dangerous day." He followed Macbeth out of the room.

Elen spent most of the morning with Gruach. After the first shock and tears had passed, the queen spent her time pacing back and forth in her chamber, wringing her hands in silent grief.

Fionna arrived at mid-morning.

"Where have you been?" Elen hissed as they met in the antechamber. "Gruach is furious with you."

"The baby was sick," Fionna said, not meeting Elen's eyes.

"Have you seen Grania?"

"Who?" Fionna looked distracted. "No. I have not seen her, I have never seen her, not for two days." And she went in to the queen.

One by one the queen's other ladies appeared, talking in hushed tones about the tragedy.

"And now Grania is missing," one said. "I heard half her clothes and all of her jewels are gone from her room."

"Perhaps she has run away with Fergus," suggested another. "What a foolish thing for them to do, just when the queen had finally convinced Macbeth to let them marry."

"Be quiet, the queen will hear you."

Finally, Gruach appeared in the antechamber, pale but self-possessed.

"We are all going to the chapel to pray for Bancho," she announced. "Elen, you look exhausted. You are dismissed until tomorrow evening. Let those who were not present last night or earlier today wait on me now."

Elen went to the chapel with the others. She knelt a long time, praying for the repose of Bancho's soul, and for Fergus' safety, wherever he might be, and for poor, silly Grania who had once done her a kindness in the days when Duncan was king. Her prayers completed at last, she started back alone to her own quarters, across the courtyard.

Bancho's body was being brought into the palace grounds. Elen turned her eyes away from the sight of his bloodied face. She did not want to remember him like that, the victim of an unworthy death. She wanted to think of him as she had seen him so many times, sitting in his favorite spot in the great hall at Laggan, his booted feet up on a stool, a brimming cup of ale in his hand, his great, booming laugh ringing out. She blinked hard. She would not cry in public. Bancho would not like that.

Two other bodies were carried in and dumped unceremoniously onto the ground next to Bancho. She had not heard that anyone else had died. Had Fergus, too, been found? If so, whose was the third corpse?

She hurried forward to look at the dead men. She stopped short, her hands flying to her face in fear. It could not be, but it was. She had only seen them for a moment, in semidarkness, but still she recognized their faces. They wore the same clothes in which she had seen them before. She was certain of their identities. These were the two rough-looking men she had seen two nights ago in the back corridor that led to the royal chambers.

Then she saw Drust, Talcoran's aide, directing the disposition of the bodies. She hurried to him.

"Drust, what is this? Who are these people?" she asked, the words tumbling out of her mouth in rapid confusion.

"These are the villains who killed your friend the Thane of Lochaber," Drust told her.

"But why?" Elen stared down at the lifeless bodies, then turned her attention to Drust. "Why?"

"Mistress," Drust said, "we believe that Fergus hired these two ruffians to kill his father. We think what happened is that these men set on Bancho and he killed one of them. The second man killed Bancho. Then Fergus killed his father's murderer so he could not talk and implicate Fergus. Fergus's knife was found in the man's back. Fergus has disappeared. We think all of this happened last night, while the king held a banquet in Bancho's honor and wondered why his guest had not arrived."

"No. No, it can't be." Elen backed away from the gory sight on the ground before her. "Fergus would never do such a thing. He loves his father."

Drust stepped close to her, too close for any servant but her personal maid. There was no disrespect in the movement, only urgency. He bent his head to hers.

"That is the story, mistress," he said, his voice little more than a whisper. "I think before you dispute it in public, you should speak with my lord Talcoran, and ask what he wants you to do. Please, mistress, for your sake and his, take my advice."

Elen could not speak. She nodded to Drust and then ran across the courtyard as fast as she could, ran as if the devil himself were pursuing her, into the palace, along the hallway, until she reached the safety of her own rooms. There she slammed the bedchamber door behind her and leaned against it, panting.

"My lady?" When a startled Ava rose from the chest in the corner into which she had been folding one of Elen's gowns, Elen screamed, flinging out her hands to ward off whatever was coming toward her.

"Mistress, it's me. It's only Ava." The maid caught her hands, steadying her. "I won't harm you. Mistress, what is it? You are so pale."

"Ava. It is you. Oh, thank heaven." Elen swallowed hard, trying to control her panic. She must be careful what she said.

"It's Bancho," she said. "They have just brought him back to the palace."

"Oh, mistress, you should not have seen that. Sit down here. Let me get you some wine."

Elen took the cup Ava offered and drank the contents down without stopping.

"It was evil," she muttered.

"Mistress?" Ava was plainly worried about her.

"There was something evil, some vile thing hovering about those bodies."

"Because it was murder." Ava crossed herself, then crossed herself again. "When a son kills his father, that is the worst kind of evil. Of course you felt it."

"I don't believe—" Elen stopped, recalling Drust's warning. "Leave me, Ava. When Talcoran returns, tell him I wish to speak with him."

She felt feverish and ill. She threw off her gown, poured cold water into a basin, and splashed it on her face and shoulders. Then she began to pace as Gruach had done earlier.

Fergus had spent more than half a year at Laggan, living in her home, and in all that time Elen had not heard him say one word against Bancho. They had been happy to see each other when Bancho visited Laggan. No matter what anyone said, Elen was certain Fergus was innocent of his father's death. He must have fought off the attackers, trying to save his father. That would explain his knife in one man's back. But where was Fergus now?

When Talcoran finally returned, she tried to question him.

"Leave it alone," Talcoran told her roughly. "It is safer thus."

"Has Fergus been found?"

"He has fled. We think Grania has gone with him. Macbeth says he believes they planned the murder together."

"That's ridiculous. Grania hasn't the wits to plan a needlework pattern, let alone a murder." When Talcoran did not answer, Elen went on, "I for one don't believe it. Fergus loved his father, and what good would it do him to kill Bancho if he must flee and be an outlaw? There's no profit in that. Bancho's lands and title will now revert to the crown.''

Elen stopped, staring at Talcoran's haggard face.

''It is Macbeth who profits,'' she said slowly. ''Bancho's lands and titles are Macbeth's now, to keep or to bestow on someone else. Bancho was Macbeth's general and his men loved him well, perhaps too well for Macbeth's comfort, but Bancho's soldiers are now Macbeth's men. My cousin Macbeth.''

''Believe the story you have been told,'' Talcoran said.

''Gruach knew, or suspected, what he planned, and tried to stop it by arranging that marriage for Fergus and Grania,'' Elen went on, unable to stop the terrible direction of her thoughts. ''Macbeth hid his true intent behind the marriage arrangements and the feast for Bancho.''

She wondered if she should tell Talcoran about the two men, the murderers she had seen on their way to the king's chamber. She decided against it. The knowledge might be dangerous to Talcoran, and she would not put him in danger.

''There will be others,'' she said, ''who will surely ask the questions I have asked, and who will find the same answers.''

She had not finished speaking before Talcoran grabbed her by the shoulders and shook her so hard that she cried out, frightened.

''Don't ever speak of your doubts to anyone else,'' he ordered. ''Don't speak of them to me. Don't even think of them!'' He caught her against his chest, hugging her so hard she could not breathe. ''Sometimes I fear for you, my love. You are both too wise and too foolish.''

As abruptly as he had embraced her, Talcoran let her go. Elen was so upset she hardly registered the fact that he had just touched her for the first time in months. There was something more important than the sad state of their marriage to think about. This, after all, was Macbeth's man. She had to ask the question that tortured her.

"What do you know of this affair, Talcoran?"

"I *know* nothing. I have dark thoughts which I will not speak," was all he would say. "Do as I command you, Elen, and never mention this again."

16

Winter 1043 to Summer 1045.

Conal mac Duff had no qualms about discussing Bancho's death, especially when he and Fionna visited Elen and Talcoran in their chambers. Assured of privacy, he spoke freely.

"Despite those rumors about his contacts with Earl Siward—and they may be true—still Bancho was loyal to Macbeth," Conal insisted. "There is something very strange about all this. I think someone at court wanted him dead. He was too powerful and too well loved."

"I would not say that to anyone else if I were you," Talcoran warned. "Macbeth is none too fond of you these days."

"Do you think I'll be next?" Seeing Talcoran's shocked reaction, mac Duff laughed. "I'll be careful. It seems to me that even your loyalty to our king is stretched a bit thin just now."

"He must do what he thinks is best," Talcoran said.

"Best for Alba or for Macbeth?" Conal's question was almost teasing.

"It is the same thing, my friend."

"I agree with Conal," Elen said, "even though the king is my cousin."

"Be quiet, woman," Talcoran ordered. "I will have no traitorous words from my wife."

Elen saw Fionna look from her to Talcoran and back again with a puzzled expression. They must be careful, Elen realized, or clever Fionna would soon discover how it was between her and Talcoran, and Fionna's knowledge was the one blow her sorely damaged pride could not tolerate.

Macbeth provided a noble funeral for Bancho and offered a huge reward to anyone bringing Bancho's murderous son to justice. But he never had to pay it. Within a few weeks, the king himself was advising them all to put the sorry business of Bancho's death behind them, and the incident ceased to be talked about.

On the surface at least, life at Macbeth's court returned to normal, though Elen and a few other friends continued to mourn for Bancho, and she wondered, each time she looked at her royal cousin, if she had discerned the truth about her old friend's death. There was no one to whom she dared voice her thoughts, and when Conal and Fionna returned to Fife, Elen was more lonely than ever.

At Christmas of 1044, Macbeth held a great feast. Most of the nobles were present. Even Thorfinn the Mighty had come from the storm-battered islands of Orkney to celebrate with his cousin and friend the King of Alba, and as he said, to drink the darkness down until the days began to lengthen again.

Elen met Fionna in the great hall before the feast began.

"How good it is to see you again!" Fionna exclaimed. "Conal and I have been in Fife so long I feared my friends had forgotten me."

"Never." Elen embraced her warmly. "I have

sorely missed you."

"Conal wanted to stay away from court for a while. He grows impatient with the intrigues and silly feuds of some of our nobles. Elen, may we talk privately sometime soon? I have something important to tell you."

"Of course. We could slip out now to one of the anterooms."

"No, we can't, for here come the king and queen. We'll do it later." Fionna swept into a low curtsy as Macbeth and Gruach passed by, followed by Thorfinn, Talcoran, Conal, and the other nobles who were the king's close friends and advisors, and then the queen's ladies who were in attendance on her that day.

"How tall Lulach has grown," Fionna remarked, eyeing Macbeth's slender stepson.

"He is sixteen. I find it hard to believe." Elen watched Lulach fondly. "I remember when he was just a frightened little boy, and now he is beginning to grow a beard, and his hair is darker. He begins to look like a man."

"Do you think Macbeth will make Lulach his heir?"

"That is the question everyone has been asking since he finished his studies at Loch Leven and returned to court. It seems certain now that Gruach will have no more children. Since Lulach is not Macbeth's own son, but the child of two of his cousins, Talcoran feels he will be acceptable to those nobles who favor royal succession by the old laws."

"And since Lulach is Gruach's son and Macbeth's stepson," Fionna added, laughing, "there will be few complaints from those who hold with this new idea the English have, of succesion by direct descent. What a clever man our king is. He can have it either way."

"Except for those who favor Duncan's sons. There are a few who feel that way, including Duncan's father Crinan, who would like to see his grandson Malcolm on the throne."

"Elen, don't even whisper that in this court. And certainly not to me. I must give Macbeth no cause for suspicion, else I could put Conal and the children in danger." Seeing Elen's sharp glance, Fionna added bitterly, "Well, I am the one who has the traitorous brother, am I not?"

The feasting began then, and they had no chance to talk further. The palace cooks had outdone themselves with roasted venison, grouse, a whole roasted boar, beef, fish, pies of minced meats and spices, breads and sweetmeats, apples and nuts, dried berries and clotted cream, and bottomless pitchers and jugs of wine, ale, beer, and mead.

Thorfinn's skald, Arnor, had come with him to entertain the courtiers with songs and poems about the brave Norsemen. He and Macbeth's harper soon began a contest of their musical and poetical abilities that threatened to go on all night.

In another part of the hall a magician performed his tricks, and in a clear space before the lower tables, wrestling matches were held.

When the eating was done and the guests had settled down to earnest drinking and entertainment, Fionna motioned to Elen. Together they made their way to a room set aside for ladies of the court to use to refresh themselves. It was crowded with chattering women, not a place in which to exchange confidences. They left the room and walked along an empty corridor.

"How cool it is here, after the hot banqueting hall," Elen said, breathing deeply. "What is it you wanted to tell me, Fionna?"

She had expected to hear that Fionna was

with child again, but it was not that. She was
stunned by what Fionna did say.

"I have had a letter from Patric."

"What? How could he do such a thing?
Doesn't he realize how dangerous that could be for
you? Suppose someone found out? Does Conal
know?"

"I have told no one, not even Conal. The
servant who brought the letter did not know what
it was. It was sent to a monastery here in Alba. I
won't tell you which monastery. The letter was
passed to me from the abbot, so there is nothing to
connect it to Patric."

Elen knew the letter must have gone through
Dunkeld. King Duncan's father Crinan was lay
abbot of Dunkeld. He had retained his position
after his son's death and enjoyed King Macbeth's
protection. Elen had heard rumors of plots
against Macbeth being hatched at Dunkeld,
though none of them ever came to fruition. No
doubt Macbeth had his informers among the
monks there. Any ruler with his wits about him
would.

"Elen, are you listening? Patric has been
living at the English court and in Northumbria,
where he has been Earl Siward's guest. He and
Siward seem to have become good friends. Patric
is still unmarried."

"Why should I care about that?" Elen's voice
was louder than she had meant it to be, considering the content of this conversation. She
spoke more softly. "I don't want to hear any more
of this, Fionna."

"He says," Fionna persisted, ignoring Elen's
growing agitation, "that Fergus of Lochaber is
safe in Wales. Patric met with him a few months
ago."

"Fergus?"

"Aye. I thought you would want to know that. Patric writes that Fergus told him he and Bancho were ambushed the night Bancho was killed. Fergus was wounded. He fled when he realized Bancho was dead, and he took Grania with him."

"That is no news. We guessed as much."

"Fergus believes Macbeth ordered Bancho's death, and that the feast Macbeth arranged for that night was a trick, to deflect any hint of blame from Macbeth."

When Elen made no reply to this news that Fergus had reached the same conclusions she had about his father's murder, Fionna continued her recital.

"Grania died in childbirth. She was with child when they left here. In fact, that is why she went with Fergus. Both she and the child died."

"Grania dead? That silly, giddy young girl?"

"At least she was with her love," Fionna said gently. "Patric said they did marry as soon as they could."

"Poor Grania. Poorer Fergus. He has lost everything—father, wife, lands, title. How sad."

"Yes." Fionna waited expectantly.

"How is Patric?" Elen asked at last.

"He says he is well. He also said he hoped one he cared for but could not name is well and happy. That could only be you, Elen."

"Why did you tell me that, Fionna? Why?"

"Because he begged me to," Fionna said simply. "But only if you asked about him. I was not to offer information that might upset or anger you."

Elen clenched her fists hard at her sides, fighting off the image of Patric that now rose up before her. She had thought she could not remember his face, and yet there he stood in her imagination, just as she had last seen him. Those

close-cropped auburn curls, that square chiseled
jaw, those bright blue eyes . . .

"No!"

"Elen, I'm terribly sorry. I didn't dream it
would distress you so. I should not have told you.
You and Talcoran . . ." Fionna's voice trailed off.

"Yes," Elen said between set teeth, "I love
Talcoran. I have borne his children. I never think
of Patric. I have forgotten him. It was Grania,
dying alone in a foreign land, that distressed me.
That, and remembering Bancho." Elen tried to
calm herself. She believed that she had done so.

"Let us return to the feast," she said.

She sat beside Talcoran while the harper sang
and the magician performed. Her mind and heart
were filled with memories of Patric. She was
tormented by an unreasonable desire to see him
again, to hear his deep, laughing voice, to feel his
lips on hers.

She was scarcely aware that the feast had
ended, or that she and Talcoran had returned to
their apartments. She found herself in her bedchamber not knowing how she had gotten there.

She heard Talcoran in the reception room,
talking to Drust. Talcoran, who was her husband,
who was kind to her, who would rather sleep alone
for the rest of his life than chance giving her
another child that might kill her.

Patric had left her without a good-bye. Patric
was a traitor. If Patric came through the door she
would . . . she would throw herself into his arms
and beg him to make love to her, as they should
have made love long ago when they were both
young, before madness and war overtook Alba and
she had been made to marry a stranger who
was . . . who was the man she loved above all

others, whose caresses she longed for each night and must now live without.

"I'm going mad," she whispered to herself. "Mad. I can't bear it any longer."

There was a pitcher of mead on the table. Elen filled a cup and drank it down, then swallowed a second and a third.

"Mistress, are you ill?" Ava was watching her, puzzled.

"Undress me," Elen said.

"Do you want your robe?" Ava asked when Elen was naked, covered only by the smooth black hair that spilled over her shoulders and down to her hips.

"No, it's too hot in here. Leave me like this. Go to Drust, Ava. Go and make love with him all the night long. If you love him, don't deny it, and don't wait."

"Mistress!" Ava was shocked.

"Go!"

Ava slipped out the door as Talcoran came in. Talcoran, not Patric. Talcoran, who was her husband, whom she loved. Her sudden desire for Patric was a momentary aberration, some trick of the devil perhaps. She would not fall victim to it.

Talcoran took in her naked state with raised eyebrows.

"I came to say good-night. You seemed unwell this evening. You eat so little these days."

"I am in perfect health," Elen told him, lifting yet another cup of mead to her lips.

"Still drinking?" he asked lightly. "You will have a sore head in the morning." He watched her for a moment or two, his dark grey eyes taking in every line of her slender nakedness before he turned to go.

"Good night," he said over his shoulder. It

seemed to Elen he went reluctantly.

"Don't leave me," she whispered, but he was already gone.

There was a fire in her veins, a smoldering, barely suppressed need that tortured her. It would not go away. It was more than three years since she and Talcoran had lain together shortly before Aiden's birth. No wonder she thought of Patric. It was a marvel that in all that time she had not found someone else, someone to ease the febrile yearning and at least make it possible for her to sleep at night. As quickly as it came, she rejected the idea with revulsion. It was Talcoran she wanted. She was his wife. He had no right to deny her his affection, however good his intentions might be.

She would go to him, beg him to take her back into his bed. No, she had tried that once and his refusal had been so humiliating that she had never attempted it again.

She poured herself another cup of mead, lifted it, then banged it down on the table. Mead would not help her. She needed a clear mind. She had to think of something to change her situation.

She recalled a conversation she had once unwillingly heard between two of the queen's ladies, who had twittered in delicious outrage over the peculiar demand made by the husband of one of them. Elen had declared such a thing to be impossible, unnatural, and quite probably sinful, even with one's own husband. With malicious pleasure the two ladies had proceeded to enlighten her, after which a scandalized Elen had placed the unwelcome information firmly in the back chambers of her mind and turned the key on it.

Now she opened her mind, let the idea out and examined it anew. It no longer seemed so revolting. In fact, it might offer a way for her to be close to Talcoran again, if he would accept the idea.

She draped a plaid woolen shawl about herself and headed for the room in which Talcoran now slept. She would act before she lost her courage.

Talcoran sat in a chair, the harsh lines of his face cruelly accentuated by the single oil lamp that burned beside him. He was deep in thought. She picked up a stool, placed it before him, and sat down.

"Elen. What are you doing here?" He made as if to rise, his loose robe falling open as he moved. Elen placed a hand on each of his bare knees.

"Talcoran, we must talk. Please don't send me away."

He sat back in his chair and waited.

"You have been cruel to me," Elen said. "You banished me from your bed without asking my opinion, but I am the one who must take the risk."

"I will not discuss this with you."

"Have you had other women?" By the look on his face she saw that he had, and the knowledge was like a knife in her breast. "Shall I find other men because my husband no longer wants me?"

"I have not said I do not want you. The others mean nothing. I use them, and only because I cannot have you."

She put her head down on his knees. After a while she told him what the court ladies had said, that scandalous, exciting, possibly sinful thing they had informed her about. She heard his gasp as she spoke. When she lifted her head at last, she saw that whatever he might say, Talcoran was not at all averse to her suggestion.

She slipped off the stool and knelt between his knees. She pushed aside his robe and lowered her head. He stiffened, making a futile gesture as if he would push her away, before his hands became entangled in her hair, and with an ecstatic moan he surrendered to her.

For the next few weeks Elen went about her duties in a happily dazed condition similar to that she had known when first she and Talcoran had married. She smiled at trifles, and discovered that even the most irritating problems of daily existence melted away when she thought of Talcoran.

He came to her room almost every night. Although it was she who had opened the gates of imagination, Elen marveled at the inventiveness of his mind, the suppleness of his hands and body, the tender passion of his mouth. There was one thing only he would not do, the thing she wanted most, for he still feared getting her with child. She decided it was a small price to pay. She had her husband back again, and his loving attentions had driven the specter of Patric mac Keith out of her mind.

In the summer of 1045, King Duncan's father, Crinan of Dunkeld, finally hatched a plot to unseat Macbeth which was more than mere talk or midnight meetings in his abbey. Upon learning of Crinan's plans, Macbeth ordered the great warhorn blown to officially summon the men of Alba to war.

"I will accompany Macbeth as always," Talcoran said.

"Colin will go, too," his four-year-old son declared, unsheathing his wooden toy sword and matching it to his father's real one. His midnight-blue eyes, so like Elen's, sparkled, and a lock of straight black hair fell over his forehead as he tossed his little head, trying to look fierce.

"Put that thing away," Elen ordered. She caught Colin in her arms, tossing the make-believe blade aside. "I've seen enough of war. I thought once Macbeth was king, we would have peace."

"This revolt was not Macbeth's doing," Talcoran said. "If he had dealt harshly with Crinan at the beginning of his reign, killed him or sent him into exile, it would not have happened. This is the penalty a king pays for treating his enemies with kindness."

"I am afraid for you."

"Don't worry about me, I have a charmed life," Talcoran laughed.

Elen thought with a flash of something akin to hatred that he was looking forward to the battle against Crinan. How lovingly he polished his blade and oiled his leather helmet. How carefully he checked the strength of his square shield and tested the edges of both spear and battleaxe. He whistled a light-hearted tune as he laid out his leather battle dress, examining the metal plates attached to it. There was new armor made of chain mail coming into Alba from the continent of Europe. Talcoran preferred his older, padded leather gear that had served him so well in the past.

Cheerfully Talcoran and Drust discussed the horses they would use, and the arrangements to feed both men and beasts. As Thane of Laggan, Talcoran had responsibility to provide a certain number of men-at-arms for the king's enterprise, and frequent messages went back and forth between the court and Laggan Castle where the men were gathering.

Like small boys bored with courtly intrigues and feastings and meetings of the king's council, the nobles of Alba joyfully prepared for war.

Macbeth himself was in the best of humors, certain of victory over Crinan, whom he repeatedly referred to as "that pious ass." Lulach girded on his sword and swore to make his stepfather and king proud of him. Even Conal mac Duff, who had once said he had lost his taste for war, now seemed to be looking forward to it.

"They've all gone mad," Elen said to Fionna.

The queen had overheard her.

"Where's your courage, woman? Here's wine. Thicken your blood with it; you look green and pale. This war is just."

Macbeth had entered the room while Gruach spoke, and laughed.

"My love," he said, "you sound as fierce and warlike as one of those strange goddesses the Norsemen believe in, who carry heroes killed in battle to their heavenly banqueting hall."

"Speaking of Norsemen, will Thorfinn fight with us?" Fionna asked.

"Aye, if we need his help, but leave such matters to men, sweet lady," Macbeth told her. "War is not a woman's problem."

"It is if her menfolk are killed or wounded, or if she herself is harmed, as too often happens," Elen reminded him.

"It will be a short campaign," Macbeth promised her. "We will all be safely home by mid-summer."

In spite of the king's assurances and the cheerful confidence of the nobles, Elen felt a sense of dread. Talcoran rode off on a secret mission for the king, and in the three days he was gone, Elen neither slept nor ate. He reappeared during one of those royal feasts Macbeth was so fond of giving. He sat down next to Elen and calmly began eating from her trencher.

"This is good," he said. "I've not had hot food recently."

"Where have you been?"

"Don't ask. I'll be late tonight. I have to report to Macbeth when this is over." Talcoran looked about the crowded hall. "Everyone is here and ready. My own men have arrived from Laggan. Unless something goes wrong, we leave tomorrow."

Later, Elen lay alone in her bed, tensely listening for a sound that would tell her Talcoran had returned from his conference with Macbeth. The hours passed slowly until she dozed.

She wakened, how much later she did not know, aware of Talcoran stretched beside her. By his quiet breathing, he was asleep. She pressed against him, afraid for him, wondering if they would ever lie like this again.

"Elen?" His mouth touched hers in a gentle kiss that quickly turned into something much more.

He was abruptly, hugely erect, with a hard, pulsing need that could not wait or be denied. She heard a startled exclamation as he rolled over on top of her, his mouth seeking hers again. There was an urgency in him, a hasty desperation that she recognized as a counterpart to her own fears for him.

She was ready for him, responding eagerly to his slightest touch, for this, this was what she had wanted from him, the one thing he had denied her during their recent nights together. She rejoiced in his maleness as Talcoran gave in to the atavistic urge of the soldier going into battle, the desire to create life before taking it, to leave some part of himself behind lest he not return.

They surged together, half mad with their

need for each other, moaning in painful pleasure as the irresistible, immediate climax shook them both.

He kissed her until her mouth was numb. He caught her face between his hands and kissed her again and again as if he would never stop, and his body was still inside hers, and she cried out as one final bursting wave shook her and she gave herself to his unending kisses with tears of joy that she had known this night, this time with him.

"Oh, dear God." He had stopped kissing her. She opened her eyes. In the grey dawn light he was staring down at her in shocked horror. "What have I done to you?"

"We have made love."

"You know what I mean. How could you let me do that?"

"It was impossible to stop you," she teased. "Was it so terrible?" She wrapped her arms around him and held him fast. After a while she felt him relax against her.

"What's done is done," he told her philosophically. His mouth brushed down the length of her throat. "Whatever damage there will be from this has already happened. I do not need to leave for some hours yet, and who knows when I will return, or in what condition? I see no point in wasting the time left to us, do you?"

17

Late summer and winter 1045.

The war against Crinan's rebels, which was to be over so quickly, dragged on for several months. Talcoran had been gone not quite ten weeks when Elen concluded she must be with child again.

"What shall I do?" she asked Fionna. "Talcoran will be so angry with me. He forbade me to have more children."

"The child is of his making," Fionna reminded her. "He can hardly blame you after he has had his pleasure, can he?"

Elen giggled, momentarily forgetting her concern.

"It was pleasure," she said, her cheeks coloring a bit at the memory. "But I am afraid. Aiden's birth was so difficult. I dread the next one. And I fear Talcoran's rage even more."

She felt well enough. She joined Gruach and the other women in a celebration when news came of Crinan's defeat and death at Dunsinane.

"We will celebrate better when the menfolk return," Gruach promised. "And then I suppose a few months from now most of you will again ask leave to go home and have babies, as you do after every war. I remember the last time."

There was delighted laughter at this, and
some rather rowdy speculation about who the
happy new parents would be. Elen said nothing.
She had told no one but Fionna about her
pregnancy, and had sworn Fionna to secrecy.
Talcoran should know first.

She did not feel well the next day, but thinking
it was only that she had eaten some bad food at
yesterday's party, she went to attend the queen.
She was with Gruach and Fionna when a second
messenger came with more details about the
battle.

"The king was unharmed," the messenger
said, "but many were wounded."

"The Thane of Fife," Fionna asked breathlessly, "is he well?"

"He is, lady." The messenger knew Elen. He
would not look at her. "Conal mac Duff is well, but
Talcoran of Laggan was sorely wounded."

"What? Talcoran? I don't believe it," Elen
cried.

"Aye, lady, it's true. He took a spear in his
side. It is not known if he will live."

"No! He can't die!" Elen staggered as if it
were she who had been struck down. She felt two
pairs of arms supporting her.

"It's all right, Fionna, I have her." Gruach
made Elen sit down. "Put your head down, cousin,
or you will faint."

"I have to go to him." Elen fought Gruach's
arms, trying to stand again. "Please, Gruach, give
me permission to leave court. I will travel to Dunsinane to be with my husband."

"You will do no such thing. I'll have none of
my women wandering around a battlefield.
Macbeth has told me about the ruffians, the
deserters and defeated soldiers who skulk about
after a fight, looting the unburied bodies and

attacking anyone they meet. I leave to your imagination what they would do to a woman such as yourself."

"I will take an armed guard." Elen would not be dissuaded. "I'll be safe enough. If he should die alone, when I might have been at his side, I could never forgive myself."

"Elen, if you disobey me in this, I will see to it that both you and Talcoran are banished from court. Will you have him recover from his wound only to learn that you have ruined him? He will not thank you for your devotion then. Neither Macbeth nor Talcoran would permit you to go on such a foolish errand, and neither will I."

Elen, knowing only too well that Talcoran would also have her pregnancy to be angry about, gave in. In her heart she knew Gruach was right. Dunsinane was no place for her. While her concern for Talcoran would have sent her to find him no matter the danger to herself, she would do the wiser thing. She spent the remainder of the day on her knees in the chapel, until her legs and back ached from the hard stone floor, and the damp chill had reached into her bones.

That night she miscarried. It was Briga, with her knowledge of herbs and ancient medicines, who finally stanched the bleeding when Elen was certain she would die.

"You have saved my life again," she said to Briga. "I won't forget it."

"It was my duty, mistress," Briga said simply.

"No one can know what has happened. Briga, Ava, I want you both to promise me you will not reveal either that I was with child or that I miscarried it."

Her servants swore what Elen wanted.

"Lady," Ava said, "how can we explain that you are unable to attend the queen today? You are too weak to stand."

"Send a message that I am distraught about
Talcoran's wounding. Say I will resume my duties
the day after tomorrow. Gruach may seem to be
annoyed, but she will understand. Briga, you will
concoct one of your herbal remedies for me, so
when I return to the royal apartments I will
appear to be in good health."

"Yes, mistress."

"I will see no one but Fionna. No other
visitors."

They left her alone to rest, but her disordered
thoughts would give her no peace. She was over-
whelmed with guilt. She had desired Patric, lusted
after a man not her husband. She had gone to
Talcoran and demanded readmittance to his bed,
not because she wanted him, her husband, but because she had wanted Patric, and because her
body had clamored for physical release from that
need. Now heaven was punishing her. Talcoran
might die, and the baby he had given her, possibly
his last child, was gone, too, and it was all her
fault, because she had wanted Patric. She hated
the very thought of Patric.

Let Talcoran live, she prayed, let him live and
I will care for him and love him and give him
another child though it cost me my life.

When Fionna came, Elen made her, too, swear
not to reveal her pregnancy or its end. Talcoran
must never find out. It would destroy the close-
ness they had so recently recovered. If he knew
what had happened, his fear for her and his
strength of will would combine to keep him permanently from her bed.

If he lived.

She sent three of the men Talcoran had left to
guard her off to Dunsinane to find him.

"See him face to face if he is able," she

instructed them. "Bring me word from his own
lips that he is healing. Failing that, speak with
Drust. Every other day, one of you will return to
me with news of him."

Two days later the first of the men returned to
tell her Talcoran was indeed grievously wounded
and might well die. Subsequent reports suggested
that though extremely weak, he was improving
slowly.

Frantic with worry over him, Elen spent her
days trying to convince Gruach to let her go to
Dunsinane. In the end it was Macbeth who
reunited them. He sent a letter directly to Elen,
telling her Talcoran would live. He had ordered
Talcoran taken by litter, in slow stages, to Laggan.

"He spoke in his delirium of the sweet air and
sunshine of that place," Macbeth wrote. "I think it
best to send him there to recover, though his con-
valescence will be long, and I will miss him at my
shoulder for every hour of that time. Show this
letter to the queen and tell her it is my wish that
you and your son should leave the court and join
Talcoran at Laggan, to stay with him there until he
is completely well."

"Mistress, what is it?" Briga had rushed into
the bedchamber at Elen's loud cry. Elen flung her
arms around the woman, the king's letter crushed
in her hand.

"Talcoran will live!" Elen was laughing and
crying at the same time. "We are going home,
home to Laggan. He will be there. Briga, I'm so
happy."

The following day, Elen, Colin, Briga, and Ava
departed for Laggan, accompanied by a troop of
Talcoran's men-at-arms. They traveled as quickly
as they could, urged on by Elen's impatience to be
with Talcoran again. She hoped they might over-
take him along the way, but he was at Laggan half

a day before she arrived.

"He is very tired, lady," Drust told her. "We carried him to his bed. He should be sleeping. It would be good to let him rest."

Elen paid no attention to Drust. She was half-way up the steps, hurrying to her husband. He was not asleep. He lay propped up in bed. He was so still, and so very pale. His cheeks were hollow. There were dark blue circles under his sunken eyes. A dirty bandage was wrapped about his chest.

"Oh, my darling." Elen threw herself on him, not noticing when he winced in pain. She kissed him hungrily, then sat back to look at him. A skeletal hand reached up to stroke her hair. She caught it and pressed it against her lips.

"Elen." His voice was a hoarse, weak croak. "I regret . . . I cannot . . . greet you . . . as I would like." He produced a sad parody of a smile.

"I am here to make you well," she told him brightly. "By the king's command."

"I fear . . . that is . . . .impossible."

"Would you have me disobey the king? I'll do no such thing. You will recover, my love. I'll see to it." She looked about the room. "This place needs cleaning."

"I'm too tired. No maids in here. Let me sleep." He closed his eyes.

"For today and tonight you may. We'll clean tomorrow. But I will have Briga in here to look at your wound and put fresh linen on it right now. Then we will bathe you and trim that beard that's half-way down your chest. And cut your hair, too."

Briga came, and scowled at the filthy wrappings over Talcoran's wound. It took a long time to remove them. They were stuck to his flesh, and crusted with blood and dirt.

Talcoran lay quietly, giving no indication of

the pain he must have felt when Briga tugged at the cloth. He was hardly like Talcoran at all. Most of his fierce spirit seemed to have fled through the wound in his side.

Elen turned her head away when the last bit of bandage was gone. Then she made herself look. This was her husband, and she would care for him. She would be brave for his sake.

The wound in his right side was a long red gash, the edges of which had been crudely sewn together. Even with her small fund of knowledge in such matters, Elen knew the attempt at repair was inadequate and the wound was not healing properly.

Briga stood, looking grim, contemplating the damage.

"This needs marigold petals," she said softly, as if she were thinking aloud. "An ointment of dried yarrow leaves and swine's grease."

"I want to watch what you do," Elen said. "I want to learn."

"First, we will need boiling water and linen cloths to cleanse this." Briga gestured toward the wound. "I cannot undo what the surgeon has so badly sewn. My lord Talcoran, you will always have a thick scar in that spot. What I can do for you is hasten the healing and make you more comfortable."

"Do whatever you think is right," Talcoran told her, his low voice oddly lifeless.

Elen worked with Briga, cleaning the fiery red wound with herb-infused water, and then dressing it with a thick, greasy salve Briga had compounded. Elen gritted her teeth and choked back the bile that rose to her throat as they poked and prodded the tender flesh, but she kept at it, and at last Talcoran lay peacefully, his wound wrapped in fresh, clean linen. Elen drew a fur covering up to his chin.

"Sleep now," she said. "I'll bring you food later."

"Not hungry," Talcoran whispered through blue-white lips. He had made no sound during all of their sometimes necessarily rough treatment of his wound.

"I will prepare an infusion of bitter herbs," Briga told Elen. "It will improve his appetite."

"I'll sit with him tonight."

"No, mistress. Have a care for your own health. From what I've seen of Laggan Castle today, there is much work for you outside this chamber. I will stay with Lord Talcoran this night."

Briga was right. While they had been at court they had left Laggan in Dougal's hands, but Dougal, try as he might, was now too old and too slow to see to all that must be done.

Elen took firm control of Talcoran's domain, managing to do it without injuring Dougal's tender pride. She sent Drust and a few of Talcoran's men to collect ovedue rents, and when that was done, she put Drust in charge of the castle's men-at-arms, who, in their master's absence, had taken to lounging about the great hall all day drinking and playing with the serving wenches. She gave Drust strict orders to turn those men into soldiers again before the Thane of Laggan was up and about. Drust took on the task with relish.

Elen dismissed some of the more sluttish servants, hired the younger daughters of some of the farmers who worked the fields of Lagganshire, promising them fine dowries when they married, and set about cleaning Laggan Castle from tower to storage cellars.

She tried to make Talcoran do their accounts,

thinking he needed distraction. He could not spend every day just lying in bed, looking out the window. Talcoran had never been very concerned about such matters. He could count well, but he could barely read and write. He had left the account books to an inept secretary, who, during the winter just past, had run away with one of the kitchen wenches, taking along for dowry half a dozen silver cups that had belonged to Elen's father. It was too late to recover the silver, but the account books could be repaired and made more accurate, if only Talcoran would take an interest. He did not, and soon Elen was doing that task, too.

She thrived on all the work she had undertaken. She slept well and ate heartily. Her healthy body had apparently recovered completely from her miscarriage. Her mind was constantly occupied with the management of Lagganshire. As the results of her efforts became more and more obvious, and she found herself ruling an efficient, productive domain, she felt a sense of competence and well-being she had never known before. Even her guilt over the last winter's brief desire for Patric had begun to dissipate.

"I'm content here," she said to Briga one evening. "I don't care if we never go back to court."

"You will have to return, as soon as our master is well."

"If he ever does recover. It's taking so long."

"Mistress, I confess when I first saw that wound of his, I thought he would die of it. It was a terrible injury and sapped most of his strength. We ought to be patient with him."

Talcoran did eventually leave his bed. He spent the warm autumn afternoons sitting in the sunshine, watching old Dougal teaching Colin to use his tiny sword.

"He's too young," Elen objected. "He's just a baby."

"Leave him alone, Elen. It's only a game," Talcoran said, letting her see he was annoyed by her interference.

To please him, and to placate his uncertain temper, she stopped voicing her objections.

Elen moved back into Talcoran's bed. For a long time they did not make love, but as the nights lengthened toward winter it was comforting to sleep next to him and to feel his warmth. His listlessness and his strange irritability would disappear as his health improved, and then they would be close once more.

The harvest was gathered, the household was well prepared for the winter to come. It was the old Celtic new year, the festival of Samhain, when the spirits of the dead walked abroad for one night. As Christians, they now called it All Hallows' Eve. The servants had celebrated it with extra ale and beer, and noisy games designed to keep evil spirits at bay.

In the master's room it was quieter. A huge golden moon hung in a luminous sky, casting its light across the bedchamber floor and over the bed where Talcoran lay.

"It's a night for ghosts." Elen shivered as she threw off her robe and slipped under the furs.

"And what of living men?" Talcoran asked, sounding more like his old self than he had for months. "Is it a night for them, too?"

She saw his face in the moonlight, black and silver, almost like a ghost in its thinness. But he was alive. It was warm, human flesh that fastened itself upon her mouth, and human hands that touched her, stroking embers into glowing flames once more. It was a human body, a distinctly *male* human body that covered hers and with fierce love brought her to the edge of a delight all the sweeter, all the more intense because of the fear she had so recently had for him, for his very life. He was alive now, as only Talcoran could be alive, hard and tense and almost frantic in his need of her. He moved against her and she melted with love for him, urged him into her, welcoming the growing tension within herself, knowing it would end in glorious unity, Elen and Talcoran, one being. Soon now, soon . . .

Something was wrong, horribly, dreadfully wrong. He was gone from her and she was empty, bereft, and the pain was unendurable. He was gasping above her and she felt something wet and sticky on her belly and she knew what he had done.

"Don't, don't," she begged, but it was too late.

"I can't do it," he whispered, panting. "I can't chance hurting you. I don't want to lose you."

"You have already hurt me!" she cried, trying to push him away.

He did not hear her. His brief burst of strength expended, Talcoran had fallen asleep. Elen lay in her beloved husband's arms while he slept, and her heart and her mind were empty and cold, and she felt totally alone. She wondered in despair if they would ever truly be together again.

She tried to discuss it with him the next morning, reminding him of the many things they had done and enjoyed before he was wounded, that had been pleasurable to her, too.

"Unmanly things," Talcoran said, his temper flaring as it did too frequently since his wounding. "I will decide such matters, Elen, and you will be an obedient wife and do as I wish. Do not tempt me with such ideas again."

She did not argue further. She understood his churlish inflexibility on this matter had something to do with his injury. Perhaps he felt diminished by his physical weakness and by the need for his wife to manage his affairs until he recovered. Only in this one aspect of their life together, their lovemaking, did he still exercise complete control. She would not dispute his authority in their marriage bed. She would leave him that, for the sake of his fierce pride, until he was completely well again.

18

Autumn 1046.
Scone.

She never learned how he discovered it. When she asked them, Fionna, Briga, and Ava all swore they had said nothing. It might have been some ill-chosen turn of phrase on her part, some careless piece of evidence, a putting together of bits and pieces of information. Somehow, Talcoran had learned of Elen's pregnancy and miscarriage.

It was the worst possible time for it to happen. At Talcoran's insistence they had returned to court in the summer of 1046, although he was still not completely recovered from the terrible wound he had taken the year before. He would admit to no disability, although he tired easily, and when his side ached in bad weather, he limped. There were nights when he put his arms around Elen and could do no more than that, and he pretended it was all he wanted. Elen knew better. Still, those times were easier for her than the nights when he used her as he had at Samhain, and left her empty and lonely even though he was beside her.

When Earl Siward of Northumbria, backed by English trooops, made a feeble attempt to invade Alba, Macbeth would not allow Talcoran to ride with the army.

"You are too valuable here," Macbeth told him kindly. "I leave you to sit on my council. Like the good soldier you are, you will guard my back."

The kindness rankled.

"Even Lulach, a weakling of eighteen, is included in the army," Talcoran fumed, "and I, at thirty-three, am treated like an old man who cannot even sit his horse."

"Macbeth needs you here," Elen said soothingly. "He needs someone he can trust completely. The campaign won't last long."

"What do women know of armies and campaigns?" Talcoran said cruelly. "I am a warrior, not some snivelling courtier."

"Which is exactly why Macbeth wants you at court."

He glared at her, then left the room. Elen shook her head sadly. He was so different since his wound. He was even rude to Gruach later that evening, after the army had left to fight Siward.

"His wound aches," Elen apologized. "He does not mean what he says."

"It is hard to be left behind," Gruach said. "Perhaps Morigan can divert him. If she fails, he's hopeless. Bring your needlework and sit by me, Elen, while the harper plays. We've not talked for a long time."

Grateful for her cousin's sympathy, Elen took her place on a stool near Gruach. She watched Talcoran from time to time as the evening progressed. He sat in a corner of the queen's reception room, talking with the queen's lady, Morigan. The beautiful, red-haired niece of the Thane of Mar was only lately come to court. She had been widowed after a year of marriage and was expected to make a good second marriage, since her husband had left her considerable property. Elen had heard whispers about her, that she was overly fond of men.

Elen saw Talcoran smile at Morigan and bend his head to say something to her. If Morigan could charm him and put him into a better mood, she would thank the woman and be her friend no matter what the gossips said of her.

Talcoran became increasingly cheerful as the days passed. Elen thought that he had reconciled himself to not marching with the army. Certainly he was busy with matters of state, with meetings of the king's council and conferences with other nobles that often lasted well into the night. She saw him less and less.

He had new clothes made for himself. They were not the dark grey or black he had always worn, but dark green silk for the tunic, and bright red wool for the cloak.

"How handsome he looks," she said to Fionna. "His health is better, too. There is more color in his cheeks."

"And sparkle in his eyes," Fionna added dryly. "Indeed, there is a definite *gleam* in Talcoran's eyes these days."

"I hope so," Elen laughed. In a fit of despair one day, she had confessed to Fionna a little about her unhappy relationship with Talcoran, and had been advised to be patient with him, for men often had such problems, especially after a serious wound, which injured the spirit as well as the body. "I begin to think you were right, Fionna. Perhaps we can be happy again, and soon, too."

"Elen, sometimes I worry about you." Fionna's voice had taken on a certain sharpness. "You have a marvellous capacity for never seeing what you don't want to see. Were you a king, you'd lose your throne and your head within a year."

"What's this? Elen a king? What a funny idea." Morigan had joined them. Her easy laughter bubbled up. "Fionna, why should Elen want to be a king?"

Now Talcoran was at Elen's elbow, smiling down at her. She returned the smile and took his arm. He covered her hand with his and she gave a little sigh of happiness at this affectionate gesture. Talcoran did not often show his love for her in public.

"I was saying," Fionna said in that same sharp tone, fixing her sparkling blue eyes on Talcoran, "That not being of a suspicious nature, Elen would make a dreadful king. She is too trusting."

"But she is a wonderful wife," Talcoran said.

That night they made love, and it was almost as it had been when first they married. Until the end, when, nearly too late, he left her alone as was his custom now, and she beat at his shoulders and cried out that she hated him, hated him.

"That may be," he told her, "But you are my wife, my chattel, and you will do as I wish." And with that, this newly cold and cruel Talcoran, this stranger she loved and hated at the same time, rolled over and went to sleep.

Elen was not quite so simple as Fionna imagined. She was aware of Talcoran's interest in Morigan. At first she thought it would be good for him. A joking conversation, a little flirtation with Morigan would lift him out of his despondency, would make him feel more manly. They slept in the same bed each night so she did not doubt his fidelity. But after a time, he began coming later and later to bed, and she sensed a strange odor about him, another woman's seductive perfume, and knew it was Morigan's.

She was afraid. A nobleman of Alba had power of life and death over his wife. Talcoran could send her away to a convent, divorce her, even kill her if he wanted. It was not likely he would kill her, for she was too closely connected to Macbeth for that, and she knew that whatever their differences Talcoran cared about her. But he could divorce her to marry Morigan, who was eighteen and could give him children, the sons he wanted. Because he had Colin, grandson of the last thane, Talcoran could keep Laggan, to pass it on to his eldest son. Elen, should he divorce her, would be left with nothing.

The tense weeks crawled by, with Talcoran growing ever colder and more distant. Elen did not know what to do.

Ava came to her one morning with a perplexed expression.

"Mistress, it has been eight weeks." Ava counted on her fingers. "That long since your woman's time has come on you. Are you with child?"

"That's impossible. It can't be."

"Oh, yes it is." Ava counted again, explaining patiently, and Elen remembered the night when Talcoran had almost, almost, forgotten to be careful.

"I've been so distracted, I never thought of this," she said. She was terrified and happy at the same time. Could she give Talcoran another son after all? And Talcoran, what would he say, what would he do?

"Tell no one," she cautioned her maid. "I must find the right time to inform Talcoran."

These days there never seemed to be a right time to talk alone with Talcoran about anything. Another week passed while Elen worried about how to do it.

And now, on top of everything else, Talcoran had learned about her miscarriage.

"Am I so feeble a creature that my own wife dares to lie to me?" he roared. "How could you keep such a secret for so long? I had a right to know."

"You were grievously ill, Talcoran. And by the time you were well enough to know it, it was in the past. I did not want to distress you. I was afraid if you knew," she added honestly, "you would forbid me your bed again."

"So I would have. You could have died, Elen. I may never forgive you for this. Do you think I'm some half-man to be manipulated like that?"

All the fears and heartache, and all the thwarted desires, of the past year and a half boiled over at last.

"Yes!" Elen replied hotly. "That miserly bit of yourself you deign to bestow on me in our bed is less than half a man, less than half of Talcoran. I deserve more. I want all of you, not an occasional bone tossed under your table as though I were a dog. Forgive me? You should go on your knees and beg *me* to forgive *you* for everything you've done to me!"

His open hand cracked across her cheek. Elen stumbled, caught herself on a chair and pulled herself upright. She knew other men beat their wives, but Talcoran had never struck her before.

"From now on, you will get none of me, woman," he snarled. "You will keep to your chamber at night, and I'll keep to mine." He headed for the door.

"Before you leave, my noble lord, there is something you should know." Elen's voice dripped scorn. "I have another secret to tell you. I am with child again."

Talcoran turned white. He approached her like some tense, wiry beast, stalking its prey.

"Whose?" he demanded. "Who is the father?"

"Unlike you, I have not betrayed my marriage vows. I have known no man but you, Talcoran. The child is yours."

"That is impossible."

"So I thought, but it is so." A flicker of amusement crossed her face. "Perhaps whichever soldier friends of yours have been advising you in such matters should be warned their methods do not work."

The faintest hint of answering humor showed in his dark eyes before he sobered.

"It was no ordinary soldier," he said. "It was the Thane of Mar."

"That seems appropriate to me. I trust you did not serve his niece in the same way."

Talcoran's eyes slid away from hers.

"No," he said shortly.

There was an uncomfortable silence until Talcoran cleared his throat and spoke again.

"I have treated you badly."

Elen knew it was as close to an apology as Talcoran could ever come.

"Indeed you have," she said.

"About Morigan. It is finished."

"There is no need to explain. We began our marriage promising to be honest with each other and we have both failed miserably. But we could begin again. I see no reason for you to stay away from my bed, Talcoran, now that the thing you feared the most has happened."

"I am still afraid." Talcoran shook his head. "I fear nothing in war, not death however hideous, nor anything that happens after death. But I am terrified of losing you."

Elen saw in his face that it was true. Whatever their quarrels, Talcoran loved her. He was her husband, and she must, she did, love him.

"I am afraid, too," Elen said, "But less so

when you hold me. Never leave me alone again, Talcoran. Promise me that, and let us try to be happy together once more."

In late November, Macbeth returned in triumph from routing Earl Siward. A few nights later, Gruach, after loving him into complaisant good humor, made a tactful suggestion, and in December, the Thane of Mar's niece was married to a wealthy Norwegian jarl and sailed away to live in that icy land. Elen, happily involved with Talcoran once more, scarcely noticed that Morigan had left.

19

Siward the Strong, Earl of Northumbria, spun around on his booted heel when the door behind him opened.

"Ah, Patric, it's you. Come here to the window. Look at that." He pointed to a pair of young men engaged in swordplay in the practice courtyard below. "Watch now. Ha, ha! Good work, Malcolm. Not many lads of fifteen could do that. What a warrior he'll make in another year or so."

Siward and Patric mac Keith stood shoulder to shoulder at the narrow window. Siward was of almost gigantic size, towering half a head above Patric's own great height. He was a burly, beefy, barrel-chested man, with hair and beard the color of brass. He was both violent and unscrupulous, but he ruled his earldom with rough justice. Having made Northumbria securely his possession, his present goal was to place his orphaned nephew Malcolm mac Duncan on the throne of Alba. Siward considered Macbeth a usurper, and welcomed into his earldom those who had fled Alba when his brother-in-law, King Duncan, was killed. He had quickly befriended Patric, appreciating the bravery of the man who had safely brought his young nephews to him.

"We could have used Malcolm in Alba this summer," Patric said, following the swordplay below them with considerable interest.

"We could have used a few hundred more English troops," Siward corrected him sourly. "That's what we needed. But King Edward was too miserly for that."

"More troops would have made no difference. It was a foolish invasion, ill-planned and poorly captained."

Siward's eyes narrowed at the insult. His hand went to his sword hilt.

"And now," Patric went on, "Macbeth has no doubts left about your intentions. He will be even better prepared against us when next we attack him."

Siward's hand left his sword.

"You always were a plain-speaker," he said.

"Honestly is all I have left," Patric replied.

"What, out of silver again? Too many wenches?"

"I bought information with the silver, not women. It's not good news, my lord."

"Don't tell me all of Macbeth's nobles are loyal to him? Even your brother-in-law?"

"Especially Conal, and I'll make no attempt to subvert him."

"You're mighty squeamish for an outlawed traitor."

Patric shrugged. He knew Siward well enough not to take offense.

"You need to know the truth," Patric said. "And the truth is that you cannot conquer Alba. Not now. Macbeth has made the land both peaceful and prosperous. He sits securely on his throne, backed by his nobles, who hold him in high regard. You were ill-advised to invade Alba last summer, and you would be a fool to try it again."

"That is plain enough. Very well, my truthful friend, what do you advise me to do?"

"Wait. Eventually something will occur that will enable you to divide the Alban nobles so that some at least will come over to your side. Or perhaps Macbeth himself will provide an excuse for you to attack him."

"Waiting is the hardest thing for a soldier to do."

"You have nothing to lose by it."

"Only time."

Patric nodded toward the youth in the courtyard, who had now taken on a second opponent, having throughly bested the first.

"Malcolm has time."

"Ah, but I am older than he." Siward sighed. "Have I got time?"

On June first of the Year of Our Lord 1047, Elen of Laggan gave birth to a daughter. The child was born in her chamber at court, with Fionna, Briga, and Ava attending her. Elen's labor was short, the delivery remarkably easy.

Talcoran, who had spent the last months torn between fear for Elen's safety and the desire for another son, poked uneasily at the pink, elfin creature. His daughter wrapped her tiny hand about his finger. A wide grin split Talcoran's dark face.

"She's beautiful," he said.

"I know." Elen sat up in bed. "Give her to me. I want to nurse her."

Talcoran watched for a while.

"How happy I am," Elen said softly. "With your permission, I would like to call her Grania."

"I'm not sure that's wise."

"It's a common enough name."

"Not at this court. I have a better idea. We'll

call her Gruach, and ask the queen to be her god-mother.''

And so the child was named Gruach, but Elen, during all of her daughter's short life, called her Grania, in memory of the friend who had once carried a message for her.

In the Year of Our Lord 1050, Lulach, now twenty-two, was betrothed to Gertha, a niece of Thorfinn the Mighty.

"I really don't want to marry anyone," Lulach told Elen, "But I must do my duty.''

They were strolling along a sheltered walk near the chapel. Elen tucked her hand into Lulach's arm with the easy familiarity of old friends.

"So you have always done, my lord," she said. "Even when you were a little boy. How long ago that seems.''

"I used to dream I would grow up and marry you, Elen. Did you know that? You were always so kind to me.''

"I'm too old for you, Lulach, even if I weren't married already. Gertha is young and pretty, and she will give you sons.''

"You know Macbeth plans to make me his heir, now that I'm old enough to sit on the council?''

"I've heard rumors.''

"Do you approve, Elen? When the time comes, will you be my loyal subject?''

"Always, dear Lulach. I promise.''

She gazed after him thoughtfully when he left her. How sad that a ruler as strong as Macbeth should have for stepson and heir someone so weak as Lulach. She remembered Malcolm calling him Lulach the Fool, and Lulach's impotent, youthful fury at his overbearing cousin. It was not that

Lulach was stupid, only that he was unsuited to rule.

I love him, and one day I will bow to him as my king, she thought. But, please God, not yet. Not for a long, long time.

With his stepson safely married and his kingdom at peace, Macbeth decided to make a pilgrimage to Rome. Thorfinn of Orkney had already left on a journey through Norway, Denmark, and the continent of Europe. The cousins planned to meet in Rome. Talcoran would travel with Macbeth.

"Six months?" Elen exclaimed. "What will I do without you?"

"You will manage Lagganshire for me. You did it well enough when I was wounded five years ago. Dougal can still help a little, and Colin is nine now, so he can be of some use to you. After I leave, take him and little Gruach to Laggan. The court will be quiet while the king is gone. Gruach won't need you. You can come back here when it is time for me to return."

"I'm more fortunate than you," Fionna said later. "Conal isn't going to Rome. He is one of the regents on Macbeth's council, so we will remain at court. I would rather go home to Fife."

Elen spent a quiet summer at Laggan. Ava was lonely for Drust, who had gone with Talcoran, and was poor company. As a result, Elen spent much time with Briga, learning more from Briga's seemingly inexhaustible fund of knowledge about herbs and medicines. They took three-year-old Grania with them and tramped the nearby hillsides to find wild herbs or dig roots. They brought their harvest back to the stillroom, where they hung plants to dry or made the distillations that would be used later to cure winter ailments.

Even with all of this activity, and the management of Talcoran's estates besides, she had too much free time in which to be lonely. She missed Talcoran, especially in the evenings and at night.

She too often found guilty thoughts of Patric intruding on her, and wondered if she would never be free of him. It was just over ten years since last she had seen him, yet he would not leave her alone. She was glad to return to court in October, to await Macbeth's—and Talcoran's—return.

"It's amazing," Conal mac Duff said. "Alba is quiet, and there has not been the slightest stirring from Northumbria."

"Siward must have realized at last just how strong Macbeth is," Elen said.

"Perhaps. It's more likely he's biding his time." Conal smiled. "I'll be glad to see Talcoran again. I wager you will be, too, Elen."

"It's a good thing you didn't go to Rome, Conal," Fionna teased him. "I don't think I could endure six months without you. I hate to be separated for even a few days."

Conal laughed. "You don't have to worry about that, my love. I'm not going anywhere without you."

Macbeth's return to Alba was a triumph. He and his companions rode into Scone wearing their brightest clothes, to the cheers and applause of the people who had come to line his route, hoping for a look at their king.

Macbeth was met by his council of regents, by his heir Lulach, whose serene, pale-blonde wife Gertha stood by his side, and by his queen with her ladies. Elen spied Talcoran in his usual position just behind Macbeth's right shoulder. He had a new velvet cape, trimmed in fur, and wore a broad-brimmed felt pilgrim's hat. She paid no attention to anyone else, not even the king. She could not take her eyes off Talcoran.

He had seen her. He looked straight at her. Her heart began to pound harder, but she remembered to behave with dignity. She was not a silly girl any more, whatever her heart said; she was twenty-seven years old and the wife of a great nobleman. She forced herself to stand quietly.

Macbeth formally greeted his council, then came to meet his queen. He took Gruach's hand and together they led the procession into the church for the service of thanksgiving for the king's safe return.

It was a long service. Elen could not see Talcoran from where she stood. She concentrated on her prayers, thanking heaven profusely for sending Talcoran safely home to her.

The service was over at last, and the royal company filed out of the church. Elen was free until the banquet later in the day. She searched, but could not find Talcoran in the crowd. When Drust appeared at her side, she could have hugged him for joy.

"My lord will join you in your chambers shortly," Drust said. "He has some brief business with the king first."

Elen forgot dignity. She hurried as fast as she possibly could, and by the time she reached her own door, she was running.

"Ava! Briga! Where are you?"

"Here, mistress."

"I want the children prepared. Their father will be here soon. Bring the tub in, and hot water. He will want to bathe before the feast. And food. Cheese, and that dark bread he likes, and mead."

"It's all here, just as you ordered earlier, and the children are ready, too." Briga laughed at her excitement. "We've only to bring in the hot water."

"Do it now. I want everything ready when he comes."

"Did you see Drust?" Ava asked hesitantly.

"Yes, I spoke to him. He is well. You may go to him after Talcoran has dismissed you all."

Talcoran arrived before the bathtub was quite full, Drust entering the room behind him. Little Grania ran to her father and threw her arms about his neck as Talcoran tossed her into the air. Young Colin tried to restrain his eagerness and look manly, but in a moment he, too, was clasped in his father's embrace. Over their children's heads, Talcoran's eyes met Elen's.

"Good day, wife."

"My lord." Trying not to giggle, Elen made a deep formal bow.

"Briga, it's good to see you again," Talcoran said. "Take the children away. Now. Drust, Ava, you go, too."

"Master," Ava protested, "The tub. You will need more water."

"I care nothing about that. Leave us."

Elen's heart was beating hard again. Talcoran took two steps toward her. She was in his arms before the servants had left the room. She knew she had missed him. She had not realized just how much until that moment.

Their mouths met. She felt his hands in her hair, removing all the pins, loosening the braids and untwisting the heavy strands until her hair fell down over her shoulders. He buried his face in it, breathing in the delicate herbal scent she used. Then his lips were on hers again. Her knees buckled. Passion, unleashed after so many months of separation, rocked them both. They sank to the floor, tearing at each other's clothes in unthinking haste, strewing discarded garments around them as they went. His mouth bruised hers. He moaned half-words and broken phrases.

"Need you ... Elen ... no one else ... so long."

He flung up her skirts while she pulled at his breeches with shaking fingers, hating anything that delayed their joining. At last they were both free. With a wild, uncontrollable eagerness, he entered her to a frenzied, screaming climax that was immediate and devastating.

They clung together like victims of some great earthquake, quivering and dazed at what had happened to them. They could not separate. They stayed together, and his mouth, grown tender with the release of his need, now held her gently, caressing her into a soft, melting sweetness, while his hands renewed their familiarity with the soft-ness and roundness and beloved secrets of her body, until the fire blazed up once more, carrying them into that glorious agony where they cried out their love for each other over and over again until they lay limp and sobbing and at peace.

Elen recovered first.

"We are expected at the feast," she reminded him, stroking one hand across his bare chest. "You will want to bathe. I should call the servants."

"No," he murmured. "I want no one else here. Only you."

She sat up reluctantly, searching for her shoes and shawl.

"I think I'll need to change my dress," she said, looking down at her crumpled skirts. She wriggled away, laughing, when he tugged play-fully at the laces at one side of her waist.

"I'll help you finish undressing, and you help me bathe," he suggested, beginning to roll down one of her stockings. "You may wash my back."

In a remarkably short time she was barefoot and clad only in her undershift. Ava had left a bucket of steaming hot water on the hearth, and this Elen dumped into the tub before Talcoran lowered himself into it. She gave him a bowl of the soap Briga had made, scented with fresh-smelling herbs. He lathered his arms and shoulders, then carelessly splashed water about to rinse himself.

"My back, please," he said, handing her the linen cloth.

She scrubbed at him until he leaned back with a sigh of contentment.

"You may as well do my chest, too," he said. "That's fine. A little lower. There, wash that, too."

As Elen leaned over the tub, he caught her by the waist and pulled her in on top of him. Soapy water splashed onto the floor.

"Talcoran! Don't!"

"You need a bath, too, after all that exercise," he said gravely.

He pulled her about until she was straddling him. He was soapy, slippery, and he wanted her again.

"Elen." His mouth was only a breath away from hers. "How I have missed you," he whispered.

He moved, just a little. She moaned and closed her eyes.

Macbeth's homecoming feast went on for half the night. The banqueting hall was smoky with flaring torches and candles and damply burning logs. It was hot and noisy from all the people there.

Elen, in a fresh gown of moss-green wool trimmed in gold, watched Talcoran with Macbeth. The dignified, reserved man who stood by the king's chair engaged in quiet conversation was very different from the lover who had taken her so passionately a few hours ago, and who would, she had no doubt, possess her again as soon as they returned to their rooms.

They were all alike under their stiff silk or woolen garments and their smooth, polite faces. Every man of Macbeth's company, even the priests who had gone to Rome with him—for many of them were married—had surely lain with his woman that afternoon. Elen had herself spread fresh lavender-scented coverings on the queen's bed, and had smiled at Gruach's eager anticipation of her husband's return.

We hide it so well, she thought, but we all yearn for the same thing. Gruach, and I, and servants like Ava—what we want most is our men home safe and in our beds with us.

Talcoran came to her again when the feasting was finally done, and made love with her with the same urgency he had shown earlier. Afterward, they lay until past dawn, talking while the candles guttered low. He told her about Rome, about going with Macbeth to meet the Pope, and how Macbeth, riding through the great city, had scattered money to the poor like seed in springtime, calling it a joyful penance, and then had received from the Pope absolution for all his sins. She told him of Laggan, of the fine harvest recently gathered and his increasing wealth, and he said he was pleased and proud of her. And then they made love again, and he slept at last, his head on her breast.

Bruised, aching, but happily satisfied, Elen vowed to herself as she drifted toward sleep that she would never, never again think of any man but Talcoran, only him, her beloved husband . . . her love. . . .

20

Summer 1053.
Fife.

Fionna was very ill. She had borne a second daughter in mid-June, while she and Conal were at home in Fife. Confident of her prompt recovery, Conal returned to court a week later, expecting Fionna to follow him in early August. He received instead a weary servant, who arrived late one night, having ridden to Scone without stopping.

"The baby has died," a distraught Conal told Elen and Talcoran. "I can't understand from what my man says exactly what is wrong with Fionna. I can't go to her. Macbeth needs me at court just now. Elen, would you go to Fife in my stead?"

"Talcoran?" Elen looked at her husband for permission.

"We owe Fionna a great deal," he agreed. "I have no objection. When will you go?"

"Tomorrow. I'll leave Ava here to keep watch over the children while I'm gone, and take Briga with me, along with a chest of her herbs and potions. Perhaps she can help Fionna."

"That is what I had hoped for." Conal looked more cheerful after Elen's suggestion. "You needn't use your men-at-arms for this, Talcoran. I'll send two of my men along for Elen's protection on the way. She won't need more than that. Thanks to Macbeth, the roads are safe for travelers."

Castle Kennoway was situated on the coast of Fife, on a cliff overlooking the Firth of Forth. Conal kept a well-armed and always alert detachment of men there to guard it against the Norsemen who still sometimes attacked by sea. When Elen and Briga arrived, they found Fionna, a priest, thirteen-year-old Keith mac Conal, twelve-year-old Ewen, and Elen, whom Fionna had named for her friend, and who was now eleven.

"I am mighty glad to see you," Ciniod, the captain of the guard greeted Elen. "We have feared for my mistress's life. The priest is with her now."

Fionna's hot, damp chamber smelled of illness and unwashed linens.

"No wonder she's so sick," Briga said in exasperation. "I'll find a couple of serving women and we'll put clean linen on the bed and strew fresh herbs around to purify the air. Then I'll make a nice hot infusion for her to drink, and we'll wash her and comb her hair."

"Oh, no," the priest objected as Briga tore down the heavy strips of woolen cloth that had been fastened over the narrow windows. "You mustn't do that. You will let the air in. It will sicken her more."

"Nonsense," Briga said. "It is bright summer and the breeze is warm."

"My lady of Laggan, stop your servant," the priest implored. "I fear for this poor woman's life."

"We are here by order of both the king and the Thane of Fife," Elen said. "Briga knows what she is doing. I suggest that you leave. We are going to unclothe Fionna and bathe her.''

"Bathe her? Heaven protect us all!" The scandalized priest fled the room.

They worked over Fionna for the rest of the day and well into the evening. First they sponged her with herb-infused water, trying to cool the fever that racked her body. Then they forced her, sip by unwilling sip, to drink cups of steaming herbal brew, which Briga said would make Fionna sweat and thus dissipate the fever.

"There is little more you can do here, mistress," Briga said at last. "Why don't you try to sleep? I'll sit with her until morning."

Elen was too tired to object. She made her way to the chamber assigned to her, where she fell into a heavy, dreamless slumber.

Fionna was only a little better the next day. Elen and Briga took turns sitting with her and making her swallow Briga's herbal medicines and hot drinks. It was several days before they could be sure she would live.

"I have never seen a fever like that," Elen said.

"I have," Briga told her. "It happens too often after childbirth, and usually it kills. It is fortunate we arrived when we did.''

The bright weeks slipped away toward autumn while Fionna slowly recovered. Elen found Kennoway a peaceful place. She enjoyed walking along the cliffs, frequently with her namesake Elen, or with Ewen. Ciniod always sent a man-at-arms to attend her when she went out.

"You never know what dangers may come by sea," Conal's captain said darkly.

Elen was not overly concerned by Ciniod's worries. She was too happy breathing the sharp, salty air, watching the blue sea and the gulls circling above. Her heart was light. Fionna was getting better. Before long, Elen could return to Scone, where Talcoran and her children awaited her. In the meantime, each day was a new delight.

One day Fionna got out of bed. She took only a few steps before declaring she was dizzy and needed to lie down again, but each day after that she was able to walk farther. Within a week, she was sitting in the great hall. Her appetite had improved.

"Most assuredly, you will live," Briga pronounced. "You will not be completely well for some time, and you must be very careful to eat well and stay warm this coming winter, but I no longer fear for you."

"I do not know how to thank you," Fionna told her. "Or you, Elen. You came to me when I was in desperate need."

"We are friends," Elen said simply. "You have helped me in the past."

"I have some advice for you both," Briga said. "You are too old to have more children. You, mistress Elen, are twenty-nine next month, and you, lady, are thirty-two. You both have given your husbands sons. Do not risk your lives again. Let me provide an herbal potion for you that will prevent conception, and drink it regularly."

"Talcoran would never allow that," Elen protested.

"Aye, mistress, I remember well that after poor Aiden was born, your husband would not let you use it, but if you had, you would have saved yourself and him much grief."

"I cannot deny that."

"A man need not always know what his wife is doing," said Briga, eliciting laughter from both women.

Elen had seen Fionna safely into bed a few nights later, and was returning to the great hall.

She passed a chamber set aside for Conal mac
Duff, which no one else was allowed to use. He
kept the records of his estates in there, and some
gold, and the door was always locked.

Tonight, a bar of light showed under the door.

Elen stopped. Had Conal arrived in Fife un-
expectedly? If he had, she felt certain he would
have gone to Fionna at once. If not Conal, who else
would dare to use his room? Some thief? Should
she call Ciniod, and have him bring armed men to
check the room? Or perhaps it was Ciniod himself,
making certain all was well.

She pushed at the door. It swung silently
open. A candle sat on Conal's big, polished table,
where he wrote out his accounts. She could see
nothing more. She entered the room. It appeared
to be empty. Why was a candle burning in an
empty room?

She heard the door click shut behind her. She
froze. A gleaming dagger flashed before her eyes,
and an instant later its point pressed against her
throat.

"One sound," said a harsh whisper at her
back, "and you are dead."

She heard the man move, heard the bolt on the
door being closed. The knife at her throat did not
waver.

"It is your misfortune," the harsh whisper
said, "that you arrived before I locked that."

"I saw your light," she whispered, risking her
life to speak.

"I will remember that and be more careful the
next time." He moved, the knife at her throat
making her turn so that she looked directly into
the candle. Her eyes dazzled by its bright flame,
she could see nothing but a dark shape when he
stepped in front of her. The dagger shook, then
steadied.

"Dear God," the harsh whisper came again. "Why are you here?"

Something about the man, his great height perhaps, or the set of his broad shoulders, was oddly familiar. He wore a hooded cloak, the hood pulled up to hide his face. She strained to see his features.

"I know you," she whispered. "I'm sure I do."

"Were you anyone else, those words would mean your death."

"Who are you?"

"Will you promise me you'll not cry out?"

"I promise," Elen said, curiosity overcoming her fear. "Show me your face."

He kept the dagger at her throat. With his free hand he pushed back the hood.

"I can't see," she said. "Are you from court? No, I'd remember you if you were."

He moved closer to the light, still keeping the knife pointed at her, and now she saw him clearly.

Auburn curls, with a bit of silver at the temples. Deep lines radiating from bright blue eyes. A magnificently luxurious mustache. A once tender mouth grown older, harder. A square jaw with a cleft.

She must not faint. There was danger here, and she must keep her wits about her.

"Patric."

"Aye, it's me."

"What are you doing here?"

"I believe I asked you that first."

"Fionna was sick. I came to nurse her."

"Fionna. What's wrong with her? Where is she?"

Elen told him.

"Thank God for you and your nurse," he said.

"Now explain to me why you are here, Patric."

"I came to see my sister."

"Don't expect me to believe that, you lying traitor! You have no right to place your feet on Alban soil. You're plotting something, aren't you?"

He chuckled and raised an eyebrow, but the old, bright smile did not come.

"You have grown hard, Elen. This is not the sweet, shy maiden I left thirteen years ago."

"No, it is not. I have changed. It began when you deserted me. Traitor!" She hurled the word at him again, her voice rising with unleashed anger.

He caught the hair at the back of her head, pulling her face so close to his that she could see every line in it, and now the dagger was back at her throat, its point pricking into her tender skin.

"Be quiet!" he ordered. "Fionna's life depends on your silence. And your own life, too."

"Did Fionna know you were coming here?"

"She knew nothing." He glowered at her for a moment, then let her go with a savage push. She stumbled against the table, rocking the candle. She caught it and steadied it with shaking hands. A drop of tallow splashed onto her wrist, burning her. She gave a smothered cry, and rubbed at the spot, trying to ease the pain. Her chest was so constricted with fear and something else she dared not admit to, that she could hardly breathe.

"Where is Fionna?" Patric asked, still in the same harsh whisper.

"In her bedchamber. She is sleeping."

"I have to trust you, Elen. If you say one word about seeing me, you and Fionna and her children will all die."

"Will you do the deed yourself, traitor?" She regarded him with contempt. He was hard and cold and cruel. How could she ever have loved such a man?

"Not I," he said. "But there are others who

will not let you live if I am betrayed."

"It might be worth it, if they'll let me see you drawn and quartered before I die."

There was a surprised silence. When he broke it, there was a sad note in his voice.

"Do you hate me that much, Elen?"

"More!" she hissed at him.

"I'm sorry. I thought you understood. I must go now. I'll see Fionna and then I'll be away from here. I depend on your silence."

"Don't ever come back!" she whispered viciously.

He paused by the door, listening carefully before he slid open the bolt. He grinned at her, and for just a moment all the old boyish charm and confidence was there, tugging at her heart.

"Oh, but I will come back," he said, teasing her as he used to do. "Will you be waiting for me, love?"

He was gone.

"No," she moaned, still whispering, though the need for it was over. "No, no, no."

He had to be spying. He was surely in Alba to stir up trouble against Macbeth. Perhaps he was even planning to kill the king.

She ought to send a message to Talcoran, telling him about Patric. But was Patric alone, or did he really, as he had threatened, have companions—men who would intercept any messenger, then come and kill her and Fionna and the children? Patric had entered Kennoway Castle by some secret means, she was sure of that, and his companions would know the way, too, and would enter and kill them before Ciniod and his men could prevent it.

And if her messenger got safely to Scone and found Talcoran, what would happen then?

Talcoran would tell Macbeth, and then Conal, Fionna, and their children would all die anyway, for Macbeth would never believe Conal was unaware of Patric's presence in Alba, or uninvolved in whatever Patric was doing. Elen had heard Macbeth making sarcastic comments to Conal about his brother-in-law often enough to know that. Even she herself might not escape. Macbeth might think she had been helping Patric, because she had once loved him. And Talcoran, would he think she had betrayed him?

There was nothing she could do except follow Patric's orders and keep silent.

She tried to talk to Fionna the next morning, but got only one word out before Fionna put up a restraining hand.

"Say no word to me, nor to anyone else about this," Fionna said.

"How can you?" Elen exclaimed, disregarding Fionna's caution. "By allowing him here, you betray both your husband and your king, and put the lives of all your family in danger. How can you defend him?"

"I swear I didn't know he was coming." Fionna, still weak from her recent illness, burst into tears. "He is my brother, and I love him. I haven't seen him for five years."

"*Five years*? Do you mean you have done this before?" Elen was stunned by this revelation.

"We have met here only three times since Duncan's death. Patric comes by sea. There is an old, forgotten entrance into the castle through one of the caves in the cliff below, that he knows about. It is perfectly safe."

"It can't be safe. He is a condemned traitor. Does Conal know about this?"

"I think he suspected the last time, but he said nothing to me. Two of the servants told me he had asked odd questions about my actions. Conal knows how close Patric and I were and how unhappy I have been about his exile. I think he understood."

"More likely he did not want to know for sure,' Elen said. "Such knowledge could condemn both of you to death, and your children with you. You must never do this again, Fionna."

Fionna did not answer.

"Where has he gone?" Elen asked.

"I don't know. He didn't tell me."

Elen was uncertain whether Fionna spoke the truth or not. She began to regard her dear friend with new eyes.

Patric was wicked, a condemned man. Elen hated him. She was sure she never wanted to see him again. It was odd that as she went about the business of caring for Fionna and directing the management of Fionna's household, Elen's footsteps took her so often past that door Patric had lurked behind. The door remained unlocked. Elen knew that, for she had tried it several times. She wondered if Patric's secret entrance opened into that room.

Two nights after Patric's visit, she could contain her curiosity no longer. After everyone else had retired, she wrapped a shawl over her nightdress and crept along the passage from her room, the candle she carried flickering weakly in the gloomy darkness.

She found the door she sought, pushed it open, and entered. Holding the candle in one hand, she began to examine the stone walls, running her free hand along the cool, moist surfaces. She could find no evidence of a concealed door.

There were several wooden chests in the room, in which Conal stored his documents. They were all locked and were so heavy she could not move them to search behind or beneath them.

She put her candle on the table and stood looking about the room, bewildered. How had Patric entered?

"Are you waiting for me?" Patric leaned lazily against the now closed and bolted door.

She did not cry out. Something in her had known he would come—had, indeed, been waiting for him.

"I told you not to come back here," she said.

"I am leaving soon."

"How did you get in?"

"That is my secret. Did you think I walked through the walls, like a spirit? I always use the door, my love."

"Don't call me that."

"Why not, since that is what you are?" He rounded the table, approaching her. He was too near.

"You put your sister's life in danger by coming here," she said wildly, backing away from him.

"Only if you reveal my presence. You won't, will you, Elen?"

"It is my duty."

"I know about duty." His blue eyes rested hungrily on her. His hard face softened. "How beautiful you are. You are more lovely now than you were as a young girl."

One huge hand moved to caress her cheek. She pulled away another step.

"Elen, you loved me once. In the name of that love, keep my visit here a secret."

She could not speak. She shook her head and put out one hand as if to hold him off.

"Elen." He advanced again, trapping her against the edge of the table.

He was now so near that she could feel the

heat of his body. She was nearly overcome by the masculine scent of him that she could remember so well from those few passionate months of her youth, when all of life had been before them, before everything had been blighted and twisted by war and death. Standing this near to him, the years fled away, and she could almost believe she was sixteen again, and he was twenty.

She swayed toward him, pulled by remembered desire. One kiss, one embrace, and that desire would flare up anew, would consume them both. She could see the answering longing in those blue eyes that never left her face.

He reached out, and his large hands held her face, softly, gently, like some delicate flower that must not be bruised. She knew he would kiss her. Her trembling mouth eagerly awaited his touch.

He was dangerous. She had to protect herself from him, protect her marriage vows. She must be true to Talcoran. She closed her eyes against the sight of Patric, but his face was burned into her brain. She felt his forward motion, knew his lips were almost on hers.

"Talcoran," she whispered, "Talcoran."

Patric dropped his hands. She sensed him moving away from her.

"I beg your pardon, lady." His voice was soft, choked with emotion. "I forgot for a moment that you are not mine. You never were mine. Forgive me."

She drew a deep breath and steadied herself, then opened her eyes and looked at him.

"There is nothing to forgive," she said. "Nothing happened."

"No? I think you are wrong about that." For a moment his expression held the old teasing humor she remembered so well, then he became serious again. "Where is Fionna?"

"Sleeping in her bedchamber."

"Will you tell her I am here? I dare not walk freely about the castle. I was nearly caught the last time." As she began to protest, Patric stopped her. "I am leaving, Elen. I will not return to Alba until I come with Malcolm at the head of a victorious army. I would say farewell to my sister before I go."

Knowing Fionna's love for this man, Elen relented.

"Very well. Remain here. I'll send Fionna to you." She went to the door.

"Elen, wait." He did not move from his position across the room from her, but she felt as if he had taken her into his strong, warm arms. Her eyes filled with tears. "I can be found with Earl Siward in Northumbria. If ever anything happens, if you need help, send for me and I will come."

The tears trickled down her cheeks, but she paid them no heed. She kept her head high and spoke calmly.

"I am wife to a great nobleman, a man who is loyal to his king. My husband loves me, and I love him. How could I ever need help from an exiled traitor?"

"So was I loyal to my king, Elen. My rightful king."

She pretended she did not see the pain on his face.

"I hope I never see you again," she said, and left the room.

21

"Elen, you are so distant from me, even when we are together like this." Talcoran moved restlessly in the big bed. "You have been this way ever since you returned from Fife."

"Do I not please you?" Elen ran her fingers lightly along his arm and up to his shoulder. He was as firm-muscled and strong as he had been in his youth, and as vigorous in bed, but there was a sprinkling of grey in his thick black hair and his beard, and there were deep lines about his eyes. He pulled her back to him and kissed her again, a warm, satisfied kiss.

"You please me more every year," he said. "But sometimes I wonder if you are merely doing your duty."

"It is not only my duty to warm your bed," she assured him, "It is also a great pleasure. You are the best of lovers."

"When will you tell me about Fionna?" he asked.

She knew he felt her stiffen. She tried to sound natural.

"I have told you, my dearest husband. Fionna was terribly sick. Briga and I nursed her. She recovered. We returned to you. A few weeks later, Fionna returned to court."

"And now you scarcely speak to her. Gruach has noticed. Even Conal has mentioned it to me. You were like sisters. Now you are more like strangers."

"It is a woman's thing. It will pass."

"I have never known you and Fionna to quarrel before," Talcoran persisted. When he got no response from Elen, he returned to his original query. "I want to know what Fionna has to do with the way you treat me. You are no longer truly mine."

"But I am." She began to fondle him. Perhaps if they made love again, that would distract him from such a dangerous subject. "I am all yours. I love you. I do. I love you so much. My darling. My dear husband."

He responded as she wanted him to do, and a few moments later he entered her, caught up in his intense need for her that never seemed to diminish.

"I love you," he whispered later, "And I know you are faithful, but you are worried and you are keeping something from me. One day I will discover what it is."

Talcoran began to watch her carefully. He was even more observant when Fionna was present. Conal noticed.

"It is only something between women," he said to Talcoran, but the once warm friendship between the two men now also showed strain.

Elen was unaware of the change, nor did she notice that she and Talcoran made love less and less often. Her thoughts were elsewhere. Gruach chided her for absentmindedness, and her children teased her that they had to speak to her twice before she answered a question.

She was possessed by a feeling of foreboding. Patric's visit to Alba had had some purpose other than a meeting with his sister. That purpose would have a result, though what it might be, Elen could not imagine. All seemed perfectly normal, Alba was peaceful, Macbeth was secure on his throne, yet Elen waited tensely. Something would happen.

"We will have war again," Macbeth said. "I have written to Frankland, to hire Norman mercenaries. We will need more men than Alba can supply to fight the huge army the English king is assembling for Earl Siward."

They were in a reception room of the royal quarters. Elen and Fionna were in attendance on Gruach, and the room was crowded with Macbeth's nobles and their ladies. Lulach and Gertha were present. Both had greeted Elen with a friendly kiss.

"War again," Lulach sighed to Elen. "Why can't they ever do anything but fight when there is a disagreement?"

"This war is being forced on us," Elen said, annoyed at Lulach's attitude. "It is for your sake as much as anyone's, my lord. It is your inheritance that is at stake here."

"We must assemble the largest army possible," urged one noble, "and destroy this blasted Siward once and for all. If we do not, he will continue to invade us regularly."

"I agree," Macbeth replied. "Let us be done with the English menace so that we can continue our lives in peace."

"And yet," Conal objected, "we might make a treaty with Siward as you once did with Thorfinn. Perhaps you could give him some small portion of land for Malcolm to rule. If you would permit

Malcolm to become a noble of Alba, Siward might be pacified. If Siward's army marches on Alba there will be terrible bloodshed and devastation wherever it passes. We could save ourselves much misery by avoiding warfare altogether."

"Aye, that's right," agreed a few nobles, mostly those whose lands lay in the probable path of Siward's army. "Conal is right, my lord."

"No, no," a larger group of men protested. "Siward will not negotiate. He wants to put his nephew on the throne of Alba. Let us fight. We will make an end of Siward now, before he grows even stronger."

Macbeth laughed, throwing back his golden lion's head to let the rich sound pour out.

"Your lands are safe enough, Conal," he said, still laughing. "Surely you don't fear Siward and that stripling Malcolm will unseat you from Fife?"

"My lord, I fear for this land of ours, and for our wives and children."

"I can't believe you have become a coward, Conal." Macbeth's face suddenly darkened with anger. "Have you been suborned by Malcolm's wealthy English relatives? Or perhaps by your traitorous brother-in-law? Are you tainted with his stench? Would you like to see Malcolm inherit Lulach's place when I am gone? Is that it?"

"I only make a suggestion for us to consider," Conal replied calmly. "You have always been willing to listen to other men's ideas, my lord."

Elen, hearing Macbeth's accusations, felt her heart nearly stop. She stole a glance at Fionna, who looked unusually pale, with her lips pressed tightly together. Did Macbeth know that Patric had visited Alba and had stopped at Kennoway to see Fionna? It was whispered that Macbeth knew everything that happened in his kingdom. Had one of Fionna's people seen and reported Patric's presence? What if Talcoran learned that she, too, had met with Patric? Would he ever forgive her? Consorting with traitors was treasonous activity, punishable by a hideous death. Elen felt the blood drain from her face at the horrible thought.

"Are you sick?" Gruach's hands steadied her, and her sharp voice brought Elen back to reality. Lulach also came quickly to her side, to lend her his supporting arm.

"Elen?" Talcoran started toward her, a worried look on his face.

"It's nothing. I'm fine now," Elen assured them all.

"Are you with child again, cousin?" laughed Macbeth, his good humor restored by this diversion. "With your attentive husband, it is not unlikely." He paused suggestively.

"I—I'm not sure, my lord."

The king chuckled and turned back to his men, forgetting her. Elen saw Talcoran staring at her. He knew well enough she was not with child, for she had refused him the last two nights, pleading womanly indisposition. She lowered her eyes under her husband's dark, thoughtful gaze.

"Why does he do it?" Elen demanded. "Every time Macbeth and Conal are in the same room lately, Macbeth questions the poor man as if he were on trial. It's so unfair. You and I both know Conal is loyal to Macbeth. Macbeth should know it too, after so many years."

"But Conal's brother-in-law was not loyal," Talcoran answered her.

"How ironic," Elen murmured.

"What is?"

She could not tell him. She was sure Conal knew nothing of Patric's most recent journey to Alba, which she was now certain had something to

do with Siward's invasion plans, and which was
the most probable cause of Macbeth's sudden
enmity toward Conal.

"Elen, do you know something? Tell me." Talcoran shook her, frowning.

She could not meet his eyes. Guilt over the
secret she had kept from him for so many months
welled up, producing anger. She struck at Talcoran's hands, and pushed him away.

"I know nothing."

"My dear love, I, too, am unhappy about this
state of affairs. I am torn in two by it. Conal has
been my friend for years, yet so has Macbeth.
Elen, I feel certain you are hiding something from
me. Tell me what it is and let me help you."

"I cannot. Just as men sometimes have
divided loyalties, so have women."

"Your first loyalty should be to me."

It was true. He needed her love and her whole-
hearted loyalty. It was as essential to him as his
own loyalty to Macbeth, from whom he had had all
his rank and riches, and whom he would follow to
the end of life, always faithful. He would be
faithful in the same way to Elen, if only she would
talk to him, tell him what was troubling her. She
would not. She only put her arms around him and
laid her head on his shoulder and held him tightly.

They made a strange kind of peace, leaving
their differences unresolved, and after they had
agreed to quarrel no more they made love, and it
was beautiful and inexpressibly sad, and when
Elen slept at last, Talcoran lay beside her, longing
silently for the honesty and trust they had lost.

Macbeth's quarrel with Conal mac Duff
became worse. Macbeth would not leave it alone,
but kept picking at Conal's pride with a tactless-
ness unusual in him.

Macbeth and a party of his friends, including Conal and Talcoran, rode out to hunt, taking a brief respite from the plans for war that now occupied most of every day. A short distance from the palace their way was blocked by a team of oxen struggling mightily to pull a heavily loaded cart up a hill. The royal party rode around the lumbering team. Macbeth paused, watching it.

"Do you need help?" he asked the driver.

"No, my lord. I'll do right well, thank ye." The man cracked his whip smartly over the animal's backs.

"A handy thing, a whip," Macbeth said cheerfully. "I have an idea. Let's harness Conal in place of the oxen, and see if he can do the job. I'd like to see you use the whip on him. What do you say, Conal?"

There was an astonished silence before Macbeth, laughing merrily, dug his spurs into his horse's flanks and rode on. His men trailed after him, watching each other with embarrassed expressions. Talcoran, lingering behind the others, looked at Conal with raised brows.

"I'll not go on," Conal said. "That was one insult too many. It grows too dangerous here. He will never forgive me for being Patric's brother-in-law, nor believe I have had no contact with Patric."

"What will you do?"

"I'll go home to Fife and stay there. Fionna and I will be gone before you return this evening. I'll not go into battle for a man who thinks I'm a traitor. I'd have to guard my back as well as my face."

"Farewell." Talcoran put out his hand, and Conal took it.

"Goodby, my friend. We may not meet again. I am no traitor."

"I know that, else I would not take your hand. Good luck to you." Talcoran pulled his horse around and galloped after Macbeth.

Talcoran recounted the story to Elen that evening.

"Why does Macbeth treat him so?" Elen cried.

"Because Patric mac Keith has been seen in Alba." Talcoran's dark eyes impaled Elen on her own guilt. "Macbeth believes Conal has met with Patric."

"Has he proof of that?" Elen's voice shook.

"No, but Conal's hasty departure from court has convinced Macbeth that Conal is in league with Patric and Siward. We are riding after him at dawn." Talcoran's face was pale under his tan.

"Dear God, help him and Fionna," Elen breathed. She put her arms around him. They clung to each other, knowing what would happen to Conal and his family were Macbeth to prove him guilty of treason.

The troop of men who rode into Fife with Macbeth returned two weeks later.

"Your friend Fionna is a remarkable woman," Talcoran said, unbuckling his sword belt. "Briga, bring me some ale. Ava, I'll want a hot bath."

"Is Drust safe?" Ava asked.

"Aye, wench, he's seeing to the horses and equipment. I have no doubt he'll find you as soon as he's finished. Now, fetch my water."

"Talcoran, tell me what happened," Elen demanded. She waited anxiously while he downed half a tankard of ale at a gulp.

"That's good. It was a thirsty ride. Fill it again, Briga. I'm not teasing you, love," he said to Elen. "I just need a while to collect my thoughts.

So much has happened. Help me off with my boots."

Talcoran flung himself into his chair and stuck out one foot.

"Do you know what that wench Fionna did?"

"I would very much like to hear," Elen said impatiently. She knelt and tugged at Talcoran's boot.

"She shut up her castle, tight as a wineskin, and kept us waiting outside the gates for half a day. She would not even allow Macbeth's unarmed messengers inside.

"Then at evening she appeared on the walls. What a picture she made, with her red-gold hair and her bright green cloak blowing in the breeze. For such a little woman she looked right tall and royal that day. An admirable sight. She has courage." Talcoran paused to sip at his ale.

"But where was Conal?" Elen asked. "Wasn't he with her?"

"No." Talcoran laughed, remembering. "She was alone except for the captain of the guard."

"Ciniod," Briga said softly, refilling his cup as she listened.

"Aye, Ciniod. Fionna stood there on Kennoway's wall, her captain at her back, looking down on us like some fierce warrior woman out of the old legends. Macbeth demanded that she open the castle gates to us, and she refused. 'Not yet, my lord,' she said, and laughed at him."

"Laughed at Macbeth?" Elen repeated in wonder. "Only Fionna would dare do that. What did Macbeth reply?"

"He ordered Conal to come forth and meet with him. At just that moment a soldier ran up to Fionna and said something to her. We could hear her laughing.

"Macbeth called up to her again. 'You're mighty gay,' he said, 'For a woman with a traitor's heart and a traitor husband.'

" 'We are neither of us traitors,' Fionna shouted down to him. 'We were your loyal subjects until you drove us away by your mistrust and your insults.' "

"That was brave of her." Briga, like Elen, had been listening breathlessly to this story. "What happened next, my lord?"

"Macbeth lost his temper," Talcoran told them. "He roared in a mighty voice, 'Send out your husband, lady, or by God, I'll tear your castle apart stone by stone until I find him!'

" 'You will not find Conal mac Duff in Kennoway, Macbeth,' Fionna told him. 'While I have kept you talking here, he has escaped through a secret passage to a cave in the cliff. Do you see that little sail, far out at sea? There are my husband and our sons, fled safely to England. You yourself have driven them to Malcolm and Siward.'

"I have never seen Macbeth so angry," Talcoran went on. "We stormed the castle that very hour, battered down the gates, and took it. Ciniod, the captain of the guard, was one of the first to be killed, and after he was dead, the others had little heart for fighting. It was only a small garrison, and we outnumbered them by a hundred or more. They surrendered."

"What of Fionna and little Elen? How could Conal leave them alone like that?" In her concern, Elen could hardly frame the words.

"There was only room for three in the boat, and Fionna insisted the men go. She told them Macbeth would be merciful to a woman. I'm not sure she was right about that," Talcoran said. "So far, Fionna and her daughter are both alive and unharmed. But Kennoway Castle is no more. We camped nearby while Macbeth had it razed to the ground. He forced Fionna and young Elen to stand there, day after day, and watch it done.''

"He is a cruel king!" said Elen angrily. That lovely spot in Fife, where she had walked listening to the sea's wild song, and the gulls' crying, gone. It was hard to comprehend. "Cruel," she said again.

"Not at all," Talcoran insisted. "It was what they deserved for defying Macbeth and making him look foolish. It is not wise to play tricks on kings."

"What will happen to Fionna now?"

"There were those who advised that she and little Elen be put to death at once. There were others who did not agree."

"And which were you, Talcoran?"

"I remember when our son Colin was born," Talcoran answered. "When our Grania was born, Fionna was with you then, too."

"You don't believe this charge of treachery against them, do you?"

"No, I do not." Talcoran had an oddly mischievous look on his dark face. "Do you know, wife, I am homesick to see Laggan once more before I ride off to war. Shall we go tomorrow?"

"Laggan?" Elen was dumbfounded at this suggestion. "What has Laggan got to do with Conal mac Duff and his wife?"

"There is no time to explain now. We must join Macbeth in his chambers shortly, and I need a bath. Where is Ava with my hot water?"

Elen and Talcoran dined privately with Macbeth and Gruach. Macbeth was pleased with the success of his expedition into Fife, even though his principal quarry had escaped. He had confiscated all of Fife. Conal's title of Thane was now empty.

"I'll find someone to bestow it on once we have vanquished Siward," Macbeth said confidently. He raised his golden cup to toast Talcoran. "You haven proven your loyalty once again, though Conal mac Duff was your friend."

"I have considered your suggestion for disposition of Conal's wife and daughter," Macbeth went on. "You are correct, my friend, when you say living hostages will be more useful against Conal than a dead wife he would want to avenge. I will not harm them, but I want them confined a safe distance from Fife, so they cannot be rescued."

Macbeth now turned to Elen.

"I am curious, cousin. Did Fionna say something to you when you visited her last August? Did you suspect her loyalty and her husband's? Is that why you broke off your friendship with her so abruptly?"

Elen, taken aback, answered honestly and without thinking.

"I have never heard either Fionna or Conal say one word in opposition to you, my lord. I think you have been mistaken about them."

Macbeth regarded her coldly.

"Then what did you quarrel about?" When Elen hesitated, he barked, "Must I remind you that I am your king? Answer me, woman, and if you value your life and the lives of your husband and children, answer me honestly!"

"Will you become a tyrant, cousin?"

"If that is what is necessary to retain my throne against Malcolm and Siward, then yes, I will! You know something of what went on in that household at Fife, and I demand to know what it is."

In the face of Macbeth's rage, Elen knew

absolute terror. Her teeth began to chatter with a sudden chill. She saw Talcoran looking at her with unreadable eyes.

"Well?" shouted Macbeth.

"We quarreled about her brother," Elen quavered.

"Who?" Macbeth's anger seemed to grow at this answer.

"About Patric of Bute," Elen said, her voice a little stronger. "I was betrothed to him once."

"I remember." Macbeth's cold gaze was fastened on her face. "What about that damned traitor?"

"That's just it," Elen said, seeing her way out of the abyss that for an instant had yawned before her, and seizing it. "I said the same thing, that Patric was a traitor. Fionna took offense. She reminded me that whatever Patric had done, he was still her brother, and we quarreled about that."

"Is that all?" Macbeth's blue eyes narrowed, watching her closely.

"That is all, my lord. I swear it. I saw no sign that she approved of his treachery, only that she was deeply hurt and unhappy about it, and that she feared for his life, as any sister would."

"And you, Elen. You once loved the traitor Patric. How do you feel about him?"

It was a question she could not answer, not even in her own mind.

"Well, cousin?" This time Macbeth's voice was soft, almost silky in quality. Elen knew this was the most dangerous question of all, and she must answer it wisely.

As she hesitated, Talcoran made a motion with one hand.

"My lord—" he began. Macbeth interrupted him.

"Be still, my friend. You are too kind to your wife. You love her too much, you protect her too carefully. Let Elen answer for herself."

"The same could be said of you, my lord," Elen said pertly, hoping to throw him off guard. "You are also known to hold your wife dear."

Her response had no effect on her inquisitor, but it brought a surprised laugh from Gruach, who had been uncharacteristically quiet during Macbeth's questioning.

"Answer the question," Macbeth said softly.

By now Elen had had a chance to think and to gather her wits together.

"I feel pity," she replied. "The same pity I would feel for a condemned man who has lost everything."

"The condemned man has repented and been shriven of his sins before he dies," Macbeth told her. "Patric of Bute has never repented."

"But he has lost everything, including me and my dowry," Elen reminded him. "I am right glad to be the wife of my lord Talcoran, and we are both—*both*"—she emphasized that again—"completely loyal to you and grateful to you for the gifts and honors you have bestowed on us, dear cousin."

"I told you so," Gruach said softly.

"Good." Macbeth let out a long breath. "That is what I needed to hear, that neither your former friendship for Fionna nor the affection you once had for her brother will influence your duty to me. Tomorrow I will give Fionna and her daughter into Talcoran's custody. Take her to Laggan and keep her secure there. See that she has no communication with England. When Talcoran returns to me, for I need him by my side when I go into battle against Siward, then you, Elen, must guard Fionna for me. Will you do this?"

Elen bowed before her king and cousin.

"I will, my lord, to the best of my ability."

"Did you know Patric was in Alba?" Talcoran watched her from across their bedchamber as he spoke.

"Dear husband, you have been away for several weeks, and I have missed you. Will you not come to bed?" Elen sat down on the foot of their bed and looked invitingly at the angry man who now approached her.

"Answer me, woman."

"I thought I had answered everything when Macbeth questioned me earlier tonight." She caught his hand and pulled him down to sit beside her. "Don't you trust me?"

"Why is it that whenever Patric mac Keith is mentioned you distract me by coaxing me into bed?"

"Perhaps it is because I find him a disagreeable subject of conversation." Elen placed her husband's hand on her breast. "Isn't this more pleasant?"

"You know it is." Talcoran bent his head to kiss the soft flesh that rounded the surface of her nightdress. She caught at him and held him close.

"I have been away too long," Talcoran whispered as he pushed her down onto the bed.

22

Summer 1054 to Spring 1055.

Talcoran stayed at Laggan only a few days before riding southward to rejoin Macbeth.

"Let me go with you, father," Colin mac Talcoran begged. "I'm strong, and you know how good I am with my sword."

"Not this time," Talcoran said. "Remain here and protect the women."

"Women," Colin scoffed, with all the fine scorn of a thirteen-year-old male.

"Two of those women are royal prisoners," Talcoran reminded him. "Macbeth and I both are depending upon you to guard them well."

"Take care, Elen." Talcoran kissed her cheek and mounted his horse, a descendant of the great, prancing brute he had ridden when first she knew him. "I'll send messengers regularly. You will be well informed."

She watched his back as he rode away. He had loved her well the night before. Her body was pleasantly satisfied, but a doubt lurked in her mind. She feared he no longer trusted her as completely as he once had done.

Dear Lord, she prayed, let him return safely

and I'll never give him cause to wonder about me again.

Elen settled down to her usual summer duties at Laggan, and to keeping a watchful eye on Fionna, who showed no interest in escape, but instead whiled away the time by helping Elen as if they were still on the friendliest of terms.

Talcoran's messengers came regularly with news. Earl Siward had crossed the border into Alba and was steadily fighting his way northward. The Norman mercenaries Macbeth had requested from his ally, the King of the Franks, had arrived. They were a rough lot, but eager for battle. Gruach had been ill, with a high fever and a cough, but was somewhat better now, though the cough remained. She had told Talcoran that she sorely missed Elen, and even Fionna. Lulach sent greetings to Elen.

July was over and August had begun. There were no messengers for several days, and then one morning a dust-streaked rider appeared with a letter dictated by Talcoran. Colin and little Grania, Fionna and her daughter Elen, Briga and Ava, and the aged Dougal clustered around Elen as she broke the seal and opened the parchment.

"What does it say?" Colin asked breathlessly.

Elen read quickly.

"There was a battle on July twenty-seventh," she reported.

"And? And?" Colin was nearly dancing in his excitement. "What else, mother?"

Elen raised stricken eyes from the pages in her hands.

"Macbeth has sustained a major defeat," she said, and saw their faces fall. She went on reading. "Siward attacked by land, and at the same time sent his warships into the Firth of Tay to make a second assault from the sea. Talcoran says our men fought bravely, even the mercenaries. It was a terrible, bloody battle. Both sides took heavy losses. Earl Siward's elder son Osbeorn and his nephew Siward were both killed, along with many of his followers."

Fionna gasped, a trembling hand clutched to her throat at this news, and Elen knew she feared for her husband and brother.

" 'Although Siward and Malcolm won this time, it will do them little good, for many of their best men are gone,' " Elen read. " 'Malcolm has been re-established as King of Cumbria, and has secured to himself most of Alba south of the River Tay. He now makes his headquarters at Dunedin, on the Firth of Forth.' "

"I should have been there," Colin complained.

"Thank God you were not," his mother told him.

"What of Macbeth?" Briga asked.

"Talcoran says he has retreated northward. The court is now at Aberdeen. Not one noble or soldier went over to Siward's side. How proud Macbeth must be of that."

A second letter arrived two days later, this one for Fionna. Talcoran sent word that he had learned both Conal and Patric were unharmed.

"What a good man Talcoran is," Fionna said. "How kind of him to write to me."

Talcoran himself appeared in late September.

"Siward has withdrawn to the south," he said. "There are rumors he is ill. There will be no more fighting for a while. We are safe enough in the north. Macbeth is gathering a new army to reconquer southern Alba. I will take more of our men with me when I leave."

"Take me, too, father." Colin made his usual plea.

"Stay here this winter, my son. Perhaps next spring you may join me."

Talcoran made love to Elen two or three times each night of the week he spent at Laggan. It was as if he could not get enough of her, or perhaps he needed that assurance of her love for him. She knew that, however much he loved her, he did not entirely trust her, and her heart ached at the knowledge.

Winter that year was unusually cold and snowy. Drifts piled up in the mountain passes in November, so deep that Laggan would be isolated until the spring thaws. With Talcoran at court and no news of Macbeth's fortunes or Siward's activities coming to them, the folk at Laggan Castle drew in upon themselves.

Shortly after Christmas the usual minor winter illnesses began. Elen and Briga doled out medicines from the stillroom. Except for the bad weather, it seemed an ordinary winter until Dougal became sick. Elen tended her late father's aged servant with loving care, but on the third day he died.

"There was nothing more we could have done," Briga comforted her. "He was too old and weak to fight the illness."

"Let us hope the young are stronger." Fionna had joined them by the fire in the great hall. "My Elen is feverish."

By the next day, seven-year-old Grania was sick, too, and the day after that Colin took to his bed. Ava and two of the kitchen wenches were next. Each day, more members of the household fell ill. The last lingering constraint between Elen and Fionna disappeared as they worked together with Briga to nurse the sick. They were no longer prisoner and keeper, but the friends they had always been at heart.

Fionna's twelve-year-old daughter Elen died. Her grown-up namesake and godmother held Fionna in her arms as the two women mingled their tears. The following night Grania coughed her life away, and it was Fionna who held a grieving Elen.

"I have only one child left!" Elen cried. "If Colin dies, too, what will I do?"

"I think he will live," Briga said. "He is stronger than the girls were, and he seems to be a little better today."

"Poor Fionna. I'm sorry," Elen said, her arms about Fionna's waist, her head on her friend's shoulder. "You've lost a daughter, too, and you don't even know where your boys are. Oh, Grania, Grania." Elen burst into tears again.

In those bitter days, Elen's only happiness was that Colin was slowly getting better. He had lost a great deal of weight, his thinness bringing out more obviously than ever his resemblance to his mother. His midnight-blue eyes were ringed by dark shadows, his youthful cheeks were hollow. Briga and Elen continually plied him with treats from the kitchen, hoping to hasten his recovery and to add some flesh to his too-slender frame.

By the time the sickness had run its course, they had lost one of the kitchen wenches, two other servants, and a man-at-arms. Ava survived in a weakened state. Elen made Nechtan, one of Talcoran's Pictish men-at-arms, her new captain of the household guard to take Dougal's place.

After the snow had melted in the spring, Talcoran returned to Laggan. He said nothing when told of Grania's death, but Elen saw his mouth twist into a hard, bitter line. The daughter she had borne him when he had expected another son had become his special joy and delight, a child of laughter and sunshine not the least intimidated by her father's stern reserve, who climbed over him, teasing and cajoling and loving him. Talcoran wept no tears for his daughter, but that night he came to their bed and took Elen with a cold, savage fury, as though he were punishing her for the loss of Grania. And he still mistrusted her.

"You have believed nothing I've said since that night Macbeth questioned me," Elen accused him. "You are unfair to me, Talcoran."

"Macbeth may have believed your story, lady, but I do not. I know you too well. Something else happened while you were in Fife. Tell me what it is, so I can trust you again."

She could not do it. If he knew her, she knew him, too, and knew he would tell Macbeth that she and Fionna had both spoken with Patric. It would mean their lives, for after Siward's invasion of the summer past, Macbeth would never accept their explanations that the meetings were innocent. Talcoran might be punished by death, too, since he was responsible for his wife's actions, and Colin's future, if he were allowed to live, would be bleak. No, whatever the cost to her marriage, she could not tell Talcoran what he wanted to know. She had to protect him and their son.

Siward the Strong, Earl of Northumbria, was dying. His nephew, Malcolm mac Duncan, was in Dunedin, but Patric mac Keith had come to York in the spring of 1055, at Siward's summons, to bid him farewell.

"You will stay with Malcolm," Siward said, attempting to heave himself up in bed. "When I am buried, return to him."

"As I promised his father, so I promise you. I will remain with Malcolm until he is King of Alba."

"Soon. It shall be soon." Siward gave way to a fit of coughing.

"We must be patient, my lord, until the time is right. We misjudged the Scots. They remain faithful to Macbeth, as we now know to our cost."

"You always council patience," Siward said irritably. "Have you never in your life been rash and impetuous?"

"Often, when I was young, but the years have taught me to wait. Time is on Malcolm's side, my lord. He is only twenty-four. Macbeth is fifty this year, and Lulach, his heir, is weak."

"Time," Siward huffed, "Is what I have no more of, my friend. How shameful it is that I could not have died in one of my battles. But I have lived on, to die at last in my bed, like a cow in its stall." He struggled to sit up.

"I will not have it," he cried. "I will meet death as a warrior should. You, there, aid me." He motioned to an attendant, then began to gasp and choke.

"My lord, you should rest," Patric cautioned.

"Time enough to rest when I am in my grave. Help me to stand. Help me, I say!"

The old note of command was back in his voice. Siward's attendants dragged him to his feet. He flung his right arm over Patric's shoulder to keep himself erect.

"Bring me my armor," Siward ordered. "Put it on me."

With Patric supporting him, the attendants buckled on Siward's breast plate and then the heavy leather belt with his huge broadsword.

"My helmet and shield." Siward swayed alarmingly, but Patric held him upright while his helmet was placed on his head. Siward took his heavy shield upon his left arm.

"Give me my axe," he said, and a servant

handed him his gilded battleaxe. He let go of
Patric's shoulder to take the axe in his right hand.

"Now stand back," Siward commanded. "This
battle I must fight alone."

The men in Siward's chamber backed away
from him. Patric was near to tears with
admiration as the mighty warrior stood alone.
Siward's once-strong arm lifted his huge battleaxe
with great effort. Higher and higher it rose.

"Ahhh—!" With a loud cry, Macbeth's
implacable enemy, the great Earl of Northumbria,
fell dead.

Patric rode from York to Dunedin as soon as
Siward had been buried. He knew there would be
conflict over the succession to Siward's rich
earldom. He was glad to be away from it.
Northumbria was no longer his concern. Malcolm
was.

He had time to think as his horse galloped
northward on the road the ancient Romans had
built when they ruled Britain. At first his thoughts
wee mostly of Malcolm. The spoiled, savage little
boy Patric had first met at Duncan's court had
grown into a pleasure-seeking, quarrelsome
warrior who wenched and fought and drank even
harder than his roughest soldiers did. At twenty-
four, Malcolm was a hostile, immature man.

When Patric, frustrated and angered beyond
endurance by some wild escapade of Malcolm's,
had expressed doubt that he was worth the
sacrifices necessary to put him on the throne of
Alba, Siward had assured him that heavy responsibility would steady Malcolm. Worse men had
proven themselves great leaders when their time
came.

He devoutly hoped Siward had been correct
in his assessment of Malcolm's character. Patric

had lost much of his youthful idealism during the hard years of exile. He wanted to believe Malcolm was worth the price he himself had had to pay to keep his promise to Malcolm's father.

Elen. In the two years since he had seen her in Fife, she had been often in his thoughts. Too often. He could see her still, if he closed his eyes, her raven-black hair wound about her head and fastened with gold pins, her pale skin luminous in the candlelight. He could hear her voice, filled with contempt for him.

Whatever she thought of him, he loved her, would always love her. It was because of her that he had never married. He had said it was because a homeless, penniless exile needed no wife or heirs. His only possessions were his horse and his clothes. Everything else he got he spent in Malcolm's cause. What woman would want such a life? Siward had once called him mad, and Patric had laughed and said perhaps he was. In his heart he knew it was because he wanted only Elen. There had been women aplenty, when he needed them to satisfy his healthy lust, but he had cared for none of them.

He came at last to the wall the Romans had built to keep out the warlike northern tribes and rode past it with scarcely a glance. He stopped for a night at a filthy inn, and in the morning, after breaking his fast with stale bread and dry cheese and sour ale, he rode on, into the hills of southern Alba. It was Malcolm's land now.

It was right that the eldest son of a king should succeed his father. Once this rule was established, Patric believed there would be an end to the assassinations and treachery that had plagued Alba for generations under the old Law of Tanistry.

It was only a matter of time until Malcolm

was installed at Scone as king of all Alba. When that happened, when Patric had finally discharged his oath to King Duncan, he would be free to live his own life. He did not know what he would do then. He wanted to be sure Fionna, his only blood kin, was reunited with her beloved Conal. He could protect Elen, and her lands and family. Malcolm owed him much, and Patric would have no hesitation about requesting a favor from him. Elen would be safe to live at Laggan with her husband, that brave and honorable Talcoran to whom she was so loyal.

And then what? Perhaps he would be killed in battle and all his worries ended. That, thought Patric as he rode through the gates of Dunedin, might well be the simplest solution of all.

23

Early June to August 10 1057.

Thorfinn the Mighty had died.

"Malcolm knows Macbeth has lost a great ally," Talcoran said. "That is why he has chosen this time to invade again. I will leave Laggan the day after tomorrow, to join Macbeth and his army."

"Father, you must let me go with you this time. I'm sixteen years old now. You can't refuse me again." Colin mac Talcoran stood tall and slender before his father, the dark blue eyes that were so like Elen's shining with youthful enthusiasm.

"Yes," Talcoran said, nodding agreement. "You will be my aide. You and Drust."

"No," Elen protested. "Talcoran, he is our only child. Let him stay here with me."

"Will you coddle him and make him a weakling, as Gruach has done to Lulach all these years? My son will be an honest warrior like his father."

"Please. If anything were to happen to him, I'd die. Talcoran, I beg you."

"Nothing will happen to me." Colin laughed. "Mother, you worry too much."

"Talcoran—"

"Be done with this whimpering, woman. Would you unman him? Where's your spirit?"

"Lost with my other children. You and he are all I have."

They quarreled again that evening.

"You are a poor mother," he snarled at her. "You would make your son a coward. He goes with me, and that's the end of it."

He did not come to their bed on his last night at home, but sat drinking in the great hall with his men. When she would have apologized and made peace with him the next day before he left, he stormed at her, making her angry again.

"Guard Laggan well until I return," he said. "And keep a close watch on Fionna. It is possible that if Malcolm's army reaches far enough north, Conal will try to rescue her. See that you have a care for my honor if you are forced to deal with him."

He mounted his horse and rode off without kissing her good-bye. Colin gave her a hasty peck on the cheek and followed his father.

Elen retained her anger for only a day before it became remorse. She would make everything up to Talcoran when he came home. After Malcolm was finally defeated she could rid herself of the guilt of years and tell Talcoran what she had kept from him for so long, that she had once met Patric at Conal's home in Fife. He would be angry with her at first, but then he would understand, and he would trust her once more. They would be happy again, safe at Laggan, together.

The messenger tracked mud and rain water across the stone floor of the great hall.

"You are not from my Lord Talcoran," Elen said, taking the letter from his hands.

"No, lady, I am sent by the king."

"More instructions about the lady Fionna, no doubt. There is a pitcher of ale on the table. Help yourself." Elen broke the wax seal and began to read. There was silence except for the gurgle of pouring liquid as the messenger filled a cup.

"*No!*"

Elen's shriek echoed through the hall. The messenger started and dropped his cup of ale. Fionna and Briga ran from the stillroom, Ava nearly flew down the stone steps from Elen's bedchamber, Nechtan appeared with three men-at-arms.

Elen lay senseless on the floor, a piece of parchment beside her outstretched hand.

"Seize that man!" Nechtan ordered. "If you have harmed my mistress, you will die most painfully."

Briga hurried to Elen's inert form and knelt to touch her with skillful hands.

"She has fainted," Briga said, glaring at the messenger. "What did you do to her?"

"It wasn't the man. It was the letter." Fionna had picked up the crumpled parchment and begun to read it. She cried out in pain.

"What is that cursed thing?" growled Nechtan, who could not read and had a superstitious dread of the written word.

"It is from Macbeth. Talcoran has been slain in battle, and his son, fighting bravely at his father's side, was also killed. Talcoran's aide, Drust, was sorely wounded trying to save them, but he will live. The retreat by Macbeth's army was so rapid that their dead had to be left behind, to be buried at Malcolm's mercy."

Fionna's face was wet with tears. She put a comforting arm around Ava, who was weeping uncontrollably. "Dear Talcoran. Our dear, honest friend."

On the cold stone floor, Elen moaned and turned her head, eyelids fluttering. Fionna took charge.

"Nechtan, have your men carry your mistress to her bedchamber. Ava, attend to her. See that she's kept warm. Briga, make up your strongest soothing potion. Elen will need it. Someone send for the priest. Elen will want prayers said for both men's souls, and for Drust's recovery, too."

"Lady, you are a prisoner here," Nechtan challenged her. "You will be locked in your room until we have orders from the king about you."

"Don't you dare!" Briga inserted herself between Nechtan and Fionna. "This lady may be a prisoner, but she is a friend to our mistress. We will follow her orders until our own lady regains her senses. If you are overly harsh with her, I can guarantee you will be punished for it."

Nechtan's eyes fell before Briga's determined fierceness. He motioned to his men to lift Elen and take her upstairs.

"Thank you, Briga," Fionna said. "Once again you have served your mistress well. Ava, stop that crying and go undress your lady and put her into bed."

It was Fionna who ran Laggan for the next week, while Elen was immobilized by grief and guilt.

"We parted in anger," she said over and over again, the unstoppable tears pouring down her cheeks. "I would have explained when he came home. Talcoran, my love. And Colin, my baby, my brave, foolish little boy. How can they both be gone, lying in some unmarked grave far from home? Oh, Talcoran . . . Colin . . . Talcoran . . ."

Nothing Fionna or the others said or did could ease her pain, and as the days went slowly by, Fionna began to fear for her friend's sanity.

Patric mac Keith picked his way through the jumbled debris and the bodies scattered across the silent battlefield. He and the two men-at-arms with him were looking for any fallen warriors they could recognize as having belonged to Malcolm's forces. Malcolm wanted his own men sorted out and given decent burial. It was a grisly search, but it had to be done, and done soon. Squinting, Patric slanted his dirt-streaked face upward for a moment, scanning the painfully brilliant blue sky for the carrion birds he knew would be circling above the field, waiting patiently for the living to abandon it.

"There's no one left here to interest us," one of the men-at-arms said. "Our people will have all been retrieved by now."

"I suppose you're right." Patric had turned to go, relieved to be finished with a task he hated, when his attention was caught by a proud youthful face, beautiful even in the stillness of death. Something about it caught at his heart. He stepped closer. The sightless eyes were a peculiar midnight blue, fringed by thick dark lashes. They had been turned in the last moments of life upon the black-clad warrior who lay half across the lad with his left arm outflung over the boy's shoulders, as if to protect him from the fatal blow.

Patric drew in his breath in a long exclamation of sorrow at the loss of the bright promise he saw in that young face. As he gazed he was suddenly overcome by a sense of deep foreboding. Stooping down, he pulled the warrior's body away from the boy and turned the older man gently onto his back.

"Oh, God," Patric groaned, "no, not him."

"These are Macbeth's men," the man-at-arms said, "and not our concern. Let the crows feast on them."

"The crows have feasted enough since we came to Alba. I knew this man. He was a brave warrior and a worthy opponent." Patric stood, facing the two men with him, and both stepped back a pace at the blaze in his eyes. "Find a cart, one big enough to carry two bodies. And select six of my men who are willing to undertake a long journey."

"Journey? Now? But Malcolm wants the entire army to advance northward," objected the first man-at-arms.

"I'll find what you want, my lord," offered the second, who was more observant and had noted the pain in Patric's blue eyes. "Six of your own men-at-arms, to escort him home again and see him decently buried. That is what you want, isn't it, and the boy with him?"

"Aye." Patric turned away, not wanting them to see his face. "I'll wait here for you, to give the men instructions."

"I'd be willing to lead them on the journey myself," said the second man. Patric nodded, and they left him.

"Ah, Elen," he whispered, wiping away the unmanly tears that came despite his effort to stop them. "For your sake, love, I wish it had been me. Better I should die than have your heart break over this loss."

He knelt down on the muddy, blood-soaked earth and gently closed the boy's eyes before saying a prayer for both father and son. By the time he had finished his men had found him. He gave them detailed orders in an unfaltering and commanding voice.

A second letter from Macbeth came to Laggan
a week after the first one. Elen would not look at
it. She lay on her bed as she had done since the
news of Talcoran's death had come. She stared out
the window with empty eyes, seeing nothing,
while she turned Talcoran's charmstone over and
over in her hands.

"You must open it," Fionna urged, trying to
make her take the letter.

"Why? It's only more bad news. I don't want
to hear any more."

"You can't ignore the king," Fionna said, and
broke the seal herself. "We are summoned to
return to court. It seems Macbeth has decided
your dangerous prisoner will be more secure
under his royal eye. We are both to resume our old
positions as ladies to the queen. Gruach has been
ill and wants us by her side. Elen, did you hear
me?"

"It doesn't matter," Elen said.

"Oh, but it does. You cannot stay here at
Laggan and mourn for the rest of your days. You
had better start making the arrangements for our
journey."

"You make them."

"I wish you would bestir yourself, my dear."

"I cannot."

"Then I will do it all." And so Fionna the
prisoner conferred with Nechtan, the captain of
the guard, and with Briga and Ava, and a few days
later they left Laggan to join Macbeth and his
court near Aberdeen.

Nechtan, who had come to regard Fionna with
an odd mixture of amusement and respect, led the
way. He took with him a dozen well-armed men
for protection and demanded Fionna's promise
that she would not try to escape.

"Else I must chain you," he said, and watched Fionna burst into laughter.

"I am honored by your high opinion of my courage," she replied. "You have my promise. Nechtan, I am seriously concerned about your mistress. She is in a sad enough state just now. I would do nothing to distress her further."

"Thank you, lady. I have seen that you are a good friend to her. I will trust you for the moment."

Ava and Briga went with them, and there were several pack horses loaded with the women's clothes and other household belongings.

The way was long and difficult. They rode due north at first, to avoid Malcolm's troops, who were said to be ravaging the countryside south and east of Laggan. The old pathway through the mountains was no longer safe. They turned east after a while, and rode through rough, unfamiliar land until at last on a gray day they came to the castle that was now Macbeth's headquarters.

Again it was Fionna who took charge, ordering the arrangement of the two small rooms assigned to them, dealing with Ava's fears about Drust, who was still seriously ill from his wound, and trying in vain to rouse Elen from her torpor.

"Why should I bother?" Elen asked. "There is nothing left for me now. My life is over. I wish I could die myself."

Fionna regarded her friend with horror, and then went to confer with Gruach. She returned to their rooms later, telling Elen it was the queen's order that they begin attending her that very day.

"Get up and dress yourself," Fionna said. "We have work to do."

Elen grudgingly did as she was told. Even in her continuing grief, she dared not refuse the queen.

"I beg you, dear cousin, let me return to Laggan. I would mourn Talcoran and Colin alone, in our home."

Gruach coughed, holding a linen cloth to her mouth. She had grown shockingly thin, and there were bright spots of red on her cheeks.

"It is too dangerous in that area now. Malcolm's troops are moving northward. I cannot let you go. I need you with me, Elen." Gruach moved restlessly about the room, her unnaturally brilliant eyes darting from Elen to her other ladies and back again. "I am ill, surely you can see that, and I am so lonely. Macbeth is busy every day, planning for the next battle with Malcolm. Lulach is with the army, and his wife Gertha is not over-fond of me. She thinks I have too much influence over my son. Perhaps she is right, I don't know any more." Gruach wrung her hands, sending Elen a piteous look.

"You are like a younger sister to me, Elen. We have been close for so many years. Don't desert me now." She gave a wry laugh and coughed again. The linen cloth came away from her lips stained with red. "It won't be for long, I promise you."

Choked with sudden tears, Elen could make no response. Gruach, seemingly unable to remain still, wandered about the room again, coming back to Elen at last. Her thin fingers plucked at the bloodstained cloth in her hands.

"If we let you go back to Laggan, you will turn to the English," she muttered. "Your father always favored Duncan over Macbeth, and now that Talcoran is gone, you will turn to Duncan's son over your rightful king."

"No, cousin, I swear I will not." Elen was shaken out of her self-absorbed grief, not only by

Gruach's outrageous accusation, but by her physical condition.

"How can I know if you speak the truth?" Gruach asked. "You and Fionna will remain here, in attendance on me, so I can watch you both. You cannot hatch treasonous plots if you are under my eyes every day. It is one service I can render Macbeth. One last service to my love."

She gave way to another fit of coughing, the desperate spasms racking her frail body. She sank into a chair, unable to stand any longer. Her ladies hastened to wipe the froth of blood from her lips and offer wine for her to sip. Elen watched her helplessly.

Lulach's wife Gertha came into the room. She and Elen had always been on good terms. Where some of the ladies of the court had been cold to Gertha when first she came to Alba, Elen, because of her own affection for Lulach, had sought Gertha out, welcomed her, and made a friend of her. The tall, large-boned young woman with the silver-blonde braids and the proud, chiseled profile had accepted Elen at once, for behind her cool exterior she was lonely and frightened in her new home. Now she greeted Elen warmly.

"You have been too long absent from us," Gertha said with her heavy Norse accent. "I have missed you. We need you here."

"What in heaven's name is wrong with the queen?" Elen whispered.

"The doctors say the fever is consuming her lungs. She has grown steadily worse for months. She coughs up blood more often now. She will not live long and she knows it." Gertha regarded her mother-in-law with sad eyes. "Poor lady."

"She seems so agitated. She says things she must know are not true."

"It is the sickness. She does not sleep well. She wanders about the castle at night because she breathes more easily when she stands. After such a night, her thoughts are often muddled. Only when Macbeth is with her does she rest."

Elen saw the truth of Gertha's remarks at that evening's meal. Gruach sat beside her husband, holding her restlessness in check, though Elen could see her wringing her hands as she tried to keep them quietly in her lap.

While the ranks of his nobles were noticeably depleted, Macbeth himself did not seem to be greatly changed by his recent defeat in battle. He still kept royal state. The walls of the great hall had been hung with tapestries, and the food, no longer as lavish as his feasts had once been, was presented with the usual ceremony. Everyone present spoke and acted as if Malcolm's latest victory were only a temporary setback.

"We will retake everything Malcolm now holds," Macbeth told Elen confidently after the meal had ended and they had a few moments to speak together. "It is just a matter of time. There are some who do not believe that, a few who fear I will lose my throne and who have defected to Malcolm, hoping to preserve their estates if he wins this latest war."

"Never say defeat, husband," Gruach urged nervously. "You must not think of such a thing."

"I do not, my love." Macbeth laughed easily, putting one large strong hand over her thin ones. "You will see. I will rule all of Alba again, with you by my side."

"Then it must be very soon," Gruach said, her voice low.

There followed an uncomfortable silence. Elen broke it, rousing herself out of her depression.

"Talcoran would never have deserted you, my lord, no matter what the cost, and neither will I." Her eyes filled with tears. "Talcoran was a good husband to me, and a loyal subject to you. I am glad you made me marry him. You were wiser than I when you made that decision for me. I grew to love him deeply. I love him still." She stopped, unable to go on. She was surprised to see Macbeth's eyes glistening with unshed tears as he answered her.

"I thank you for those words, cousin. How I wish I still had Talcoran to guard my back when I ride into battle." He paused, swallowed hard, and then went on, his voice becoming stronger as he spoke. "I will not be defeated by those soft Englishmen. I'll make them all sorry they invaded my Alba. And I swear to you, Elen, that Talcoran's death, and Colin's, will be avenged. You have my word on it."

Elen was forced to put aside her grief over her husband and son in order to deal with the imminent death of another who was dear to her. Gruach's condition grew steadily worse. She would not allow the doctors to come near her, saying their bleedings and purgings only made her weaker, and she was weak enough already. Let the physicians tend to Macbeth's wounded men, and leave her to die in peace.

But she was not peaceful. Her restlessness increased with each day that passed. She ate nothing unless urged repeatedly by Elen or her other ladies, or by Macbeth himself when he was present. When she did eat, she would take only a single mouthful before declaring she could swallow no more. Even Briga's most delicious herbal brews could not tempt her. No one who saw her could doubt she was dying. She grew ever thinner, and her face was chalk-white, bloodless except for the scarlet patches on each cheek.

"I am so tired," she said one afternoon. Her thin fingers shook as she pulled at the linen cloth she now carried with her everywhere. A thread had unraveled from the edge, and she worried at it until it was loosened completely from the fabric, then rolled the single thread into a tiny ball and broke it off. She stood looking at it as if wondering what do do with it.

"Lie down and try to rest," Elen said, taking the cloth from her hands and leading her into her private chamber. Gruach stretched out upon her bed, but soon rose again and wandered into the reception room.

"I can't breathe when I lie flat. Where is Lulach? I want to see my son."

"I'll send for him." Elen went searching for a man-at-arms to carry a message to Lulach. When she returned to the room Gruach was pacing back and forth in great agitation.

"Where is he? Is he coming? I must see him."

"He will be here shortly. Sit down and rest, dear cousin. You will wear yourself out." She put an arm around the thin shoulders and led Gruach to a chair. The sick woman sat down, then quickly stood and began pacing again.

"Why should I rest? A few days, a week at most, and I will be gone." She caught at Elen's hands. "You are so patient with me. I have often been harsh with you, but you repay me with goodness."

Elen took Gruach into her arms. She felt the frail bones under Gruach's dry, hot skin and sensed the heavy laboring of her exhausted heart as Gruach laid her head on Elen's shoulder. The golden braids were thin now, and heavily streaked with grey. Elen thought her heart would break all over again from her feelings of helplessness and from the pity evoked by the ruin of her cousin's strength and beauty.

"You have helped me more than you know," Elen told her, holding her close and kissing her hot cheek. "In caring for you I have begun to put aside some of my grief over Talcoran and Colin. Before, I could think of nothing but myself and my loss."

"And now you worry about me. That's not much better." Gruach pulled away, laughing, then started to cough and could not stop.

When the hemorrhage began, Elen called frantically for the serving women, who came running with basins and cloths. By the time Lulach got there the bleeding had stopped and Gruach was lying exhausted on her bed, too weak to rise. After sending the servants away, Elen piled more pillows behind her to ease her breathing a little, then left mother and son alone.

As she went into the reception room, Gertha arrived, out of breath from running. She was followed by a priest, who entered the bedchamber. Lulach reappeared.

"She is making her confession," he said. "Where is Macbeth?"

Fionna was just entering the room. She took in the situation in her usual competent way.

"I'll send word to him," she said, and left again.

The priest returned to the reception room.

"The queen wishes to see you again, my lord," he said to Lulach. "Also your wife, and this good lady." He nodded to Elen.

"Come with us, father," Lulach begged. "She will be glad of your presence, too."

The four of them crowded into the small room. Lulach knelt down at one side of the bed, his mother's hands clasped tightly between both of his. Gertha stood behind her husband, supportive hands resting on his shoulders. Elen knelt beside Lulach, while at the foot of the bed the priest murmured unceasing prayers.

"I have loved you all," Gruach whispered, her voice a fragile, rasping sound. "Elen, my dear cousin, and dearer friend. You, too, Gertha, though you have not always thought so. You have been a good wife to Lulach. If my love for him made you unhappy, I ask your forgiveness."

"I give it freely." Gertha reached out and laid one hand atop her husband's hands which still held Gruach's bone-thin fingers. "There is little to forgive, because we both love Lulach."

Gruach smiled, then fastened her eyes upon her beloved son's face.

"He will make you King of Alba after him," she whispered, and Elen could see in Grauch's heaving chest the effort each word cost her. Her voice was so faint they all leaned forward to hear. "You are the next rightful king, and he promised. Macbeth always keeps his promises. Depend on him, Lulach. Where is he? Macbeth? My love?" She looked around and made as if to rise, then slumped back upon the pillows. The light flared up once more in her grey eyes. Then her lids dropped and the life went out of her so softly that Elen was not certain she was gone until the priest moved around the bed and bent to listen for breath or heartbeat. He shook his head, looking directly at Elen.

"The queen is dead," he announced.

In the silence that followed, Elen bent her head in prayer. When she rose, she and Gertha both had to help Lulach to get off his knees. He did not want to release his mother's hands, but Gertha insisted, gently yet firmly. When he was finally standing he burst into tears, his arms about both women.

"Come, husband," Gertha urged. "Come to our rooms. This place will soon be crowded and such grief as yours should be private." She led the sobbing Lulach away, while Elen went to find the servants to tell them to come and prepare Gruach's body for burial.

When Macbeth finally appeared, Elen was on her knees again, praying at Gruach's bedside. Candles had been lit at the head and foot of the bed, and Gruach's pale face was serene in their flickering light. Macbeth knelt beside Elen and put his face in his hands. Thinking he would want to be alone, she moved to leave. He caught her elbow and held her in her place.

"Stay," he said. "She would want you here."

At last, a long time later, he stood and helped Elen to her feet. He showed no embarrassment at the wetness on his cheeks, nor did he deign to wipe it away.

"I should have been with her," he said. "I have been so preoccupied these past months that I have had little time for her."

"She understood, my lord."

"Perhaps she did. We shared so much, she knew how deeply I loved her. Still, I should have been here. And now I have not even time to mourn her properly. Malcolm is advancing on us. We will meet in battle in a day or two and his strength is the greater now. He has called up an enormous army from his English allies. But I will win. I must, for this Alba I love so much, for the old ways that Malcolm would heartlessly destroy, and for Lulach's right to rule when I am dead. Gruach would understand that, too, I think."

"She would indeed, my lord. You are a good king to us."

"If Malcolm wins this war," Macbeth sighed, "Men will say I was a wicked king. He will see to that."

"Those of us who have lived under your rule," Elen told him gravely, "will never forget that you brought years of peace and prosperity to Alba. We will remember you with love."

It occurred to her with horror that she was speaking as though he were certain to die in the coming battle. With a little cry, she put out her hands to touch him, to reassure herself that he was still solid and alive. She found herself in his arms, held close against his strong warmth, and the dark premonition that had been forming in her mind vanished.

"My dear and faithful cousin," he said, his deep voice husky with emotion. A moment later he released her. "See to her burial. I entrust to you my love's remains." He nodded toward Gruach's body, and then he was gone.

Gowned in deepest blue wool, for she would not wear black mourning on this occasion, Elen stood alone just beside the entrance of the castle the next noontime, watching Macbeth and his men ride out to meet Malcolm. The day had begun grey and misty, but now the sun had begun to break through, glinting on armor and weapons, enveloping the scene in a golden haze that made everything seem shimmering and unreal.

She remembered other times when she had stood thus while he rode off to war with his proud army behind him. It was a smaller army now, reduced by death and injury and a few desertions, but it seemed to her that its ranks were swelled by the ghosts of his earlier companions. She thought she could almost see, riding in his accustomed place just behind Macbeth's right shoulder,

Talcoran of Laggan with his son Colin. And there, through the softening mist, was that not the sturdy bearded figure of Bancho of Lochaber? And that was surely Thorfinn the Mighty of Orkney in his huge bearskin cape. And those others, whom she could just glimpse now and then, so many others, who had been Macbeth's friends, who had loved him and had been willing to give their lives to defend an ancient way of life. Surely they were here to lend their aid to him now? Remembering all of them, Elen's eyes filled with tears.

As he came abreast of her, Macbeth reined in his horse, pulled off his gauntlet, and reached down to take her hand. She felt again the vitality and strength of him.

"See," she told him, standing on tiptoe to stretch higher so she would be nearer to his heart, "the sun is coming out. That's a good omen, cousin."

"A good omen for someone," he agreed. "I pray it is meant for us. Take care, Elen."

"Go with God, my lord." She watched him spur his horse, and kept her eyes fixed on his blue-mantled back as he rode down the line of warriors, until the press of men and horses blocked him from her view, and the mist closed in again, and the army disappeared, like the ghosts she thought she had seen, leaving behind it a great, empty silence.

PART III

MALCOLM'S KINGDOM

A.D. 1057-1058.

24

August 15 and 16 1057.

The wounded soldier screamed as Briga finished sewing his wound and applied a hot herbal poultice to it. Elen began to wrap his side with a strip of linen.

"Lie still," she ordered. "You are not so badly hurt. You will heal quickly with this treatment."

"I can't stay here. I have to escape. Lady, you don't understand. Malcolm's army is coming here. Ah, such an army. I've never seen so many men. You should run away, too. It won't be safe for you when they come."

"Will it be any safer in the countryside?" Fionna asked briskly. She was busily bandaging the shattered arm of the boy who lay next to Elen's patient. "We are noblewomen, and we will remain here, inside these walls, where we will be treated with respect by whoever rules this castle."

The soldier in Elen's care laughed bitterly.

"For your sake, lady, I hope you are right," he said, "But as for me, I am leaving as soon as I can stand."

The great hall was full of maimed, weary men, who had staggered or been carried from the battlefield at Lumphanan, a short distance away.

Elen had been told that the stables were packed with wounded, too.

Drust, who was still weak and recovering from the injury he had taken in the battle before this one, limped across the hall with a bucket of hot water.

"Thank you," Elen murmured. Drust squatted beside her on the stone floor, grunting a little and pressing his hand to his side.

"Lady," Drust whispered, "I have heard a rumor that Lulach's wife and her women are preparing to leave this place. Perhaps you should go with them."

"Don't be silly. Where could they go?"

"To Moray, lady. To Macbeth's old stronghold. Lulach is Mormaer of Moray now. The folk there will support him."

"Drust, Macbeth is Mormaer of Moray. Lulach cannot hold the title until—" Elen stopped, overcome by the full realization of what had happened. "Macbeth is dead," she finished in a hushed tone.

"Aye, lady," Drust said, "and my lord Talcoran, were he still alive, would ride to Lulach's aid."

"So he would. I will think about it, Drust. For now, we have work to do." Elen moved on to the next wounded man. By the time she had a few moments to think of what Drust had said, Gertha was gone.

"Wise woman," Fionna said dryly. "I am not at all surprised. Don't worry, Elen, we will stay in our quarters when Malcolm takes the castle. I will appeal to him for the safety of all of Gruach's ladies. If we offer no resistance, we will be safe."

"Perhaps Conal will be with Malcolm."

"I hope so." Fionna's blue eyes shone. "It has been three years since I have seen him."

It did not happen as Fionna had hoped it

would. With Briga and Ava, they barricaded themselves in Elen's rooms when Malcolm's men stormed the castle. Elen watched through the window as a seemingly endless stream of men threw themselves against the gate and forced it open. Another relentless river of humanity swarmed over the walls. It was finished quickly. Elen heard a cheer as something was lifted on a pike and stuck above the castle gate. She saw yellow-gold hair and beard, lightly streaked with silver, blowing in the breeze. Even in death the gruesome trophy was plainly the head of a king.

"Macbeth," Elen whispered, grasping at the sill to hold herself upright. She turned away from the window, unable to bear the sight.

Someone was battering at her chamber door. She could hear shouts and the sound of something heavy being dragged along the stone floor outside.

"They are breaking in!" Ava screamed, flinging herself behind Elen for protection. "Oh, dear God, help us now."

Some weightly object thudded against the stout wooden door. The bolt shook but held. The weight thudded again. Ava began to scream once more. Briga caught her by the wrist, dragging her away from Elen.

"Be quiet," Briga ordered sternly, and Ava's cries diminished to tearful whimpers.

The metal bolt was being torn from the door frame. With every blow against the door, it gave a little more. Elen and Fionna stood hand in hand, waiting.

With a loud crack, the door flew open and half a dozen blood-stained soldiers erupted into the room, their swords drawn. They stopped, startled at the sight of four women, and then began to smile mirthlessly. Elen shuddered at the sight of those grimy, grinning faces. She sensed an

answering tremor in Fionna's body before Fionna
stepped forward.

"We are noblewomen. My husband, Conal
mac Duff of Fife, is fighting in your army," Fionna
said, her voice remarkably steady. "I wish to
speak with your officer in charge."

One of the men spat out a few words that Elen
could not understand, though she thought it was a
curse.

"They are heathens," Ava moaned. "They
don't even speak Gaelic."

"They are English," Fionna said, and spoke to
the men again in that language.

Elen spoke a little English, but she found it
impossible to comprehend what was being said.
When one of the men caught Fionna's arm with
one hand and tore her gown off her shoulder with
his other hand, Elen did not need words to understand what would happen next.

Fionna slapped her attacker's face. He threw
her across the room. She stumbled against a stool
and fell to the floor.

The room exploded into violence. Elen lost
touch with what was happening. The noise was unbearable. Men were shouting and throwing the
furniture about. She heard Ava screaming, saw
Briga struggling with a tall, dark-haired man,
watched Fionna swing the stool at the man who
had hit her.

Someone had Elen by the shoulders. A beery,
hot breath blew against her face, coarse lips
buried themselves in her neck. She fought with all
her strength, but could not get free of the dis-
gusting creature who held her. He bore her to the
floor, pulling at her clothes. She could feel him
moving against her. It was too horrible to be-
endured. She had to stop him. She bit his bare wrist,
sinking her teeth in as deeply as she could. With a

cry of pain, he loosened his grip on her and drew back his arm to strike her. She closed her eyes, anticipating the blow.

Then the weight was gone from her. Elen opened her eyes. The man hung above her, a surprised expression on his face, until he was slammed into the wall. He slid slowly down the wall and sat on the floor, his eyes closed.

A long, tanned hand reached out and lifted Elen to her feet. She gaped at her rescuer, only slowly recognizing the handsome, lined face, the brown hair and beard, now streaked with grey, the solemn grey eyes.

"Conal?"

"Yes. Are you hurt?"

"I don't think so. Fionna, where is she?"

"Safe." Conal mac Duff smiled at something across the room.

Elen suddenly realized how quiet it had grown. The six soldiers who had rushed into her room now lay on the floor, unconscious. Some were bleeding. Ava was weeping softly in Briga's arms. But, where was Fionna?

Fionna was clasped in the embrace of an auburn-haired giant. Her plump little hand stroked his face as she nestled against his chest.

"Wouldn't you think," Conal asked Elen seriously, "that she would want to greet her husband first?"

Fionna flew across the room and into Conal's arms.

"You were busy rescuing Elen," she told him. "I didn't want to disturb you."

"Take my advice and kiss her," Patric said. "It's the only way to keep her quiet."

With a smothered laugh, Conal swept his wife off her feet and planted his mouth firmly over hers.

Elen stared at Patric, feeling the hatred rising inside her until she wanted to scream it out.

"Did they harm you?" he asked, taking a step toward her.

She ignored him. She went to her serving women.

"Ava," she began. Ava cried harder.

"She'll be all right," Briga said. "She's only frightened. These good men arrived just in time. I thank you, my lord," Briga added to Patric.

"It was a pleasure," Patric said. "Elen, are you sure that man didn't hurt you?" He put out his hand to her. She backed away.

"Don't touch me," she grated through clenched teeth. "Stay away from me, you traitor."

"I am no traitor," he replied mildly.

"No? You and that English army you march with have killed the best king Alba ever knew. His head rests on a pike above the gate out there. Your English army, not two months ago, killed my husband and my son. They were loyal to their king." Elen drew herself up proudly. "I am still loyal to Macbeth and to Lulach, and I, Elen of Laggan, say that you are a damned traitor!"

"I know about Talcoran and your son. Elen, I'm sorry. Let me tell you what I—"

"Sorry won't bring him back to me, will it?" she interrupted as she saw him approaching her again. His presence was no less intolerable to her than that of the soldier who had seized her a while ago. "Why should Talcoran be dead when you still live? I hate you! Don't come near me." She made for the door. He grabbed her around the waist and pulled her back into the room.

"Don't go out there. It's unsafe," he said. "They are still fighting."

"It's unsafe here, with you in the room," she snarled, her teeth bared at him in rage. "Take your filthy, bloodstained traitor's hands off me!''

Patric dropped his hands and stood back.

An anxious face appeared at the broken door. Drust looked about the room and swore softly. Ava, seeing him, began to cry loudly once more.

"What in the name of all the saints happened here?'' Drust asked.

"Just a little misunderstanding," Patric told him. "Are you one of the lady of Laggan's servants?''

"I was her husband's aide until he died," Drust answered.

"Good. You will need help to drag them out." Patric gestured toward the men on the floor. "Then someone to stand guard until the door is repaired."

"I'll find Nechtan and his men, my lord." Drust left, and Patric came to Elen.

"I won't touch you," he promised, "but I will stay here to guard you until your servant returns."

"I don't need your help."

"Need it or not, you have it, Elen."

The wounded of both armies had been moved to one side, clearing a space in the center of the great hall. A high-backed chair had been placed there for Malcolm's use, but he refused to sit. He moved among the wounded, speaking to a man here, exchanging a coarse jest with another, holding the hand of a dying soldier.

He wore Macbeth's gold circlet upon his head, and Elen, coming into the hall between Conal and Fionna, was reminded of Macbeth striding victorious into Burghead with Duncan's crown sitting lopsidedly on his golden hair, and tossing it carelessly upon his bed.

That was seventeen years ago, she reminded herself, and this is another world. Malcolm will change everything. We must begin by speaking English, I suppose, since I have heard he speaks little Gaelic.

She studied the new king of Alba. He was twenty-six years old, an extremely tall, thin man, with dark brown hair and piercing grey eyes. His hair was uncombed, his leather tunic bloodstained and slashed open on one arm where he had taken a minor wound.

"Conal." The king's loud voice rang across the hall. "You found your wife, I see."

Malcolm came to meet them. Fionna made a deep curtsy and Conal bowed. Elen remained upright, staring at Malcolm as he took Fionna's hand and raised her.

"I'm glad you are safe," Malcolm said to Fionna, his English speech strange to Elen's ears. "My friend Conal was much concerned about you."

Malcolm's calculating grey eyes now met Elen's, and his smile disappeared.

"Who is this?" he demanded.

"I am Elen of Laggan, widow of Talcoran, Thane of Laggan, and cousin to King Macbeth," she replied boldly, before anyone could speak for her.

"Oh, ho—a rebel still." If Malcolm's voice was amused, his face was serious.

"I am no rebel," Elen insisted. "I am a loyal subject to my rightful king."

"Your king is dead, lady. I am King of Alba now."

"Then I ask a favor of you. I am newly widowed and I wish to return to my home, where I will live in retirement and cause you no trouble. Give me permission to take my women and my men-at-arms and go to Laggan. I will leave at dawn."

"You ask a favor as though you were making a demand."

Elen stood proudly before him, not flinching at his hard expression. She remained silent while Malcolm regarded her with distaste.

"You cannot return to Laggan," Malcolm said. "It is no longer yours. As of this day, Lagganshire and everything in it is my own property."

Elen gasped as if she had been stabbed.

"It was thanage, was it not?" Malcolm went on. "Though it was held by your grandfather and father, inherited by your husband through you, and would have passed to your son had he and Macbeth lived to be subject and ruler, still Lagganshire was always crown property, administered by its thanes for the crown. As king I have the right to take it back, and that I now do."

"I am pleased to learn you are so well schooled in the laws of Alba," Elen told him coldly.

"It is my country, too," Malcolm said. "I must find a new administrator for Laggan."

Elen would not so easily accept the loss of her beloved home.

"I would remind you that my father, that very Colin of Laggan for whom my son was named, was thane to your own father, King Duncan. He died fighting at Durham for your father. For his sake, you should return Laggan to me."

A look of surprised admiration came into Malcolm's eyes.

"I like your spirit, lady." Malcolm passed one hand across his face. "I am weary, and I have many other pressing matters to consider just now. I will think about Laggan when I have more time. I will let you know my decision later. In the meantime, since you remain rebellious, I must make you a royal prisoner. I place you in the custody of my loyal subject, Conal mac Duff. I trust he and his good wife will keep you secure."

"The Thane of Fife?"

"He is a thane no more. He is Earl of Fife now," Malcolm told her. "When I am installed at Scone all of my thanes will become earls, and the land once held in thanage will be given to them by royal grant."

"Like the English," Elen murmured.

"Why not?" Malcolm laughed. "I grew up in England, lady, and the English were kind to me."

"You mean they used you for their own purpose against Alba."

Malcolm raised a warning finger.

"Never interrupt your king, mistress. And never speak such words to me again or I'll call you traitor. The English had their purposes; I had mine. The English king gave me a home when I was an orphaned exile, and he treated me well. He provided me troops with which I won back my throne. Is it not natural that I should look kindly upon the English and adopt some of their methods of government, now that I have come into my rightful inheritance?"

"For that home," Elen told him, "for that English manor of Colby which King Edward gave you, he will now expect you to pledge your fealty to him. And then he will say that you have pledged him Alba, too. Before you know it, the kings of England will claim that they are the rightful rulers of Alba, not you and your descendants."

Malcolm began to laugh at her.

"By God, you are a quarrelsome wench! I pity the man who weds you." He sobered suddenly. "I will pardon your boldness, because I know you are in great distress, having lost your nearest kin and suffered attack upon your person. But mind your manners with me in the future, for I will not forgive you a second time. Leave me now, and do not come before me again until I order your presence."

Elen fled through the castle, so intent on reaching her own rooms before she broke down completely that she did not see the tall figure coming toward her. She ran right into him.

"Elen, what's wrong? Has someone hurt you?" Patric inspected her tight, strained face with a worried expression.

"Malcolm. Your king." She spat out the words.

"He has not touched you?" Patric knew only too well Malcolm's predilection for beautiful women, and Elen, even in grief and anger, was very beautiful to his eyes.

"He doesn't need to. Malcolm wounds without touching. He has taken Laggan away from me."

"I see. Why would he do such a thing?"

"He says I am a quarrelsome wench." Elen sniffed, stopping the threat of tears.

"I wonder why he said that?" Patric tried not to smile. Elen was too angry to notice.

"I reminded him," she went on, "that my father fought and died for his father."

"That was clever of you. Malcolm appreciates loyalty. Was he impressed?"

"I don't know. I lost my temper and scolded him."

"Scolded the king?" Patric shook his head. "Oh, Elen."

"He deserved it."

"I am sure he did."

"What are you laughing at? I've lost my home. What am I to do now? How could he take Laggan away from me?"

"You are the only noble he has treated so

harshly, and there are two reasons for that. First, you refuse to submit to him as your king, and second, you are obviously female. Beautifully female." Patric's large hand rested on her shoulder. She tried to shake it off, but he would not release her. "You know a woman cannot hold thanage in her own right. But Malcolm will treat you more kindly if you kneel and pledge your loyalty to him. He might leave you something of your father's property if you will do that."

"I cannot, no more than you could give your oath to Macbeth."

The hand on her shoulder shook her hard, but Patric's voice was soft.

"You are incredibly stubborn, my sweet."

She was so distressed that she scarcely noticed the endearment, or the concern in his blue eyes.

"I will not change," she stated flatly.

"I know you well enough to believe that. It might help if I spoke to Malcolm in your behalf. He is well-disposed toward me."

"He should be, after all you have done for him. Patric, you would do that for me, try to make Malcolm treat me more kindly?"

"That and more. I'll ask him to give Laggan back to you."

"You will? Oh, thank you." She smiled up at him, her earlier despair wiped away by new hope. "Thank you."

She was so grateful for his promise of help that when he put his arms around her, she did not resist. It was only a friendly kiss, a soft touching of his lips to her cheek. There was nothing wrong with that. She felt his arms tighten, just for a moment, before he set her gently aside.

"I'll do whatever I can for you," he said, and

then he walked quickly down the corridor and disappeared from view.

It was only later that she remembered that he was a despicable traitor and she hated him with all her heart.

"Elen, do be careful," Fionna cautioned. "Malcolm has a notorious temper. Do not anger him again."

"What do I care? I have lost everything. There is nothing more your new king can do to me." Elen pointed out the window of her chamber. "Look what he has done to Macbeth. How long will that—that *thing* hang there over the gate?"

"It will be taken down tonight." It was Conal who answered her. "Malcolm has ordered Macbeth's body removed to Iona. He will be buried there."

"Has he admitted then that Macbeth was rightful ruler of Alba?" Elen asked in surprise.

"He has acknowledged by his order that Macbeth was *in fact* ruler of Alba for seventeen years," Conal said. "It is a slight difference."

"But an important one."

"Elen, you must realize that Malcolm is king not only as eldest son of Duncan, but also as the nearest qualified male descendent of Kenneth mac Alpin," Conal told her patiently. "Malcolm rules Alba by both direct descent and by the Law of Tanistry. No one can possibly quarrel with his right to be king."

"There is Lulach. He is nearly four years older than Malcolm."

"Lulach is not fitted to be king, and you know it." Fionna was becoming exasperated at this argument between her husband and Elen. "If Lulach will make submission to Malcolm, then

Malcolm says he will be given the Mormaership of Moray."

"Lulach has that anyway, by right of heredity," Elen snapped.

"Not under this king, my dear. There will be great changes in Alba now."

Fionna was glowing with happiness as she spoke, rejoicing in the knowledge that both her husband and her brother had been restored to her, and that her sons Keith and Ewen, who had been with the army in the south of Alba, were safe and would rejoin her in Fife when she returned there. Her red-gold curls were frosted with a few silver strands, and there were lines about her eyes, but at thirty-six, Fionna in her new-found joy looked like a young girl again. Typically, she did not gloat over the abrupt reversal in their positions, but treated Elen with the same kindness and friendship she had always shown. It was this kindness that Elen, in her unhappiness, found hard to accept.

"Ava," Elen said when Conal and Fionna had left her alone, "I cannot wander freely about this castle now, but you can. Find Drust. Ask him to learn everything he can of Lulach's whereabouts and his activities. Perhaps Drust can get a message to Lulach or Gertha. Tell him to ask how I can best serve my lord Lulach."

"Yes, mistress." Ava looked more cheerful than she had for some time. "Drust will be happy to hear this of you. He does not like Malcolm."

"Neither does Lulach," Elen said, "as you and I remember well. Malcolm is not secure on his throne while Lulach lives. If I can help Lulach in any way, I will."

25

August to September 1057.

The new royal court was to move to Scone before
proceeding even farther south to Dunedin. It
seemed to Elen that every person in the castle was
busy with Malcolm's plans, bustling to carry out
some new, detailed order Malcolm had given. The
king himself, preoccupied with affairs of state,
had apparently forgotten Elen, who spent her time
assisting Fionna in a half-hearted way.

Fionna worked daily, directing the inventory
and then the sorting, packing, and removal of
household goods. The gold and silver cups and
plates, pitchers and basins, the tapestries and
beds and carved chests of Macbeth's and Gruach's
royal household were to be sent to Scone.

"If Malcolm makes no decision about you, you
will go on with us from Scone to Fife," Fionna told
Elen. "Officially, you are a prisoner, but you are
my best friend still. It will not be unpleasant, my
dear."

Fife is too far south, Elen thought. I have to
get away from here before the court moves.

She had been sorting through some of her own
clothes. She pulled a heavy bracelet from the
bottom of the chest, and looked at it for a long
time before she remembered what it was. Patric

had given it to her at their betrothal ceremony so many years ago.

I'll keep it, she thought cynically. Perhaps it will buy a winter cloak to keep me warm in my old age. She tossed it back into the chest and dumped her old red woolen gown on top of it, and promptly forgot it.

It was nearly three weeks after her interview with Malcolm that Ava finally brought her news of Lulach and Gertha.

"Thank heaven," Elen said. "We are leaving for Scone soon. Did Drust find Lulach?"

"Yes, mistress. Lulach is in northern Moray. He sent you a message."

"Tell it to me quickly before someone comes looking for me," Elen ordered. "I am seldom alone these days."

"Lulach has been proclaimed king by the people of Alba," Ava informed her. "He will make his capital in the north of Moray, where he has the greatest support. He sends word that you will be welcome at his court, and Gertha—Queen Gertha—promises you will be her chief lady."

"How can this be?" Elen asked. "I have heard nothing of this. Do you suppose Malcolm knows?"

"Of course he does. It is not to his advantage to make it common news, is it? People like you, who don't like to see the English flocking into Alba behind Malcolm, would go over to Lulach's side if they knew he had set up his own court in the north. Drust says Malcolm's control of the country is not as complete as he would like everyone to think."

"I must go to Lulach, and it will have to be soon, before the court starts south."

"There is a lot of confusion, mistress. Everyone is running around packing and moving things into the baggage carts. We could be gone a long time before anyone missed us."

"We?"

"Drust and some of his men and I will go with you. I will not stay behind when you are in danger, mistress, and I have been away from Drust too often in these last years."

Elen accepted this without argument.

"Did Drust suggest a time for us to escape?" she asked.

"Three nights from now. Drust will have horses, your own mounts from Laggan, moved outside the castle to wait for us. He said we should go after midnight, when most people are asleep."

"I agree. We will need warm clothes, and food for the journey."

"I can manage that. Chose just a few of your own old garments, mistress, things Briga won't notice gone if she should open your clothes chest for some reason. Drust says we shouldn't tell Briga about this plan."

"Not trust Briga? Why, I'd trust her with my life."

"But not with this information, lady. Briga is too friendly with the lady Fionna. She might reveal our plans, thinking it was for your good to keep you with Malcolm's court."

"I suppose you are right, though I don't like it. Very well. Come back later and I'll give you some old garments. If anyone should question us, we'll say you asked for them for one of the women in the kitchen."

Throughout that day, Elen hid her increasing nervousness and devoted herself to assisting Fionna. She slept little that night. Ava appeared early in the morning.

"It is all arranged, mistress. We will leave after midnight tomorrow night. Drust will come to your room to guide you out of the castle by a back way."

"Good. Don't look so furtive, Ava. I'm frightened, too, but we must hide it."

"What is all this whispering?" As Fionna entered the room, Elen and Ava jumped apart. Fionna laughed. "You two look like conspirators."

"It's nothing," Elen said. "Just some gossip from the kitchen. You should not tell such scandalous tales, Ava. You may go. Here, take this bundle with you. It's the old clothes you asked for."

"Aren't you going to tell me?" Fionna teased when Ava had left.

"I'd rather not repeat what Ava said."

"Oh—well." Fionna dismissed the supposed gossip. "That's unimportant. The king has summoned you."

Elen's heart lurched, then began to beat with unnatural speed. Could Malcolm have discovered her plan to escape?

"Elen, you are as white as a ghost. Malcolm won't harm you. Hurry, he has ordered you to appear at once."

"My hair. My gown."

"No time for that. You look lovely as always, and this is certainly not a formal court. Come along, you mustn't make the king wait."

Malcolm was seated at a trestle table in the great hall, a pile of parchment documents and several half-unrolled maps before him. His secretary stood at his elbow, holding still more documents. Malcolm's priest stood at his other side.

Elen was surprised to see the priest. Malcolm was far from being a religious man. He must have a specific reason for having a clergyman at hand when Elen was called before him. She wondered what it was. She was also puzzled by the presence of both Conal and Patric.

"Elen of Laggan, come forward," Malcolm called, his loud voice interrupting her thoughts.

Elen glanced at Fionna, who had come into the hall with her, and who now shook her head to indicate she had no idea what Malcolm would do. Conal also looked puzzled. Patric's face was perfectly blank. He stared straight ahead, his eyes on Malcolm, and gave no sign that he knew Elen was there.

Elen moved forward until she stood alone, facing Malcolm. He scowled at her.

"You are one of my most difficult subjects, cousin," Malcolm said.

He had never called her cousin before, not even when his father was alive. Elen was filled with sudden hope at Malcolm's use of the term. Perhaps Patric had reminded Malcolm of that relationship, had convinced him not to take Laggan away from her after all.

"I have decided what to do with you and your inheritance, dear Elen," Malcolm continued, speaking in measured, formal tones. "All of the lands in the north of Lagganshire, and in Moray and Cawdor, which once belonged to Talcoran, Thane of Laggan, which were given to him by Macbeth, must revert to the crown, and I will dispose of them as I wish. That seems fair to me, since Talcoran was Macbeth's man.

"I exempt from this reversion only that portion of Lagganshire originally belonging to Colin, Thane of Laggan, who fought bravely for my father and died in his cause at Durham. This exempted portion I now give freely to that same Colin's daughter, Elen, despite the fact that she is a woman."

Elen blinked in surprise. She had never heard

of such a royal grant being given to a woman. She knew, for she had had the management of them, that Talcoran's estates were huge. She did not like to lose them, but Laggan, her home, would still be hers. That was what mattered. She could forget her plan of escaping to Lulach, and instead take her servants and return to Laggan and never see Malcolm, or Patric, again. She would find some way to help Lulach from Laggan.

"I regret to say," Malcolm continued, "that there was strong resistance when my soldiers besieged Laggan Castle. It was necessary to damage it and even to burn part of it in order to take and hold it. The owner must make repairs at her own expense. I trust you will be so happy to hold your ancestral lands again that this will not overly distress you." Malcolm watched her, waiting.

"No, my lord," Elen said. Swallowing her pride, she knelt to him at last. "I have no complaint, and as your subject, I thank you." Malcolm nodded, pleased.

"I knew you would submit in time," he said, looking with obvious satisfaction on her lowered head. "You may rise."

Elen stood and faced him. Malcolm's secretary handed him a parchment document. Malcolm signed it. The secretary then melted a stick of red wax, letting it drip onto the parchment, and Malcolm pressed his ring into the wax. He gave it back to the secretary, who passed it on to Elen.

"I make one condition to this grant," Malcolm said, just as her fingers touched it.

"I might have known," Elen muttered under her breath. She clutched the document to her heart. So long as she held it, Laggan was hers.

"Patric mac Keith, come here," Malcolm

called, and Patric moved to stand beside Elen. Malcolm looked upon him with genuine affection.

"Patric, you have been my loyal friend for many years. You deserve a reward for all you have sacrificed for my sake. Therefore, I give you those lands in Lagganshire that were once Talcoran's."

Elen watched the king's secretary repeat his previous actions with a second document, which Malcolm signed and sealed, and the secretary delivered into Patric's hands. So, Patric had made a bargain with Malcolm, to divide her inheritance in this way. She did not like the idea of Patric as neighbor, but if that was the price she must pay to have Laggan Castle and the surrounding lands truly belong to her, then she could live with Malcolm's decision, and would even thank Patric for his help.

"This is a vast area I have given to the two of you," Malcolm said when Patric finally held his grant. "I wish to be assured that it will all be properly administered by the strong masculine hand of one who is completely loyal to me. Therefore, I create Patric mac Keith Earl of Laggan, and I order him to marry Elen of Laggan today."

"My lord!" the priest at Malcolm's shoulder objected, "This lady has been a widow for only two months. Her period of mourning should be longer. And then the banns must be posted and we must observe a waiting period to give anyone who objects to this marriage an opportunity to come forward. Elen of Laggan cannot marry for at least one month."

"There will be no objections," Malcolm said. "And I waive the banns."

"You cannot do that, my lord. This is a church matter."

"I have done it, priest. Marriage is a legal

contract between two parties. The church has nothing to do with it save to bless the union after the contract is sealed. These two will marry in three hours."

Before Elen could gather her wits to do or say anything, Malcolm pointed a finger at her, jabbing it into the air as he spoke.

"That is my one condition, lady. You agreed to obey me when you knelt to me just now. You have Laggan back and it is fully yours. Let there be no protests from anyone. You may go."

26

September 8, 1057.

"You tricked me!" Elen cried.

She had fled toward her chamber after Malcolm dismissed her. Patric, following, had caught her and pulled her into a nearly empty storage room.

"You don't understand," Patric began. She cut him off.

"I trusted you! You promised to speak to Malcolm for me. Instead, you asked for Lagganshire for yourself. And Malcolm, that wicked, deceitful man, who was determined to have me kneel and submit to him, gave me to you in the bargain, just to make it legal by the old laws, as well as by his new English rules. Do you think I don't know that once I marry, my property becomes my husband's property? You and Malcolm conspired together to give Laggan to me, and then to take it away again. And I, fool that I am, knelt to Malcolm and called myself his subject, just as he wanted."

"It did not happen that way, Elen," Patric said. "I wish you would listen to me."

"Once a traitor, always a traitor. I should have known you would betray me again if you saw the chance to gain something for yourself."

Patric's patience snapped. He caught her hands and pulled her against himself. His bright blue eyes spat angry fire at her.

"Would you rather marry the younger son of the Lord of Warkworth?" he asked. "That is what Malcolm had planned for you, to pay you back for your intransigence, until I intervened."

"That cross-eyed, fat-bellied English snail?" Elen winced at the thought, but she would not give in. She was too hurt and angry. "The one who sleeps with little boys? Aye, I would a thousand times rather bed with him than with you."

Patric choked back sudden laughter.

"What, and have the young, half-English slugs he gets on you inherit your beloved Laggan some day? I think not. Now listen to me, Elen. You will marry me today as Malcolm has ordered. You will be a wife to me in every way. You may even come to enjoy it before too long."

"I will not. I'll never be your wife!" She slapped at him, and then began to scratch.

"I've had enough of this nonsense." He caught her, pinioning her arms. Enraged by this restriction, she bit his lip when he kissed her, drawing blood.

"Was your marriage to Talcoran so perfect," he ground out, "that you now find it impossible to accept another man?"

"My marriage to Talcoran is not the issue here. Your treachery is."

"Answer me." He held her still, and she was forced to look at him, though she wanted to run and hide from the rage and pain in his eyes as he waited for her answer.

"No," Elen said, speaking slowly, forcing her mind away from the day's unhappy events and remembering the past, "No, it was often a difficult marriage, but in time I learned to love Talcoran, and he always loved me."

It seemed to her that a little of the anger went out of him at her honest words.

"Elen, I don't expect you to forget him and all that happened when you were wed to him. That was an important part of your life and I would not take it away from you."

She considered that a moment.

"Did you never marry in all those years?" she asked.

"No. There were women." He grinned at her with a touch of his old, boyish deviltry. "Quite a few women, but none of them was you, and so I never wed. I have never loved any woman but you."

He thought he saw a softening in her expression. He kissed her again, and this time she did not resist what he was doing.

"Ah, Elen, tonight when you are mine at last, I'll teach you what love is."

"I will never love you. I hate you."

"I have good news for you that may soften your heart. We will go home to Laggan a few days after our marriage."

It shocked Elen to hear him call it his home.

"Are you so eager to take control of your new estates?" she said sharply.

"And of everything else that will be mine." His hand brushed along the curve of her cheek and she flinched at the possessive touch. "Malcolm has given us permission to leave court. We will go the day after tomorrow and travel part of the way with the royal procession."

"How kind of the king," she said sarcastically. "My father never needed Duncan's consent to retire to his own estates, nor did Talcoran need to ask Macbeth."

"We will be better off away from court, I think. Your sharp tongue will lead us both into trouble if we stay. Have you much to take with you? My man Resad is arranging for the baggage carts. Will you ask Briga to tell him how many chests she will pack?"

"I have but scanty possessions these days, my lord. Those English soldiers from whom you rescued Fionna and me ruined most of my clothes and furniture in their ravaging about my rooms. Since then I've had no means of acquiring other gowns."

"I will remedy that as soon as I can. You may have whatever you want, Elen. You need only ask."

"I'll ask of you only that you leave me alone."

"I can't do that. I love you. I want to marry you, and I will make you want me."

There was no escaping him. Patric took her into his arms again and kissed her passionately, caressing her and murmuring words of endearment. She let him do what he wanted, but she refused to respond.

She told herself that she loathed his touch, indeed hated the very sight of him. She looked forward to their wedding night with dread, fearing that she would lose her self-control and be swept away by his passionate demands. She fought her own body's reactions to him with every ounce of her will.

Patric stood holding her, his large hands clasping her buttocks, pushing her against his hips, his face buried in her throat. Her arms lay listlessly about his neck. It took all of her strength to deny the urge that was building in her. She wanted to move against him, to run her fingers through his thick hair, to open her mouth when his lips touched her again and take him into herself.

He felt her begin to shiver with the effort to deny her own feelings. He let her go.

"You will love me again," he said.

"No, I will not."

"About Talcoran and your son," Patric went on as if her determined words had not been spoken. "I should tell you what I have ordered done." Perhaps if she knew that he regretted the loss of both men, and mourned with her, perhaps that would help to bring her to a more reasonable acceptance of their marriage. He had his mouth open to speak further when she cut him off.

"Never mention that good man to me again," she said coldly. "I will not hear his name, or my son's, on your traitorous tongue."

Well, Patric thought, resigning himself to patience, she would find out soon enough. Once they got to Laggan she would know he had had both Taloran and Colin taken home. He could wait.

Elen had no special gown for her second wedding. As she had told Patric, her wardrobe was in poor repair. She rejected an orange-red silk gown because it was too cheerful, and chose instead a plain dark grey wool, with narrow bands of silver embroidery at the round neck and tight wrists. She refused to wear the golden hair ornaments Talcoran had once given her. She put them into the wooden box with his charmstone, and when no one else was in the room for a few minutes, she gave it to Ava.

"Hide this, and when you can, put it in the bundle of clothes I gave you."

"Mistress, what shall we do? You can't escape if you are married."

"All the more reason for me to go. I can't abide that man, Ava. I despise him. He and Malcolm have betrayed me. No matter what Malcolm's grant says, once I marry Patric, Laggan is mine no more. Malcolm tricked me into submission. I reject him as my king."

As usual, Ava began to weep loudly. Elen shook her, her own fears threatening to burst out of control.

"You must be brave," Elen said. "Tell Drust our plans are unchanged. I cannot avoid marrying Patric. If I tried, Malcolm would probably have me locked up so securely that I would never see daylight again. I will marry Patric, and heaven help me, I will have to lie with him tonight and tomorrow. But late tomorrow night, after he is asleep, we will escape this cursed place. Drust can easily discover where Patric's chambers are located. I will meet him in the corridor outside them as soon after midnight as I can."

"Yes, mistress." Ava hid Talcoran's box in her ample bosom. "Now you should bathe. Briga is helping the lady Fionna to dress, and when that is done, they will both come to robe you."

When Elen descended to the great hall to marry Patric, her appearance was as severe as a nun's. She wore no ornaments in her tightly braided black hair, and no jewelry at all. Her only decoration was the silver embroidery on her grey gown.

Patric wore a plain dark green tunic and a heavy gold chain that was a recent gift from Malcolm.

Elen refused to look at him. During the reading of the marriage contract in the great hall, she stared at the floor and her responses were barely audible. She hesitated so long at one point that Malcolm's priest, in nervous, unhappy attendance, whispered to her, "Lady, you must say yes."

"Yes." The word was filled with quiet despair.

When Patric kissed her lips at the end, she made no response.

The marriage contract agreed to and signed and sealed, the bridal party proceeded to the castle's tiny chapel for mass, Malcolm leading the way. Elen and Patric, Fionna and Conal, two of the ladies who were all that remained of those who had once attended Queen Gruach and whose fates were soon to be similar to Elen's, crowded into the cold, airless room, along with a dozen or so of Patric's friends and a few servants.

Elen saw Drust standing with Ava at the back of the chapel. She stared hard at him. He nodded, but made no other sign to her. Elen had given Ava that night free, to enable her to have adequate time to talk with Drust in private. When the time came for prayers, Elen's thoughts were on Lulach and her escape plan, not on her new husband.

Malcolm had ordered a festive banquet, but after several weeks of feeding the nobles who temporarily lived there, and partially supplying the army that camped outside its walls, the castle larder was nearly bare.

"It is a good thing we are moving to Scone in a few days," Malcolm said. "We will go hunting tomorrow to provide some fresh meat until we do leave. Patric, can I prevail upon you to accompany us, or will you be rising late?"

"I'll be happy to join you, my lord," Patric spoke without thinking, and paid no attention to the laughter his response had generated. He was more concerned with Elen than with the others at Malcolm's banquet table. When first she sat down, Elen had swallowed several large goblets of wine as quickly as she could. When she called for more,

Patric stopped her.

"You've had enough," he said. "I do not want a senseless bride in my bed."

"Better for me if I were," she replied.

"Sweet Elen, you will enjoy this night." He would have kissed her, but she turned her head away.

"Ah, no," he said. "I am your husband now, and you cannot refuse me."

He turned her face toward his own. He did not hurt her, but there was no fighting his strong hands. He kissed her slowly and thoroughly, to the great amusement of the onlookers.

"By God!" Malcolm laughed, toasting Patric with an over-full golden cup that splashed wine on those near him. "You have found the best way to deal with a surly wench like that one. To your health, Patric. I wish you luck and strength. I think you'll need both."

Patric had insisted on dispensing with the traditional custom of the wedding guests bedding the bride and groom.

"That is for couples younger than we are," he had told both Conal and Malcolm earlier. Then, calling upon their friendship for him, he made them party to his arrangements. When it was nearly evening and most of the guests were far gone in drink, Patric made his move. By previous agreement, on his signal, Malcolm captured the company's attention with a wild story about his adventures in exile, while Patric half dragged, half led Elen out of the great hall, and Conal made sure that no one followed them.

"I don't want to go yet," Elen protested.

"If you make much more noise, we will have all those lords and ladies, and their servants, in our bedchamber to watch us. Would you prefer that?" Seeing her white face and frightened eyes, he added more gently, "You cannot stop what will happen this night, dear wife. Let it be between the two of us alone."

She went with him with lagging feet. There were two guards stationed at his apartment door.

"Are they to keep me in?" she asked. "Will you hold me a prisoner for the rest of my life?"

"I do not expect to hold my wife by force, Elen. These men are to keep pranksters out and assure our privacy. I thought you would want that. They are posted only for tonight."

"Nechtan, what are you doing here?" Trying to hide her relief that Patric's chamber would be unguarded the following night, Elen had stopped at the door, and now recognized the captain of her household guard.

"I serve the Earl of Laggan and yourself, my lady. I wish you happiness of your new marriage." Nechtan saluted her, then opened the door to Patric's rooms.

They were sparsely furnished, but neat and clean. There was a small reception room and a larger bedchamber. Patric's personal servant, Resad, and Briga awaited them. Briga had removed Elen's belongings from her old room to this one.

"You may use the bedchamber to undress," Patric said. "I'll join you in a little while."

Elen let Briga remove her clothes and wash her with cool, lavender-scented water, then wrap her in an ivory silk robe. She fumbled at her own hair until Briga took over and unfastened the heavy braids, untwining and combing them. When Elen's hair flowed down her back in a thick cloud, Briga stepped back, satisfied.

"Will you get into bed now, mistress?"

"I . . . no, not yet. Is there any wine?"

"My lord of Laggan's manservant has

prepared food and drink for you. I think he will bring it shortly." Briga edged toward the door.

"Don't go." Elen clutched at Briga's arm.

"Your husband will be here soon, mistress."

Elen looked at Patric's large bed with panic-stricken eyes. She began to tremble.

"I can't," she whispered. "I can't."

"He won't harm you," Briga said. "I think he is very fond of you."

"I despise him. I hate him. I don't want to lie with him."

"We will change that this very night." Patric stood in the doorway, a soft wool cloak draped over one shoulder. It barely covered his nakedness when he walked calmly into the room. Even the imperturbable Briga caught her breath at the sight of his tall, muscular form.

Patric's servant hurried into the bedchamber, deposited a tray loaded with food and drink, and left quickly.

"You may go, too, Briga," Patric said.

"Yes, my lord. Good night. I wish you both well."

Elen watched with sinking heart as Briga departed, leaving her alone with this giant of a man, this hated husband who strolled to the table where the tray of food rested and poured himself a cup of wine.

"Would you like some food, Elen? You ate nothing earlier."

"Wine." Elen licked her dry lips. "I want wine."

"No more wine for you until later." He sipped from his own silver cup, his eyes on her face.

"I am thirsty," she said.

"Then drink water."

"I hate you."

"You grow tiresome, my love. Think of something else to say. Something sweet."

"Sweet? To you? I'd rather die."

"You may die of love before this night is over." He set down the cup. "But have no fear, I will resurrect you."

"On top of everything else, you are a blasphemer."

"Elen." He laughed, opening his arms and beckoning seductively. "Come here, my dearest wife."

Elen backed away. Perhaps she could reach the door and escape from him. Then she remembered Nechtan and his man, stationed just outside. She was trapped.

Patric began to walk toward her. The blue cloak, slung so carelessly over his shoulder, billowed to one side as he moved, revealing his muscular flanks. Her eyes fixed upon his eager manhood. A surge of warmth shook her. She fought it down. She would not give in to him, no matter what she felt, no matter what he did to her.

She tore her eyes away from his body and began searching for a weapon. On a table near her were some clay bottles and jars containing the herbal preparations Briga made for Elen to use on her skin. Her fingers closed around a bottle.

Patric moved nearer. She threw the bottle at him. He ducked, and she picked up a jar and threw that, too, then another. He kept ducking the missiles. Each time he dodged, he came closer to her.

She picked up the last object on the table, a vial of perfume. She let it fly. It sailed past Patric's head to crash against the opposite wall. The pungent scent of lavender filled the room.

"You would make a wonderful soldier," Patric told her, "but it's time to surrender."

He reached for her. She ran under his outstretched arm, picked up the skirt of her robe, and headed for the other side of the room. He lunged after her, catching the trailing sash of her ivory silk robe, tugging on it until it came away in his hands. The robe slipped down, nearly falling off her shoulders. She gathered the edges together across her breasts.

He was coming after her again. She stumbled against a wooden stool, caught it up, and hurled it at him. He slowed until it hit the floor, then stepped over it and calmly continued his pursuit of her.

He stalked her around the room, never taking his eyes off her, always stepping aside at the last minute as she threw at him everything she could get her hands on. Dishes from the tray of food flew through the air, then the silver wine cup he had used. Her aim was getting better; the cup hit his shoulder and he swore at her.

She picked up the pitcher of wine from the tray. Faster than her eye could follow, his hand shot out and took it from her.

"Now," he said, "you go too far."

His fingers touched hers. Crying out as though his flesh had burned her, she snatched her hand away and retreated further. She came to a carved wooden chest, and pushed against it.

"That's a bit too heavy for you to lift," he said.

He had her cornered between the chest and the wall. She ran at him, her hands clawing. He swerved, so that her nails missed his face and sank into the cloak on his shoulder. Snarling like an animal at bay, she tore it off him, and flung it aside.

He reached for her waist, his hands clutching at the silk robe. She slipped out of it, dodged again, and, naked now, whirled away from him.

Too late she realized her mistake. She was

backed against the bed. She stood there panting, her skin glowing with moisture from her exertions. Her hair hung over her shoulders, the rosy-brown tip of one breast parting the heavy flow. Her midnight-blue eyes darted frantically about the room, seeking something, anything, to fend him off, to keep him away from her.

"How you have changed," Patric chuckled. "Where is the meek virgin I once terrified with my kisses?"

"She disappeared when you deserted me," Elen panted.

She could feel his breath on her skin. His hand brushed the bareness of her arm. With a wild cry, she leapt onto the bed, scrambling toward the far side and temporary safety.

He caught her. He grabbed her ankle, and then his arm was across her throat, forcing her onto her back. He was on top of her, his bare skin plastered to hers as he captured her mouth and thrust his tongue into her, devouring her.

She could not move. His hands held her head on either side as he savaged her lips. His strong thighs held her lower body securely between them, his hot, throbbing manhood pressed against her belly.

"Elen," he gasped between hungry kisses, "I need you so badly. I've waited for you for so many years. Kiss me back. Oh, Elen, love me. Please say you love me."

"I hate you." She struggled weakly, knowing it was a useless attempt. He was going to possess her.

His mouth trailed along her throat, his breath hot on her sensitive skin, making her moan and shudder. She felt the first flickering of pleasure when he caressed her shoulders and moved to touch her heaving breasts.

"Patric," she whispered softly.

"Yes, my darling." He lifted his head. She scratched at his eyes. With the instantaneous reflexes of a veteran fighting man, he caught her wrists, forcing her hands down to her sides.

"I grow tired of this battle," he growled. "You belong to me, and I am going to make you enjoy it."

"I won't. I won't."

"Oh, yes you will. You've slept alone too long, and you are hungry for love. You won't admit it, but you are."

She closed her eyes. She could not stop him, but she need not look at him. It seemed to her that he had a dozen hands. He held her wrists tightly so she could not strike at him again, and yet his hands were all over her body.

He teased at her breasts until she gasped in tormented pleasure in spite of her determination to feel nothing. His fingertips stroked and pulled until her nipples were hard and aching and then his mouth fastened on her and she gritted her teeth to hold back the excited cries that rose to her throat and threatened to burst from her, giving him encouragement.

Now he was doing things to her legs, his hands sliding down their slender length. She bit her lips and clenched her eyelids tightly closed as he placed moist, lingering kisses on her calves and the backs of both knees. She felt him shifting his position, but still she could not move, nor would she open her eyes to see what he was doing. She kept her body stiff, her arms rigid at her sides.

His mouth, that damned, tormenting mouth, was now scorching across her belly and he was caressing he hips and her upper thighs. His mouth was moving lower. He parted her thighs. She could not move her hands to fight this delicious torture. She had no idea how he was holding her.

She dared not lift her lids. She knew if she met his eyes she would have to admit the unbearable truth, that she longed for him, ached for him, hungered to feel him inside her, thrusting, heaving, forcing her to say the unthinkable words, the words she had vowed never to utter again.

She felt his hand move between her thighs, felt his fingers probing, touching her. In spite of her determination not to react, her body, just for an instant, betrayed her. She pushed against him and his fingers slid into her. She could endure it no longer. A wild, reckless need shook her. Her self-imposed restraint dissolved. She broke her grim, painful silence.

"Patric. Oh, Patric, please." She moved on his hand again, her frenzied body demanding more.

"Open your eyes, Elen. Look at me."

She felt his warm breath. His mouth was almost on hers. His fingers continued their maddening motions.

"I can't. Please, please," she moaned.

He withdrew his hand. She screamed at the loss, and her eyes flew open. She saw his face next to hers, his blue eyes blazing with the intensity of his own barely restrained passion.

She felt his hardness pressing against her. Forgetting everything but the desire that now enveloped her, she surged upward to meet him, opening her body to receive his. He plunged down, down into the warmth, and she closed about him and held him in that sweet captivity.

"Elen, my love." His lips skimmed over hers and she gave her lips to him as she had given the rest of her body, feeling more intensely the thrust of his tongue and the hot sweetness of his mouth because of her previous denial of her own deep longing.

He began to move slowly, trying to delay the ending, savoring the long-dreamed-of pleasures of her body. Caught in the excitement he had engendered in her, Elen moved with him, lifting her hips to meet each thrust. Her hands, at last released from their mysterious confinement, fluttered lightly along his spine, sending ripples of delicate sensation throughout his body.

Elen sank into the honeyed heat of his love-making, giving herself with open pleasure now, forgetting hatred and pain and loss while Patric conjured up a storm of emotion that built like thunderclouds in August, higher and higher, until at last, as though with a great bolt of lightning, the storm broke, and Elen was whirled away in thunder and lightning to some elemental place where nothing mattered but feeling, sensation, the touch and taste and heat of Patric's body in her and on her, possessing her totally. She heard her own voice, though she did not will herself to speak.

"I love you," she moaned. "Patric, I love you."

Her body vibrating with the most exquisite tremors that went on and on and seemed as if they would never stop, the thunder roaring in her ears, from far away she heard his joyful response.

"And I love you, my sweet, sweet Elen."

The storm quieted at last. He held her more loosely, their limbs still entwined, his breath warm on her cheek. He planted soft kisses all around her mouth, then fixed his lips on hers, glorying in his victory.

"I knew you loved me," he whispered.

"I do *not* love you." She pushed at his shoulders, and tried to wriggle out from under him.

"You said you do," he reminded her, kissing

her throat and shoulders. "I heard you, my darling."

He was still on top of her, and try as she might, she could not get him off her body.

"I do not love you. I hate you!" she said angrily, still trying to push him away. "You made me say that, you did things to me. You held my hands so I couldn't protect myself."

"I did not hold your hands, not after the first few moments. If you had opened yours eyes, you could have seen that you were free. You imprisoned yourself, my love."

He kissed her again, his mouth smothering and finally quelling the outburst of rage that followed this revelation. Her breasts were crushed against the soft hair that grew on his wide chest. Each time he moved, whether to kiss her in some new place, or simply to take a breath, his hair tickled at her nipples until they were hard. He noticed.

"You want me again," he said with absolute certainty.

"No, no," she moaned. She tried to move her hips and legs. She had to separate herself from him before the threatening storm inside her broke a second time. Her efforts did not free her, and they only aroused him. She felt him growing, and he held her with a determined strength that increased her inner turmoil.

"You made me say it," she accused him again, her breath ragged with rising desire.

"Then I'll make you say it once more," he promised.

And he did.

Afterward, she lay glaring at him. He owned her body, but that was all he would get, and after tomorrow he would not even have that any more.

The realization gave her a sense of power.

"I didn't mean it," she told him coldly. "I lied. I hate you, Patric mac Keith. I will hate you until the day I die."

27

September 9, 1057.

From the safety of his bed, Patric surveyed the wreckage of his bedchamber, hiding his amusement at the expression on Briga's face.

"You had better clear this away before your mistress gets up. I don't want her to cut her feet. Will you want a bath this morning, my darling?" he asked the woman beside him.

"I certainly do," she responded. "I want to wash away any sign that you ever touched me."

"Why bother, since I'm only going to touch you again?"

"How can you want a woman who feels about you the way I do?"

Elen flounced out of his reach. Picking a clean patch of floor to place her feet on, she rose from the bed. Patric looked at the slim line of her back and felt himself grow warm.

"It's because I know how you feel about me, really feel about me, that I do want you. No matter what you say afterward, Elen, when we make love, your body is honest with me." Patric stretched out on the bed, his long legs crossed. "I think I'll stay here and watch while you bathe."

"Then I'll stay dirty." She bent to pick up her silk robe from the floor, revealing the full, creamy-skinned curves of her hips and buttocks.

Patric seriously considered sending Briga out of the room. He wondered if there would be time enough to do battle again with his passionate, defiant wife before he must dress and join the king for that morning's hunt. The swing of her long hair as she threw it carelessly back from her face, the glimpse of a rounded breast just before she covered it with her silk robe had almost decided him in favor of the idea, when Resad and a second manservant appeared with bread and cheese and ale, a joint of cold beef and a basket of apples, so they could break their fast.

"Oh, good," Elen said. "I'm ravenously hungry. I'll wash and dress later, Briga, after our master leaves." She put a piece of cheese on a wedge of brown bread and began to eat, sitting on the end of the bed.

Patric sat up, and, pulling aside her hair, placed a kiss on the nape of her neck. His right hand crept around to cup her breast.

"Leave me alone," she said, getting up and moving to the opposite side of the room.

Patric shrugged. He would wait until tonight. When they were alone together once more he would make her say again what he wanted to hear. He believed that sooner or later she would admit in a calmer moment the truth of the words that had been torn out of her as she lay writhing in ecstasy in his arms the night before.

He got to his feet and stretched, chuckling to himself at Briga's gasp. Elen stared at him, then quickly averted her eyes. Patric picked up his blue cloak, wrapped it about his waist, and left the women to themselves.

Ava came to Elen at mid-morning.

"Drust says the journey to Scone has been

delayed again," she repeated. "There has been some fighting on the road south of here. Drust expects King Malcolm to take a band of men into the area tomorrow to pacify it."

"Patric will surely be among those men," Elen said. "If I leave our bed in the middle of the night, and Patric rises early to go with Malcolm, he'll see that I'm gone."

"That will ruin our plan, mistress."

"Patric mac Keith is not going to stop me." Elen thought a while. "I know what to do. Tell Drust to be ready just after sun-up tomorrow. We will leave after Malcolm has ridden south. This is better than our first plan. We can travel faster in daylight, and we can be gone an entire day before anyone notices we are missing."

Malcolm, Patric, and Conal returned early from the hunt. Elen met Patric in the great hall.

"I've heard the news," she said. "Do you ride with Malcolm?"

"Yes, at dawn. We'll be gone for several days. Is there any food?"

Elen brought him a platter of cold meat and bread and cheese, and a pitcher of ale.

"Sit with me," he said, pulling her down beside him on the bench. "Did you miss me this morning?"

"Not at all," she replied.

He laughed softly, his left hand stroking her thigh.

"I should remedy that, so you long for me in the next few days and greet me eagerly when I return."

Elen's mind was working rapidly. She could throw him off her trail if she were clever, giving herself and Drust and Ava even more time to reach Lulach.

"I am sorry you must leave, Patric. I am

anxious to return to Laggan. It is harvest season,
the busiest time of year. I should be there. So
should the new master," she added.

"I understand," he said. "I promise it will be
only a few days' delay, and then we will travel to
Laggan as fast as we can. I want to see to it that
the damage Malcolm's men did is repaired before
winter comes. There will be much work to do to
ease the hardship of your—our—people. I will
need your help, my love. You are more
experienced in such matters than I am. We'll do it
together, shall we?"

Patric's hand covered Elen's where it rested
on the trestle table. He gave it a squeeze, smiling
at her. Elen, surprised and a little shaken by the
genuine concern Patric had expressed for Laggan
and its people, smiled back at him.

He lifted her hand to his lips, kissing it, then
turning it over to run his tongue across her palm.
She trembled, feeling the melting warmth begin
deep within her. She let her hand remain in his
until he let it go to cut himself another slice of
bread.

"Will you spend the rest of the day with
Malcolm?" she asked as they rose from the table.

"There is much to do in preparation. It is certain there will be more fighting on the southern
road."

"Oh," she said, trying to look and sound disappointed. "I thought you might ride with me, or
at least take a walk. I long to go outside these
walls, but Fionna says it isn't safe for a woman
alone."

"She's right. I don't have time to ride, but we
can walk a little now, if you like."

"Yes, thank you. I have been inside this castle
for more than a month, and it feels like a prison to
me. How I long for Laggan," she added, casting a

sidelong glance to see how Patric was taking this newly friendly approach of hers.

"You will be at Laggan soon enough, my sweet," he said.

The guards at the gate saluted Patric as he and Elen walked through. A short distance from the castle was an orchard. They made their way toward it. The scent of ripe apples hung heavy on the crisp autumn air. The hills to the west were purple, the sky above them a deep blue. Between the castle and the orchard, the earth was bare, with many freshly made mounds. Malcolm's army had not camped in this small area.

"How desolate the land looks," Elen said.

"It's better than it was before," Patric replied. "The dead are buried, and the discarded equipment has been collected. It hardly looks like a battlefield now, and the grass will grow again when spring comes."

"Malcolm's battlefield," Elen muttered. "He leaves destruction wherever he goes."

"Will you never forgive the poor man?"

"Forgive? It's because of Malcolm that you betrayed me. You left me for him."

"I had to keep my promise to Duncan. You know that."

"You were a traitor to *me*," Elen insisted, her night-dark eyes blazing with anger too long submerged. "I loved you then. I would gladly have gone into exile with you, but you never asked me. You just left a message with Fionna, releasing me from our betrothal. How do you think I felt when I heard that? Can you wonder that my love turned to hatred?"

So that was at the heart of her antipathy to him. She thought he had been careless of her love for him. Overcome with sorrow for those lost years, Patric would have embraced her, but she stepped aside, putting a gnarled old apple tree between them. He faced her over a low-hanging branch.

"I could not ask you to go with me," he said. "It was too dangerous. I knew that once I left Alba, I would be an outlaw with no home, no place to lay my head but by someone else's charity. You were so fragile, so shy and gentle. How could I ask you to share such hardship, possibly even a cruel traitor's death if we were caught?"

"You were mistaken in my character. I am not so fragile. I have survived my own dangers and hardships."

"I have recently begun to realize just how strong you are." Patric rubbed at a sore spot on his jaw, where she had hit him the previous night. Then he grew serious again. "That was a long time ago, and I had good reason for what I did. Let me point out to you that had you gone into exile with me, like me you would have been proclaimed traitor and outlaw, and Macbeth himself would have confiscated all of your property and given it to someone else, as he did with mine. You still have Laggan. Malcolm returned your home to you. Can you not forgive him, and me, too, and let us forget the past?"

"I will think about it," she whispered. She changed the subject abruptly. "May I go riding while you are gone?"

"I told you, it's not safe. You have enough to keep you occupied, helping Fionna with the packing."

"I would take Drust and two or three of his men with me, and Ava for chaperone. We could go in the early morning, before Fionna needs me. Please, Patric. It would be so wonderful to get out of that stuffy castle, just for a little while."

"I don't think it's a good idea."

"And if I ride every day until you come back, I'll be used to riding again, and I won't slow you down on our trip to Laggan."

"You would do it for my good, would you? What a sorceress you are. I think you could cajole me into anything you want."

He stopped to kiss her, and she did not object. She leaned against the roughness of the tree trunk and opened her mouth to him. As his hands wandered upon her, she let him think she wanted him, while she told herself over and over again that she did not enjoy it, she was only doing this so he would be agreeable and let her go riding tomorrow, so she could escape him and join Lulach.

"Let us end our walk here and return to the castle," he whispered. "I want to make love to you, and I prefer to do it in the comfort of our bedchamber."

His arm was about her waist, urging her along. She dared not hang back or delay. She did not want to anger him. He hurried her back to the castle, through the gate and the great hall, then up the stone staircase and into the room they now shared. He bolted the door securely behind them.

"I have wanted to love you in mid-afternoon," he said. "Candles are not enough. I want to see your beautiful body in daylight."

His kiss was deep and sweet, drugging her like heady mead. She was afraid of the light, for in it she might reveal too much to him, but she knew she could not stop him.

He lifted her gown over her head, then bent and quickly unfastened the ribbons at her knees, pulling off both stockings and shoes with one gesture, leaving her wearing only a linen undershift that clearly revealed the rich contours of her figure.

His hands sought her breasts. She nearly swooned with pleasure when he pulled her shift down off one shoulder and set his mouth on one round globe. His hand pushed at her other shoulder, and her shift dropped to the floor. By the time he finally lifted his head, her arms were around his waist and she was clinging to him breathlessly.

"Your tunic scratches," she said as soon as she could speak. From shoulder to waist her skin was red from rubbing against the rough wool, and the heavy buckle of his belt had made an indentation on her stomach.

"You had better remove it," he said, watching her with narrowed eyes, as though he did not quite trust this newly compliant Elen.

"I?"

"Yes, you. Undress me, Elen."

She wanted to tell him to undress himself. She reminded herself she had to keep him in a good mood so he would not forbid her to go riding the next day. She bit back her irritation. Reluctantly, she began working at his buckle. It came unfastened at last. His arms were still around her, his hands resting lightly on her waist.

"Let me go," she said, "and I'll put it on the chest."

"Drop it."

The heavy leather slipped out of her fingers and thudded on the floor.

"Your neck chain," she said, lifting the thick gold links of Malcolm's gift.

"Leave it on. My tunic next, please."

"How can I take it off if you won't let go of me?"

"One arm at a time," he chuckled.

She pulled the hip-length garment up to his armpits. With great solemnity, he gave her first

one arm and then the other so she could pull off
the sleeves, then ducked his head to allow her to
remove it entirely. At no time did he let her out of
his grasp. She dropped the tunic onto the floor on
top of his belt.

She kept her eyes away from his wide, heavily
muscled chest, pretending to herself that she did
not want to lay her head upon the mat of soft hair
that covered it. She concentrated instead on his
boots.

He wore long, tight woolen trousers in the
Norse style, and soft leather boots wrapped with
strips of leather to hold them to his calves. He
stood quietly while she unfastened the wrapping
and drew off the boots.

It was time to remove his trousers. She
fumbled with the drawstring at his waist, trying to
ignore the obvious bulge just below her hands.
She could not unfasten the knotted cord.

"Shall I help?" he asked, laughter in his voice.

"I can do it," she snarled, momentarily forgetting she was trying to please him.

"Whatever you wish, my love, but don't take
too long. I'm growing ever more eager for you."

With a muttered oath, she gave another tug
and the knot untied. She pushed the trousers
down his long legs. She could not help herself, her
hands caressed him as they slid along, feeling the
tight muscles, the strength of him. She knelt to
pull off the trousers, and then she looked up at
him.

He stood naked before her, his erect manhood
thrusting proudly outward, awaiting her next
move. He presented an irresistible temptation.
Still kneeling, she touched him, feeling the velvety
softness, and then the hard, throbbing length of
him, and the softer part that lay beyond. She
gathered all of him into her hands and nuzzled

gently at his flesh. He smelled of cinnamon. She pressed her mouth against him, her tongue flicking over his now hugely distended manhood.

With a loud cry, he caught at her shoulders, pulling her up, clasping her tightly to him while he rained kisses over her face. Still holding her, he backed toward the bed. It was only a short distance. He fell across the fur coverlet, pulling Elen down on top of him. She lay there, her head tucked under his chin, feeling the hardness of his body beneath hers, while his hands moved along her spine to fondle her softly rounded hips.

She forgot she hated him and was trying to trick him. She was filled with tenderness and an intense awareness of her own insistent need. She pushed herself to a crouching position atop him, her feelings showing plainly on her face.

"You, too, my love?" He laughed up at her. He took her by the hips, lifting her and then impaling her upon himself. She cried out, startled at the sudden action, her eyes wide.

"Like this, Elen." He moved within her, eliciting another cry. She began to ride him, feeling her passion surging out of control, while he played with her breasts relentlessly until she fell upon his chest, heaving and sobbing in her fulfillment.

He gave her only a brief respite before he clutched at her hips and rolled over, pinning her under his great weight, their bodies still locked together. And now he took his pleasure, surging into her with endless need, reawakening her desire and carrying her with him to even higher peaks of ecstasy, over and over again until she was suffused by a rapture so intense it was painful, and she could neither think nor speak, but only feel, and there was nothing else in the world for her but Patric and her need for him, and the pleasure they gave each other.

She came back to herself only slowly. She lay crushed underneath him, scarcely able to breathe. She could feel the beat of his heart, the warmth of his breath against the curve of her throat, and she tried to press herself against him even more closely than she already was.

He stirred. He did not move from atop her body, he simply raised himself a little, as though he could not bear to separate himself from her. His mouth found hers. It was a tender kiss, deeply satisfying.

"Elen," he whispered, "I love you so."

"Don't." She began to struggle against him, suddenly angry with herself for her weakness. "Don't make me say it. I can't. I mustn't love you. Please, please."

But when he made love to her again a little while later, she did say it, over and over again. She told herself it was to lull any suspicions he might have.

He fell asleep at last, and she lay under his arm, knowing herself for a traitorous, heartless creature. She could not look at him, even in sleep.

She would leave on the morrow, betraying him as he had once betrayed her. She had to leave him. There was nothing else she could do. She, too, had her loyalties, and they were with Lulach.

"I'm sorry," she whispered softly, so as not to waken him. "Oh, Patric, I am so sorry."

28

September 10 to Christmas 1057.
Moray and Laggan.

It was barely light when Patric rose and began
dressing to go with Malcolm. In the glow of the
candles Resad had lit, Elen knelt on the bed and
watched her husband buckle on his sword.

"It will be a clear day," she said, glancing out
the window at a pink and gold sky.

"Good. That will make travel easier."

"Yes, it will," she replied, thinking of a
journey other than the one Patric had on his mind.

Patric picked up his blue cloak and swung it
about his shoulders.

"Go back to sleep if you want, my love. I've
given you precious little rest these last two
nights."

"I'd rather go riding. Please say yes, Patric.
Drust will take good care of me."

Patric's mind was on the day's journey, and
the battle that lay ahead of him at its end.

"Whatever you like, my dear. Just be careful."
He strode to the bed and caught her face between
his hands. His lips lingered on hers, relishing her
eager response. "Say you'll miss me, Elen."

"I will try."

"I think that's an improvement." He kissed

her again, laughing, then started for the door. "I'll have Resad tell Drust to saddle a horse for you."

"Don't bother. Resad has too much to do, since he's riding with you. When Ava brings my hot water, I'll send her. She likes an excuse to see Drust."

"That will be easier, I suppose. Good-bye, my love."

With a wave of his hand, Patric was gone, and Elen breathed a sigh of relief. She had not wanted to chance Resad's noticing anything odd about Drust's too-elaborate preparations for an hour of riding.

Patric flung the door open again, startling her in the midst of her guilty thoughts, but it was only to let Ava enter with a steaming pitcher of hot water.

"Here she is. Enjoy your ride, my darling."

"Is he really gone?" Elen asked.

"I think so, mistress. He only stopped to help me. King Malcolm was shouting for him when I passed through the hall."

"Malcolm is too impatient. Thank heaven I won't have to see Malcolm, or Patric, again."

"Are you sure you want to leave?" Ava inquired. "You seemed awfully fond of him yesterday. I thought you might have changed your mind."

"I was pretending, Ava, so he wouldn't be angry and refuse to let me go riding."

"I just wondered. He is so strong and handsome, and they say he is a mighty warrior. Is he a mighty lover, too?"

Elen refused to think about Patric and his lovemaking any longer. He was the enemy. She thrust him from her mind.

"I'm not interested in love, I am only concerned with joining my rightful king, and that is

Lulach. Now help me dress. I want to be gone before Fionna and Briga arrive and start asking questions or want to come with us."

Malcolm's troop of soldiers had departed by the time Elen rode out of the castle gate accompanied by Ava, Drust, and two of Drust's men who were also firm in their loyalty to Macbeth's heir.

In accordance with the scheme Elen had devised the day before, they rode south, following after the soldiers until they were well out of sight of the castle. Then they doubled back, riding west of the castle, skirting the edge of the forest and hills to a pre-arranged rendezvous. There, two more of Drust's men waited, with pack horses loaded with food and their bundled possessions.

"Any trouble?" Drust asked the men.

"None at all," came the answer. "Half the men-at-arms were preparing to ride with Malcolm, the other half have been pressed into service to help the Earl of Fife's lady pack for the move to Scone. No one even noticed us leave."

"It won't matter after this morning anyway," Elen said. "I have dropped enough hints about Laggan to make even an idiot understand that is where I want to go. It should be a long time before anyone thinks of Lulach and northern Moray."

"So now," Drust said, "we lose ourselves in this forest and head north instead of southwest. And King Lulach will have five more good fighting men who are faithful to the old ways, for his army."

"And two brave women," Ava added.

"Of course. Two women," Drust agreed. "Let us ride on, and remember to stay out of sight, so there will be no one to report which way we have gone."

It took them three days to reach Lulach. They

kept away from all habitations and did not even light campfires at night, lest Malcolm's troops, whom Drust had learned searched the countryside for clues to Lulach's whereabouts, discovered them. When they were found on the third afternoon, it was by three of Lulach's men. They sat upon their horses and gaped at Elen's party.

"What are women doing here?" demanded the leader, a dark, dangerous looking man, whose name, Elen later learned, was Bran.

"I seek my cousin, King Lulach," Elen told him. "Will you take us to him?"

"I might if I knew who you are," he sneered at her.

"I am Elen of Laggan. These are my people." Elen recited the names of her companions.

"You were wed to Talcoran," Bran said, his manner now more polite. "He was a good man. Lulach will be pleased to see you. Follow me."

Bran chose a well hidden path through the trees, which they followed until they came to a clearing, where Lulach had made his camp by a swift-flowing river.

"The king's tent is this way," Bran said, leading the newcomers toward it. As they reached the tent, Lulach stepped through the flaps.

"Elen!" he cried. "Is it really you?"

Elen was hardly off her horse's back before she was clasped in his arms.

"I knew you would come. I knew it." Tears filled Lulach's pale blue eyes. "I told Gertha you would never desert us."

"Where is Gertha?"

"Here, with me. She and the children are in the next tent. You have come just in time," Lulach said. "We are riding north tomorrow. We'll spend the winter in Burghead. I see your faithful servant is with you. Ava, I remember you and your kindness to me. And this is Talcoran's aide, is it not? But who are these others with you?"

Drust, who had knelt to kiss the hand of the man he considered his rightful king, now rose and presented his men-at-arms.

"We will serve you in any way you wish, my lord," Drust told Lulach, "Though I consider it my first duty to ensure the safety of my lady, which is what my lord Talcoran would have wanted me to do."

"Drust was badly wounded early in the summer, fighting beside Talcoran," Elen explained, "and he is still not completely well. I would like to keep him near me."

"Then I appoint him your personal guard," Lulach said. "As for these other men who came with you, I leave that to Drust."

"They all wish to fight for you, my lord," Drust said.

"I am happy to have them. Discuss with Bran where they can best serve," Lulach replied. "Now, Elen, come and see Gertha."

Gertha sat with her children and her one lady-in-waiting. Six-year-old Maelsnechta played with a toy sword that reminded Elen too poignantly of the tiny weapon her own Colin had once had. Deirdre was practicing embroidery stitches, her four-year-old fingers fumbling with an outsized needle. Gertha embraced Elen as warmly as had Lulach.

"I promised you would be the first of my ladies and you will," she said. She beckoned to a red-haired woman. "Do you remember Clare? She was with Gruach and now attends me. You two will have to share a tent for the present, but once we are at Burghead, you will have your own rooms."

Elen met the rest of Lulach's nobles at the

simple evening meal. She knew most of them, and her spirits lifted to see the goodly number of men who had remained steadfast after Macbeth's death.

"If these people are all supplying men to you, then you must have a large army," she said to Lulach.

"It will be even larger in the spring," Lulach replied. "Clare's husband Domingart has gone to Orkney to arrange for more men. Gertha's cousins are joint earls of Orkney now, and they support my claim to the throne of Alba. They have good reason to do so. If Malcolm defeats me, his next act will be to invade Caithness and Sutherland."

"Malcolm's father once tried to take those lands from the Orkadians," Elen reminded him, "and lost his life as a result."

"But Duncan had Macbeth and Thorfinn allied against him," Lulach said. "If I were dead, and Malcolm had more soldiers from the English king, he could easily take all of this land, right up to Pentland Firth. We both know Malcolm's warlike nature, Elen. He won't stop until he reaches the sea."

"You will stop him," Elen said, alarmed at this pessimistic view.

"We will try, but Malcolm is strong." Lulach brightened suddenly. "Would you like me to find you a husband from among my unmarried noblemen? Choose whomever you like, and I'll command him to marry you."

"I can't. Malcolm made me marry Patric mac Keith." Elen recounted the circumstances of her hasty wedding.

"I am sure there are those who would say you were wrong to run away from your husband," Lulach said, "But Patric was a traitor to Macbeth, and he and Malcolm tricked you. Once I've defeated Malcolm, I'll arrange an annulment, and then you may chose any husband you want. Of course, he might die in battle before then."

"Patric killed?" Elen had never considered that possibility before.

"You hated him enough to leave him, so it shouldn't matter to you."

"Of course not. You are right, Lulach. It doesn't matter." But a voice deep in her heart said, *it does matter, it does, it does.*

"Conal, Patric, thank heaven you have both returned safely."

"How are you, Fionna?" Patric spared his sister a quick kiss while his searching glance took in the company in the great hall. "Where is Elen? Why isn't she here to greet me?"

"She's gone."

"Gone where?" He saw the expression on Fionna's face. "What happened? Why didn't you stop her?"

"Patric, calm yourself. I'll tell you what I know, though it isn't much. She left secretly, and we believe she had ridden to Laggan. She told both Briga and me several times that she felt she should be there. She apparently was concerned about the reports of heavy damage done to the castle and the farmlands by Malcolm's army."

"She said as much to me the day before I left," Patric agreed, "but I told her we would go together as soon as I returned. I don't understand why she couldn't wait a few days. Go on, Fionna, tell me the rest. When exactly did she leave? And with whom? Though now I think on it, I'd wager I already know the answers to both of those questions."

"She went the very morning you rode away with Malcolm. It was well planned, Patric. Briga said Elen had your permission to ride with Drust and Ava, but they took four others along, men from Laggan."

"That seems reasonable," Conal observed. "Drust is always careful of Elen's safety."

"They took food and clothing," Fionna continued. "And they rode south."

"To River Garry and then west to Laggan," Patric said. "I'll send a messenger at once, to be certain she arrived safely. I'll leave first thing in the morning, and when I get my hands around that beautiful throat of hers—"

"I have already sent a rider to Laggan," Fionna interrupted. "I did that the morning after you left, five days ago."

"Then we won't hear any news for another three or four days at least. I can't wait that long."

"You are tired and hungry." Conal caught Patric's arm as he raced for the stairs. "Eat with us—look, the food is being brought in now—and get a good night's rest. In the morning we will talk more sensibly and decide what to do."

"Conal is right, Patric. Sit down," Fionna ordered. "Here, drink some wine."

"She would never have done such a foolish thing when she was young," Patric said, gulping at his wine.

"She is much changed since then. We all are, but in the last three months Elen has lost four of her dearest kinfolk. Make no mistake about it, dear brother, she did love Talcoran, and she doted on young Colin. She was ill for days after she learned of their deaths. Then Macbeth and Gruach both died, and she lost Laggan, too, and was forced to marry a man she had thought of as a traitor for many years. I think she is half mad with grief. She's not thinking clearly."

Patric stared glumly into his wine cup.

"You may be right. I've been none too gentle
with her." He paused, recalling his wedding night.
"Thank you, Fionna. I'll try to remember what you
have said."

But he could not restrain himself the next day.
Taking Resad and some food, he rode south. Two
days later he met the messenger Fionna had sent
to Laggan. After hearing the man's report, Patric
returned with him to Malcolm's headquarters. He
had begun to accept the fact that Elen's true intent
had been to leave him. She had cajoled him into
believing her heart was softening toward him, and
it had been a trick.

"If she's not at Laggan, where can she have
gone?" He prowled about Conal's rooms. "I have
got to find her."

"We are finally leaving for Scone tomorrow,"
Conal said. "Malcolm wants you with him."

"How can I go south with Malcolm when I
can't find my wife?" Patric flung himself into a
chair. "I am going to ask him to let me stay here
and search for her. Elen, Elen, where are you?"
His fist pounded on the chair arm.

"She will be safe, you know." Fionna tried to
comfort him. "She had five armed men with her.
Drust is no fool. He will be careful of her."

"*Fool.*" Patric went perfectly still, thinking.
His eyes met Conal's. At the same moment, both
men said, "Lulach."

"Oh, no," Fionna breathed. "She wouldn't."

"Wouldn't she?" All of Patric's anger and hurt
were in his voice.

"Well," Fionna admitted, "We do know how
much she hates Malcolm."

"She has always been close to Lulach," Conal
added.

"Then I must ride north," Patric said.

He asked Malcolm's permission that night.

Unwisely, he chose to do so in the great hall, before all of Malcolm's company, because the king was in a good humor at dinner. Malcolm laughed at him.

"What did you do to her, that she ran away after you had bedded her?" Malcolm demanded, his loud voice calling the attention of the entire court to Patric's marital problems. "Can't you control your own wife? No, you may not stay here. You will ride to Scone with me, and then, after a while, if I need you no more, you may go to Laggan. What you do there, on your own lands, is no concern of mine." And he remained adamantly opposed to entreaties made by both Patric and Conal.

"That was unnecessarily cruel," Fionna declared later. "Malcolm should not be so rude to you. He owes you too much."

"Which is why he is rude," Patric said. "Gratitude is a bitter brew for a king to swallow. I'll do as he wants, go to Scone, and then I'll go to Laggan and stay there all winter. I'm sick of royal courts."

"I have some men I can lend you," Conal offered. "We will send them out in the morning to search for news of Elen. They can report to us at Scone."

"Thank you."

Conal's men discovered nothing. The very lack of information convinced Patric that Elen had gone to Lulach, and had cleverly hidden her tracks.

He could think of nothing but Elen. He ached for her. The memory of her soft, passionately responsive body and her unwilling, tormented declarations of love haunted him, fueling his anger against her.

As soon as Malcolm would allow it, Patric

departed Scone and rode to Laggan. Fionna and
Conal had heaped gifts upon him, saying he would
need furniture and linens and other household
gifts.

"I have heard the most awful stories about
Malcolm's army ravaging the castle," Fionna had
said. "You may find nothing there but the bare
walls. But whatever the condition of your home, I
think you would rather have a new marriage bed,
would you not?"

Patric had hugged her, touched by her sen-
sitivity and by her implied belief that Elen would
return to him. Because Fionna knew Laggan well,
Patric had let her give instructions to the servants
who would accompany him. Fionna and Briga held
long conferences, and when the time came for
Patric to leave Scone, Briga went with him. They
were followed by a train of pack horses, and
guarded by Nechtan and a large party of armed
men, for Malcolm had not yet completely subdued
the countryside, and travel could be dangerous.

Because of all the baggage, the journey was
tediously slow. Patric chaffed and swore at every
delay, but at last they arrived at the castle that
was now his home.

He scarcely remembered the place. He had
spent three nights there eighteen years ago, and at
the time he had been more interested in Elen than
in her home. Now he reined in his horse and sat
looking at the surrounding hills and the limpid
blue loch. Beside the loch, Laggan Castle brooded,
grey and solid.

"It looks just the same," Briga said as they
approached the high-walled citadel.

Inside, it was much changed. One wall of the
great hall was blackened where fire had scorched
both timbers and stone, and the trestle tables and
benches had been badly damaged or broken. The

servants who had survived the attack had made a half-hearted attempt to clean the walls and repair the furniture, then had given up.

The master's bedchamber was a shambles. Malcolm's marauding army had destroyed everything in the room during a wild night of drinking and wenching. Patric kicked at the fragments of a chair and cursed.

"I can't sleep here," he said. He looked at Briga, who had followed him into the room.

"The other chambers are just as bad. Everything in the stillroom was destroyed," she reported. "Only the kitchen is usable. We can all sleep there for the time being."

Nechtan appeared at the open bedroom door.

"My lord, I would speak with you. There is a problem at the stables."

"Yes, I'm coming. Briga, I leave you in charge of everything indoors that is within a woman's domain. My sister says you are dependable. Here are the keys. Keep them until my lady comes home."

By the time they met again in the damaged great hall that night, over a scanty meal of cold game birds, bread and ale, Patric had a long list of problems he had found on his new property. He listened closely to Briga's comments and advice.

"Nechtan," Patric said to the man he had that afternoon confirmed as captain of his household guard, "I'll gladly take your suggestions, too. You will be aware of details not in Briga's knowledge. If we all three work together we can make Laggan even more beautiful and productive than it once was, so that when our lady returns to us, she will be pleased with what we have done."

He would not admit even the slightest possibility that Elen might not return. He wanted to ride to Lulach's camp, wherever that might be, and drag her home. Instead, he was forced to remain at Laggan. There was so much to do, and he was now solely responsible for the well-being of the people of Lagganshire. While he and Briga, Nechtan and Resad, labored together, gradually eradicating the evidence of war and hardship from the castle and its surroundings, repairing, rebuilding, supervising the harvest and storage of food for the winter, Patric sent a few trusted men to search out Lulach's headquarters and find news of his missing wife. It was nearly Christmas before he heard anything definite.

"She is at Burghead, my lord. When I rode north I stopped at a farmer's house to rest, and there I recognized another traveler, a friend of Drust's, who had become separated from a hunting party. The man went with Drust and your lady when they rode to join Lulach. He was eager to talk about Laggan. I think he was homesick. I gave him a little news of his old friends here, and then I asked him about my mistress. She is well, and has been made Lady to Lulach's wife. The man says she is devoted to Lulach and Gertha, but whenever he sees her, she seems sad."

"And what did you do with this talkative fellow?" Patric asked.

"There seemed no point in killing him. I suggested to him that it would be unwise to let his new companions know he had spoken to someone loyal to King Malcolm, and hinted that we might meet again sometime, when I could give him more news of his old home. We parted on friendly terms."

"Good fellow. You acted wisely." Patric beamed at his man. "Now that I know where Elen is, I can plan how to get her back."

"It might be well to wait until spring." Nechtan had also been listening to the man's report. "Burghead is so well fortified that even King Malcolm's army would have difficulty taking it, and though it is warmer in that part of Alba than it is here, and there is not so much snow, still the winter storms can be treacherous."

"We think alike, Nechtan. I hate the thought of Elen at Lulach's court, but in the spring he will have to move out of Burghead and go south to protect his southern border from the army Malcolm will send against him, and he will very likely take his womenfolk with him. We can rescue Elen before the two armies do battle, before she is in any serious danger."

And when I get my hands on her, Patric added silently to himself, my dear wife will regret the day she left me.

29

December 1057 to March 1058.
Burghead and Scone.

It was cold and damp at Burghead, and there was never enough food. Gertha's Viking cousins had sailed down from Orkney to celebrate Christmas with Lulach, and at long nightly feasts had consumed most of the supplies stored in the fortress.

Lulach had not begrudged the Norsemen their food and drink. He was trying to negotiate a formal alliance with them so they would send men to help him fight Malcolm when spring came.

In addition to her constant hunger, Elen suffered from the cold. Her wardrobe was inadequate for the winter conditions. She had brought with her only two gowns and the dress she had worn for travel. They were not warm enough. She had spilled wine on the warmest of the dresses.

"I'll wash it," Ava said, "But I don't think the stain will come out, and it won't be dry for tonight's feast."

"I have my old red wool gown. I put it in this chest when we first arrived. Go on, Ava, wash that and don't worry about me. I can dress myself."

Elen took the red dress out and unfolded it. As

she did so, the bracelet Patric had given her for a betrothal gift years before fell out of the skirt and clattered on the floor. Elen picked it up, feeling the weight of the gold, running her fingers over the smooth, cool surfaces of the stones with which it was set. She pressed it against her cheek as if doing so would bring Patric himself closer to her. Her eyes were misty.

"I'm being silly," she whispered to herself. Walking to a nearby table, where her comb and a small hand mirror lay, she picked up the wooden box containing the charmstone and the gold hair ornaments Talcoran had once given her. She stood a long time, weighing the two objects, one in each hand. At last, with a deep sigh, she put Talcoran's box into the clothes chest and lowered the lid. She clasped Patric's bracelet around her left wrist. And then she put on her red woolen gown and went down to Lulach's feast.

Hasteen, a pale-haired Norwegian giant, had taken a liking to Elen. He managed to sit next to her at every feast, and spent his evenings trying to charm her. On the night he tried to kiss her, Elen pushed him away so roughly he nearly fell off the bench.

Hasteen was not offended. He broke into loud, drunken laughter.

"I would like to marry you," he declared. "A woman like you would make strong sons. We would have a good time in bed, I think."

Elen grimaced at the thought. She reminded herself she should be nice to this Viking for Lulach's sake.

"I cannot marry you, Hasteen." She tried to put a touch of regret into her voice. "I already have a husband."

"Where is he?" Hasteen demanded, his hand

on his sword hilt."

"He fights for King Malcolm."

"That is worse than no husband at all. You
sleep here, he sleeps at Scone. Only a bad husband
would let you leave him."

"He is not—" Elen bit off the words she had
started to say.

"I give you a promise," Hasteen told her. "If
we join Lulach in his war against Malcolm, I will
seek out your husband and I will make you a
widow, so you can marry me. Would you like that,
my beauty?"

"Will your leaders join Lulach?" Elen asked,
to change the unpleasant subject.

"I do not know. That one is weak." Hasteen
nodded toward Lulach. "Perhaps the rulers of
Orkney will decide it is wiser to make a treaty of
friendship with Malcolm than to support one such
as your Lulach."

Elen shivered and rose from her place at
table. Hasteen reached for her. She slipped out of
his grasp.

"Where do you go?" he inquired.

"I have forgotten to do something," Elen said.
"I will return later."

She hurried away to her chamber, and bolted
the door behind her, lest Hasteen should follow.
She needed to think. The Viking's words had
terrified her. What if he did find Patric, and killed
him? It was an unbearable idea. She wanted no
harm to come to Patric because of her. Her
nervous fingers stroked the gold bracelet, which
she now wore constantly.

Lulach would not make a good king for Alba.
She had always known that, but in her grief at
Macbeth's death, and her blind anger at Malcolm
and Patric, she had cast that knowledge aside. In
the three months since she had joined Lulach, she

had seen his nobles daily quarreling among themselves, while Lulach, inept and weak, was helpless to stop them. Elen was certain that a group of Lulach's men were using him to advance their own fortunes. Lulach's decisions were often contradictory, frequently confusing, and usually not obeyed. Gertha was stronger than her husband, and more sensible, but she was a foreigner, and no nobleman would take orders from a woman under any circumstances. When spring came there would be war again, and Elen was convinced that, Viking allies or not, Lulach would be the loser.

She had been wrong to come to Lulach. She would remain, having made her choice, and publicly she would show only loyalty to Lulach's cause, but hers was now a heart divided.

She thought too frequently of Patric. Finding herself in a similar situation, she had begun to understand a little of what his life in exile must have been like. She had lately found herself becoming more and more sympathetic toward him.

He had told her he had never stopped loving her through all those years they had been separated. She had destroyed that love by her own actions, for how could he want her after what she had done? Her flight to Lulach, that act of disloyalty to Patric and to Malcolm, would separate them forever. She lived each day with that bitter knowledge. And now, when it was too late, she admitted to herself that she loved Patric. A part of her had never stopped loving him, not even when she thought she hated him.

Alone in her cold bedchamber, Elen wept for poor, foolish Lulach, whom she still loved like a brother whatever his faults, and for herself and Patric. She could see no end but tragedy.

"Patric, it's so good to see you. It has been a long winter." Fionna embraced her brother warmly. "Is there any news of Elen?"

"She is with Lulach. I was ready to ride north and rescue her when Malcolm's summons came, and I had to abandon my plans."

"Rescue? Is that what you call it? Are you sure she wants to be rescued?"

"She is my wife," Patric said, his mouth tightening, "and by heaven, I'll take her home to Laggan at this war's end, if I have to kill Lulach's entire army myself to do it."

"This war may not be so hard nor so long-lasting as we once thought," Conal said. "Have you heard about Malcolm's proposed marriage?"

"I only arrived at Scone an hour ago and came directly to your apartments. I've heard no gossip yet. Why is Malcolm marrying? It's an idea he has never relished."

"For the same reason all kings marry—to get an heir and to seal an alliance," Fionna said.

"There is always Donald for heir," Patric observed. "He is the next eldest of Duncan's sons."

"Donald has lived in the Hebrides too long," Conal said. "From Malcolm's point of view, Donald is tainted by exposure to the old tribal customs. As for Maelmuire, Malcolm has made him the ruler of Atholl, and the royal baby brother is quite content with that honor. A new day requires a new kind of king, and Malcolm believes in direct succession. He needs a son he can train as he wants."

"You are right," Patric said, "And I would have realized all of this myself, had I not been pre-occupied with other things. So Malcolm will marry. Who will the new queen be? You mentioned sealing an alliance, too."

"Ingebjorg of Orkney."

"Thorfinn's widow?" Patric whistled in surprise. "She's a good deal older than Malcolm."

"Not too old to bear him a son," Conal said. "Such a marriage will bring with it the friendship of Thorfinn and Ingebjorg's sons, who are now co-rulers of Orkney."

"So Paul and Erland will give their mother in marriage to Malcolm? That means they will stand with Malcolm rather than with Lulach, whose wife is only their cousin."

"Exactly. The contract is all but signed, and Malcolm seems eager enough to marry."

"Still, Lulach is safe so long as he remains in Moray," Patric said. "My information is that the people of Moray are united in their support of him. Lulach is Macbeth's heir, after all."

"Malcolm has a plan. I don't know what it is; he's keeping it to himself," Conal revealed.

"It had better be a good plan," Patric replied. "I want Lulach beaten, and I want my wife back."

In early March, Malcolm's army left Scone and marched into Moray to meet Lulach.

30

April 2 and 3, 1058.
Strathbogie.

"I will not do it." Patric faced Malcolm, a dangerous gleam in his blue eyes. Beside him, Conal nodded in agreement.

"Neither will I. This is unworthy of you, Malcolm."

The king looked up from the map he had been studying. He leaned back in his chair and stretched out his legs, his arms behind his head. Patric knew Malcolm was not so relaxed as he appeared to be.

"It is necessary. There will be no peace in my kingdom while Lulach lives. There would always be those men, particularly in these northern parts of Alba, who would rally behind him and try to place him on the throne."

"Lulach has a son," Patric reminded him.

"Maelsnechta will be disposed of, too," Malcolm said. "Lulach will be buried beside Macbeth at Iona."

"That royal graveyard grows crowded very quickly," Patric muttered under his breath.

"Do you fear for that renegade wife of yours, Patric?" Malcolm's laugh was unpleasant. "Is that why you oppose me in this? You should have taken my advice and divorced her last winter. You would still have Laggan, and you would be free to marry again. There are any number of my lords who would be willing to marry their daughters to you." Malcolm's attention returned to his map. "Here, I think, is a good place to trap Lulach."

The dozen or so other lords in Malcolm's tent agreed enthusiastically. The plan was approved with no more discussion. Only Conal and Patric dissented.

"Ambush and treachery," Conal said in disgust. "Lulach is no common outlaw, he is a prince of Alba, with a true claim to the throne. You should meet him in fair battle to decide who will rule. Give him warning and allow him time to draw up his men in proper formation, as is the custom among civilized rulers."

"Lulach is not ruler of Alba. I am, and I reject his claim. With the Norse and English reinforcements, my army outnumbers his by six to one. However I meet him, I will certainly win, but why should I waste more warriors than I must on a large battle I don't need to fight? An ambush is good enough for Lulach. I'll save my men for the task of pacifying the entire north of Alba." Malcolm's cold grey eyes flicked from Patric's set face to Conal's and back again. "You will not order your men to march with me?"

"No, my lord," Conal said evenly.

"No," Patric said.

"Were you any other men, I'd have you put in chains," Malcolm told them. "You are too scrupulous. Lulach is a usurper. Very well, I see I can't move you. I'll give you another assignment, then. While I engage Lulach, take some of your men and capture Lulach's womenfolk. I want Gertha and her children brought here to me. Hand the other women over to your men. They can do whatever they want with them. Patric, you may have Elen back again. If you are wise, you will strangle her at once.''

Patric and Conal left Malcolm's tent together.

"Kings!" Patric exploded once they were out of Malcolm's hearing. "I'm sick of them and their damned royal ambitions. When this war is over, I am going home to Laggan, and I may never leave it again. I've had enough of courts and kings."

"I share your disgust, but I will stay at court and use my influence to moderate Malcolm's ambition. He has the potential to be a good king, but he is young and inexperienced. At least," Conal added, "we are still free men. I thought he would have us jailed for treason."

"He needs us," Patric grumbled. "His position is not so strong as he pretends."

Conal considered this.

"He is right about the need to remove Lulach, but I cannot stomach the thought of that poor fool being led to the slaughter like a sheep."

"Lulach should be warned," Patric said. "He deserves a chance to die like a man."

"Patric—" Conal's tense voice held a cautionary note. Patric cut him off.

"If we bring Gertha and her children back here, Malcolm will kill them as soon as Lulach is dead.''

"You cannot help them, my friend."

"I can at least try. I cannot go myself. If I leave this camp before he does, Malcolm would guess at once what I was doing. Conal, I want you to leave me now. For Fionna's sake as well as yours, I don't want you to know anything about my plans."

Conal put out his hand and Patric took it.

"Good luck," Conal said, and went away to his own tent.

Patric found Nechtan.

"I have a mission for you," he said. "When you

return, you are to make your report to no one but me."

Lulach had brought his entire household south from Burghead. Gertha and her two children shared a large tent. Nearby was a smaller tent, which Elen shared with Ava, and a third tent for Clare and her husband Domingart. He and Bran were Lulach's closest advisors.

Elen had grown friendly with the quiet, serious Clare. On this day they were both in attendance on Gertha, when Lulach and Domingart appeared.

"My scouts have located Malcolm's army a short distance southwest of here," Lulach said. "We will meet him in battle in a day or two."

"My lord," Clare said nervously, "Do you think Queen Gertha and the children should be placed so near an enemy army?"

"I hadn't thought of that. Perhaps you are right. But I want Gertha near me. And you, Elen."

"We will stay with you, my lord," Gertha said firmly. "Knowing we are nearby and that our safety depends on them, our soldiers will surely fight even more valiantly than they otherwise would. And when victory is ours, your family will be here to celebrate with you."

"Yes, I think you are right, my dear. Stay then. You will be safe enough here. Malcolm won't make war on women and children."

Elen disagreed with Lulach. She was not afraid for herself, or for Gertha, who made her own decisions. It was the children who concerned her. When Lulach and Domingart left Gertha's tent, Elen excused herself and followed them, intending to plead with Lulach to send the children back to Burghead, where they would be safe.

As she stepped out of Gertha's tent, Drust moved into place beside her and accompanied her. She saw there was a heavier than usual guard about Lulach's tent, and men were entering in more than usual haste. Lulach must be holding a meeting of his captains. Her request would have to wait until later. She went to her own tent. As Drust pulled back the flaps to let her enter, Elen heard him utter a startled exclamation.

"Is something wrong?" she asked.

"No, lady, I only remembered a chore I forgot to do. Will you stay in your tent now? I'll return soon to guard you."

"I will, and Ava will be with me."

Drust watched Elen inside, then turned and strode quickly to Lulach's tent. The guards there, who knew he often carried messages from Elen to Lulach, let him enter without question.

"Nechtan!" Drust stared at the man kneeling before Lulach. "I thought it was you I saw being dragged in just now. What are you doing here?"

"Be careful," Bran warned. "He was heavily armed."

"He can hardly hurt me on his knees with you holding a dagger at his throat," Drust responded calmly.

"Do you know him?" Bran demanded.

"I do, and I think he would do King Lulach no harm, even if you were to let him stand."

"Drust, who is he?" Lulach asked.

"He was the captain of your cousin Elen's household guard at Laggan. He now serves her husband. Nechtan, have you a message for my lady?"

"Not for her, but for Prince Lulach," Nechtan said.

"He is *King* Lulach," Bran declared, giving Nechtan a hard push.

"Let him stand," Lulach said. "Let him deliver this message from my cousin Malcolm."

"It is not from Malcolm that I come," Nechtan said, straightening his tunic, "But from Patric mac Keith."

"What has he to do with King Lulach?" asked Domingart.

"My lords, I am sent to warn you that Malcolm plans an ambush tomorrow. He will kill all of you if he can, as you march to meet him, while you are yet unprepared for battle."

Lulach, white to the lips, tried to speak, but could get no words out.

"How do we know your message is not in itself some kind of trap?" Bran demanded.

Nectan ignored him and spoke directly to Lulach.

"My master told me to beg you to believe me, in the name of the love you have always borne for your cousin Elen and the love she has for you. You are greatly outnumbered by Malcolm's army. You have time to flee northward if you would save yourself, my lord. Whatever you decide to do, my master begs you send the women and children back to Burghead. I was to remind you that you should want your son to survive."

"Even if I die." A little color had come back into Lulach's ashen face. "Patric mac Keith would not flee from danger, would he?"

"No, my lord."

"Nor would Macbeth. Neither will I."

"But, my lord!" Domingart cried, "It is a trap."

"It's no trap if we know Malcolm's plan," Bran growled. "We should stay and fight."

"We will," Lulach said in a surprisingly decisive tone. "Nechtan, can you read a map? Do you know where Malcolm plans to meet us?"

"Yes, my lord." Nechtan walked to a table where several maps lay open. He looked at them in silence for a while, then laid one finger on a spot. "Here is the place. My master knew no more of the plan than its location. He and the Earl of Fife refused to take part in it, and so they were not given information about it."

"I don't think we should trust this man," Bran said. "Perhaps a little torture would wring more information from him."

"I have told you the truth, my lords."

"We'll find that out before we kill you," Bran snarled.

"No," Lulach said. "I will not repay a kindness with torture and death. Nechtan, will you linger to take some food with us? No? Then you are free to go, with my blessing and my thanks."

"He may have been a spy," Bran said after Nechtan had left. "We should follow him."

"Sir," Drust said quietly, "I know that man well. I believe he spoke the truth."

"I agree with you, Drust." Lulach had apparently lost all of his earlier fear.

"Do not tell the women about this message," he ordered. "I don't want to frighten them. We will arrange for them to go north at dawn. We'll get little sleep this night, my friends. We have a new battle plan to devise. We will show Malcolm how bravely the men of Moray can fight."

Malcolm positioned his army so that its center faced a narrow valley through which Lulach's forces must march to reach the open plain where Lulach would most likely choose to meet him. Lulach was to believe Malcolm would wait until both armies were drawn up in battle order, a period of at least one day. But Malcolm did not plan to wait. His right and left flanks were stationed out of sight on the hillsides above the valley. A fourth part of the army, composed of Norsemen from Orkney and Norway, had been dispatched with orders to ride around the hills unseen, and after Lulach's army had entered the valley, block off its northern end so there could be no retreat.

"He'll be boxed in," Malcolm said, his contempt for his cousin plain to hear. "I know Lulach. He's stupid and weak. When he sees me, he'll surrender and I'll kill him, and that will be the end of it. But just in case some of his men decide to fight, we will be well prepared. If anyone tries to escape at the other end of the valley, the Norsemen will cut them down. It should take less than half the morning. This will be a glorious day."

"A shameful day for Alba," Patric said as he and Conal left the tent that served as Malcolm's headquarters.

"There is nothing we can do now but follow our orders," Conal replied. "We must take some of our men and go capture the women. I pray heaven we don't find them."

They made a wide circle around Malcolm's army, and in late morning found Lulach's nearly deserted camp. Dismounting, they crept along the side of a hill, sheltered by rocks and bushes, until they were near enough to look down into the cluster of tents.

"No sign of women," Conal noted. He pointed. "That is where the wounded will be brought—see the supplies of bandages—and there are the extra horses."

Nechtan, on Patric's other side, agreed.

"That empty place next to the largest tent is where Queen Gertha lived. There were smaller tents around it for the ladies. They are all gone now, my lords."

"Then we will assume your visit here was not in vain, Nechtan." Patric started back toward the horses and his men who waited some distance away. "We had better capture those poor souls who are left down there, and take them back as prisoners to appease Malcolm. It's hardly worth attacking them."

Lulach's followers put up a surprisingly strong resistance. It was several hours later when the few survivors were tied together with rope and prodded toward Malcolm's camp. Patric personally destroyed the evidence that clearly indicated the women had fled toward Burghead. He hoped by doing so to delay Malcolm's inevitable pursuit, thus giving Gertha and her party a better chance of reaching safety.

"God, Conal, I'm sick of killing. This was ridiculous, and that senseless ambush—they'll all die in that valley." Patric ran his hands through his hair. "I'm glad I warned them. At least Lulach was able to make a choice about meeting Malcolm. And I'm glad the women escaped. Elen—"

"Let's go," Conal said.

As they rode back toward Malcolm's encampment, the sounds of battle grew louder. They were drawn toward the noise. In silent agreement the two friends and Nechtan turned their horses and rode toward it, signaling their men to take the prisoners on to the camp.

By the time they reached the valley, the slaughter was almost done. Bodies littered the hillside. The noise was retreating northward as Malcolm's army pursued the last remnants of Lulach's men into the arms of the waiting Vikings.

"Have you come to see the end of it?" Malcolm called. He was on foot, his red-gold banner, held by an aide, flaring out above him in the breeze. He towered half a head above the men who formed a circle about him. "Join us. You are welcome, though the men of Laggan and Fife will get no booty from this day's work."

As Patric and Conal and Nechtan drew nearer, Malcolm turned back to the sagging hulk before him.

"Here are my men, cousin," Malcolm said sweetly. "They have captured your wife and babes. After I've finished with you, I'll kill them, too."

Lulach, held upright between two strong soldiers by the stumps of his arms, flung back his head. Over Malcolm's shoulder he could see Patric and Conal, still mounted on their horses, and behind Patric, Nechtan.

Lulach's eyes locked on Patric's. Patric shook his head, denying Malcolm's words. He saw by the ghost of a smile twisting the bloody gash that was once Lulach's mouth, that Lulach had understood him.

"No," Lulach gasped. "They are safe. Safe. They have escaped you, fiend."

"We'll see about that. You will not escape me, Lulach the Fool." Malcolm raised his sword arm.

Lulach's feet were so badly mutilated he could not stand by himself, but with a final effort he drew himself up between the two men who supported him and waited for Malcolm's blow. His eyes never left Patric's.

"Thank you, my friend," Lulach said clearly.

Malcolm's sword arm slashed down.

Patric turned his head away from the thing that lay on the ground before Malcolm, and looked instead at a nearby flowering tree just coming into bloom. The air was soft and warm that day. It was spring, and new life was flooding back into the land. The shattering irony of it was not lost upon him as he thought of cold treachery and bleak death. Glancing back toward his king a moment later with his face carefully composed, he watched as Malcolm wiped his blade and sheathed it.

"That was a fool indeed," Malcolm said. "Did you hear him? He thanked me for killing him, the weakling. And now I have won. Alba is mine at last."

A cheer went up from the men surrounding Malcolm. It carried along the valley until it echoed back to him in the voices of his men returning from the annihilation of the last of Lulach's army.

No, Patric thought, you misunderstood him. It was Lulach who won this day. At the end Lulach found within himself a true man's valor and faced you without flinching, while you, my noble king, had to defeat him by treachery.

"Let us go from here," Conal said, touching Patric's shoulder.

"Aye." Patric pulled his horse around, and together he and Conal and Nechtan made their way back to their own tents.

31

April 1058.
Moray and Laggan.

"My oath to Duncan is fulfilled. Malcolm sits firmly upon the throne of Alba, and I am free at last. Now I must find Elen before Malcolm does," Patric said. "I know him; he'll go after Gertha as soon as he has finished celebrating this victory, and if he finds Elen, too, he will kill her along with the others. I cannot let her die."

"Go now, before he comes back from the battlefield," Conal advised. "Take just a few of your men with you—you will be able to move faster that way—and order the rest to march back to Laggan at once. I'll make some excuse to Malcolm for you."

"What excuse?" Patric laughed cynically. "Malcolm will accept none."

"I think he will be too happy about his victory over Lulach to be very angry with you. Malcolm knows you are loyal in spite of this disagreement. Once you and your men-at-arms are safe at Laggan, behind your mountains, I wager he'll do nothing but send you a few angry letters and then forget the incident."

Patric did as Conal suggested. He put Nechtan in charge of the fighting men he had brought from

Laggan, with orders to march home as quickly as possible. Then he took his personal servant Resad and two men-at-arms and rode toward the northwest.

They had not traveled very far before night fell, but Patric was comforted by the knowledge that Malcolm could not start after Gertha before the next day, possibly even later. In the meantime, he would locate his runaway wife and take her to safety.

He and his men were mounted and riding again as the first light streaked the sky. They found the women shortly before noon. They sat on a hilltop and watched four overloaded baggage carts and a dozen horses and riders plod slowly along the road below them.

"They don't escape very fast, do they?" said Resad.

"They're damned lucky we aren't a troop of Malcolm's men. If we were, they'd be dead by now. They don't even have a decent guard posted."

"What do we do now, my lord?"

"Follow them. There is only one person among them that I'm interested in. I'd like to see the others get safely to Burghead. I'm sure that is where they are going, and once they are there, the men of Moray will protect Gertha and her children from Malcolm."

They trailed behind the ragged little caravan, keeping out of sight. Soon the carts and horses stopped by a stream. The horses were being watered, while the fugitives ate a light meal. Patric and his men did the same.

"Now we begin to be lucky," Patric said softly, as the carts set off again, leaving five horses and their riders lingering beside the stream. Patric recognized Drust and Ava, and two fighting men. The fifth person was Elen. "There is the one I want. Let the main party get a little farther ahead of them. We will do this with as little bloodshed as possible."

Elen's people had finished watering their horses and were about to ride on when Patric and his men charged them with swords drawn. Drust saw them first. With a loud warning cry, he spurred his horse forward to meet them. One of Patric's men dealt him a slashing blow. Drust tumbled to the ground, clutching at his bleeding arm and trying to roll to one side, out of the way of his falling horse. Patric's man raised his arm to finish him. Elen forced her horse between Drust and the other man, risking her life to save her faithful servant.

"Stop it!" she screamed. "Leave him alone!"

"Angus, hold!" Patric caught at his man's arm in the nick of time, preventing him from killing Elen. "Put down your swords and you won't be harmed," he shouted at Drust's two men. He was much relieved when they quickly obeyed him.

Ava was on her knees weeping hysterically over Drust. Elen slipped off her horse and went to them.

"It's not so bad," Drust said, his hand over the cut.

"No, it only needs to be bound tightly to stop the blood," Elen agreed. "Ava, get those linen cloths out of my saddlebag."

Ava paid no attention to her, but continued to cry loudly. Elen stood looking down at Ava and Drust with a white, set face. They had all been captured so easily, and now Patric would take them back to Malcolm. All of their lives were forfeit, Gertha and her children might well be caught with equal ease, and all Ava could think to do was weep. It was too much for Elen's badly strained nerves. Suddenly she lifted her hand and slapped Ava so hard that the woman went sprawling onto the ground.

"There is no need for that, lady," Drust said quietly, reaching out his good arm to Ava. "She is only worried about me."

"Is this what you want?" Patric handed Elen the linen. She took it without a word and without looking at him. She was ashamed of what she had just done. Ava was plainly terrified and could not help crying. Now Elen became aware of Patric's men and her own servants standing about eyeing each other tensely. She pulled herself together and bound Drust's arm, stanching the blood, and then she stood, still not looking at Patric.

"I assume I am your prisoner," she said, expecting him to order all of them bound. She was surprised he had not done so at once.

Patric said nothing. He was still behind her. She heard his indrawn breath. He seized her left wrist, raising it until her sleeve fell back, revealing the gold bracelet he had once given her.

"So," he said softly, and dropped her wrist.

"If you are going to kill me, do it quickly," she told him.

"Malcolm advised me to strangle you," Patric said, "and for a while I was tempted to take his advice."

Elen gulped. She saw the desperation on Drust's face, the fear in Ava's eyes. She knew there was no hope of rescue. Gertha had made them all agree that anyone who lagged behind was on his own. Gertha had not enough men with her to protect everyone, and the safety of her son Maelsnechta was of paramount importance.

"Now that I see you, I'm not sure just what to do with you," Patric added.

Elen turned and faced him at last, looking full into his eyes. She had not forgotten how handsome

he was, how exciting. She fought the urge to throw
herself into his arms.

"What about these others?" she asked.

"They did help you to escape me, did they not?
Malcolm would say they should die for that."

"Let them go," she said, "and I will go with
you peacefully and face whatever punishment I
must endure without a struggle."

"You will go with me whether I let them go or
not."

"Drust was Talcoran's aide for years, and he
and his men have been faithful to me. Ava has been
my maid since I was fifteen years old. I cannot let
harm come to them because of me."

"You should have thought of that before you
led them astray."

"Patric." Elen tried to think of some plea that
would move the granite-faced man before her. She
found it in the past. "Do you remember Bancho of
Lochaber?"

"I do."

"Once, long ago, Bancho let you take your
men, and three little princes, out of Alba. He did it
because it was the honorable thing to do. The deed
eventually cost him his life. Had he known the
price, he would still have done it. If you remember
Bancho, you know that I speak the truth."

"What has that to do with me now?"

"Let these people go, in Bancho's memory.
You owe that debt. They can do little harm to
Malcolm, and little good to Gertha, but their lives
matter to me."

She thought she would die of anxiety before
he answered her, so heavily did her heart beat, so
hard did his blue eyes stare into hers, searching,
searching. For what? There was nothing in her for
him to find. She was empty. Lulach was dead. All
hope was gone for her own life. She could only try

to save the lives of the servants who had been her friends for so long.

"That same Bancho," Patric mused, "was most foully murdered by order of your beloved Macbeth. Yet you have remained loyal to Macbeth and his heir over Malcolm."

"Is Malcolm perfect?" Elen asked, a touch of acid in her voice in spite of the need to placate Patric. "I heard of the ambush Malcolm planned for Lulach. I can guess how Lulach died."

Patric winced. "No one is perfect, least of all a king."

"Set them free. Please."

Patric forced his eyes away from Elen's face and looked at Drust.

"Can you ride?"

"Aye, my lord. The wound is but a simple cut."

"Then take a message to Gertha. Tell her Elen of Laggan has returned to her husband. Tell her we both wish her well."

"Thank you," Elen whispered.

Ava brought the small bundle that was all of clothes or other possessions Elen had left, and gave it to one of Patric's men to fasten at Elen's saddle. Drust mounted Ava's horse and lifted her up behind him, taking his own injured animal by the reins, to lead it without burden. Patric nodded, and his men stepped back, allowing Drust's men to reach and mount their own horses.

"Good-bye, mistress." Ava wept.

"Good-bye," Elen said, fighting back her own tears. "God keep you safe. Drust—oh, Drust—"

"God keep you, too, my lady." Drust wheeled his horse, and he and his men rode away.

"Now, my lord," Elen said to Patric when the others were safely gone, "kill me quickly and be done with it."

"Did I say I was going to kill you?"

"You are Malcolm's man. I told you, I know what he did to Lulach, that treacherous ambush. I also know what you did to Lulach's camp. A rider came to us, a barber-surgeon who escaped you and your muderous henchmen. He told us how you killed as many as you could and drove the rest back like cattle to face Malcolm. You led the attack. How I hate you for that."

Elen's voice broke. She tried to control herself. She would not weep before this enemy. Patric must not know how weak and tired she felt, nor must he guess how confused her feelings toward him were. She had thought she loved him until she had heard of the attack on Lulach. Now she did not know what she felt. It tore at her heart to believe he had been party to such a cruel and dishonorable trick.

"You believe that story?" Patric was glaring at her.

"I know what happened, you brute. Go on, kill me. Women, babies, and defenseless old men are your favorite victims, aren't they?" She spread her arms wide and waited.

"Get on your horse," Patric ordered in tones of utter disgust. "You damned fool, mount, I said! Resad, help her, she looks like she's going to faint. If I touch her, God knows what I'll do to her."

Elen got into the saddle somehow. Patric and his men closed about her so she could not escape, and they moved off in the opposite direction from the one taken by Drust.

Patric drove them hard. He was eager to reach the safety of his own lands. He spoke to Elen only when it was absolutely necessary. When they stopped at nightfall she faced him as bravely as she could.

"This is not the way to Malcolm's camp," she said. "We are going in the wrong direction."

He did not answer her.

"Where are you taking me, my lord?"

"Laggan," he answered shortly.

"I thought I was Malcolm's prisoner. Am I yours instead?"

Patric shrugged and said nothing.

"What are you going to do with me?"

"I haven't decided yet."

"Patric." She laid a hand on his arm. He removed it as if it were an unpleasant insect.

"Sleep," he said. "We rise at dawn."

The men took turns keeping watch. They watched Elen as well as standing guard against attack, and she slept little, knowing their eyes were always upon her.

She grew more and more frightened as they traveled southward. If Patric had killed her quickly when he found her, she could have borne it. She had been certain Malcolm would win against Lulach, and she had been prepared to die when that happened. She had thought Patric would be merciful and it would be over with one swift stroke of his sword. This silent ride with her cold, distant husband was terrifying. She wondered how he would punish her. Men had been known to lock disobedient wives into small rooms and keep them there until they died. Perhaps that would be her fate. Or he might turn her over to Malcolm, to face a mock trial and a traitor's death. The uncertainty ate at her frayed nerves.

"Your master is a cold man," she said to Resad on the second night, while they shared a loaf of hard oat bread and some warm ale for the evening meal. "He is cold and cruel."

"You know nothing about him, lady." Resad's voice was sharp. "It is because of my master that you, and the lady Gertha and her children, are still alive." Then he told her how Patric had sent

Nechtan to warn Lulach. "That is why the women and children were sent away before the battle began," Resad finished.

"Lulach was still ambushed."

"He and his men went prepared. They inflicted more damage on Malcolm's army than anyone expected. Because of my master, your Lulach died like a man, not an animal, and all the women and children got away."

"I don't believe this. Patric loves Malcolm. He would never do such a thing."

"Ask Nechtan when you see him. He is the one who went to Lulach." Resad went away, leaving Elen to her thoughts.

They reached Laggan at sunset the next day.

"I thought it was ruined," Elen said. "It looks the same. No, it has changed. There, the north wall. Patric, what have you done to my home?"

"We'll talk later." Patric spurred his horse and rode ahead, leaving Elen with Resad.

"Will you tell me what he has done to Laggan?" she asked.

"He spent last autumn and the winter repairing all of the damage Malcolm's soldiers did, so it would be ready when you came home," Resad answered.

"But he knew I would never come home again."

"Not so, lady." Resad's mouth twitched before he resumed his customary serious demeanor. "He has always believed you would return. You have, and Laggan is ready for you."

The black smoke stains had been cleaned off the stone walls of the great hall. There were two new beams to hold up the repaired roof. Flames danced merrily in the firepit, their warm glow reflected in the polished wood of the new trestle tables and benches, and two high-backed chairs that replaced the ones destroyed when the castle was taken. Beyond the firepit Elen could see signs of further work being done on one of the walls.

"Welcome home, my lady." Briga greeted her at the entrance to the hall.

"I am a prisoner," Elen told her. "Do not call me your lady."

"My lord," Resad said to Patric, "Nechtan and his men are arriving."

"I want to speak to Nechtan," Elen declared. She would quickly discover if the story Resad had told her was true.

"Later." Patric's voice was cold. "You and I will speak later, too, when I am free. For now, I have work to do. Go with Briga. She will show you to your room. Remain there until I come to you."

Elen followed Briga. She had expected to be conducted to one of the tiny rooms near the tower, but instead, Briga led her to the master's chamber.

It was much changed. At Patric's command, a fireplace with a finely carved stone mantel like those he had seen in England had been built into one wall. Following Fionna's orders to Briga, the room had been cleared of all signs of damage and cleaned thoroughly. The new bed, Fionna's present, had been set up on the opposite side of the room from the location of the old one. It had been hung with blue wool curtains, and a piece of blue silk brocade covered the fine linen sheets that were also a gift from Fionna.

Several beautifully carved clothing chests sat about the room. There was a wooden armchair with a blue silk cushion on its seat, and a long table with a second chair, where a lady could sit while combing her hair. On the table stood a shimmering silver mirror with an ornate frame, and two silver candlesticks, all gifts from Conal mac Duff.

Dried lavender was strewn among the rushes on the floor. It released its fragrance into the air when Elen walked across it.

"Who changed this room?" Elen demanded irritably, forgetting her captive status.

"Mistress, we had to clean it after the soldiers were gone." Briga explained about the destruction wrought by Malcolm's men, and Elen sighed. It was one more thing to hold against the hated king.

"The Countess of Fife sent the new furniture. It is her wedding gift to you," Briga said. "She even gave me instructions on where to place each piece."

"Fionna is responsible for this?" Elen looked about the room with less hostility than she had shown at first.

"I hope you like it, mistress."

"I do. But am I to be kept here, in the master's chamber? Where will your lord sleep?"

"I do not know." Briga did not meet Elen's eyes, and Elen wondered if Patric had taken a mistress and slept with her in some other room. It would be her own fault if he had.

"Would you like a bath, lady? You must be sore from riding so far." Briga appraised her mistress's bedraggled appearance. "We brought to Laggan the clothes you left behind when you—er, when you went away, so you can change into something better than that."

"I do look dreadful, don't I?" Elen's low laugh ended the unnatural formality between them. "Oh, Briga, it's so wonderful to see you again. If you are here to talk to, my imprisonment may be bearable."

Elen soaked for a long time in a wooden tub of hot water into which Briga had tossed dried herbs. Their fragrance, released by the steam, drifted through the bedchamber, mingling with the scent of applewood burning in the new fireplace and the lavender on the floor. When she had finished bathing, Elen wrapped herself in a linen towel and sat before the fire while Briga dried her hair with a silk cloth to make it shine, and then combed it.

"Shall I braid it, my lady?"

"No, leave it loose. Since I am to remain in this room, no one will see it."

"You are fortunate. You have no grey hairs at all," Briga said, "And only a few tiny lines about your eyes. In spite of all that has happened to you recently, you look much younger than your years."

"That is partly your doing, Briga. It's all your herbal creams and lotions. I even took some with me when I ran away. I made some creams for Gertha and her ladies. Your name is famous in Moray." The lightness left Elen's voice when she added, "Gertha. I wonder where she is now?"

"You are too thin." Briga broke the silence that followed Elen's sad question. "You should eat more."

"There wasn't much food in Lulach's camp toward the end."

Elen looked more closely into the polished silver mirror. Thin or no, her figure was not quite so firm as it had been. There was a soft blurring of the once-angular outlines, the small round breasts not quite so high and taut, the waist a trifle thicker, the abdomen a little more rounded after four pregnancies. But Briga was right about the rest. Her hair was a shiny, raven-black mantle that hung to below her hips. Her skin had retained its creamy, translucent lustre, though the midnight-blue eyes were shadowed by sorrow.

Elen realized without a trace of vanity that she had grown into a beautiful, mature woman. There was no pleasure in the knowledge. Her beauty meant nothing. She had no love upon whom to bestow it. She would live out her life alone, imprisoned here at Laggan or somewhere else, and after Lulach's final defeat, it mattered little. Briga handed her a deep blue robe of fine, soft wool.

"That's not mine. I've never seen it before."

"It is what my master wants you to wear."

Elen slipped into the robe, and Briga adjusted the belt. The wool was deliciously warm against her skin.

"Now what shall I do?" Elen asked.

"You are to wait here until my lord comes. He will speak with you later."

"Must you go? Sit down, Briga. Tell me what has happened in my absence. I thought Laggan had nearly been destroyed, but everything I've seen is so beautiful."

"It was in a sorry state when we saw it last autumn, mistress."

Elen sat spellbound while Briga recounted in detail Patric's activities as Earl of Laggan.

"When King Malcolm is at Dunedin we are so far removed from him, and his law, that my master is quite independent," Briga finished. "He has repeatedly said he wishes to live here at Laggan, and will not go often to court. I think that is because he was homeless for so long. He loves this place, mistress."

"I'm glad." Elen had no chance to say more. The door opened and Patric entered. He, too, had bathed, and he had put on a fresh tunic. His silver-tinged auburn curls were still a little damp. He was so handsome, so vital, he took her breath away. Elen felt a deep, stabbing pain in her heart as she realized how much she had given up when she left him.

"I will leave you alone, my lord." Briga jumped to her feet.

"Thank you." Patric's eyes were fixed on Elen. She did not rise from her chair, and after a moment he took the seat Briga had vacated.

"First, you should know that Malcolm gave you to me as a prisoner," he said without preamble. "You will not have to face him."

"Thank God." Elen closed her eyes, relief washing over her.

"Now that I have relieved you of that fear, perhaps you will explain to me why you left me so suddenly and so secretly," he said in a dangerously calm tone of voice.

Elen's fingers clenched the carved arms of her chair so tightly that her knuckles went white. He was not going to make this meeting easy for her, and she could not blame him. She was well aware of the deep injury she had done to his masculine pride. He had taken her to his bed, told her over and over that he loved her, and then she had run away from him. She realized that the only weapon she dared use now was honesty. She tried to answer him with a calmness matching his own.

"I had to do it. I owed it to Lulach, and to Macbeth. I should have gone with Gertha after Macbeth was killed, fled before Malcolm's army took the castle, but I hesitated, and then it was too late, and we were forced to marry . . . you know all that. I don't expect you to understand, Patric."

"But I do understand. Did I not do something similar for Duncan? You have told me how badly my leaving hurt you then. You deliberately inflicted the same pain on me as soon as you had the opportunity."

"I wasn't trying to hurt you, only to do what I thought was right." Before he could respond to that, she changed the subject. "Please don't keep me in suspense any longer. Tell me how you will punish me."

He did not answer. He sat looking at her, wondering what she would do if she could read his thoughts. He had been so furious with her before he got her back that he had entertained himself by contemplating several terrible forms of punishment he might inflict on her. Then he had seen her again, wearing his bracelet, and he had heard her plead for her servants' lives, and his heart had begun to melt.

His anger had cooled further during the ride to Laggan. She had not complained once about the scanty food or the long days in the saddle, or the need to sleep on the ground each night with only her cloak for cover. Respect and admiration and then a new kind of love had gradually replaced his rage, until now he could not bear to think of hurting her.

He had begun to understand that the fragile, delicate creature he had held so tenderly in his boyish memories all the years of his exile, and had thought he had finally married, had never really existed. He had idealized the girl, and the woman who was Elen of Laggan was much changed from whoever the real girl had been. Her mature beauty was more tantalizing, the tortured depths of her character more intriguing and mysterious, than he had ever imagined a woman could be. He now loved her with all the depth and complexity of his own adult heart, and he recognized that it would take a lifetime to know her completely.

He could have her tonight if he insisted, but he wanted something more than her body. Much as he desired her, physical union alone was not enough. He wanted her to love him as he loved her. He was willing to wait until she had recovered from grief and loss and would let him show her how much he cared. But, he told himself, if he was going to do that, he could not stay here with her any longer or he would pull her into his arms and never let her go. He stood up.

"I will not sleep here tonight," he said. "I'll have Briga bring you some food."

"Am I confined to this room?" She looked puzzled.

"Only at night. During daylight hours you may go wherever you wish on the castle grounds, provided that Briga is with you. And," he added with a warning glint in his eyes, "You may not go riding. The men-at-arms and all the stableboys have been told that. Do not embarrass yourself by attempting it."

"You needn't worry. I have no place left to go, have I?"

"I hope you will be content at home." He left her on that, and a little while later Briga brought her a tray of food and a pitcher of wine, and stayed with her until it was time for bed.

She spent an uneasy night. Patric had not answered her question about her punishment, and she could not understand his attitude toward her. He did not seem to be angry, only cool and distant. Based on that, she felt he would not be cruel in his decision about her, but she could not be absolutely certain.

She spent the next morning inspecting the castle with Briga as guide, so she could see all the changes Patric had made. She was forced to admit that most of them were for the better. She particularly approved of the new fireplace, a huge stone structure that had recently been begun in the center of one long wall of the great hall.

"It should be finished well before next winter," Briga said, "And we can cover up the old firepit. Then the hall won't be so smoky. It will all go up the chimney, and the masons say it will be warmer because the smoke holes in the roof can be closed. There are new tapestries to be hung, too, once the workmen have finished."

Patric was absent from the midday meal. Nechtan reported he had gone to visit one of the tenant farmers and would not return until late in the day.

When Elen took the captain of Laggan's guard aside to speak quietly with him, she discovered that Resad had been telling the truth. It was indeed Patric who had warned Lulach of the ambush that killed him.

"The orders Lulach gave that night were good ones, worthy of a king," Nechtan told her, "And after he had made provision for the women he gave me safe conduct out of his camp when his men would have tortured me for more information. I hope this comforts you, my lady."

"More than you know, Nechtan." After Elen had dismissed him, she spent a long time thinking over what he had said, and contemplating Patric's possible motives in the affair.

By midafternoon she had tired of being indoors, and she and Briga walked to the loch. But the grassy shore reminded her of her children and the way they had played there, sometimes with Fionna and her little ones. Elen did not linger. Instead, she went to a nearby hill overlooking the loch, to the cleared area where her mother lay buried along with little Gruach and Aiden, and with Fionna's daughter Elen.

"Has Patric insisted on changing this, too?" she cried, anger flaring out of the pain she felt. The burial space had been enlarged and edged

with carefully cut and matched stones. She had
seen at once that her mother's and the children's
graves were neatly cared for. But there were two
new graves, marked with a tall stone. "How dare
he use my family's plot for his own men?"

"Not his men, mistress," Briga said. "They are
your men. My master Talcoran and young Colin lie
there, at Lord Patric's orders."

"Talcoran?" She looked more closely at the
stone. A Celtic cross decorated with an interlaced
pattern had been carved on the front of it. In a
panel below the cross, the figures of two mounted
warriors bore square Pictish shields. She walked
around the stone to see the back of it, too, and
discovered it had been carved in the Pictish
manner with circles and fishes and paired serpent-
like lines. The graves had been placed so they
faced the loch and the beautiful wooded
mountains beyond, looking into the heart of
Pictland. "How could Patric know whose bodies
these are?"

"He found them both on the battlefield after
they had been killed, and had them sent home. He
thought you would be here and would be
comforted to have them at Laggan. Unfortunately,
Laggan was attacked before they could be buried,
but the priest hid the coffins below the altar in the
chapel, where even Malcolm's wicked soldiers
would not dare to trespass. When Lord Patric and
I returned here last autumn, he had the graveyard
enlarged as you see, and gave them proper burial.
The stone carvers were ordered to make the cross
before they began their work inside the castle."

"Patric did this for Talcoran and Colin?" It
was difficult to absorb. She had thought their
bodies would be looted after their last battle, and
thrown into some common grave with the other
fallen men of Macbeth's defeated army, and that

belief had made her sorrow even harder to bear.

"I think he did it for you, too, mistress. He speaks most respectfully of my master Talcoran, but he speaks of you with love."

"Talcoran. Colin." Elen fell to her knees. The tears ran down her face, but this was not the bitter, hopeless weeping she had done when first she learned of their deaths, it was instead a healthful, cleansing outpouring. Talcoran was home. Colin was home. Patric had seen to it.

"Mistress, please, you will make yourself ill."

"No, Briga, I'm making myself well again." She let Briga raise her after a while. Later, she walked back to the castle with her servant and friend. At the entrance to the great hall, Elen stopped.

"Briga, will you trust me? I promise not to run away, nor will I do anything I ought not to do, but I need a little time alone to think about what I have learned today. Grant me that time, please."

"I believe you. I do have something to see to in the kitchen." Briga smiled, a conspiratorial woman's smile. "Mistress, I think you should know that Lord Patric has had no other woman in all the months he has lived here without you."

The moment Briga's back was turned, Elen ran to the master's chamber. Briga had opened her bundle of clothing the night before and had taken the few crumpled and stained garments away to be cleaned and repaired. Elen's personal belongings she had arranged on the long table. They were there now, before the gleaming mirror and candlesticks Conal mac Duff had sent her. There was her bone comb, a tiny jar of herbal salve to put on cuts or blisters, and the small carved wooden box she had made certain to take with her on the flight toward Burghead.

She lifted Talcoran's charmstone out of the

box, held the cool white pebble and turned it over and over, seeing the painted blue circles on it through blurred eyes and remembering the night he had given it to her.

Toward the end of the afternoon she left the bedchamber and made her way down the stairs and out of the castle when no one was looking, to return to the little cemetery. There she knelt between the graves of her husband and her son.

"It's time to give it back," she said, and kissed the charmstone and laid it on Talcoran's grave. "I loved you. I will always love you, and the children we had. I did the best I could, Talcoran, but the war is over, and Malcolm has won, and I must live with that. I hope you would understand. I believe you would have forgiven me, if I could have told you everything."

It was becoming darker, and the April evening air was cool, but Elen did not notice. She was at peace for the first time since she had learned of Talcoran's death nearly ten months before. She sat on the ground with one hand on Talcoran's grave and one on Colin's, while the night grew deeper around her and the guilt and pain ebbed from her forever. She did not move until she heard the quiet footsteps. Then she rose and went to meet him.

"Briga thought you might be here," he said.

"I know I disobeyed, leaving the castle without her," Elen began.

"It doesn't matter. Briga explained."

"How can I thank you for this? To do such a thing for an enemy."

"I tried to tell you months ago, but you were too upset to listen. Elen, Talcoran was no enemy of mine. We were almost friends, long ago. All honest warriors recognize and respect each other, even when they must fight on opposite sides."

"He once said something similar about you," Elen said, recalling Macbeth's great feast at Forres Castle when he was newly made king. "I spoke disparagingly of you, and Talcoran said if Duncan had won the war you would be the king's honored friend, and he would be the one called traitor. He would not let me speak ill of you that day."

"I would not willingly have known you married to any one but me," Patric told her, "But of all the men Macbeth might have chosen for you, Talcoran was the best."

"I loved him." She was almost defiant about it, but the despair of recent days was gone from her voice.

"I know you did." There was no reproach in his tone.

"I love you now."

"Are you certain?"

"Yes. Seeing this place, knowing what you did for us, and for Lulach, all of this has released me from the past. I've said good-bye." She stopped, to swallow the lump in her throat and blink away the last remaining tears. "Will you forgive me for leaving you and have me for your wife, Patric?"

He flung his head back and took a deep breath, looking into the darkening sky. Above the loch a brilliant star sparkled, its intense blue-white light reflected in the quiet waters. A little below and to the right of it twinkled a smaller, dimmer star.

"I will," he said. "Come."

He led the way down the hill toward the castle. He stopped before the entrance and looked up again. The stars were brighter now, and starlight glimmered on Elen's black hair like a lover's tender caress.

"How beautiful Laggan is," Patric murmured

his eyes on the two stars, and then on Elen's upturned face.

"It is home," she responded. "Welcome home, Patric."

"Welcome home, my love." He took her hand, and they went through the entrance together.

Epilogue

On the first day of February of the Year of Our Lord 1059, the Countess of Laggan, despite having reached the advanced age of thirty-six, presented her husband with a healthy son. By mutual consent the child was named Duncan. On March 3, 1060, the Earl and Countess of Laggan produced their second child, a daughter, named Fionna Elen.

They lived happily at Laggan for more than fifty years, seldom traveling to the royal court, but visiting Fionna and Conal mac Duff in Fife at least once a year.

Elen lived to the age of eighty-five. A week after her peaceful death, Patric mac Keith, first Earl of Laggan, quietly followed his only love into the next world.

Historical Note

On April 25, A.D. 1058, Malcolm III was inaugurated as King of Alba at Scone. He reigned for thirty-five years. In 1059, he married Ingebjorg, Thorfinn's widow, who gave him his eldest son, Duncan, and then died. In 1068, Malcolm married Princess Margaret, sister of Edgar the Atheling and grand-niece of that same King Edward who had once given him refuge in England. Under the influence of his saintly second wife, who bore him six sons and two daughters, Malcolm gradually tempered his more violent character traits and enjoyed a happy married life, at last becoming the great king his youthful supporters had believed he could be. It was during the reign of Malcolm's and Margaret's youngest son, David I (1124-55), that Alba began to be commonly called Scotland.

Lulach's widow was allowed to live peacefully in Moray with her children. Maelsnechta, Mormaer of Moray by inheritance from his father, lived until 1085. His descendants held the title of Earl of Moray.

Author's Note

The character of King Macbeth was vilified by his successor, Malcolm, and by subsequent historians until this charismatic leader was reduced to the tyrannical murderer shown in Shakespeare's great play. Macbeth's contemporaries were more charitable toward him, calling him a wise and just ruler who was no more bloodthirsty than other kings of his time, and his claim to the throne of Alba was unquestionably stronger than Duncan's.

The following are all historical characters: Macbeth, Gruach, Lulach, his son Maelsnechta, Earl Thorfinn the Mighty of Orkney and his Ingebjorg, Thorfinn's friend and lieutenant Thorkill Fostri, Earl Siward the Strong of Northumbria who was Macbeth's great nemesis, King Duncan and his sons Malcolm, Donald, and Maelmuire, Duncan's father Crinan of Dunkeld and nephew Moddan, and Macdowald, who revolted against Duncan.

Historians dispute whether mac Duff the Thane of Fife ever lived. My depiction of him is purely imaginary, and my version of his escape to England is loosely based on Sir Walter Scott's romantic account of the incident.

All other characters in this book are entirely fictional.

GLOSSARY

Alba.
One of the ancient names for Scotland. At the time of
this story, the Western Isles and the northern provinces
of Caithness and Sutherland belonged to the Norse earls
of Orkney, while a portion of what is today southern
Scotland was claimed by England and was in constant
dispute.

Ard Ri, or Adrigh.
The High King, who was elected from among the tribal
chieftains.

Duncan mac Crinan.
Designated heir to the crown by his grandfather in an
attempt to change the ancient Law of Tanistry, he ruled
as King of Alba from 1034 to 1039.

Dunedin.
The Gaelic name for Edinburgh.

Dunfermline.
Duncan's seat of government, near the Firth of
Forth.

Firth.
An inlet or arm of the sea. The word is related to the
Norse word *fjord*.

Law of Tanistry.
In order to keep a mature male on the throne, the crown of Alba passed not to the son of the late king, but to the king's brother or cousin. Only after this successor had died could the son become eligible, a system which frequently led to murder and family feuds.

Loch.
Gaelic word for lake.

mac.
Gaelic for "son of." For example, Patric mac Keith meant Patric son of Keith.

Macbeth.
This was a personal name. It was common from the 11th to the 14th centuries and was spelled several ways. It means "son of life." His full name was Macbeth mac Finleac, Macbeth son of Finleac. The rightful king by the old Law of Tanistry, Macbeth represented the tribal and northern people of Alba, in contrast to Duncan and his family, who favored succession by direct inheritance and were affiliated by marriage and customs with the south and the much-hated English.

Moray.
Macbeth's lands in the north of Alba.

Mormaer.
The title means "sea steward" and was originally connected with coastal defense. The mormaers were considered sub-kings, or king's deputies, and collected the royal revenues. The rank was hereditary.

Picts.
The ancient inhabitants of Scotland, conquered by the Scots of Dalriada in A.D. 843.

Scone.
Near present-day Perth, this was the location of the palace of the High Kings of the Picts. When the Scots and Picts were united under Kenneth mac Alpin, Scone

became his capital, and, later, the sacred place where kings were crowned.

Stone of Destiny, or Stone of Scone.

The coronation throne of the Kings of Alba. The stone described in the old chronicles was hollowed out like a chair, with carvings in the Pictish style, very different from the stone King Edward I of England carried off to Westminster Abbey in 1296.

Thane, Thanage.

Thanes were high officers of the king who administered portions of the royal lands. They themselves held substantial estates within these lands. The title was hereditary, and the lands they held were called shires. Important noblemen and bishops could appoint their own thanes.